FAULTLINE 49

A NOVEL BY DAVID DANSON

GUY
FAUX
BOOKS

"I say that there is a deliberate conspiracy, by force, by fraud or by both, to force Canada into the American Union."

John A. Macdonald, first Prime Minister of Canada

"In a world darkened by ethnic conflicts that tear nations apart, Canada stands as a model of how people of different cultures can live and work together in peace, prosperity, and mutual respect."

Bill Clinton, 42nd President of the United States

"Sovereignty has changed so greatly because of the phenomenon of globalization, where all issues become transnational."

Allan Gotlieb, former Canadian Ambassador to the United States

"There is no security threat to Canada that the United States would not be ready, willing, and able to help with. There would be no debate. There would be no hesitation. We would be there for Canada, part of our family."

Paul Cellucci, former US Ambassador to Canada

— — —

ISBN-13: 978-0-9881640-2-4
ISBN-10: 0988164027

— — —

Published by Guy Faux Books, an imprint of Guy Faux Book Company Limited, Toronto.

Cover design by Joseph Travers MacKinnon and Carlo Schefter
Frontline reports compiled and edited by Joseph Travers MacKinnon

TABLE OF CONTENTS

I'd like to acknowledge my parents for their unwavering support, input, and assistance; Sam for her loving patience, Carlo for a second set of eyes, and Nick for waiting with me at the checkpoints.

Dedicated to all the innocents who have suffered and died in North America during the Canadian-American Conflict as a result of misguided vengeance and imperial ambition. May men and women of good conscience put an end to the occupation of western Canada and aid in the rebuilding efforts of a splintered nation—neither rogue nor tyrannical—forced to defend itself against the forces of greed, fear, and paranoia.

EDITOR'S NOTE

The first edition of this book was printed by William Lyon MacKenzie Books in Toronto, Ontario. Unfortunately, in November 2011, US occupying forces raided the publishing house, destroying the first run before it could be shipped. Since all of the data and the original material (i.e. Danson's original manuscript, photographs, recordings, and notes) were remotely stored, this censorship, although inconvenient, merely delayed the book's release. The US Federal Court's embargo on David Danson's unpublished reports on the North American Conflict, on the other hand, proved to be a greater obstacle.

Gagged until some progress was made with the Ninth Circuit Court of Appeals, we decided instead to try a foreign partnership to release David's timely accounts from the frontlines. Guy Faux Books, with the assistance of a rogue printer in England, ultimately decided to publish *Faultline 49*. They interpreted the book as subversive and wanted to brand themselves as nonconformists. They took on the project, and ironically, did so with the tacit support of the Crown.

Despite printing with a foreign press, we were still unable to publish all of the intended documents due to the illegal confiscations and the state censorship David's reports have been subjected to over the past decade. Where reports are absent or have been largely censored, the following line can be found: "embargoed report." Over thirty-pages-worth of reports and data were redacted by court order. Whether or not this volume and the content contained herein will likewise be recalled and censored is up to our politicians and adjudicators. Until such decisions are made, Danson's intimate account—the only of its kind—will stand as a complex counter-narrative engaging with the conflict that radically reshaped North America from 2001-2012.

This book alternates between a first-person narrative and a string of detailed macro-accounts of the conflict. In the first person narrative, journalist David Danson elucidates elements of Bush's well-intentioned but poorly executed intervention in Canada, and enables additional perspectives in the media coverage and the debate surrounding the conflict (i.e. the point of view of the Yukon Sprites, Canadians living under the occupation, and the US 173rd

Airborne). In the macro-accounts referred to as the "Genesis" chapters, Danson provides an executive breakdown of the conflict as it evolved in North America, documenting the connections between one man's insidious revenge plot and the criminal war it precipitated.

—*Joe MacKinnon, Compiler and Editor*

THE AUTHOR

David Danson is an American journalist, author, war correspondent, and peace activist, specializing in Canadian and American politics. He moved from Valletta, Malta, to Seattle, Washington, in 1979. (His departure coincided with the withdrawal of British troops from the archipelago.)

David worked as a fact-checker for KOMO-TV until offered a scholarship from the University of Toronto. Although he was not particularly familiar with Canada, David's great uncle—a Canadian politician and decorated war hero—guaranteed him asylum and a warm welcome. Granted his uncle's assurances, David accepted the University of Toronto's offer and moved to Scarborough, Ontario, where he studied and received his Bachelors in English Literature in 1983. In early 1984, David moved back to Seattle where he worked part-time as a reporter for *The Seattle Times,* using his writer-friend (who was straddling positions at KOMO-TV and the *Times*) as an *in*.

David returned to school in 1987 to study journalism at the University of Oregon. After completing his Masters in Journalism and spending some time as a freelance researcher, David travelled to Iraq to document the tensions leading up to the Gulf War, marking the beginning of his career as a war correspondent. David's coverage of the Gulf War earned him a lot of flak from the White House, including insinuations that his reports—on civilian casualties resultant from American smart-bombs—were unpatriotic. David, fearing military imprisonment on account of formal accusations that he'd propagated Iraqi misinformation, decided to quietly return to Seattle.

Learning of David's status as a bona-fide shit disturber and mindful of his repudiation by the American government, *The Network* (a left-leaning multimedia news agency based in Atlanta) secured Danson, who, by 1992, had returned to writing for *The Daily Telegraph, The Toronto Star,* and *The Seattle Times.*

He has since worked for *The Network* as a frontline reporter, documenting the tensions in Bosnia, Chechnya, Kuwait, Rwanda, and Somalia. David is the author of *Neighbourhood Watch* (1995), *Xenophobia* (2005), and *Faultline 49* (2012). He is currently under house arrest in Great Falls, Montana.

FAULTLINE 49

BUSHWHACKED

Toronto, Ontario
January 26-27, 2006

COALITION FORCES CROSSED THE RIVER two hours after sundown and set up camp at the base of the ravine. Yells, rock 'n' roll, and hickory smoke swept over the craters and defunct mines, finding us in the mansion, crouched in squalor, both unable to relax.

Bruce Kalnychuk (a.k.a. "the Green Legend") tapped on his watch, superstitiously attempting to stall time. "God damn it," he muttered. He ratcheted his mirthless stare sideward, and caught me watching him curse the inevitable. "This is not the end, you know," he intimated. I nodded and planted my head against the exposed brick. He continued mumbling—something about the immortality of an idea—and I shut my eyes, feigning sleep. "David? You mean to tell me you can sleep at a time like this?" No longer comforted by the unattended sound of his voice, Bruce sighed and started to smoke.

A faint band of light cut through the chink in the wall where sniper fire tested the masonry days earlier. The barrage of high caliber bullets penetrated two feet of wood and steel, far enough to rewrite the story conveyed by the seventeenth century tapestry mounted inside. Days before, the linen had depicted Hannibal, proud and bloody, poised to take the Trebbia. The remaining gold and red weave told only of some ahistorical slaughter. Lingering smoke from the Legend's unpiloted pipe gave form to the light, which, piercing the Roman dead, met the chipped floor between us.

I clamored to the aperture, despairing at what I knew I'd see. The tree line breathed as more troops shuffled forward to scout the path of least resistance. They bustled up the access road, and inspected the empty machinegun nests and makeshift roadblocks on the south side of the mansion.

The Legend's remaining Yukon Sprites had abandoned their posts along the road, realizing that the new outdoor reality shaped by the Coalition's saturation bombing did not bode well in their favour. Airstrikes had wiped out virtually every anti-tank and anti-personnel mine, rendering the Sprites' trenches and pillboxes indefensible. With Bloor Street taken and most of the Sprites' appropriate firepower eliminated, Coalition tanks could launch an unstoppable multilateral advance on the stronghold.

Canada's "unlawful combatants" were running out of places to hide. The Sprite's cause was no longer something they could walk away from. One way or another, they would have to mount a last stand, though most knew better than to select this barren road— this broken promise of escape—to be their Thermopylae.

Sewers, breached by the barrage, exposed their contents. The morning sun cut through the sparse limbs of the trees bowed over the road, and heated the stagnant waste. The aroma was exacerbated further by the irradiation of human remains.

The nebulous gore, windswept across the wrinkled asphalt and slush, warmed with the road. American soldiers ascending the hill— assigned the task of scouting a safe way to the mansion and evacuating the block's civilian remainder—were preoccupied with the stench. From our perch, we spied two discontent "enemy" soldiers express their displeasure with the smell, employing exaggerated gesticulations. They then broke into laughter, waving away the aromatic decay like adolescents responding to flatulence.

Recoiling into the room, we busied ourselves with insincere small talk: what possible machismo retreats (an oxymoron?) *we* could resort to; what to make of the Canadian Spring; whether they'd have Sprite-engineered marijuana in prison, and whether prison was even an option. More or less, *we* put off coming to terms with the gravity of the situation.

The Legend evidenced his denial by feeding the cloud hanging above us with heavy exhalations. His bloodshot eyes sunk deeper into their wrinkled pods, ambushed white, and his posture began to slump.

While the hopeless *hashshashiyin* deflated before me, I shuffled through a stack of photographs re-presenting a flattened Banff, humouring the notion that I could survive the ordeal and turn those morbid collectibles into something saleable. After re-prioritizing the deck for the hundredth time, I returned to my rudimentary view-finder to determine the source of the commotion outside.

Boxes of Russian ammunition, French weapons, bullet casings, and broken Canadian bodies littered the road to the safe-house. One of the American recon grunts climbed atop of a ruined G-Wagon and signalled for the war machine, creaking out of view, to claw up the hill. It churned through the failed barriers and ammo boxes, and crunched over mounds of ice, as it approached the battered mansion's front entrance.

The iron-cast gates were reinforced by burnt-out squad cars and sandwiched between rusted anti-tank obstacles (i.e. Czech hedgehogs). They disavowed access through the only gap in the one-metre-high stone hedge, which enclosed the entire property and bled mortar onto the neighbouring area. Wherever stones had been displaced, whorls of razor wire had overgrown the void like steely ivy. Though the building could easily have passed for an indomitable fortress by any medieval standard, the solidity of the mansion and its extension was purely illusory so far as we were concerned. It was a 3400-square-foot rattrap.

The tank was positioned forty-feet-away and its cannon aligned with the front door. It groaned mechanical phrases, none of which were cryptic. Each utterance suggested more of the same— variations on the theme of butchery. The mansion's remaining glass hummed and its façade trembled, finding poor resonance with the reverberation of war.

Two armoured troop transports lumbered up the hill to join the tank. A respectable-looking officer dismounted the closest carrier, and began screaming orders. Muted by the tank's engine, it was nevertheless clear from his hand-signals that he wanted the bodies—strewn across the road—to be piled respectably. I was too far off to lip-read, but his body handily conveyed the message: "Clean this shit up!" Several men shouldered their rifles, and began tossing corpses with "YS" designations as well as unmarked guerillas into a roadside ditch.

As soon as the men had unloaded a fourth body into the shallow trench, one of the bearers collapsed, trailing a red mist behind him. His arms were at his sides when he fell, so that when his face met the ground, his helmet tumbled away, revealing a dispirited young man. Blood poured out of some hidden entry or exit point, weaving a red halo through the snow. Anxious screams were again dwarfed by the tank's engine, though they somehow managed to reach us, perhaps subconsciously.

Before acclimatizing to the threat, the tank and those in the vicinity were sprinkled by a flurry of little pincers. The source: a pair of AK-toting wraiths who darted from room to room in the apartment building opposite our position (likely with the hopes of

17

adjusting for a better vantage point on the convoy). Tracer-fire continued down in bursts, failing to make any additional mortal connection.

Taking a pause in the onslaught as a cue for heavy retaliation, the Abrams' cannon swung creakily counterclockwise, adjusted, and reciprocated with full force. The beast bellowed several times, opening the far side of the apartment to the sun's rays. Metal nets and rebar kept the skeleton of the disemboweled building together as bricks and concrete loosed by the demolition cascaded down into the street, chased by a grey cloud of particulate.

The soldiers, no longer slouched in cover against the Abrams, worked to set up a perimeter. Violent cartographers in black and green investigated the remnants of the insurgents, spread like butter over brick, shingles, ice, and splintered wood.

As they mapped out the destruction, a medic sprawled the recently felled soldier onto a stretcher. The wound was fatal, evidenced by the medic's haste in enshrouding the body in a black-canvas bag. (A Blackhawk MedEvac or "turkey"—an airborne equivalent to a meat-wagon—would pick up the body and transport it either to a New York Army hospital or the American camp on the Toronto Lakeshore.) Incensed by the morning's setback, the vociferous officer yelled at his men in a volume competitive with the adjacent war machine in idle.

Notwithstanding the mansion's size, the only remaining, dependable structure extended from the front door to the kitchen, and to the room directly above the kitchen, accessible only by an unreliable rope-ladder. Within the shattered exoskeleton, piping crisscrossed above our heads in Byzantine patterns—low enough to take out my good eye—casting a maze of capricious shadows with the help of little enduring fires, likewise restless in their wood-brick coffers.

Members from the now-disbanded 48th Highland Regiment, on their way back west to support the First Canadian Division, had helped us cannibalize furniture, brick, and stone, in order to devise a rudimentary insulation against shrapnel and other unsavoury airborne elements. (They had figured us for members of the resistance. Had they known my host's true identity, the shrapnel would have belonged to them.) After they went on their way, we salvaged more stones that had been displaced from the retaining walls in earlier skirmishes, in order to seal the windows. These makeshift partitions permitted a fleeting sense of security.

We knew that our attempts to buttress our Alamo were meaningless against the threat of a "bunker-blaster" or a mortar strike. After all, if cinders from the upper floors were able to find us crouching there and dash my notes and records documenting the most recent, imperial ambitions-in-play, then surely something more ominous could find us. It was evident to me, from this sudden deviation from the standard, excessive violence defining the spirit of the past decade, that the opposing force was exercising restraint. The reasoning for the specificity of the mortar strikes and the brevity of the Etobicoke shock-and-awe campaign? *A tactical strike may preserve the hide, but only a live-capture preserves the creature.* The Legend was being fenced-in and kept alive so that he could be executed before the American people.

Instead of gawking about or staring death in the mouth, we continued to brace for one last hurrah. Neither one of us wanted to participate in the frenetic struggle a cornered animal engages in when confronted with the truth of its own mortality, recognizing its unavoidability. Escape would inevitably result in a substitution of one futile act of desperation for another. Upon his arrival in Toronto, the Legend had taken precautions to enable a respectable final fight or flight. Unfortunately for him, few of them had been effective.

AFTER HEARING that John Qi had confessed under torture the whereabouts of the Yukon Sprites' stronghold in Etobicoke (a Toronto district), the Legend was pressed to make a deal with members of the Canadian resistance. He traded the Sprites' most recent shipment of FN[1] assault rifles for an airlift from the mansion to a safe-house in Kirkland Lake via Algonquin Park, and an explosive, out-of-town diversion affording him time to reorient and rebuild his forces.

Few had imagined that the airlift would make it to Etobicoke from the Sprite base on Manitoulin Island, given the American dominion over the air in eastern Canada, which had previously

---

[1] The FNFAL or Fusil Automatique Léger - Light Automatic Rifle was the standard weapon issued during the 1950s to the Canadian Armed Forces.

prevented any and all unscheduled aerial movement. Noting the chopper's arrival as miraculous in a time and place beyond miracles, the Legend was especially wary about climbing into the archaic Sikorsky Sea King helicopter, although time was of the essence: it was necessary to present the fly-codes to the pilot within thirty seconds of touch-down, otherwise the pilot would take off or sabotage the electronics to the point of irreparability.

Aware of the urgency and potential danger of immediate contact, the Legend sent his doppelganger, Anthony Smithwick, with the codes to the chopper, ahead of the intended evacuees. The pilot opened the door and, smiling, waved in the code-carrying Kalnychuk look-alike. Together, they disappeared into the dark cabin. Gunfire crackled, illuminating the outlines of two bodies caught in a struggle. There was shouting followed by more gunshots, and then the Legend's crumpled likeness slumped out the side door.

Seeing that the pilot was attempting to get the bird airborne, a gang of Sprite onlookers swarmed the chopper, and tore the pilot out kicking and screaming. Kalnychuk ordered them to bring him into the mansion for questioning.

Initially, all suspected that he was an American agent, sent to quash the perceived terrorist threat; however, the pilot—suspended by meat hooks—reassured that he was merely following orders given by the leader of a schismatic Sprite faction. Clearly, at least one Sprite cell had turned, along with a member of Kalnychuk's immediate posse. An impediment to old friends and past his best-before-date, Kalnychuk had been betrayed in exchange for political asylum. While I'm sure he had assumed as much would happen eventually, he hadn't anticipated how quick his own officers would give him up.

The pilot's orders: *Terminate Kalnychuk's command with extreme prejudice and return with proof of kill.* He had not been given a reason for the order, just a blacked-out file with a photograph and a location. He claimed he did not know how he had gotten past American AA guns or the drone patrols over Lake Huron, but postulated someone or something had found a way to captivate the attention of the US Forces elsewhere. After the interrogation, however, one of Kalnychuk's engineers reported that the Sea King had been modified to incorporate stealth elements.

Special coatings had been applied to the skin and all hard angles on the fuselage had been curved in order to absorb and scatter reflections of radar beams used by the USAF and US ground crew to track and identify aircraft. This was not simply some thuggish hit from a rival faction; this was an extremely expensive venture, bankrolled either by the US or the Canadian government. Unsuccessful with their intimate assassination, Kalnychuk knew that his enemies would simply escalate to using cannons, napalm, cruise missiles, et cetera.

The Legend still had to deal with two dead bodies and a lame-chopper. The bodies were less of a concern, evident from his indifference: "Just wrap them up, and heave them down the ravine." The chopper, on the other hand, seemed to be some bedeviled favour. It did not have enough fuel to reach the Sprite's alternate safe-house, a good six-hundred kilometres away, and even if it did, the Sprites at Fort Skye hadn't radioed-in for days. As far as Kalnychuk was concerned, he'd be headed to an archeological mound of smoldering ruin. *Kalnychuk, like Midas, had a destructive, silencing touch.*

Recognizing the vehicle as the only hope for his men, the Legend—determined to go out in a blaze of glory on the ground—secured safe passage from Toronto to Bancroft for his Lieutenant Colonel and three of his captains. The officers assigned their remaining men to valiantly defend Kalnychuk until out-matched by Coalition ground forces, and then to seek refuge with accommodating resistance members in the Toronto area.

Bruce's right hand man, Jason, was the only trained pilot on base, so Bruce assigned him the obvious role, and reluctantly bid him farewell. After saying their goodbyes, Jason saluted Kalnychuk and joined the others on their exodus. Kalnychuk saw the chopper off, and with it his remaining hopes and ambitions. All that remained was hate and fear.

Kalnychuk, emotionally defeated by the betrayal, invested all his Canadian Tire money (a symbolic gesture) in additional barricades. Once satisfied by his efforts to delay destiny, he cleaned his AK47 rifle, and sat me down to tell the rest of his story. While we chatted, his remaining troops secured the street, littered anti-personnel mines in the ravine backing the mansion, and set up road blocks at the western intersection and at the eastern mouth of the road. I feel

I should have been more anxious given that I was entombed with the loneliest and most-wanted man in the world, but I found myself surprisingly relaxed. There's a good chance the heroin hadn't fully run its course.

SAVE FOR THE SPACE occupied by the Kalashnikov rifles, folded and leaning against the radiator, the surrounding walls were blanketed with notes, newspaper clippings, and maps of the *American* northwest. The single kitchen window, hidden behind a palimpsest of perforated plywood and obituaries, permitted a winter breeze to creep in.

The morning chill, not yet completely dissipated by sunlight, was a comfort to already numb fingers. When the frost began to melt off of my stitches, the thawing, irritated flesh began to throb. This intense pain, in conjunction with the numbness in my digits, was a helpful reminder that I was still in it—*still alive.*

Pandemonium in the front-yard instigated Kalnychuk's twitch. He shook it off, tacked a small colour photograph of the murdered woman we encountered in the safe-house to the wall, and then proceeded to douse the last few litres of our starter kerosene over his head and onto the carpet. It was not apathy that held me back from some grandiose humanitarian rescue, but an understanding of his motivation and decision. This was a man who knew too much and meant too much to the wrong people. Tired of cutting a wake so turbulent that it subsumed all in its path, friend and foe alike, he wanted to bring a close to a short public life of suffering on his own terms.

He returned to the aperture in the wall. "This guy is sticking it to me by the book," he murmured, transfixed on the peopled horizon. "He's got his boys concealed; a good view of the killing ground; all 'round defence; a rendezvous point, including routes to and from it; an administration area; a withdrawal route; and ancillary sentry positions there, there, and there." He pointed them out with the nod of his head. "At least they had enough respect not to send an amateur." He wiped kerosene off his brow. "You know it took 'em half-a-trillion dollars to get me?" He started pacing. "Bah! How'd it come to this, eh David? 'True north strong and free' my ass. How free or strong are you feeling right about now?" The kerosene trickled down his neck, and he spat the rest of his despairing farewell. "You ought to get the fuck out of here with the truth of it.

They planned all of this, right down to the very last detail. Don't let the world forget that it was imperial ambition and greed, not solidarity, which brought the occupation." The prospect of survival overshadowed the rapport we had developed during my attachment.

We said our goodbyes. I emptied his duffle bag of defunct C4 charges, and filled it with whatever notes, drawings, and recording equipment it could fit. It was a light load, on account of the majority of my borrowed recording equipment (i.e. Dictaphone, "voice-tracer" cassettes with hours of interviews, and a USB microphone) having melted in an unfortunate "camp" fire.

My drug-induced euphoria had vanished along with my childish fancy. While he paraded around, soaked in suicidal promise, I mulled over the possibility of salvaging my work and cashing in on my injuries, my trauma, and my shame. Goodbye to this hell, I thought, and a big hello to my Pulitzer—or more plausibly and pragmatically: life imprisonment. Regardless, leaving the Legend likely meant deviation from his tragic course. He knew, as well as I, that only one of us was truly destined to die in that dilapidated deathtrap. He did not dare ask me to share in his measure.

The boys in the camouflage fell back to the apartments still smoking from the Abrams' last bombardment, with views on all previously viable escape routes. The mansion was surrounded. A barrage of knocking commenced at the front door. Between radio chirps and "copy-that's," the authoritative voice in the field demanded his surrender by name through a megaphone.

Panicked, I tried the knob on the kitchen door to no avail. I don't know why I tried, given I saw Bruce nail and gird it shut. "There's no opening the door. There, over and through the window," grunted Bruce. He ambled over to me, and then handed me a crowbar greased with accelerant. Leaning against the adjacent wall, he watched as I pried my exit, inspecting my bandages and the divots in my cheek. "Remember: a limit on vision does not mean a limited world. Do what you can David. All the best to you and your little family," said the oil-drenched man.

Limited vision is hardly what's going to constrain my world tomorrow, I thought; furthermore, liberty and agency will be unlikely sentiments shared behind reinforced steel and prison concrete. As for my little family, I had neglected to tell him that

Audrey took off with Samuel after I fucked-up. If I made it out, I would return to cardboard boxes and moth balls or a deep dark cell, living the truth of my dad's prophecy: "That network and that American succubus will leave you with nothing! No money. No faith. No hope."

Kalnychuk caught my guilty stare and smiled. "Why've you froze, boy? Fuck off." He knocked me off-kilter with a forceful push. "It's not your war, though I appreciate your trying. Pull the timber closed behind you." He threw his head back as if to repurpose some long forgotten, now jumbled aphorism. "Press forward to the end and falter not!"

As I let the board bend back into place, I felt my enduring honour devoured by shame. In some quantum-alternate-reality, maybe I would have followed the story to its logical end, and found myself written-in as a footnote in the biography of someone more consequential. The weight of my double-edged guilt (i.e. for betraying an acquaintance and for becoming acquainted with a murderer) was not, however, enough to anchor me to a sinking ship flying a black flag. I manoeuvred over the stone hedge and then trudged across the neighbouring lawn at gun point.

"Drop the fucking bag! Hands in the air! Check him." Three heavily armed soldiers intercepted me, and forcefully dragged me behind the firing line. They seized control of my arms, and pressed me face first against a tree where I was zip-tied for the second time in four months.

Behind me in the crumbling mansion, the cornered ex-pat erupted into a futile, nationalistic opera: "O Canada!"

Hands cuffed, they eased off of the pushing. I took their relaxation as my cue to inform them of my "American press affiliations."

"That's fine," one said, "but we're still going to have to process you. This here is a forbidden zone. No passes have been issued. Hell, God Himself can't get through here without getting screened—or one of these," he pointed to the American badge on his shoulder. *All true.*

I'd tell them that I had been coerced, hoping that my involvement with the Sprites might amount to a slap on the wrists. Deal or no deal, they'd still want all the information on Kalnychuk, including dates, troop positions, and the whereabouts of the British armour, Russian munitions, and French weapon caches.

My acquaintance—the "unlawful combatant" set to burn in that outpost—was not be permitted any of the niceties that a supranational citizen would be shown. Soldiers pressed past my guards in staggered formation, motioning to the heavily armoured group gleaning glimpses of the mansion's guts through the kitchen window, feet away from the resistance's pontiff: Bruce Kalnychuk. The headline regarding his capture would read: "We Got 'Em!"

Bruce had great difficulty singing the second half of the anthem in French. Some of the troops around the house began to snicker, indicating it was just a game to them. *Just a matter of twisting little brother's arm one more time and re-territorializing the bunks.*

"Sir, the prisoner?" The big lug goaded me into his commanding officer's line of vision with his pistol.

"Put him in the can, post a guard, and then get those fucking sights on the horizon," barked the officer.

The same herculean soldier guided me up the ramp into the back of the second armoured car. "Mister?"

"David Danson," I said softly, as if it were an apology.

"Sounds like an American name to me." I laughed at his genuine bafflement.

"I was actually born in Malta. My family's originally—"

"Your spawning ground is of absolutely no interest to me... I've got to say, you chose a particularly bad place to spend the night."

"I'd have to agree. I can't say I've ever had a walk of shame ever go this badly," I said candidly.

"Did you say how many are in the house with him?"

"I didn't."

"Well how about you tell me, right now." The soldier did not appreciate my feigned levity.

"He's alone."

"Now does Mr. Kalnychuk speak any English?"

"Who, Bruce? He's an American."

"Meaning?"

"You could try Spanish."

After mulling over my sarcasm for a moment, the soldier walked over this *intelligence* to his commander who, in turn, blared into his loudspeaker: "Mr. Kalnychuk, y'all please approach an east or south-facing window, and very slowly throw out your weapons."

The mutilated French stopped, and then a series of expletives began to issue forth from the mansion. "Go to hell you imperialist dogs!"

The loudspeaker turned to me: "Does your friend know this is his last opportunity to toss 'em down? We're in position to demolish the house with him inside." I looked past the megaphone and saw the tank, barrel aimed at the front of the mansion.

"He's not my friend. He's an interviewee," I spat, now almost entirely deaf. "Moreover, he's awfully stubborn. I don't think he'll listen to me." There was nothing left for me to say to him, anyway. Collaboration so soon after abandonment would simply add insult to injury.

An Apache helicopter threshed the canopy overhead. The officer poised to speak, but then waited for the bird of prey to disappear over the valley. "Alright. We're coming in, Kalnychuk."

Although partial to prayer, I don't think Bruce was chanting or invoking holy terror when they crashed in. He'd have likely slunk down against the radiator—purring warmth under the weight of wet clothes—and packed one last bowl of high-grade British Columbian weed into his pocket vaporizer. Feet away from some good ol' boys poised to perforate anything with a pulse, he'd reflect on the Battle for Dawson City, mapped on his body in raised purple. He'd remember his adopted country's flag the last time he saw it: emptied of significance and hoisted above a field littered with charred Abrams tanks, its red washing away the rape, starvation, and despair of the northwestern insurgents, and immortalizing the death of the nationalist project. He probably returned to his mantra, groaning basely: "You gave 'em hell—yeah you did. True north strong and free. The truth?" From the armoured car, I could still make out his last, grisly statement, intended for me: "Give it to them, David! Give it to them!"

"David will do no such thing. Last chance Kalnychuk," laughed the man with the megaphone. He gestured to his second in command, who subsequently signalled the charge.

"Move!"

The splintering of wood behind him triggered a reptilian nerve, which pressed him to ignite—to connect himself, in the most final sense, to the flame.

The radio pinned on the guard assigned to watch me purred static, and then clicked. "Go, go, go! Clear. . . Hands in the fucking air. Get down on the fucking ground… Oh shit. Put him out, put him out!" Bruce's garbled screams traveled through the radio like some macabre techno-opera. "Are you alone? Is there anyone else in there with you? . . . Is Jason on the premises?" The radio clicked again, and went silent.

I could still hear his bellowing, which penetrated the garrison-in-shambles. I was overcome with the realization: the head was gone, burnt to ash. The last of his honesty spent on a Judas—some utilitarian journalist.

My guard's radio fuzzed back to life: "We got him sir. He's a little crisp, but he can walk."

"Copy that," replied the commander. "If he can walk, he can stand trial. Good work. Get out of there."

I didn't get to see them carry out the charred remains of the Sprite's last real hope and figurehead. The ramp sealed me in with my bag and a dozen crooked smiles bathed in red light, reducing the mansion from a sliver to a memory.

KALNYCHUK'S OUTPOST was appropriated by the US Military. Not only did they get their man, but they secured the material support underpinning his rival narrative. The notes, maps, and news clippings caked onto the mansion's walls conveyed a story few have heard or are permitted to hear (i.e. the story of the Yukon Sprites and their western counter-offensive). Unfortunately, all of the essential artifacts will be destroyed or classified.

With a monopoly on the historical narrative concerning what went on from 2001-2011 north of the 49th parallel, the US government will adopt the official position that the Yukon Sprites and terrorist facilitators, alone, compromised an international friendship, undid two centuries of peaceful cohabitation, and led us all into this god-awful civil war. Notwithstanding the obvious barriers to entry in the truth and answers market, I hope my reports over the past decade alert readers to the dissonance between the simulacra the US government designed for popular consumption and the abysmal realities estranged in the process.

♠

GENESIS: 9/11

We live in an age of terror. Americans see themselves as the primary target in what is likely to be a long and shadowy war. The existential threat is fundamentally changing American society and government. Security does trump all, and before Americans will be prepared to lift the drawbridge at what has become a real border, they will have to be satisfied that Canadians take security as seriously as they do. [2]

—Colin Robertson

Geography has made us neighbours; history has made us friends; economics has made us partners; and necessity has made us allies.

—JFK

Canada is contiguous to "the center of the empire." Territorial control over Canada is part of the US geopolitical and military agenda. It is worth recalling in this regard, that throughout history, the "conquering nation" has expanded on its immediate borders, acquiring control over contiguous territories. [3]

—Michel Chossudovsky

AT EIGHT-FORTY-FIVE a.m. on Tuesday, September 11, 2001, the World Trade Center in Edmonton, Alberta, was demolished by a home-made bomb, consisting of six barrels of mixed contents—some containing ammonium nitrate and nitro-methane; others contained diesel fuel and fertilizer—triggered, ultimately, by one-hundred-and-twenty kilograms of Blastrite Gel sausages.

IN ORDER TO DELIVER his explosive *riposte* to alimony demands from his ex-wife Taylor Wensen—two months pregnant with her assistant's child—without raising any suspicion, Montana Police-Sergeant Harvey King took a three day leave from work to

---

[2] Stein, Janice, and Colin Robertson. *Diplomacy in the Digital Age: Essays in Honour of Ambassador Allan Gotlieb* (Toronto: Signal, 2011) 57.
[3] Chossudovsky, Michel. "Is the Annexation of Canada Part of Bush's Military Agenda?" *GlobalResearch.ca - Centre for Research on Globalization* <http://globalresearch.ca/articles/CHO411C.html>.

"visit sick family." A chiseled ex-Marine with a well carved niche in his community and the innocent adoration of all the officers at his precinct, King's brief sabbatical went unquestioned. Few were cognizant of his bi-polar mental disorder or his *Soldier of Fortune* subscription and the gun fetish it satisfied. By "sick family," they assumed he was referring to his comatose uncle, Abraham King, whose mental state rendered a testimony affirming King's presence on the days in question impossible.

King—apparently wishing to make the jaunt from his slummish post-marital, fast-food-jacketed apartment to the health care facility where his uncle resided more expeditious—borrowed a white delivery van from his cousin Darcy King, despite having the ability to take his squad car. When interviewed, Darcy recalled lending Harvey King his van around four p.m., which Harvey drove straight to Spruce Groves Palliative Care Centre thereafter.

Fifteen minutes after logging-in at the facility, King made a call to friends on the police force from his cell phone, reporting the van stolen. Surveillance camera footage taken from the Spruce Groves parking lot was far too grainy to identify the driver, either at the time of arrival or during the auto theft, though it's apparent from the recording that whoever stole the vehicle did so with a great deal of ease. Phone records indicate that King's cousin received a call from a road-stop at eight p.m., two-and-a-half hours away from the scene of the auto-theft. The duration of the phone call was approximately thirteen minutes.

The same delivery van crossed the border to Canada via the MT 409 at Aden, and headed north into southern Alberta early the next morning, hitting a number of fast-food restaurants along the way. The car-thief exercised tact during these rest stops: he refrained from using his credit card and spotted surveillance cameras before entering the eating-establishments, obscuring his face for CCTV.

Although the driver successfully dodged an affirmative ID, video cameras captured images of the same van parking in the lot on the northeast corner of the World Trade Centre (near the steakhouse's employee entrance), downtown Edmonton, on the day of the attack. The driver exited the vehicle, ventured east, and remote-detonated the van with an RC controller from the entrance of the Shaw Conference Center, two city blocks away.

Shrapnel found its way half-a-kilometre down Jasper Avenue and pockmarked the north side of the Hotel MacDonald—the old, grandiose railway *auberge*—as well as the Telus Building on the southwest corner of the Jasper-100 St. intersection. Fortunately, the building on the west-side of the WTCE was largely uninhabited at the time of detonation, since the lower floors were up for lease. Injuries were, however, sustained in nearly all buildings in the one-block vicinity (to be expected given the external structural damage incurred). The blast radius was approximately four-hundred metres, although most of the explosion had been internalized by the WTCE and the Westin Hotel next door.

Emergency lines were maxed with reports of the initial thud, called in from as far as the outer fringe of Sherwood Park (an industrial/residential satellite). The bomb sent the city into chaos and cacophony, triggering everything from the bellows of the animals in the Edmonton Valley Zoo to sensitive car-alarms on Whyte Avenue. Thick black smoke loomed over the downtown, already gridlocked with morning rush-hour traffic. Ash fell down in great wavering flakes without cessation. Roads and bridges were closed, forcing many Edmontonians to flee the downtown core on foot.

Fire and rescue crews slowly weaved through the frightened horde towards their flaming destination. Once at the scene, they worked feverishly to contain the fires and administer medical attention. Shocked and bewildered by the sinister screams and curtains of flesh draped from rebar and over the rubble, a number of survivors—most of whom had severe burns and lacerations—sauntered aimlessly about the flames and debris. Between the sight of the stunned and bloody group disappearing into and emerging from the smoke and fire, many of the emergency crews were convinced that, in that moment, hell had descended on Oil City.

The shock that reduced the still-living to monosyllabic drones would infect more than the one-thousand-thirty-five who were ultimately recorded as having been "adversely affected" by the attack. Over half of the thousand "affected" were wounded or maimed. One-hundred-and-sixty-three civilian casualties were recorded, the majority (ninety-seven) killed in the World Trade Centre where Ms. Wensen was working, while other victims were found in the surrounding streets and buildings. Only after the fires had been extinguished could rescue crews begin to extricate victims—some trapped in their cars and others pinned beneath tonnes of twisted metal – realizing, in the process, the human toll exacted by the explosion.

Footage of papers adrift in the dissipating cloud of dust and debris, over indiscernible clumps of human flesh, hair, and blood soaked fabrics, immediately went viral on the internet. The gore was censored in television broadcasts, but the horror was just as palpable. Even distant shots (in particular the amateur footage submitted to *The Network* by commuters on Highway 216) were harrowing, showcasing the pilaster of smoke fore-grounded by screams and panic.

Juxtaposed against the now-iconic image of the smoking skeleton of the WTCE, Canadian headlines read: "Bastards! A Changed Canada"; "Our Nation Saw Evil"; "It's Like a War Zone", et cetera. The press underlined the cataclysmic nature of the event. Contra the New York WTC bombing in 1993, this was considered by many to be a "game changer." Canada, a soft or middle-power,[4] was delivered a painful blow, from which it was expected to buck-up or whimper. Unless it jumped straight into the fight—with whom or with what, no one was quite sure—its citizens and allies would lose respect, compounding the problems faced by the Chretien Government.

To re-present the nature of this dilemma, the *Washington Post* ran Simeon Marouf's cartoon depicting a [Canadian] beaver beside his broken dam, with torrents of water rushing towards him. I doubt that Chalmers (the paper's editor) or Marouf had any idea of the magnitude of the impending flood in Canada—waters that would erode all obstacles with violence and force.

THE FIRST STATEMENT offered from the Canadian Prime Minister's Office was issued midday September 11:

> We reel before the blunt and terrible reality of the evil we have just witnessed. We cannot stop the tears of grief. We cannot bring back lost wives and husbands. Sons and daughters.

---

[4] H.H. Herstien, L.J. Hughes, R.C. Kirbyson. *Challenge & Survival: The History of Canada* (Scarborough, ON: Prentice-Hall, 1970). p 411

Canadian citizens...citizens from all over the world. We cannot restore futures that have been cut terribly short.

In a speech later in the day, Prime Minister Chretien offered the following statement: "[The attack is] a cowardly act of unspeakable violence...It is impossible to fully comprehend the evil that would have conjured up such a cowardly and depraved assault."

Chretien was visibly shaken. The political sheen and candour were gone. Cameras rolling, he jutted his uneven chin into the awkward silence and expectation that emanated from his sweaty, information-starved audience of journalists, politicians, law, and military officials. The Prime Minister's hesitation permitted focus to fall on the trivial minutia underpinning the scene: the confusion mapped onto his body, made manifest in the wrinkles on his mangled suit and the indecision of his remaining plugs of hair; Opposition leader Stockwell Day's athleticism (he was seated off to the side) secreted between bowed shoulders and beneath a furrowed brow belonging to one twice his age; the scores from the NHL exhibition games scrolling across the banner, interrupted by "Canadian Prime Minister Speaks..."; and the *FOX* and *CNN* reporters, relaxed as ever, trading business cards in the third row (I was not very impressed by those miserably cavalier fuckers). The disheveled PM held the podium for support, and began to issue what was rumoured to be a stern warning to the so-called enemies of freedom.

Ahead of his voice, riddled by breaks in pitch and shaken by a staccato grind through the prefatory statement, his hands began to tremble. At the airport bar in Glasgow, where my colleagues and I sipped on browns as we waited irritably for our puddle-jumper to Toronto, *The Calgary Herald* reporter to my right jotted his disgust heavily into a pocket-notebook. Fear and loathing in Glasgow; perhaps fear and shame at Parliament Hill, and more of the same on either side of Edmonton's Iron Bridge. In this moment of shared vulnerability, the perceived weight of each subsequent syllable grew exponentially. Where was the courage? The glowing heart? The Shawinigan Handshake of the street-fighter-cum-national-leader?

Chretien's pitiful trembles turned into intentional gesticulations in tandem with the rhythm of the speech, and his sickly hands became fists. My Calgarian acquaintance choked on his Canadian Club in disbelief when the old Quebecer began slamming the podium. "This damnable act of cowardice will not go unpunished. If the evil is domestic, the perpetrator will pay. If the evil is international, the perpetrator will pay," he bellowed to a room of Canadians, no longer content with playing placid, cow-eyed multilateral pacifists. Stars supplanted the tears, and the crowd emitted a primal, anticipatory growl. "Vengeance! From the darkness, *nous avons vu et entendu*—and we've seen enough. Measure for measure, and then some." Remembering his own mother was a Franco-Albertan from the Edmonton region, Chretien continued: "Canadians—Albertans—Edmontonians—should not fear the dark..." He searched the rafters for the god he forsook and then the audience for his wife Aline's confidence, "for the rejoinder will be a brilliant spectacle!"

The contents of the speech were sufficient to conclude that the Canadian government registered the explosion downtown Edmonton as an act of terrorism. Since there were no bodies tarred and feathered on Whyte Avenue, Fourteenth Avenue, Bloor Street, or in Riley Park, it was safe to say that the perpetrator was still at large. Chretien's allusion to a reactive spectacle indicated to all that, despite having forgone the initial passing of the Emergencies Act (since the House and Parliament were not in session), it soon would be, and all federal and local law-enforcement agents were to be on high alert.

Since Chretien's Liberal Government knew full-well the Emergencies Act was guaranteed and would be passed without question, they announced to the public at day's end September 11 that the Canadian Forces (CF) were given the go-ahead and granted the leeway essential to ensure civil order and safety. Canadian General Ray Henault, the Chief of Defense, issued preliminary orders to the CF, and inaugurated Operation Orion. The first CF commitment was the One Canadian Mechanized Brigade Group in Edmonton. They began attuning their exercises to worst-case scenarios resultant of a second attack. Crack troops of the Royal Canadian Regiment in Petawawa were put at the ready to defend the National Capitol. Peace keeping was about to take a back-seat.

One hour after the explosion, Edmonton mayor Bill Smith put in a call to the provincial and federal governments. In addition to the Royal Canadian Mounted Police, assigned "primary peace officer responsibility in relation to criminal offences constituting a threat to the national security of Canada," the Army Reserves, alongside units from the Regular Force, were activated. Technically, the city had jurisdictional control, but the military did not want to waste time playing "who's the boss" with local police enforcement, so General Rick Hillier flew in to direct defensive and reparative action, integrating RCMP task forces into his defense-scheme. Sidelong to military strategizing, the Special Threat Assessment Group (activated by the Solicitor General who is responsible for vital points in Canada) worked on formulating an adversarial position to their still unidentified enemy, though the plan was vague since they had little to work with.

The mystery concerning *who* and *why* was greater compounded by the particularity and severity of the WTCE bombing, contra other instances of domestic terror in recent Canadian memory: the Squamish Five's Cheekye-Dunsmuir and Litton Industries bombings paled in consequence; the Oka Crisis was an entirely different kind of gong show; and the FLQ's Montreal Stock Exchange bombing was localized to a smaller affected-area with nowhere as many victims. 9/11 inaugurated a new security paradigm in Canada, one with the potential to re-infect the entire world with a Cold War-kind of fear and suspicion.

NOMOS OF THE MODERN

Toronto, Ontario
August 24, 2005

JACQUELYN was luminescent. Ponytail tight, dressed in an egg-white blouse and constellations of sweat, she kept her cool despite the cacophony of horns and murmurs of a thousand-or-so disgruntled commuters, the ever present threat of IEDs (i.e. improvised explosive devices), the summer smog (despite an idling industrial complex), and the much-discussed sniper fire. Shuffling through her playlist, she stood apart from the hordes of marginalized Canucks. She looked back and, seeing my heat-blurred form through the window, smiled. In her groove-abetted calm, she transcended the frustration written into everyone else's faces, mine included.

I was neither luminous nor transcendent, but instead sickly, corporeal, and trapped inside our boiling rental sedan, choking on my own stench, and fretting about an expired press pass and a missing letter of accreditation. The gravity of having insufficient papers was exacerbated with every minute spent under the sweltering Toronto midday sun. The prospect of my wasted effort turning out to be a waste of time weighed heavily upon me, and I could tell from my reflection in the mirror, that it also weighed heavily upon my eyelids, already puffy from one cigarette too many. Audrey had called them "asshole eyes," which, although an offhand and vulgar remark, was probably right on the money.

Electricity along the strip was out, forcing a number of restauranteurs and their respective chefs outside along with their makeshift barbeques. Quarreling smells colluded, collided, and wafted over, carrying with them hints of their volatized chemical and cultural compounds: greasy kebabs, curry, shawarma, hamburgers, bannock, and wood-smoked ribs. Hungry crowds swarmed the sweaty culinary artists, grabbing, yelling, and shoving—faces distorted by hunger and competitive zeal. Discouraged and weaker entities cycling through the crowd slowly spiraled outward, towards the pedestrian checkpoints on either side of College Street.

Hungry, hot, and tired, I slipped in and out of consciousness, alternating control with my primal brain. I'd subconsciously lock into a suggestive stare, and then fight to break it, which easily could have been mistaken for the nods. Jake, slouched on the hood of the car, tapped on the window and yelled: "Sleeping on the job again, Danson?" Surprised, I jolted back in my seat. She smiled. The expression suited her: it made her cheek-bones bulge and wrinkled her eyes. It'd be a tragedy to Botox those laugh lines, I thought. She wouldn't consider it, anyway. "I'm timeless," she used to say. I believed it. Still do.

Over a decade chasing leads on opposite ends of the spectrum, and she still hadn't begun to age, save for a few white wisps in her hair. The white seemed to allude to her wisdom as opposed to hinting at internal decay.

IN THE EARLY NINETIES, I'd attended a sustainable journalism conference in Atlanta. One snide, chain-smoking reporter budged in front of me while I was waiting to get my ID badge, and then proceeded, over the course of the afternoon, to alienate the rest of those in attendance while wearing Pat Buchanan's name tag. For whatever reason, her cavalier "don't-give-a-damn" attitude really appealed to me. At the same conference, she was asked to leave after calling Bill O'Reilly a clown and suggesting that Christiane Amanpour had the largest testicles in the room. Dissatisfied with the speakers—all unnecessarily pedantic or unprepared—I decided to join Jake outside for a smoke. The conversation was too good to limit to a single cigarette, so we went out for dinner, and then slung worse-ever stories outside my flat over a bottle of bourbon.

Since I was enamored with Audrey at the time of this first encounter, I endeavored to keep my budding friendship with Jake platonic. I'm convinced our window of opportunity closed that night, somewhere after the sixth shot and before the tenth. Probably for the best—the security of an asexual accomplice enabled us to focus on our professional relationship.

We were two beat reporters with set and disparate proximities to the story. By circumnavigating the competitive antipathy harbored by our respective networks, we pursued different techniques to our mutual advantage. As an embedded journalist, I gave her insider scoops from the frontlines, and in exchange, she spoke in absolutes, throwing her weight around on the side to set me up with great interviews and to permit me access to her network's international resources. As you could imagine, her assistance kept me mobile.

JACQUELYN MARKED THE END of her aesthetically pleasing coma with a slap against the hood of the car, and with that, she slid off. I closed my eyes in order to simulate disinterest. Even though I knew she was coming—the air getting sweeter around me—she nevertheless startled me, swatting harder than she should. "Binoculars."

"Ow."

"Oh please. I didn't hit you that hard. Could I use the binoculars?"

"The binoculars? Why?"

"Because: because I want to see something."

"You didn't need to hit me." I crooked a smile as I pulled the brim of my cap over my eyes.

"Ok, Jesus, I'm sorry, Gawd. I forgot how delicate you are. It won't happen again. Now, can I please use the binoculars? Where are they?"

"I think you mean *my* binoculars."

"Yes, of course, how silly. May I please use *your* binoculars?"

"Yeah, I don't care."

"Where are they?"

"The trunk."

"Are you serious?"

"If you want them, that's where they are." Jacquelyn sighed, shot an exasperated look at the sky, and then recomposed herself in front of me, only to feign a smile.

"Would… would you get them for me? Please."

"No."

"Pretty please?" She parodied Betty Boop's cartoonish mannerisms, batting her eyes and smirking.

"No," I said again, bluntly.

She distorted her face with an embellished frown. "You're sure they're even back there?" Jacquelyn leaned through the window, and began rummaging around me. She searched the papers on the dash, and tried to reach beneath the bench seat.

"Whoa! Watch your paws," I said, pretending to take offense to her elbow's graze of my knee. I wrenched the keys out of the ignition, and offered them to Jake out the window.

"Can you double-check the glove compartment?" The keys glistened, catching her eye. "Forget it." She peeled off the side of the car and seized them. The binoculars were buried somewhere in between or beneath the new HD-interchangeable-lens-camera, Jacquelyn's SLR and all its phallic attachments, a couple boxes of batteries, hours-worth of footage on detachable hard-drives, our Kevlar vests, two tripods, and a first aid kit. "Found it."

Jacquelyn returned to her seat and began studying interactions at the checkpoint and taking notes. Unlike the American flag beside it, the Canadian flag was at half-mast. Sympathetic responses to massacre were evidently one element within a larger debate with petty signage. "Flags, David, or scales of justice?"

WE HAD TO PASS several checkpoints in order to reach the Sky Dome, where a couple thousand refugees and displaced Torontonians were receiving food and aid. At the time, Toronto had around 2.3 million inhabitants. A minority (i.e. ten or twenty thousand) had been displaced as the result of strategic troop placements or having their homes cordoned-off. Buildings the US Army had designated as hostile were bulldozed or boarded-up. This selection process tended to be rather liberal. Pretty much every choke-point in the city was preordained hostile, which very quickly affected mobility and the public's perception of the military presence.

A mish-mash of Canadian Forces, American Forces, UN lackeys, and NATO intermediaries were dispersed throughout the city, tasked with maintaining civic order and infrastructure. Although it certainly was a different place than the Toronto I had experienced during a lengthy stop-over right after 9/11, it retained many of the qualities I referenced in earlier reports [see my transcript, entitled "Fear and Loathing in The Big Maple" on *The Network*'s website].

We were, of course, extremely late for our afternoon "tour" of the camp. Had we walked from the airport, we likely would have arrived sooner than inching forward in our gas-guzzler. The equipment we carried, however, was far too valuable to risk seizure at any of the turn-styles intended for pedestrian transitions between city sections or at subway terminals.

According to a third party research group tasked with analyzing the ramifications of the checkpoints in eastern Canada, one third of all possessions were taken by security officers between the metal detector and the perimeter gate. Given the extent of this sort of corruption, attempting Toronto on foot was statistically not worthwhile.

Jacquelyn was not particularly impressed with my tardiness—I had "overslept." She had convinced herself that, had we rendezvoused two hours earlier, we would be "there by now," though I reassured her that we'd probably only be two cars ahead. Honestly, we'd have been waiting wherever we went, and my delay was something of a necessity. The band-aid had to be pulled sooner or later. My misadventures the previous week had amounted to the straw that broke the camel's back. Audrey left me [with a chill and numbness].

THE PHEREMONES were no longer playing white rabbit to her inner Alice. Her oasis turned to desert as our love turned to sand, and I scoured the earth for fetching-stories while the hour glass grained asymmetric.

A week prior, after a bottle of Alberta Rye Whisky, I decided she had cheated on me, which I realize was not in keeping with my journalistic style—*always cross-check the source!* The reasoning: one spawn was not enough—her internal clock was ticking and she craved another, so her subconscious volition and its correspondent (i.e. an empty womb) pressed her onwards and backwards onto another's bed.

Spending too much time in the company of pigs probably jaded me, prompting me to expect comparable behavior from all inheritors of this modern imaginary, Audrey included. Projecting the barbarism of others onto my wife proved calamitous. Four texts and a phone call later, Jeffrey Byman and his accomplice Denise Leung (friends of mine from the Canadian Broadcasting Corporation) took me downtown Toronto via the subway (the TTC), recognizing my need to let off some steam.

Basking in the brilliant darkness of some loud, crowded, and lonely Queen Street-College Street-any-street-club, I mashed lips, gnashed teeth, and pressed on, deliriously, into disoriented mating rituals, and danced to initiate and inaugurate the retributive pollination of the shiniest, waxiest, most glamorous, and promising of those midnight flowers wilting under the American occupation.

The game, so-called, I felt had always been beneath me, but after a bottle of whisky, some graduate student occupied the game's place. I was Sisyphus, pushing her up the wall or she was Tantalus, with the promise of life and release before her, or she might have been Atlas—holding up my solipsistic worst-of-all-possible-worlds—losing faith with every twist. In any case, the night amounted to a horribly hedonist error in judgment and incurred irreparable damage to my relationship with Audrey.

Since my revenge did not taste as sweet as I had imagined it would, I approached Audrey the subsequent evening, provoked a fight, and then confessed, intending the truth as a last say—an all-in, so to speak. My straight, however, was bested by her royal flush: she claimed complete innocence, all in hearts.

Suffice to say, the catharsis I had expected never came. A worse yelling fight ensued, one that I could not possibly win. Recognizing I had lost more than just the fight, I sloughed off into the night, hoping a few hours' separation, some sleep, and a stiff morning breeze could possibly rectify my wrongs. Any rational, sober man would have known better.

I woke up on the couch, late, to find Audrey and Samuel gone. They'd taken their luggage, making the room seem bigger, emptier, lonelier. She had unplugged the alarm clock—whether by malice or mistake it is not important—causing me to miss my six-thirty head-start. Two hours behind schedule, I scrambled down to meet Jacquelyn, head pounding and prayerful that my entire life was not in shambles.

"I AM FREE from the tyranny of family," I half-heartedly quipped out the window to Jacquelyn. She laughed.

"I bet you'd like to think so." Jake waltzed back around to the passenger side, and clamoured in.

"What do you mean?" I inquired.

"Everything I see still screams helplessly married, father of one. Nothing about you says anything else." The smile washed off my face and I slouched onto the steering wheel. "Did she take the kid too?" I nodded reluctantly. "Free, hah!" Jake sneered. "Her smell is still all over you." She undid the buckles on her sandals and stretched her legs out on the dash. "When you're done, can you pass me his file?"

"Done what?" I pointed to two stacks of documents and signed the option with a look of puzzlement.

"Yeah, ok."

"Whose file?" I asked.

"Who else's?" I thumbed through the pile of folders until I found it. I scanned the bolded terms, and then threw it onto Jake's lap. She sat up. "Ah, ok, here we go. Kalnychuk, Bruce, born 1937. Skip ahead to…1969, Bruce meets and marries Katherine Marie Schawght, nine years his junior. They have two kids. Then…1990-something, one dies. Gulf War. Early 1992, Bruce and Kathy Marie get divorced. Do you want to tell me what happens after that? Because I know you know."

"Know what?"

"That there are certain things that happen in life…that change everything forever. The first domino to fall in the house of cards." She tossed the file into my lap. It felt like a slab of concrete on my legs. "If you know what I mean." I could taste bile on my lips.

"No, I don't."

"What I'm saying is…do you think that when Kathy Marie left Kalnychuk after his oldest son died overseas, that he packed up and said: 'I am free from the tyranny of family' to his mistress?"

"Mistress—? No."

"No, and look how he turned out." The potential of a smile on her face—the fact that she was secretly enjoying this—was infuriating.

"I'm not a terrorist."

"Not yet, no. Everybody starts somewhere." She lit up a cigarette and brushed some dandruff off of my shoulder.

"And my son isn't dead. Why would you make such a comparison? Is that supposed to make me feel better?"

"No, I wasn't trying to cheer you up. All I'm saying is, if you want to cry, don't mind me. It's not good to bottle these things up. You'll end up repressed."

"I'm not bottling anything, I'm fine."

"Just don't fool yourself into thinking you're past this. You said it yourself: your kid still lives. Therefore, you're still his dad. And your wife ran away with him to God-knows-where. Wherever you aren't, I guess. Who knows when you're going to see your kid again. How old is he?" Her sudden staidness alleviated my rage.

"Six."

"Six, wow. Tough age to lose a father. Hope all this isn't too hard on him. I wonder if it'll have any negative kind of effects on him in the long run. Like a noticeable change for the worse."

"Jake, stop. Please."

"What's Kalnychuk's other boy up to these days? Making bottle rockets? IEDs?"

"Stop."

"All I'm saying is: you can cry if you want to. Don't feel like you have to look tough. It's okay. I know you. I know you're not."

"Stay with the car. I need some air."

"Should I come?"

"No, just stay with the car. I'll be back." I kicked my door ajar and stood up into the faint whisper of the heat claiming my body, crackling at my feet, devouring the sweat on my skin.

Jacquelyn was right, but I, like the American people, felt pain, and wanted something other than the truth for remedy. I decided to rummage about, maybe pick some brains. There was no sense of urgency or need to stick around since our rental was still parked a kilometre away from the checkpoint.

THE STOREFRONTS had advanced their shadows and wares past the sidewalks, but College Street was still in the sun's umbra. I saw some US troops idling in a Humvee beside the row of cars waiting to pass into the next city section and the multitude of people, bifurcated into two groups: those waiting in line and those selling goods to those waiting, burdened with spoiled groceries, melting ice, and sun-dyed furniture.

The Humvee-gunner, poised like a sphinx, refused to speak one word to me after I announced I was a reporter. Another soldier came around, reloading his gun. *Where had the last magazine gone?* After glimpsing my badge, he asked me if I had a moment to see something "news-worthy."

"Of course," I replied. "I have all the time in the world."

"Boy, can't be easy waiting in all that, huh?" He swung his assault rifle to his side and pointed it toward the checkpoint, squinting down his telescopic sight.

"It's certainly no treat," I replied, my focus lost in navigating the broken glass and shingles masking the road.

"Just be thankful you don't live here. That's one commute to work I could not stand."

"Well, I'll tell you how it goes. Today, it's part of my commute to work. But then again, I guess you could say I'm in a permanent commute." A school of guppies scuttled past us, chasing a basketball and cackling wildly—indifferent to the soldier, his gun, and this war.

"Kids. You have any?"

"Yeah, one. Don't see him as often as I'd like."

"You're a bit of a nomad, huh. Pains me to see a guy like you. No sense of home or centre."

"And you manage to maintain those sentiments out here?"

"Hell yeah I do. America is home. And you know what they say? Home is where the gun is…The gun's everywhere." *Rah, rah, rah.* "Get your camera out. It's just up here." He yanked on a loose corner of a chain-link fence and guided me through.

"Do you know why the Canadians are flying their flag at half mast?"

"Sure do. Rangers did a number on a bunch of insurgents in Airdrie, Alberta. Only problem was that they didn't know a Canadian team was already keeping tabs on the group. The Canucks had been taking their time, trying to capture a high-priority suspect. Whether or not it's true, the Canadians say they had secured a 'no-advance, watch and standby' order through Northern Command. Regardless, they were accidentally mixed in with the US targets."

"Did they sustain heavy casualties?" I inquired, detachedly.

"Well, a US Apache ended up making a mess of some of the Canadian troops as well as civilian bystanders, including the ambulance called to the first massacre. You can imagine that the Canadians were pretty p-o'ed. They reacted by taking down the chopper. A firefight ensued between ground and air forces. Made a bit of a mess in Calgary in the process."

"A mess?"

"More civilians and private property. The usual collateral damage. Then the Canadian Military got all up in arms."

"By a technicality, aren't they always?"

"Angry, I mean. Canadian armour started shelling forward-American positions as a deterrent, and then, before our boys could

43

escalate with Warthogs and Apaches, cooler heads prevailed. Rangers and the US armour fell back to the outskirts of Airdrie. Now they're kicking around with Canadian overseers. Probably not the last we'll hear about this fuck-up, is my thinking. Word is that the rocket attack on our boys outside of Lethbridge was official CF business. A little bit of: you cut my back, I'll cut yours."

"Sounds like US-Canadian joint operations are arthritic."

Face disfigured by puzzlement, he squeezed out a response, "Yeah, sure dude."

The young soldier brought me to the scene of a recent detonation to take a few pictures. Tar had been lifted by the explosion so that it cast a shadow on the bear-track-like burn marks, particularly dark on the side where the runner had been facing. Remains from the blast and the saboteur had been shoveled up, and then covered by a white blanket and chalk-dust. Much of the blood had been pressure washed, although the perimeter of the blanket was still tinged brown. The formless mound of nameless fragments probably resembled a cannibal platter.

Scanning the site through my camera's eye, I panned to a rather startling image. In the metal teeth of the checkpoint's fence fluttered a piece of scorched fabric. In very poor taste, and I still regret my ignorance, I commented to my guide: "Your efforts to humanize the checkpoint seem to have had an explosive reception with the locals." He smiled wryly, and then began to examine the windows overhead through the sights of his rifle, searching for threats, and mulling over my facetious remark. The soldier returned me to Jacquelyn and the car after I snapped off a few more shots of the damage.

Jacquelyn traded smiles with the soldier, and offered me "kills" on her smoke as I jostled into my seat. I interpreted this as an apology for her earlier efforts to buck me up at the expense of making me feel like shit. "No thanks. Not in the mood." I watched the white-orange devour its way down the cigarette to her ruby lips, and observed the filter, ready to mark the end of our deafening silence. She threw the butt out the window and spit white, voluminous smoke.

"Find anything good?"

I waved the smoke away from my face. "Just bits and pieces." Jake raised an eyebrow, and I started shuffling through my notes.

EVERY QUESTION was barked behind an M4 Carbine and between razor wire parentheses, prompting weary travelers to adopt defensive dispositions. Everyone was ready to address the question of "why this?" or "why that?" promoting the general sense that Toronto was a city on trial.

With the widespread implementation of military checkpoints, some areas had taken on the appearance of a second—hell, perhaps a third—world country overnight. Although Toronto, from my recollection, was always relatively ghettoized (i.e. though an inclusive and multicultural city, ethnic groups clustered together in clearly identifiable enclaves), the checkpoints had concretized previously imaginary divisions. Toronto's once celebrated cultural spillage was nowhere to be seen. Families, confined to their huts in this "global village," resented their immobility, symptomatic of the occupation. Fear conditioning, resultant and component of the occupation, led many of the Torontonians I encountered to mental illness; most commonly, agoraphobia.

While the CN Tower dialed time with its shadow over the downtown's impromptu parking lots, I grabbed some sound-bites from a woman and her four children, and then returned to the car. I played back the recording on my Dictaphone: "This is no place for a child to grow up," the woman'd said. *No, probably not.* I couldn't get Samuel out of my head. I kept quietly praying that Audrey had taken him someplace safe, someplace American.

I slid into the passenger seat, and Jacquelyn leaned into me. "Hey Romeo, maybe you should leave the talking to me."

"Romeo?" I roared.

"Yeah."

"What do you mean? Is that a... codename or something?" I said slyly.

"Don't worry about it. Listen. I think it's in both our best interests if you remain relatively quiet."

"Why? Is that what Romeo means?"

"The more we construe you as a eunuch or some impotent chaperone, the more likely the ruffian at the gate will go on feeling unthreatened. This is an unwinnable pissing contest, with a pre-determined winner every single time."

I consented. She was right. Jacquelyn knew the ins and outs of socio-sexual politics. Surprisingly, she was bad with romantic encounters and resented happy couples. She despises my saying it, but the fact is that she's comparable to an impotent pornographer – one so aware of the minutia, yet lacking the pertinent agency to participate. While she understood the game from a distance, I, on the other hand, found it to be all darkness, but such is the nature of immersion, the rabbit hole.

"Binoculars?"

"Trunk." Jacquelyn sighed. "Kidding." I pulled the binoculars out from under the bench, and handed them over.

"No. Use them yourself. Look," she pointed. I snatched them back and began scoping out the checkpoint.

"Yeah, it's a checkpoint. So what?" I inquired.

"The gate. You see the big guy with the big gun. Standing at the gate. Do you see him?"

"Uhhh."

"At the gate. The gate," she said, growing increasingly impatient with my childishness.

"I get it, I get it. Yes. Okay. There he is. What about him? He's more of a Romeo than I am –hiding behind that big machine gun."

"Yes, well, I'm glad you noticed. There is no winning here, David. You can't be talking to anyone—let alone any women— because we don't want the guy with the gun at the gate to feel threatened at all. Do you understand?"

"So I'm the Romeo?"

"Forget it David. I don't think you have a whole lot to worry about."

THE CHECKPOINT that had us waiting passed, on average, twenty vehicles every hour. Most drivers would attempt the similarly congested side streets, take advantage of the more liberal ISAF-Australian checkpoints at Jane and at Bathurst (if headed north), or simply ditch their cars. Alternatively, others would wait with the unemployed masses bent on navigating the metropolis via the TTC. Fortunately for passengers of the TTC, the foreign security officers were indifferent. If terrorism occurred in the subways, Canadians would be the only ones affected. Curiously, none of the bombers ever targeted public transit, contra the understanding forwarded in *FOX*'s facetious reports about attempts on a Calgary LRT train and on a bus in Vancouver.

After an hour or more of waiting in a car filled with still air, choking on the smell of cigarette rot and melting plastic, we pulled up to the plywood booth enshrined in razor wire and buried beneath sandbags. The bald, verbose security operative had just finished his watch, and a young, blue-eyed agent came forth. "Good day sir, may I ask you where you are headed this afternoon?" His upper lip curled and his yellow teeth ground to the fore of his jaw, cleft in two by the competing midday light and shadow.

"My partner and I are—" I started. Jacquelyn shifted away from me and donned an enormous smile.

"We're going to interview some US soldiers at the Sky Dome. Doing a piece on Toronto: a Canadian-American success story. You know? It'll detail the benefits of cooperation, integration, and all that."

"Uh huh," responded the soldier. He squinted at Jake, so that I was likely reduced to a blur in his peripheral vision. He smiled. "May I see some sort of identification –a driver's license, passport or other government-issued ID?"

"My passport," said Jake.

"—And mine." I leaned over Jacquelyn to hand him my papers with a trembling, overextended arm. To my pleasure and Jake's chagrin, he overlooked the expired date on my papers. He was preoccupied, instead, with staring down Jacquelyn's shirt with a perverse intensity.

"That'll be all." He dragged the barbwire gate back, and waved us through. "Unless you want to grab a drink…"

Jake rolled up her window. "That wasn't so bad, eh Juliet?" I chuckled. Jaquelyn took out her aggression on my thigh in a series of pinches.

"Fucking depraved meatball," Jake declared, as we cleared the checkpoint and trundled along the expressway. "I should have worn a *jilbab*!"

IT WAS EASY going for five minutes until we had to exit. Our off-ramp was blocked with concrete barriers. A soldier waved us into another line of cars. They were searching vehicles one-by-one for explosives because an IED had been detonated earlier in the day. I padded my jacket down for smokes and then tossed it into the back. I got out of the car and lit a cigarette. The driver in front of us—some middle-aged Sri-Lankan Canadian by the looks of it and from the sound of his accent—got out of his car.

"I cannot wait any longer. This is nonsensical!" he belted at the top of his lungs. Whether he had to urinate or was simply fed up with his wasteful commute, he had no intention of waiting around. He walked past me on the driver's side, gave me a polite nod, and proceeded west.

"Where the fuck does he think he's going? What about his car?" Jacquelyn threw her arms about, tracing the departed's trajectory away from his car to the sky with a frustrated sweep of her hands. "Miserable asshole. That's one more obstacle in our way. David, say something to him! Stop him!"

"Stop him? Stop him yourself."

"If he doesn't come back and move this car, they'll presume it's a bomb. Won't get through anytime soon in that event."

"You really think it's going to matter? We're already sitting in a fucking parking lot."

"Maybe he left his keys?" Jacquelyn got out of the car and headed over to the driver's side of the little Civic, where the door had been left ajar. "They're here," she exclaimed.

"I'll pull it over. Jacquelyn, stay with the car," I shouted. I kept my volume low enough to avoid alerting the guards, but in lowering my voice, I also missed Jacquelyn's attention.

"Sir, can you help us? Sir!" She began waving down a nearby soldier.

I erupted into a restricted yell, "No, no, what are you doing? Everything is okay. It's okay." One of the soldiers turned to the sound of the commotion. "Everything is okay," I barked. "Jacquelyn, what the fuck are you doing?"

"Sir!"

A soldier with machinegun poised at the ready goofy-footed over. "May I ask y'all what exactly is going on?"

"The man in front of us abandoned his car. Was headed to the washroom. Smelt like shit," Jake announced.

"Which way did he go?" chirped the visibly concerned soldier.

Jacquelyn pointed west.

"Uh huh. Alright."

The officer radioed for a tow-truck and called a bomb squad. Our relation to the imaginary line ahead became asymptotic as several groups came and went, delivering conjecture about a potential threat, each calling another puzzled group over. One pair of extremely concerned soldiers kicked the bumper off of the abandoned car, because "that's usually where terrorists hide their IEDs." The polyphony of car horns behind us overwhelmed all but the loudest voices, who were instructing the quarrelsome metal choir to endure a while longer.

GOING TO THE SKYDOME seemed, at first, to be a complete waste of time. Everyone had a sob story. Families, animals, vehicles, houses, and the like had been destroyed. The carrion had already been picked clean by the scavengers that had descended earlier from the major networks. Microphones had been stuffed into these sources' faces, and to what effect? No extra-national agency had sounded the depths of the Canadian heart, because all were content to dwell on the shallows—to extol stereotype and to evidence Bush's binaries with unconvincing examples.

I walked up and down the aisles of personal spaces designated by the Red Cross, and realized that I did not belong. If I can help, then I should, I thought. But what would I achieve by submitting a ten minute piece about the woman who lost her son in an impromptu firefight in Brampton? Teach people what they already knew about the American campaign or lose a tape trying to educate people who would rather remain ignorant?

I held a recorder like a wilted flower to an old fellow's stinky rant, then decided I could not waste anymore time, so I thanked him and left. Jacquelyn hung around because she needed to give her network something more substantial than one or two sound-bites. I, on the other hand, needed to hook a big story or choose a new profession.

As I moseyed along Bremner Boulevard trying to plan my next big play, I received a text from Jake. "North-side. Five minutes. One Blue Jays Way." I bolted around, skimming the crowd-turned-marketplace that bustled around the stadium's periphery. The throng was too dense to get a visual fix on Jacquelyn. Spinning helplessly, I waited for a sign. A hand throttled by over-sized jewelry fired into the air and began waving.

Following my five-fingered Polaris, I pressed into the organic composite. Jake stood beneath her signal, close-talking to a middle-aged man wearing fatigues. "David Danson, this is Robert Wharton from *The Washington Post*. He wants to discuss a little quid pro quo you might be interested in."

"Good to meet you Robert." I reached for his hand and we shook. He was a stout man with salt and pepper hair. "You digging for bones in that graveyard?" Robert dug his hands into his pockets—likely to hide his unsightly sausage fingers—and began yelling sensitive information over the crowd.

"No. I'll leave that to the historians. I heard you have a contact in the Hell's Angels. Is that true?"

"So there's the *quid*. What's the *quo*?" I began praying that Laroux kept himself alive through Operation Springtime.

"Saw your article about empire and survivalism. Very quaint. You've got a problem with the language you employ though. It sounds, how do I say this, too bureaucratic? Too longwinded. Too academic. Anyway, if you want to brace your arguments so that you come off as less of a bore, you may want to get the scoop from one of my contacts in Washington. Toronto is a dead-end."

"How do you figure?"

"Well, it's living and therefore unrepresentative of the rest of Canada. You don't go to Fort Lauderdale if you're writing a piece on urban American thug life, right?" He leaned in closer, to the point where I could hear his tongue click against his teeth, loosing flecks left by his smelly lunch. "If you find the smoking gun stateside, you're bound to find out where to look afterwards." I looked for Jacquelyn's expression to gauge whether or not this was a real hook-up or just a grasping attempt by a desperate man for a big break. That would make two of us. "Hell, maybe when you're there, you can do me a favour: find out whether Congress actually passed a 'War Powers Resolution Authorization' granting *Senor* Bush the power to initiate military action against any national organization or individual of his choosing. That'd be good for one of your alarmist articles, huh?" He elbowed me playfully in the gut and smiled.

"Yeah, real good. Give me your digits. I'll let you know. Who's the g-man in Washington?"

"It's not the g-men you should be interested in."

"Is that so?"

"Try Kalnychuk's only son. The boy's got a history of shunning members of the press, but that's just because they don't know how to handle him properly. All you have to do is dote on his thirst." He simulated a drinking movement, laughing into the imaginary bottle. "You could also talk to some of the Homeland Security boys, but I don't know what sort of details they'll give up." I winced. "Hey man, it's a start."

Every time I turned to see how Jacquelyn was managing the information, I caught her wearing a big, genuine smile—a good indicator from one not easily fooled.

"Yah. I'll let you know." I said my goodbyes. "I'm headed back to the hotel. Going to take the subway."

"Public transportation's a conveyor belt with seats," declared Wharton. Jacquelyn laughed. "One of the few places where the consumer, consuming, travels like the goods he consumes. God, I can't stand it! All the best, notwithstanding…"

I interrupted him, grinning, picturing him with a bloody nose, "Well, goodbye."

Jacquelyn hugged me, whispering in my ear: "I can't believe you're going to let me drive back alone."

"Sorry," I replied. "Sincerely, I am."

"No you're not. But don't worry… Good start! Good start, huh David? Maybe you'll have time for a good cry on the plane." I winced again. She smiled. "Take care of yourself, David…"

♠

GENESIS: GOOD FENCES MAKE GOOD NEIGHBOURS

IN RESPONSE to the 9/11 bombing, heavily armed RCMP teams and local forces locked-down Edmonton's downtown, coinciding with the closure of all Canadian airports west of Regina, Saskatchewan. CadPat (special camoflauge created and developed in Canada) was omnipresent in Edmonton, and it freckled major intersections throughout the rest of Alberta, as well in British Columbia and Saskatchewan. CF18s and reconnaissance choppers buzzed over the Elbow, Saskatchewan, and Assiniboine rivers. With the Emergencies Act passed, the Canadian government was enabled to employ some serious force and hardware, as well as curtail certain fundamental civil rights.

Increased security resulted in decreased mobility in the western provinces. Travel across the bridges or anywhere near "critical structures" in Edmonton, for instance, was untenable on account of multiple barricades barring access. Most Edmontonians, unnerved by the bombing, expressed their satisfaction as their city was turned into a barracks, though a small minority felt threatened by the strong military presence. Mayor Smith commented on the nature of those opposed to the increase in security:

> [Those protesting outside city hall] are a bunch of drug dealers and extremists. No one of good conscience has anything to fear, and no rational person with any sense of the tragic consequence of September 11 would think of hindering our efforts to ensure the safety and security of the people of Edmonton.

The Federal, Provincial, and municipal governments recognized the necessity for greater force.

Though supportive of the police and military action, Alberta Premier Ralph Klein pressed the issue of which units from the Canadian Forces would be tasked with policing Albertans and whether or not there would be a conflict of interest. Ultimately, he was concerned with Ottawa playing regional politics, "at a time [when] Canadians should be united in cause and action." General Henault assured him that the CF would serve the interests of Edmontonians and Canadians to the best of their ability, and suggested that, "The time for nuance has passed, making way for a period of broad strokes and unapologetic excellence." Klein took additional comfort in knowing that the powerful and determined Anne McLellan was not only the Minister of Justice, but the

Member of Parliament for Edmonton West. The home team had some muscle.

On the evening of September 12, NATO Secretary-General Lord Robertson invoked Article Five of the NATO charter for the first time in NATO's history. Accordingly, "An attack on one is an attack on all... In the event of an attack...each ally will assist [Canada] by taking such action as it deems necessary." Thus, all countries in the NATO Alliance were placed on the defensive, pending an aggressive resolution for a formal confrontation (in the event that the perpetrator[s] had international associations or were protected by a particular state).

Russia's President, Vladimir Putin, was among the first of the foreign heads of state to offer condolences and to express his sympathy to Chretien, and, by extension, to the Canadian people. In his statement, Putin mentioned the need for solidarity in the face of global terrorism. Although a war on terrorism meant Putin could better justify his war in Chechnya, Chretien was cautious not to dismiss the outreach, however political.

British Prime Minister Tony Blair was outright pissed-off about the attack, and condemned it in advance of seeing the NATO brief. Behind closed doors, Blair suggested that should Edmontonians need the official or unofficial support of any of the British Army located at Canadian Forces Base Suffield in southern Alberta, "just give the word."

The US Ambassador to Canada, Paul Cellucci, passed on Bush's regards, and revealed that Bush would fly north of the border to express his sadness and support to "the Honourable prime minister and the Canadian people in person." Bush remarked in his presidential address:

> I have spoken to the Vice President, to the Governor of [Montana], to the director of the FBI, and have ordered...a full scale investigation to hunt down and to find those folks who committed this act. Our friends and allies in Canada will neither fight nor grieve alone. This tragedy is shared. Tonight and always, our hearts are with our brothers and sisters in Edmonton and in the rest of Canada. Also shared is the responsibility...to take this challenge to the free and democratic world seriously, and to send a message to the evildoers responsible. They will be brought to justice.

Although it was unclear whether the Montana governor was mentioned in the speech because of the provincial-state border or because of some other, foreknown connection, conspiracy theorists have since made much of this particular statement. Before heading to Edmonton and Ottawa to offer a supportive presence, Bush first took off to the US Strategic Command Headquarters at the Offett Air Force Base in Nebraska.

While Bush b-lined to Nebraska, continental European heads-of-state began paying lip service. French President Jacques Chirac sent his condolences, but did not explicitly promise military support of any kind. "In these terrible circumstances, all French people stand by the Canadian people," said Chirac. "We express our friendship and solidarity in this tragedy." German Chancellor Schröder and Spanish Prime Minister Aznar called the Canadian Prime Minister's Office on the 12th, offering more of the same.

Up until the 11th, Canada had been considered invulnerable. The tragedy in Alberta inspired fear and paranoia in its allies, especially those with similarly small militaries.

WHILE THE MAN the CIA fingered as "the guy" —Osama Bin Laden, the Saudi-Al-Qaeda-Wahhabist responsible for the 1998 US Embassy terrorist bombings; the October 2000 aquatic attack on the USS Cole; the 1993 bombing of the World Trade Centre in New York, and the attempted assassination of Egyptian President Marabak—had certainly risen to the top of every intelligence agency's suspect list, the glove simply didn't fit. Edmonton did not make sense as a target.

The WTCE was one among approximately three-hundred trade centres in more than seventy countries. Though it could have been misinterpreted by extremists to be a small proponent of a larger globalizing force, the Canadian 9/11 Investigation Committee knew that none of the typical groups antagonistic of western cultural and economic hegemony were deluded enough to believe that its destruction would effect the sort of change, positive or negative, they desired (not realizing the actual potential of such a "minor" incident).

The WTCE was not a stomping ground for the usual targets (i.e. oil barons and "Zionist" IMF reps). Besides the diners in Ruth's Steakhouse, the majority of the victims had been working on Canadian-focused projects or in a tourist capacity, and were diverse in terms of ethnicity and religious affiliation. Inside the complex was a tourism information centre, a chamber of commerce, an air passenger service, and a small economic development corporation. None of the investigators wanted to disparage 9/11 victims or their unquantifiable worth, but their conclusion, left unsaid, was: *Al-Qaeda wouldn't have wasted their time.* American and Israeli intelligence indicated that if Bin Laden wanted to attack a particularly symbolic WTC, his primary target would undoubtedly be the twin towers in New York.

The list of known foreign terrorist organizations that willed to incur detriment to Canada and other NATO countries was long, but Edmonton wouldn't have made a blip on any of their radars. The CIA—reluctant to consider the possibility that the 9/11 bomber was a home-bred terrorist—pressed Canadian officials to scour the East for signs of guilt and celebration. Some Canadian politicians already shared the CIA's suspicions of antipathetic Middle Eastern Arab organizations on account of their possible motivation: *to punish Canada for its enduring support of Israel.*

The first considered was Iranian President Khatami, however, he was kyboshed as a suspect because he was far too pragmatic to permit any official or unofficial operation overseas that could be directly traced back to his government. Such a bold attack on a NATO member would threaten Iranian sovereignty. Khatami wouldn't think of it; after all, he had pressed the United Nations to proclaim the year 2001 as a Year of Dialogue Among Nations.

It may have alternatively been in the interest of the Saudi Kingdom to destabilize Alberta, a competing oil exporter. While Saudi Arabia was Canada's second largest export-market in the Middle East (totalling more than one-and-one-half billion dollars in trade), an attack such as the WTCE bombing could prove monetarily promising.

An increase in security in the western provinces would slow the southward flow of oil to the US, prompting the US to direct more attention and funds across the ocean. Such a rouse could prove costly, however. If an official link could be proven between the House of Saud and the 9/11 bomber(s), NATO countries with security obligations to Canada would be forced to take up arms against Fahd bin Abdul Aziz Al Saud's nation, and likely Bahrain, Kuwait, Oman, Qatar, and the United Arab Emirates as well (bound to Saudi Arabia by their December 2000 regional defense pact). Al Saud would not subject his country or surrounding Arab nations to a potential crusade over a short-term economic advantage.

Concluding that Al Saud would have realized that bombing Canada was not in his best interest, CSIS and the CIA dismissed Saudi Arabia as a suspect. Iraqi President Saddam Hussein, on the other hand, was "good for it," according to US Director of Central Intelligence George Tenet. US Secretary of Defence Donald Rumsfeld similarly believed Saddam to have some hand in the 9/11 plot, suggesting to Canadian Ambassador to the US Michael Kergin to look for Iraqi involvement.

Canada's support of the US bombing campaign in Iraq in February had prompted the Iraqi regime to annul two-billion dollars worth of wheat purchases from Canada and to call for a boycott on Canadian goods. While Kergin believed Saddam had motive, he argued "[9/11] was not his style." Apart from an attempted disquieting of the Quebecois, it was clear Saddam did not have the time or the resources to send any bombers to a pioneer city on the Canadian fringe. After a brief investigation, CSIS and the CIA dismissed the aforementioned Arab governments as well as large terrorist organizations in the region who had tabled Canadian-directed aggression. To the CIA's chagrin, they returned their focus to American suspects, concentrating on potential individual motivations

WITNESS ACCOUNTS were pooled and used in conjunction with the surveillance videos collected from the buildings neighbouring the WTCE—in addition to ballistic reports and forensic evidence—to conclude that the explosives used in the attack were cached and detonated in a white van with Montana plates. Security surveillance provided investigators with crisp images of the plates, providing a direct lead to the bomber's regal origin, south of the border.

The CIA terminated their support of the investigation, arguing in favour of a private, American-headed inquiry. "If there is an American ingredient in this mishap," said a CIA spokesperson, "then we will conduct an American investigation."

Undaunted by the Americans' secrecy and their shift to a unilateral approach, CSIS and the RCMP collaborated and proposed a federal play for justice. At ten a.m. on September 13th,

Chretien named Harvey King the primary suspect in the WTCE bombing investigation. King's file was rushed to Interpol and American agencies to ensure that he wouldn't flee the continent.

In his follow-up to the RCMP's news brief, the prime minister lost his composure, openly accrediting the bombing to King: "This man—this cowardly dog—is guilty of mass murder! He will be held accountable for the deaths of innocent Canadians." This statement resulted in an uproar on the primary American networks' coverage. Opinionated talking-heads criticized Chretien's lack of tact.

Although the Prime Minister's Office was more or less indifferent to American opinion (especially after the revelation of the American connection to 9/11), Deputy Prime Minister Herb Gray went on *CNN* to stanch the nightmarish media-flood by explaining away Chretien's vituperative statement as emotionally charged: "Chretien's delicacy and nuance is often incommensurable to English." The Liberal government had realized that justice still waits for politics, and politicians only ever cooperate with one eye on the prize and the other on their polls.

Notwithstanding the American reaction to the "cowardly dog" statement, King arranged his alibi and surrendered himself to local authorities. It was expected to be a swift exchange and trial, especially with the broadcast of *CNN*'s interview with Roderick Tatum, Taylor Wensen's life-long confidant and friend of the Kings, who stated:

> [Wensen] had restraining orders on Harvey. Things used to be heated. She had more black eyes than excuses…He knew if she went missing, they'd come after him first thing. After the divorce, Harvey used to publically joke about how killing her and her lover wouldn't be about the money –dodging the alimony, I mean. It'd be about revenge. He's one spiteful son of a bitch.

Roderick provided officials with a compelling testimony that explained why King would have had a stake in the September 11 bombing. This should have been enough to put King behind bars or detain him some while longer, given he was the prime suspect in a mass murder investigation.

While investigators developed a succinct chronology of the events leading up to the bombing, and corroborated their suspicions, the House of Commons returned from summer recess for a September 13th afternoon sitting of Parliament. In Edmonton, firefighters continued to work around the clock to extinguish the smoldering remains of the WTCE and the Westin Hotel. In Ottawa, Chretien addressed the House:

> It is impossible to look upon the ruin of the World Trade Centre and not be moved. Be moved by disbelief; by sympathy for the victims; by outrage at the criminals; by a desire for righteous punishment; but, above all, by a firm resolve to stand up and be counted —to stand up for our people, for our values, for our way of life; to send a clear message to the cowards in the shadows who planned this crime against humanity: that their days of being able to run and hide are coming to an end. If the attac[k] o[n] September 11 [is] a shameful benchmark for the backside of human nature, the deliberate and forceful manner in which Canada…[has] marshaled our resources against the forces of terror, will be remembered as a proud benchmark of…courage and common purpose…We must be clear in our minds that this is a new kind of struggle against a new kind of enemy, and we must not allow ourselves to be trapped by the rhetoric or experiences of past wars to define our tactics or measure our success.

Chretien asked the House to work together and rush crucial reform bills to ensure the security of Canada's borders and citizens. There was no need for debate. They immediately adopted a motion condemning the attack on Canadian soil and discussed new counter-terrorism measures.

Two Hercules air-transports helped deliver members of the Senate to Ottawa the next morning, and as expected, another unanimous condemnation was delivered. Minister of National Defence Art Eggleton updated the House and proposed to send an additional five-hundred troops from the Princess Patricia's Canadian Light Infantry to southern Alberta to help the Reserve protect "key buildings and infrastructure" against possible repeats of the 9/11 attack (i.e. if King was not the sole perpetrator). Troops had already been sent, but were initially equipped only for civil support as opposed to a full-military engagement of heavily-armed border-crossers.

The front page of the *Edmonton Journal*, dated September 13th, was retrofitted with a World War Two propaganda painting of a Canadian soldier with the inscription "Back Him Up!" Ottawa was figuring out what to do, while Edmontonians were waiting for the word on who to do-in.

President Bush met with Chretien on September 14th, and publicly remarked, "We will do everything in our power to cooperate with our closest friend in an effort to rectify the horrors we've seen on the television in the past few days." Bush recognized the act as an instance of international terrorism, given there was cause to believe the perpetrator was not Canadian, and that among the dead were Japanese, Chinese, Australian, and American nationals. Although sincere, Bush complicated his message to Canadians with folksy and instinctive aphorisms, which were poorly received. Chretien did not need help finding "a snake in a grass"; he wanted King to be expedited to jail, placed in gen-pop, and worked over by flawed and capable patriots.

Despite his sincerity and promptness to offer condolences, Bush had reservations concerning an immediate extradition. After all, in his first year in office, he had dealt with a number of US-Canadian issues, including disagreements on softwood lumber, the Alaska oil pipeline through Canada, contaminated PEI potatoes, and continental missile defence, as well as Canadian scrutiny for refusing to sign the Kyoto Treaty on global warming. Moreover, King shared a still unspecified link to a Montana Congressman, so Bush had to be cautious with respect to any crossover into state politics. Stockwell Day, leader of the Canadian opposition party, balked at the delay. His indignation spilt into the House of Commons on the 15th, leaving the room a green, cream, and gold disaster.

THE UNITED STATES GOVERNMENT performed its own investigation into 9/11. The conclusions were inconsistent with earlier public confirmations. The *9/11 Report* contended that Harvey King, a model American citizen, had a verifiable alibi for the three days in question. Darcy King—declared an unreliable witness by CSIS and the RCMP on account of an obvious bias, his heavy methamphetamine use, and his suspected involvement in a number of cold cases—assented to his cousin's initial narrative of the events.

According to his statement, Darcy's van was stolen. King remained at the Spruce Groves caring centre overnight, and then on the morning of September 11, headed to Darcy's house. Benefitted by the mentally lackadaisical nurses' sense of time and materiality,

Darcy argued that Harvey was present at the caring home and had spoken with nurses on the second day in question.

The investigation hit a slight snag when King's internet search records—needed to substantiate his alleged interest in the Oklahoma City bombing, pipe-bomb manufacturing, and Taylor Wensen's whereabouts—failed to surface, which many thought would have been sufficient for a Stateside conviction and an allowance of extradition. The *9/11 Report* claimed that any incriminating evidence on King's computer had long been deleted, although in a separate police report, officer Dan Mathews revealed that King's house had been broken into (evidenced by a smashed lock), and further, that all of his electronics had been corrupted with a heavy-duty magnet. King's unspecified connection to the Montana Congressman prompted many conspiracy theorists to conclude that the WTCE bomber had help from a higher echelon or at the very least, was protected after the fact. This setback was the first of many.

Questions over whether the testimony of the American customs officer, who attested to having seen King return to the States the morning of the attack, was suppressed or even entered as evidence in the investigation prompted fury amongst the Canadian public. Mind you, before 9/11 one did not require a passport to enter Canada from the United States or vice versa, so there was no proper documentation or paper-trail. Furthermore, the number of men who resemble King crossing the border hourly—forget daily—alone is enough to call into question any positive identification. As a result, the testimony was inadmissible as evidence.

After hearing about the evidence tampering and the strangely particular witness selection in the American investigation, Chretien told reporters outside of the House of Commons that the American investigation was, "insincere and utter bullshit...They care more that I called this murderer a dog, than they care about justice for our Canadian dead." He reiterated his government's desire for King's extradition, this time specifying the necessity of a September 23 exchange. He was refused. Bush's reasoning behind the refusal was:

> [While] Americans continue to grieve with Canadians hurt by the senseless violence witnessed on September 11, it is important to remain level-headed and seek justice in a thoroughly researched fashion befitting of our nations' legal traditions.

While justice was obstructed on both sides of the 49th, the Canadian and American governments amended their terrorism laws and saw to the maximization of their defences, as well as regional and federal securities. Their foci shifted from the past to the present, and were directed towards ensuring preventative measures were in place to avoid a repeat of September's atrocity elsewhere in North America.

The UN Security Council had adopted resolution 1368 in '01, "which established a legal basis for further action against global terrorism." [5] Invoking article fifty-one of the UN Charter (re: inherent right of self-defence), Canada legitimated its demand for King and his supporters in order to stem future attacks from occurring. Disregarding the legitimacy of the demand, the US refused to cooperate, calling for the need of "damning evidence," which American agencies, ironically, both destroyed and withheld. In late September, resolution 1373 passed, which permitted the blocking of financial support to terrorist groups. However, the resolution proved impotent, as the States prevented the seizure and freezing of King's accounts. The UN was ineffectual. King was untouchable. His cousin, however…

THE EVENING OF THE FIRST refusal, two expatriate Canadians [6] living in Whitefish, Montana, killed Harvey King's cousin, Darcy King. Mistaking Darcy for their primary target, the two former Calgarians gunned him down on his way home from the Bulldog Card Room. They dragged his corpse back to Darcy's house for a positive ID. Upon recognizing the nature of their *faux-pas* in Darcy's dimly lit drug den, James Fisher and Joakim Nabokov set fire to the house in order to destroy any evidence implicating them.

Fisher and Nabokov had derived the location of Harvey King's cousin by tracking the van's plate number (shown in the *CNN* coverage where surveillance videos of the van-pre-detonation surfaced) to Whitefish, and waited for an opportune time to strike. Their chance came when they found Darcy—having led a troop of stoned miscreants to a local bar and drank his way into a stupor—

---

[5] Tirman.
[6] There were 680,000 Canadians living in the United States circa September 2001.

stumbling home alone. The police-coroner calculated that at twelve-twenty-five a.m., Darcy's partying had come to an abrupt end.

Law enforcement agents patrolling the neighbourhood—tasked with key-witness oversight and protection—apprehended two men attempting to flee the scene of the burning house. Fire crews found a badly mutilated body inside the kitchen, which had survived the worst of the fire. Inside Darcy's den, emergency crews also found child pornography and an armory of automatic firearms. Fisher and Nabokov were both charged with first-degree murder.

When news of the Calgarian "hit-men" began to circulate, anti-Canadian messages dominated the airwaves. Attempting to soothe an American populace growing increasingly hostile to their supposedly docile neighbours, the Bush administration issued a statement, stressing that the murder was a local affair, calling anti-Canadian protests "uncalled for…"

Following this hostility, Bush, who had theretofore been noncommittal, concretized his resolve to deny King's extradition. In a presidential address, Bush mutilated the Cain and Abel story in an effort to suggest that the United States, "[was] his brother's keeper," not his "un-doer," and that the "perpetrator may yet be Canadian." In the same address, he cited an intelligence report from Alaska concerning northwestern anti-American groups who would jump at the opportunity to create such a wedge between the US and her allies.

The US took a defensive posture in addition to starting the blame-game: Congress passed a forty-billion dollar emergency package for increased spending, available for infrastructure-building, the military, and for enhanced security needs.[7] Casting doubt on the conclusions reached separately by CSIS and the RCMP, Bush's statements aggravated the "adversely affected" and their surviving family members. Furthermore, Bush's insinuation that the perpetrator was Canadian necessitated a new angle: the evil that Canada and the world needed to contain was domestic as opposed to international.

---

[7] Hoge, James F., and Gideon Rose. "The Unguarded Homeland." *How Did This Happen?: Terrorism and the New War* (New York: PublicAffairs, 2001) 271.

The 9/11 attack stigmatized Canada. It created a weakness that left it exposed to the greater threat of foreign "help." Chretien's inability to successfully identify an antagonist placed him in an even more precarious position.

October arrived, and Chretien was faced with quelling the riotous protests that had cropped up across Canada, particularly in Alberta. The American Embassy in Ottawa as well as American consulates across the country (e.g. Edmonton) were forced to close their doors to the public.

While Canadian representatives waited on appeal to the United Nations, Ann Morgan, grieving widow to Frank Morgan (killed in the WTCE attack), killed herself and eight others with a rifle in a Montana-based Target retail store. Thought an accomplice to the shootings, her seventeen-year-old son, Sean Morgan, was detained, and then beaten to death by a bloodthirsty mob in the lobby of the Best Western where he was staying.

Again, the internet played an interesting part in the domino-effect of bad news. Videos emerged of the Morgans' sympathizers: vociferous North Americans who lambasted the United States, its people, and the violence that had erupted on both sides of world's longest, undefended border. Morgan's broken body likewise became iconic. The image conveyed the sense that Canadian victims were worse than forgotten: their bodies and memories were being mutilated post-mortem.

The NHL season was cancelled in anticipation of ferocious riots and violence on and off the ice, as well as a result of the Canadian players' (who proliferate the NHL) refusal to play. American flags were burnt in separate instances of anti-American protests held in Ottawa, Montreal, Toronto, Calgary, Fredericton, Red Deer, Lloydminster, Valcartier, Victoria, and Vancouver (and a host of small towns), while rabble rousers sounded war horns outside of Parliament. The American consulate in Toronto, already closed to the public, was evacuated after a fire bomb was thrown through one of its second story windows (a riot on Queen Street had spilled over onto University Avenue).

When asked what the government intended to about worsening civil strife, Chretien remarked: "Parliament will decide." While Parliament mulled over possibilities, Alberta Premier Ralph Klein began talking oil and gas:

How badly does Montanta's Governor Martz want to protect that murderer? Whoever has decided to help King evade justice does not care about law and order, Albertans or about the victims in Edmonton. Do you really want to piss off Canadians with this sort of willful neglect? With accessory to murder? Now, sick and crazy cows crossing a porous border are one thing, but energy is another. Treaties aside, the US should think about whether it wants to start tapping its strategic oil reserve, especially when it's only bound to last three months. Canadian supply heats American homes, powers American cars, and sustains American jobs. You don't think that an American treaty breach—holding King despite conclusive proof of terrorist activity—warrants a little NAFTA contract-breach? You're living in dreamland. What we want is simple. What we're prepared to do, however, is to complicate everything.

Klein's bravado prompted fury south of the 49th parallel and in Ottawa, but won him support at home. Chretien—fearing severed ties with the Americans—called Klein, but was unable to sway him. Klein was convinced that Ottawa was out to fuck Albertans, and that the US would play fair only if Canadians demonstrated some gall.

Stateside, politicians at the federal and state levels were panicking about voter satisfaction and the potential crisis that rising gas prices and energy shortages would create. The executive branch was again strongly considering delivering King to the Canadians. Congress vowed, rather irrationally, to protect "American interests," notwithstanding guilt. Tension was growing between state representatives, Congress, and the Bush Administration, leaving the US divided between differently perceived obligations and duties.

ON NOVEMBER 3, 2001, Martin Sanqmarez—a clerk from the US consulate in Toronto—appeared in an online video stream reading his kidnapper's terms of exchange, which articulated the need for retribution for victims of the WTCE attack. Without informing Chretien, the RCMP, CSIS or local law enforcement agencies, Bush sent a team of Navy SEALS to free Sanqmarez on November 5. Fourteen Canadians were captured, and later surrendered to the Metropolitan Detention Centre in Brooklyn, where they were placed in solitary confinement and made unavailable to the press.

Two Canadian law-enforcement officers died as a result of the operation, when US special operatives opened fire on what they believed to be suspects fleeing the scene, when in fact, they had been Toronto police in pursuit of an alleged kidnapper. When a member of the American special team went to inspect the kill, local resident and witness Hugh MacLeod managed to tackle him, breaking several of his ribs. Restraint was exercised on the part of the special team, and the aggressive resident's life was spared—he was simply pepper-sprayed. When the injured resident recovered, he called emergency services and tried to resuscitate the fallen officers, by which time the American team had already taken off.

Although the Americans "got the men responsible for the kidnapping," the inanity and futility of the secretive play quickly became apparent. Sanqmarez's body turned up in the Scarborough bluffs the next morning, with its throat slit. No evidence was submitted connecting the men to the murder or the kidnapping, and yet they remain—to this day—in an American detention centre. *Amnesty International can only melt so many hearts.* Canadians, meanwhile, mourned the deaths of Officer Jean-Louis Chennells and Officer G.K. Granastein.

Bush called Chretien on November 7 to express his condolences and to promise to find out how the Sanqmarez rescue operation (an op he OK'd) happened and went so poorly. Apparently, Chretien managed to call Bush a criminal twice before throwing the phone across the room. Paul Cellucci was supposed to make a public statement of condolences, but was gagged so that the operation could be spun to look like a success. Instead, Pennsylvania Governor Tom Ridge touted the operation as one among many needed "domestic" operations in the "war on terror."

FOLLOWING THE MURDER of Chennells and Granastein, Chretien was pressed to dump frustrated Defence Minister Art Eggleton because he'd lost his credibility. Progressive Conservative Leader Joe Clark had confronted Chretien, telling him he had to put the interests of the troops and Canadian citizens ahead of "the pride of the Liberal Party and name a minister whom Canadians and our troops can respect in this time of crisis."[8] Eggleton's replacement was Ian Pugliese (a.k.a. "the man with the plan"), an alleged "wild card" and patriot with a troubled personal history and base utilitarian worldview.

Pugliese began his ministry with a condemnation, calling Bush's unapologetic act of aggression "invasionary" and "war-mongering." "Canada," continued Pugliese, "has the means to protect itself. JTF2[9] was not assembled for show...I wonder if the American President would be taken aback to see Canadian special teams taking out American targets selected by Canadian intelligence operatives to further Canadian interests..."

Chretien, in tandem, lambasted US impetuousness:

> One cannot start hunting for terrorists in heavily populated areas with the blunt and clumsy force we've seen used here. And it is not hunting season. Canada reserves the right to take care of its own issues.

Chretien insinuated that further interventions done in this manner were sure to incur unnecessary collateral damage and the wrath of the Canadian Military.

Whereas traditionally, "Canadian commanders control[led] US Forces operating in Canada in conjunction with Canadian Forces," the degree of Canadian participation in the American operation to free Sanqmarez was negligible.[10] Politicians and military officials alike identified this event as infantilizing and as salt in old wounds, especially concerning the capability, size, and financial funding of the Canadian Military.

Bush and Chretien planned to meet to arrange a joint task force that would deal with the epidemic of violence and dissent along the borderlands straddling both nations, and stem unilateral undertakings where North American security was concerned. This was an obvious step, given the integration already underway (e.g. on 9/11, NORAD headquarters at Cheyenne Mountain was under operational control of a Canadian—AF Gen. Rick Findley).

---

[8] Dawson, Anne "Eggs on a Hit List"
http://www.freedominion.com.pa/phpBB2/viewtopic.php?nomobile=1&f=2&t=2766
[9] JTF2 is an elite, Canadian special task force, which grew out of the RCMP's Special Emergency Response Team. It is responsible for counter-terrorism ops and armed assistance to other government departments.
[10] Sokolsky, Joel J., and Joseph T. Jockel. *Fifty Years of Canada-United States Defense Cooperation: the Road from Ogdensburg*. Lewiston, NY: E. Mellen, 1992. Print

JTF2 was briefed and readied to form a coalition counter-terror group with American Delta Force operatives. The Canadian Defence Department also recreated the disbanded Canadian Airborne Regiment for additional muscle-power to commit to remote operations. Indifferent to the politically correct jargon expected from one in his position, Pugliese quipped to Chretien: "Troubled by that weird, warm feeling between your legs? Makes sense; it's been a while. Those're balls."

The highly controversial and picketed US-Canadian summit meeting was called off when Bush, quoting "good" albeit distorted CIA intelligence, reneged on his promise to stave off unilateral endeavours and gave Chretien an hour's notice: a US Marine Expeditionary force would join Canadian units to seize and "protect" the hydro-electric power stations in Quebec (that fed power to New York). The CIA's undisclosed tipoff (the reason for this operation) turned out to be premature.

One company of American troops, hugged by heavily armed Canadian units, was split between and stationed at three primary power stations. They were joined the next day by armoured units from the Canadian Military as well as local Quebec law enforcement. While ostensibly there to support the American force, the Canadian tanks were given orders to monitor all American activity and to engage any combatant poised to do injury to Canadian citizens, infrastructure or interests.

Bush, defensive of what many in the media were referring to as another invasionary manoeuvre despite a last minute OK from Pugliese and the Prime Minister's Office (it had not been planned through NATO or NORAD channels, and thus appeared one-sided and sudden) communicated to Chretien:

> Neighbourly security will stem reactionary violence that threatens to freeze and cripple New York and the north-eastern seaboard. If I saw my neighbour's house being robbed and the phones were dead, it would be my responsibility to take action.

Clearly, Bush did not see the irony of using a break-and-entry metaphor. He had run out of animal metaphors, and wanted to simplify the facts, invalid in some respects at the time, when NORTHCOM (Northern Command) had not yet conferred certain rights to the US in Canada, where: "Canadian and US Forces [could] cross the border in emergency situations with[out] the permission of the host government."

Chretien was forced to recognize that Canada had previously accepted—under NORAD agreements—American plans to disperse US bombers and ground support to Canadian airfields in time of crisis. The obvious criticism (i.e. hydro-electric facilities do not constitute airfields) was downplayed as semantics. Bush argued that distress signalled permission. "A neighbour does not wait till he hears screaming." By day's end November 10, an American base with Canadian support-staff had been erected near the Robert-Bourassa generating station, and Toronto's Pearson International was receiving American security forces, cautiously escorted by the Canadian Forces. Canadian troops were also stationed on Wolfe Island, across from Kingston, just to ruffle some feathers.

Canada's Foreign Affair Minister Bill Graham stressed the need for the US to parlay their assistance through the mediation of the UN, given its proximity and involvement in the issues. Graham also asked Canadians to strive to be "as Canadian as possible under the circumstances."[11] The unwelcome American muscle seemed to cultivate antipathy, where it was intended to ensure safety and peace of mind.

ALTHOUGH THE HYDRO-THREAT had been manufactured, newly emergent subversive militant factions saw the American presence on Canadian soil as an opportunity to avenge the victims of 9/11. Their retribution, however, was haphazard, anarchistic, and ultimately, self-defeating.

No single consequence was desired, just as long as someone south of the border was likewise "adversely affected." On November 16, Canadian militants disabled three Quebec-based hydro-electric facilities with strategically located explosions. Four American soldiers were killed in the attack and others were wounded, including several Quebec counter-terrorism officers.

The toll exacted by the infrastructure sabotage did not become fully apparent until the evening of the 16th. New York State, Vermont (thirty percent of its electricity came from Quebec), and much of the northeastern seaboard, were already experiencing a brutal, early winter. October had brought cold rain and regional flooding, and November brought heavy snow. Blackouts, resultant

---

[11] Roach, Kent. *September 11: Consequences for Canada* (Montreal: McGill-Queen's UP, 2003) 125.

of the explosions, left millions without electricity. Homes without the capacity for manageable fires quickly became iceboxes, and for many, tombs.

A coalition of Canadian and American engineers set to work on the disabled power stations, while twenty-thousand government employees (civilian and military) were mobilized to aid in the rebuilding efforts and in the distribution of essential goods and services to the freezing masses. Partial electricity was achieved by the morning of the 18th. Nevertheless, four-hundred-and-ninety Canadians and over twenty-five-hundred Americans died in the cold. Altogether, the electrical shutdown affected close to fifty-million people, including 1.4 million Hydro-Quebec customers.

Former Canadian Foreign Affairs Minister Lloyd Axworthy's point took on a new gravity as a result of the attack: "Military responses feed the anger, poverty, rhetoric—the climate of grievance—which create and sustain terrorist intentions." [12] The November Bombings were instrumental in the establishment of the vicious circle that persists today (i.e. invasion-reaction, occupation-reaction). In *Kingdom of Fear*, Hunter S. Thompson hypothesized about this fear-circuit and the post-border nature of the conflict: "It will be guerilla warfare on a global scale, with no front lines and no identifiable enemy...We are going to punish somebody for this attack, but just who or what will be blown to smithereens for it is hard to say."

Bush, pained by the loss of American lives, promised the American people their pound of flesh: "Any individual, state or institution found complicit in the November Bombings will be brought to justice." From Barksdale Air Force Base, Louisiana, Bush added, in his address to the American people:

> Freedom, itself, was attacked this morning by faceless cowards, and freedom will be defended. I want to reassure the American people that the full resources of the federal government are working to assist local authorities to save lives and to help the victims of these attacks...We have been in touch with the leaders of Congress and with world leaders to assure them that we will do whatever is necessary to protect America and Americans...The resolve of our great Nation is being tested. But

---

[12] Roach 199.

make no mistake: We will show the world that we will past this test. God bless America.

In addition to forcing a strong-handed response from the American government, the November Bombings led to an intensified paranoia on both sides of the border.

The threat of water-poisoning or an attack on a nuclear-plant's power generators fed the White House's fear, prompting Bush to pull out all the stops. The Ambassador Bridge between Windsor and Detroit, among others, was closed to all traffic. Riverside Drive, overlooking the US, was covered in Canadian Military vehicles and cement road-blocks, while the American National Guard had patrol boats zigzagging up and down the Detroit River. American jets pierced the clouds along the 49th, while Canadian troops unloaded anti-tank hedgehogs and barbed wire. Tension, fear, and loathing had grown to an all-time high.

The evening of November 17, the Emergencies Act took on a new shape in Canada. The particular type invoked under the act was "Public Order Emergency." The House of Commons gave unanimous support to the Act, the aim of which was to address a "national emergency" of an urgent or critical situation ("of a temporary nature") that:

> (A) seriously endangers the lives, health or safety of Canadians and is of such proportions or nature as to exceed the capacity or authority of a province to deal with it or (B) seriously threatens the ability of the Government of Canada to preserve the sovereignty, security, and territorial integrity of Canada, and that cannot be effectively dealt with under any other law of Canada.[13]

Coinciding with the press release was a statement from the PM's Office, essentially paraphrasing an earlier Canadian Prime Minister, Pierre Trudeau:

> To those who do not like to see the sight of men with guns and who wonder how far Canada will go, just watch and see. The time for anti-Canadian and anti-American childishness has come to an end. The Quebec bombings have claimed the lives of innocent Canadians and Americans. We've lost too much already to begin forsaking bonds with our friends and neighbours. Anyone who harbors or supports those involved in the

---

[13] "Emergencies Act." *Justice Laws Website | Site Web De La Législation (Justice)* <http://laws-lois.justice.gc.ca/eng/acts/E-4.5/index.html>.

November attacks is likewise culpable for the murder of innocents, and will be punished accordingly.

The next day, the spirit of the Treachery Act was reincarnated in new anti-terrorism laws, and passed with a new lingo to allow for expedient prosecutions for espionage and terrorism.

The Cabinet identified possible threatening causes (i.e. unlawful associations, kidnapping, terrorist actions, and uncontained civil strife), and called upon the Canadian Forces to bring peace to increasingly chaotic urban centres. Units from the Canadian Forces not already dispatched were armed, assembled, and given instructions to disperse to designated locations across Canada as of December 1. Chretien, responding to the November Bombings, remarked to US Ambassador Paul Cellucci:

> Side by side, we have lived though many dark times, always firm
> in our resolve to vanquish any threat to freedom and justice.
> And together, with our allies, we will defy and defeat the threat
> that terrorism poses to all civilized nations.

Many Canadian citizens felt stuck between a rock and a hard place. Civil liberties were minimized even further, and the threat of detention or worse was omnipresent. Thomas Homer-Dixon published an article in the *Globe & Mail* after the attacks where he argued that:

> Because the enemy, in this case, is so diffuse and indeterminate,
> it would be easy to turn against groups and people within our
> societies—against anybody who looks different, who expresses
> opinions that vary from the norm or who has been associated, at
> one time or another, with suspect people or causes.[14]

Indeed, there was cause to fear the politicized fear mongering, evidenced by the statistics released in Pugliese's report on international kidnappings. Not accounting for individuals and groups taken in secret US raids, there were 374 arrests made between November 17 and December 4. Anything from collusion in riots to online condemnations of the US warranted interrogations, arrests, and detention. Canadians exhibited greater anxiety about American reactions to terrorism than about home-grown terrorism itself.

Chretien and Bush announced the establishment of another joint task force to ensure the safe repair of the destroyed generators and

---

[14] Roach 116.

power transmission lines, as well as their defense against future attacks. Word of this cooperative initiative rejuvenated hope in both countries for an amicable solution; however, stark realities were in tow.

Besides the abundance of electricity exported to the US, Canada "[wa]s also the largest source of petroleum for the United States (at seventeen percent of US imports) and ha[d] the second largest oil reserves in the world—ahead of Iraq and Kuwait."[15] In addition to its available resources, Canada lacked most of the geopolitical baggage weighing down other major exporters to the US; imports from Canada were relatively strings-free.

The US hadn't found a need to install an inside man as Prime Minister, have the CIA organize a *coup d'état* or invade in order to secure the resource and the relation, because they were dealing with an agreeable, business-like folk. In late November, however, Americans were waking up panicked in cold rooms and realizing that the US, with its current foreign policy, was dependent on Canadian resources to a fault. Although few would have reached such conclusions on energy and oil immediately, it was clear by December that the majority of Americans wanted their government to change the source or the middle-man. The honeymoon was over.

♠

---

[15] Welsh, Jennifer *At Home in the World: Canada's Global Vision for the 21st Century* (Toronto: HarperCollins, 2004) 102.

XENOPHOBIA

Toronto, Ontario
August 31, 2005

SOMETIMES I'M SUCH a damnable voyeur. I rode the subway from one end of the Bloor Line to the other, scrawling down the herd's many lives, expressed in fragments. The people's story offered itself to me on the myriad faces, waving from one body to another, crashing in expressions, some of which I attempted to note: the smile on the old woman who wrinkled her purse protectively; the frown on the business man who routinely goes to St. Andrew station, and up the stairs to a de-peopled workspace, only to dream of days when he could still afford his five dollar cup of coffee; the two teens puzzle-pieced together—draped in white and blue—musing about how the Leafs will win the cup when the NHL starts up again[16], and the wet faced woman knitting a hat, whose son and daughter had gone missing.

It was evident, from the stories told through the slivers left between bodies—between the crotches and through the tiny apertures left by an arm in the crowd, a pair of legs or a back painfully arched—and in the dark reflections captured in the half-life between passenger and the troop-filled Don Valley or whatever dark passage scraped by the train into obscurity, that Toronto and its inhabitants had not given up.

The people wasted no time coping, and pressed onwards, despite thunder on the horizon and the inexhaustible supply of demoralizing "missing" posters adrift above their dusty streets. Fully aware of the hell-mouth pried open on 9/11 and all of the evil that it propagated (recorded on the stacks of newspaper matting the subway's floors), Torontonians have curiously not cowed under the pressure or been demobilized by fear, despite their proximity to the source (Toronto is on the 44th parallel). Jacquelyn suggested to me that it was the same everywhere—in Napanee, Victoria, Trois Rivieres, Kingston, Banff, Charlottetown, Churchill, Sydney, and even across the border where Americans were still reeling from the

---

[16] They still haven't.

ramifications of the November Bombings—but that did not make Torontonians' resilience any less remarkable. Like Isaac Brock before them, they appeared to share the same kind of hot blood and tact necessary to hold against fate and tyranny.

Packed like a sardine in a can going sixty-clicks-an-hour beneath Toronto's calloused skin, I realized that, notwithstanding the omnipresent forces tasked with hindering civil mobility, much of central and eastern Canada had retained its pre-war characteristics and qualities. After I charged with the incensed herd out of the train, squeezed up two sets of stairs bordered by asparagus green tile (nearly trampling people along the periphery), and emerged into daylight on St. George Street, I was reminded of a G.K. Chesterton supposition: *a dead thing goes with the stream, only a living thing against it.* Toronto was very much alive and pushing against the upsetting inevitable.

Where Canadian military and police agents were dedicated in number and in force, the peace was highly regulated. Of course, the placement of troops was highly politicized (e.g. Rosedale was better protected than Jane and Finch or Moss Park; Bay Street more so than Parkdale or Regent Park), promoting the sense that society always prioritizes the interests of its rich ahead of the masses, further fragmenting urban Canadian allegiances. Those parts of the city where peace had permitted laxer checkpoints were doing especially well, although some feared that the goodwill rampant at the turnstiles would be compromised by internal issues, such as the mounting racial and class tensions that had been developing even prior to the occupation.

A British security specialist from the *Economist* suggested to me, while waiting in a long tangle of caffeine addicts, that:

> Canadian unity against a single perceived threat has not put an end to petty crime, hate crimes, domestic violence, or murder. Those problems persist. Homicide rate's gone up to 14.5 per 100,000 people. That's up from 3.3. That's a huge fucking difference. But put it in context: in pre-war Detroit, the number was 33.8; it was 19.7 in Atlanta; and 15.5 in Chicago. It's important to understand the statistics, though. In Canada, cops are now less likely to respond to a call about some guy beating his wife to a pulp or stealing a stereo when AK fire can be heard down the block. It's not even a matter of that AK doing damage. Law enforcement has just completely reprioritized what calls they rush to because of the threat of high-intensity crime or

terror activity. They've also receive a lot of pressure from the Americans. For a city with Toronto's size and predicament, it's surprising that it hasn't got any worse, though I can assure you, it won't get any better soon.

The war had problematized living in Toronto, but it did not make it impossible.

The April 3, 2003, headline for the *Toronto Star*—circulating as widely as it had in 2000 before the occupation—indicated the resurgence and acceptability of sarcasm, hope, and humor in the east: "If You Insist on 'Nation Building', Start with the Gardiner." The Gardiner Expressway, a decrepit, semi-functional artery tracked through the City of Toronto, had been a longtime eye-sore and grievance for many local residents. With all the talk of reparation, nation-building, and reinforcement of civil infrastructure, many quipped about the prospect of US Forces bombing, and then rebuilding the Gardiner. Such dark wit suggested that members of the Canadian press were shifting away from prescriptions and articulations of strict survivalism.

While the citizens of Ontario's capital joked about the prospect of there being positive side-effects to the occupation, many Canadians proved humourless, and for good reason: some were still living day-to-day off rations, dressed in flak jackets, and feeding ammo-belts into truck-mounted machineguns, praying for strength. Those of the latter category found themselves in an especially precarious position, since the Canadian Forces were technically not backing the resistance movement in Canada, but tasked, instead, with peace-keeping, defence, and the "upkeep of Canadian sovereignty." Regionalism grew increasingly strong as lifestyles became particularly disparate. It was understood that one survived in the west and complained in the east.

I WALKED PAST a crowded cafe into the deli next door, famous for its ridiculously large Montreal smoked-meat sandwiches, piled high with mouth-watering beef brisket, embroiled in mustard, topped with "special sauce," and partnered, finally, with a dill pickle. There I spied through fading mirrors two off-duty soldiers with shoulders back and chests out—still proud of serving and protecting their dear Canada—watching an American sitcom on the wall-mounted TV while they waited for their numbers to be called.

The butcher spun a plastic bag full of a bloody something and handed it off. "Twennie six!"

The scene felt so commonplace and familiar—no different than the strip-mall nearby my home in Seattle. I began to ponder how these people were distinct from their American neighbours. Had a futile sense of nationalism wrongly sent good people to their graves in an annexed land, while the culture they left behind eroded at home, without a fight? The hazy silhouette across Lake Ontario served as a funhouse mirror-city; only, all the fun was gone, and the distorted differences prompted, instead, anxiety and rivalry.

Anti-Americanism had been increasing in Toronto since 2001, especially clear from the desecrated advertisements at bus stops, in streetcars, and along the highway. Of the many unmistakably American ads that cake Toronto's walls and telephone poles (e.g. Am. Eagle, Am. Apparel, Hollywood film posters, etc.), few survived the first few years of the conflict unscathed. If it is true that Canadians defined themselves as non-American after the war of 1812, perhaps this new conflict—nearly two hundred years later—has provided them with another opportunity for self-definition. Mustached Hollywood actresses and defiled American clothes models indicate repulsion. Whether or not this negativity will become constructive or creative is left to be determined.

DIFFERENCE AND VIOLENCE marks Canadians and Americans even presently in those sectors where interests are seemingly aligned. There was a story in *The National Post* that detailed a firefight that had begun between a shopkeeper and an American soldier, and ended with the curt and contentious response of a Canadian soldier. The American soldier had been accused with looting from an electronics store near Pape and Bloor. Initially, the soldier had fired his weapon to intimidate the shopkeeper, though the shopkeeper—like many other Canadians who had purchased automatic weapons off the black market—pursued the soldier into the street, gun-a-blazing. The *pkt-pkt-pkt* of machinegun-fire caught the attention of a Canadian unit from the Queen's Own Rifles. Four shots later, the violence had been allayed.

Witnesses attested to having seen the Canadian soldiers—led by Sergeant MacPhee—roll in, disarm the store-owner with a nonlethal rubber round, and then order Private Raylin Ashforth to drop his weapon, to which he replied: "Fuck off, Captain Canuck." When he turned his weapon on MacPhee, three rounds were rifled. Unfortunately, at such close quarters, nonlethal rounds have the grave potential to do more than disarm, especially when they find an individual's temple. Raylin died instantly.

MacPhee was later reprimanded for unauthorized use of lethal force, and the article indicated he would likely be court-martialed before a joint tribunal to appease the Americans. The story illustrated the difficulty in having a bi-national military force policing a large city. It further illustrated forced and failing distinctions between Canadian and American forces, insurgents, and the civilian population.

Another suggestion I extrapolated from the *National Post* article was that, although a saddening incident, this accidental slaying did not arouse the sort of public interest that individual slayings and tragedies piqued in 2001. It hadn't even made its way to the front page of the G-section. Whether growing desensitized to senseless violence or preoccupied with their own daily tragedies, there was little reaction to Raylin's death, just as few on either side of the border paid attention to the droves of men and women killed for god-knows-what in god-knows-where. The war demoralized both nations. Anti-war activists and peace journalists began to focus on exit strategies (i.e. how to get out of Canada without starting a civil war).

An exit strategy would be beneficial to both countries. In terrorist attacks against military forces in Canada, ninety-four percent have been directed against US-commanded forces. The resistance to martial law and military encampments in urban sectors, thus, appears one-sided and reactive. Alas, instead of prompting an American exit, such one-sided antagonism has simply concretized the US Force's resolve to stay and to further entrench in Canadian cities. As the civilian and military death tolls rise, however, it should become apparent to politicians and military officials alike that this conflict is untenable, and that the current solution is not working. In the meantime, life goes on.

My flight to D.C. was booked and my bags were packed, but I still had the evening to kill. I nursed a nice room-temperature stout at a bar near Bay and Bloor, and then—being the damnable voyeur I am—boarded another train, stomach stuffed full of kosher-beef brisket and beer, to continue to scrawl the problems of this city on a new leaf.

♠

GENESIS: A COLD WAR

[H]ow can we expect states to lay down their arms if there does not exist any way in which a state which is wronged can remedy that injustice; and how can states be expected to stay disarmed in such circumstances?[17]

   —Allan Gotlieb, Former Canadian Ambassador to the US

The easiest way to provoke Americans is to make us look like a source of threat, either by arming to the teeth against them or by allowing our border to be porous to a hostile missile, bomber or terrorist. Like it or not, that's why there will be a Northern Command and we will conform to its directions or pay a price.[18]

   —Desmond Morton

FISHER AND NABOKOV'S hackneyed assassination, the Sanqmarez kidnapping, and the November Bombings, were cited as cause for an increase in surveillance and basic security in the United States. Accordingly, the US—responding to potential terror cells located at home and in border towns along the 49th—developed a new cabinet level Department of Homeland Security (DHS), headed by Tom Ridge. Between this new overseer and the new anti-terrorism laws, "civil liberties [after 9/11] were curtailed, domestic surveillance increased, [and] military spending increased dramatically…"[19]

   The USA PATRIOT Act (Uniting and Strengthening America by Providing Appropriate Tools Required to Intercept and Obstruct Terrorism Act of 2001) was one of the more contentious byproducts of this new security paradigm. As it was proposed, the PATRIOT Act was intended to: "disrupt terrorist financial networks" and to infiltrate terrorist bases. The act passed after a week-long media campaign designed to stir Americans into panic and frenzy. The campaign successfully urged even the palest of bleeding-heart liberals into complicity. It enabled, among other things, domestic wiretapping, spying, and data interception. The act

---

17 Gotlieb, Allan. *Disarmament and International Law* (Toronto: Canadian Institute of International Affairs, 1965) 232.
18 "National Defence: A Little Common Sense." http://speeches.empireclub.org/62829/data?n=1
19 Tirman, John. *The Maze of Fear: Security and Migration after 9/11* (New York: New, 2004) 59.

was in clear breach of the Fourth Amendment to the United States Constitution, which details:

> The right of the people to be secure in their persons, houses, papers, and effects, against unreasonable searches and seizures, shall not be violated, and no Warrants shall issue, but upon probable cause, supported by Oath or affirmation, and particularly describing the place to be searched, and the persons or things to be seized.

The permissiveness of the American public was inversely related to their sense of security. Rumsfeld suggested that there were new, unfathomable dangers that required a "heightened sense of awareness." Bomb scares, faux chemical warfare close-calls, and (reportedly government-organized) juvenile pranks in the States sent relatively cool-headed people of heightened awareness into hysterics.

Despite the President's earlier suggestion that the issue was strictly domestic with some international implications, US Attorney Ashcroft's actions suggested otherwise. In late November, he revealed plans to temporarily replace ordinary American customs and immigration officials with 3,500 troops from the National Guard, who "would not function 'as troops at all.'"[20] Border Patrols were already equipped with "helicopters, fixed-wing aircraft, motion sensors, CCTV, low-level light and heat-sensing night vision equipment, stadium lighting, horizontal radar, upgraded weaponry, improved communications networks, and so forth."[21] In addition to the high-calibre weapons and technology already used by border agents, armoured vehicles (including tanks) appeared nearby border checkpoints. Unmanned-aircraft vehicle systems (a.k.a. drones or UAVs) —equipped with high-definition and infrared cameras and capable of remaining airborne for up to fifteen hours—flew circuits above areas where border controls were previously lacking. The myriad eyes and ears focused on the border and on American citizens (potentially fraternizing with the enemy or enacting revenge on unwitting Canadians) were tantamount to an Orwellian nightmare.

---

[20] Roach 137.
[21] Winterdyk, John, and Kelly W. Sundberg. *Border Security in the Al-Qaeda Era* (Boca Raton: CRC, 2010) 44.

US Border Patrol agents "went on 'level one' alert after the attacks, checking every car, truck, and person attempting to legally enter the country."[22] The Ambassador Bridge between Windsor and Detroit; the Peace Bridge between Fort Eerie and Buffalo; the Whirlpool Rapids Bridge fording New York and Ontario at Niagara, and the area south of Vancouver, north of Blaine, Washington, were transformed into fortresses. Canada attempted to follow suit, spending three-billion dollars on increased security in 2001 alone and budgeting more for 2002, given the perceived shortcomings of too little too late.[23]

In early December, a Canada-US statement on Common Security Priorities was announced in Windsor with US Attorney Ashcroft outlining special joint border security patrols, more border guards, and coordinated visa policies. Canada's Immigration Minister Elinor Caplan commented: "it will help queue jumpers, criminals, and those who pose security risks or terrorists ... before they can even get to Canada or the US."[24]

Then-Deputy Prime Minister Herb Gray was critical, and his successor John Manley especially so, pointing out the danger of too-close an engagement with the US for Canadian sovereignty, and warning, "working closely with the United States does not mean turning over to them the keys to Canadian sovereignty." Perhaps forgetful of the 1997 Manitoba Flood and the 1998 ice storm, Manley overlooked the support Canadians had accepted from the Americans in the recent past. Notwithstanding his reservations, Manley suggested that it was important for Canada to situate itself within the American security perimeter. Chretien recognized the importance of security, but scoffed at the potential ramifications: "[security] but not at the expense of the people of the country."[25]

The fearful recognition of Canada's metamorphosis into an American protectorate seeped into public consciousness, only this realization, again, came too late. *Friendly* American support was there whether Canadians wanted it or not. American support was

---

[22] Winterdyk and Sundberg, 50
[23] Winterdyk and Sundberg, 29.
[24] Roach 136.
[25] Andreas, David, and Thomas J. Biersteker. *The Rebordering of North America Integration and Exclusion in a New Security Context* (New York: Routledge, 2003) 35.

ostensibly guided by the desire to keep criminals out of the States, leaving them a Canadian problem.

Immigration Minister Caplan recognized the plan's preferential treatment of American security over Canadian security. The Canadian government set out to monitor water and food supplies, erect barriers for vulnerable sites, and ensure the protection of its sovereignty, while the United States considered how to "slap [Canada] out of its shame-spiral. That's what big brothers do."[26] To inaugurate the new program, the Ambassador Bridge was reopened to the delight of a number of small, nearly bankrupt just-in-time Canadian businesses.

Despite reopening, the Canadian-US border had undergone a catastrophic transformation in the American social imaginary, from the longest undefended border to "a source of vulnerability."[27] Congress sought to impose a "trade embargo on itself" and prevent further human/material osmosis with Canada.[28]

The clash between American isolationism and imperialism was at once obvious. In order to reconcile the two agendas, Bush's administration began thinking in terms of "Fortress North America."[29] Through "multilateral policy harmonization and a 'pooling' of sovereignty to build a North American security perimeter," the US could achieve both goals: expand in order to protect the center.[30]

It must be reiterated (I am certainly not the first): the decision to work towards a common frontier/security perimeter was not strings-free. The November Hydro Bombings revealed and embellished the American dependence on Canadian resources. In lieu of US concerns regarding Canada's ability to protect energy supply going southward, the Bush Administration wanted to circumnavigate most if not all mediation. The prospect of a drop in supply (hinted at in Alberta Premier Ralph Klein's scathing address to Montanan Governor Martz) or worse (e.g. competition with China for Canadian resources) was unconscionable. So-called

---

[26] Allan, Chantal. *Bomb Canada: and Other Unkind Remarks in the American Media* (Edmonton: Au, 2009) 86.
[27] Andreas and Biersteker 8.
[28] IBID.
[29] Andreas and Biersteker 15.
[30] IBID.

integration appeared the necessary next-step to guarantees on resource pooling.

AFTER FORTY-FIVE years conjoined to the United States under NORAD (the North American Aerospace Defence Command), Canada was upgraded with regards to American regional combat responsibility—that is, registered under the US radius of military response and interest. USNORTHCOM (Northern Command) opened its umbrella over the continent.

As a result of increasing border issues along the 49th, President Bush had fast-tracked and signed a new Department of Defence Unified Command that "established the NORTHCOM to provide command and control of the DOD's homeland defence efforts and to coordinate military support to civil authorities."[31] NORTHCOM would be responsible for "security cooperation and coordination with Canada and Mexico."

The *agreement* seemed to ramify positively for Canada. In the event of a natural disaster (e.g. flood, hurricane, earthquake or forest fire) or low-intensity conflict, American units would be dispatched to assist in reparation and civil assistance. Critics couldn't get over the Liberal Government's failure to prioritize Canadian sovereignty over an unattainable peace of mind.

Lloyd Axworthy, Canada's former Foreign Minister, suggested that the *interoperability* sought through NORTHCOM's observance in Canada would be synonymous with *takeover.*[32] Dr. Michel Chossudovsky (involved with the Bi-national Planning Group), perceiving a similar threat, summed up the consequences of NORTHCOM: "[Canada's] borders will be controlled by US officials, and confidential information on Canadians will be shared with Homeland Security"; "US troops and Special Forces will be able to enter Canada as a result of a bi-national arrangement"; and "Canadians can be arrested by US officials, acting on behalf of their Canadian counterparts and vice versa."[33]

---

[31] Bolkcom, Christopher C., Lloyd DeSerisy, and Lawrence Kapp. *Homeland Security Establishment and Implementation of Northern Command.* (Washington, D.C.: Congressional Information Service, Library of Congress, 2003).

[32] Axworthy, Lloyd. *Navigating a New World* (Toronto: Vintage Canada , 2004) 103.

[33] Chossoduvsky: http://www.globalresearch.ca/index.php?context=va&aid=8323

Chretien initially refused provisos attached to NORTHCOM; however, with the Emergencies Act engaged, he was especially prone to the influence and suggestion of Canada's Military commanders. The Bi-national Planning Group (neither accountable to the US Congress or the House of Commons) circumnavigated Chretien's refusal, taking the military's "maybe" as temporarily binding. US and Canadian military officials quickly "signed a Civil Assistance Plan enabling the military of one nation to support the armed forces of the other nation during a civil emergency."[34] The Canadian Parliament swung in an sentimental moment and voiced support for NORAD-NORTHCOM recognition after the fact— another empty gesture.

How long the assisting-nation's forces could remain on foreign soil in the event of social instability (so extreme that it warrants a full-scale intervention by a joint task force) and their responsibility to the host state were items not thoroughly addressed, but instead dog-eared for later review. Since there was not sufficient debate over the expeditious legitimization of this command structure and the preponderance of supporters accused the few visible critics of having terrorist-sympathies, the topic veered over the heads of the public. *Why worry them?* They were already consumed by anxiety concerning increasing domestic violence and a slumped economy. What's the good of a little truth if it's of no use to anyone?

Citing 9/11 and the Hydro-sabotaging as obvious reasons for a swift bi-national integration of military structures, law enforcement, and intelligence, Donald Rumsfeld openly recognized that NORTHCOM had jurisdiction over the continent, and would target and eliminate terrorist groups at will. Within the North American arena, the United States "w[ould] lead a coalition of the willing to disarm [the November bombers, terrorists in Alberta, northern British Columbia, the Yukon, and the North West Territories, as well as other enemies of freedom]."[35]

The prospect of a heavily armed, continental police force did not seem as treacherous with a large Canadian component and say on the matter, but as coordination became largely unilateral and the American cooperative element glaringly absent, Canadians grew

---

[34] "US Troops Deployment in Canada." *MetaExistence Organization | Geo Political Think Tank* <http://metaexistence.org/uscanada.htm>.
[35] *CNN* http://edition.CNN.com/2002/WORLD/europe/11/20/prague.bush.nato/

frustrated. Axworthy's anxiety regarding NORTHCOM seems prophetic in hindsight:

> [Canadians will] accep[t] analysis and prescriptions supplied by the US administration instead of engaging in their own assessment of what the serious risks are from their perspective and sharing this 'risk assessment' with their neighbor.[36]

The immediate consequences, besides the trickling of American teams into Canadian airports, and their increased presence alongside Canadian Forces at checkpoints, was the ostensible subordination of Canadian troops on Canadian soil, and the rampant and arbitrary arrests of anti-war activists. Although the nature of the military assistance was initially left up to civilian authorities, it was glaringly clear that the US Forces in Canada expected the Canadian Forces to kowtow to US interests. So far as NORTHCOM went, the Canadian chain of command had been exclusively joined to an American link.

Canadian and American troops had fought side by side in a long list of major wars and operations. North American defence co-operation dated back to the Ogdensburg Announcement (where MacKenzie King met Roosevelt on August 17, 1940, and embraced a permanent defence alliance) and the North Atlantic Treaty (1948). Their respective military leaders were inclined to believe that the North American terror activity and its eradication would amount to nothing more than a hiccup in this long-standing friendship. Canadian governments, "Liberal or Conservative, have nevertheless been consistently sensitive about a public image of Canadian subservience or satellite status stemming from the relationship."[37]

Under different circumstances, NORTHCOM may have been a blessing and a great opportunity for Canada to shine militarily, but with much of the focus on Canadian soil, it was a huge risk. Future violence or terror attacks would be met by "'military contingency plans' which would be activated 'on both sides of the Canada-US border' in the case of a terror attack or 'threat'."[38] The "what" and "who" pursued in these operations were matters for the Americans to decide.

---

[36] Axworthy 104.
[37] *Canadian Defence and the Canada-US Strategic Partnership* (Ottawa, Ont.: Canadian Defence & Foreign Affairs Institute, 2002) 2.
[38] IBID.

NORTHCOM opened up Canada and its territories to US Special Operations. Despite its vociferous critics, the media did not pick up on this rather monumental shift in American continentalism, and surprisingly, the Canadian media –save for a *National Post* editorial and a brief mention on a televised *CBC* segment– neglected to get their hands dirty with the big sovereignty fumble.

With NORTHCOM posturing to take out all of Canada's "bad-guys" (i.e. as specified by the American government), most Canadians faced the realization that security trumps sovereignty, necessity trumps preference, and fear breeds complicity.

The adoption of NORTHCOM and the dramatic increase in US security forces along the coastal US border indicated an official American contempt for Canada. Regarding shifting US-Canadian relations and the escalation of security measures taken on the northern border, *The Washington Post's* DeNeen Brown remarked: "Canada is not accustomed to being considered an enemy in the world, much less a potential terrorist target."[39] *The Toronto Star's* Richard Gwyn wrote rather pessimistically regarding the American revaluation of continental security:

> We have entered the virtual sovereignty phase of our national story…[T]he Chretien government's decision this week to adopt a common North American perimeter—US standards applying everywhere, that's to say—for security and intelligence, for immigration and for our refugee systems represents one of the most significant abandonments of our sovereignty in our history. Abandonment is the wrong term. Accepting the inevitable would be the right way to put it.[40]

Stateside, extremists in the American media (e.g. Bill O'Reilly) were quick to make sweeping generalizations and assume that the November Bombings reflected a greater anti-American resolve amongst Canadians, notwithstanding the aforementioned permissions Canadians were granting American interests in their home and native land.

On his MSNBC show, Pat Buchanan called Canada a "Soviet Canuckistan." [41] Ann Coulter regurgitated her usual slurs and

---

[39] Allan 83.
[40] Wright, Robert A. *Virtual Sovereignty: Nationalism, Culture, and the Canadian Question* (Toronto, Ont.: Canadian Scholars', 2004) 237.
[41] Allan 85.

absurdities, this time directed at Canadians in an excessively antagonistic segment on *Hannity & Colmes*, concluding that: "they better hope the US doesn't roll over one night and crush them. They are lucky we allow them to exist on the same continent."[42] With faces red with fury and embarrassment, Canadians waited as Chretien, "under intense political pressure from both right and left," decided what to "promise Washington."[43]

The "red menace"—the North American country that had been at war with Hitler years before the US committed, seized Vimy Ridge after her allies failed miserably, and sent its men into bloody, foreign lands with the western nations in two World Wars as well as in subsequent satellite wars in Korea, Cypress, Iraq, and Kosovo; that sovereign state that saved American hostages from certain death in Iran, and was saving the world from itself with aid, innovation, and force, in countless humanitarian and peacekeeping missions throughout the twentieth century; a nation that had its arm in space, its fists and firsts in professional sports, and its people protected by a phenomenally nuanced and effective constitution, rule of law, and healthcare system; the same North American country that refused to boil to tasteless its immigrants, and invested, instead, in diversity—mulled over ways to gamble sovereignty on appeasement to its southern neighbor, and watched impotently as its economy began to waver.

IN NOVEMBER 2001, trade represented forty-five percent of the Canadian economy. Eighty-five percent of that trade was with the United States. Thirty-nine states had Canada as their top export destination. [44] Sixty-five percent of foreign direct investment in Canada came from the States. On the flipside, Canada was the largest supplier of oil to the US. It provided more than seventeen percent of US crude and refined oil imports, and supplied the US with eighty-six percent of its natural gas imports.

The US wanted some way to send a message without interrupting the flow of oil or disrupting other resource-related

---

[42] Allan 92.

[43] Allan 82.

[44] Lieutenant-General Rick Findley and Lieutenant General Joe Inge, "North American Defence and Security in the Aftermath of 9/11," in CANADIAN MILITARY JOURNAL, Vol. 6, No. 1 (Spring 2005) 23.

interests. With the primary pipelines unscathed, the Americans continued to utilize NAFTA agreements to obtain discounted, priority oil from Canada. Without the Canadian connection, it would have to look to re-address its geo-political grip on the Middle East, which would require a divided attention, even more pandering to conflicted, regional desires, and a more heavy-handed sorting of Iraqi affairs. Aware that the American dependence on trade with Canada was asymmetrical, the States decided to take a chance.

Border control tightened its grip at checkpoints, which suffocated Canadian exports and halted American imports. The "increased border security resulted in a thirty-mile line of trucks at the border...depleting inventories that relied on just-in-time supplies."[45] While a NORTHCOM "Joint task force" was amassed to safeguard oil pipelines (comprised primarily of Canadian troops), transports idled at the Ontario-US border. Three-fifths of Canada's foreign trade had halted.

Closing the borders completely was out of the question, since a hermetic seal along the 49th would "trigger thousands of local US issues,"[46] thus creating a rift between federal and state governments. However, the US was content to delay deliveries and spoil millions of dollars worth of goods, while truckers waited for security clearances to enter or leave the US.

The new necessity for passports bothered only a few. The real issue was the waiting and the harassment suffered at the checkpoints. These disruptions affected exports linked to more than 390,000 jobs and $3.7 billion of annual investments.[47] Finance Minister Paul Martin scrambled to loosen borders and, at the very least, ease the squeeze at bottlenecks at checkpoints.

Politics kept bodies waiting, and necessity—defined by the Americans—kept resources flowing, despite the various riots in resource-rich settlements (e.g. Fort McMurray). The tightened border appeared to work only one way.

The Montreal Gazette's Bryan Sitka took a chomp at this perceived inequity with a front page two-frame cartoon of an American cowboy-turned-bandit donning his bandana, and hijacking a

---

[45] Lieutenant-General Rick Findley and Lieutenant General Joe Inge, 24.
[46] Dyment, David. *Doing the Continental: a New Canadian-American Relationship* (Toronto: Dundurn, 2010) 49.
[47] Rempel 163.

Canadian oil-train. The subtitle, quoting former American President Reagan, reads: "there will be no negotiation with terrorists, of any kind." Although ambiguous enough to escape censorship and condemnation, Sitka's intent was nevertheless clear: to accuse the United States of international terrorism. A number of American papers repudiated the suggestion and responded with equally cynical, stereotypical, and caustic cartoons. With the media-war pressing coals to Canadian-American wounds and further vexing citizens in a dithering economy, civil order was again at serious risk. Worse, hotheads were prevailing at the executive-level.

RUMBLINGS FROM "the fifty-first state" prompted an escalation in military presence along the border. On December 1, 2001, American armour appeared on major roads and bridges between Canada and the United States, forty yards into the Canadian side on all fronts. The consistency was registered as "an unmistakable provocation and an invasionary measure." Canadian ambassador to the US Michael Kergin subsequently remarked, "foreign intervention is interference bordering on aggression." Again, the US had not consulted with the Canadians directly or through a NATO/NORTHCOM brief. Even if the US had consulted Canada via the aforementioned channels, the advance exceeded the requirements detailed in the UN's definition of aggression (defined by the General Assembly in 1974).

The Canadian Armed Forces met the armour at every instance of border-breach. Canadian troops were stationed eight kilometres outside of every urban area near the border and, in a nation-wide exercise, arranged southward facing artillery commons.

In the first hours of the breach, the Royal Canadian Regiment reportedly escorted a US Army unit based out of Fort Drum, New York, back to American lines. The meet between CF and US Forces was symbolically and practically significant. It reified the previously imaginary divide between the two nations, and indicated that any extra-legal intervention would prove costly.

The UN Security Council registered Canada's complaint, but the issue proved contentious. The Bush Administration cited Article fifty-one (already invoked by Canada), suggesting that terrorism and civil unrest in Canada likewise threatened security elsewhere on the continent, including the well-being of seventy-five million Americans residing in the thirteen states bordering Canada. With growing civil strife, "who kn[ew]", suggested Colin Powell, "who could wield Canada's arsenal of Schedule One chemical weapons in the months to come." This suggestion was completely asinine, granted that the Canadian Forces were in control and garnered the respect and support of the majority of the civilians they came in contact with.

Some Canadian observers noted that Powell and Bush spoke about terrorism in the White House, which itself overlooked Lafayette Park, gloriously named after a murderous pirate who would satisfy any modern definition of terrorist. Terrorism, apparently, is what *other* countries do. Bush cited the recently ratified NORTHCOM arrangement as grounds for border-breach. America was simply following up on its responsibility to North American security in its territories and borderlands. The missing permission or distress call was simply accidental.

In an attempt to come off as reasonable, Bush (and Chretien by proxy) agreed to a buffer zone in order to preserve the peace and to permit a window for talks and negotiations. Chretien argued: "We must not let individual dissent and malice dictate national direction. As friends and neighbours, it is important to localize and treat as oppose to generalize and terrorize." Bush conceded his point, but responded with audacious demands:

> We want to quash all unnecessary tensions between the Canadians and ourselves, and will work vigorously to do so. Together we will identify and bring to justice individuals who desire to threaten the peace of our two nations. We want the November bombers. As friends and allies, Canadians should see it in their best interest and in the interest of North American security to comply—to offer the perpetrators up to the authorities and wash their hands of any and all terrorist taint.

The extent to which Bush intended the additional joint-initiative (tasked with delivering Canadians complicit in the November Bombings) to be Canadian-controlled was laughable. His method was not immediately transparent. In effect, his action plan to quell the violence entailed more covert American operations, unobstructed by Canadian law enforcement officials. The deal was denied. No respectable government would permit such a plan.

On December 5, a force of combined NATO strength landed (after a bi-national agreement to "keep the peace" was ratified by both governments) in Saint John's, Buffalo, Seattle, Niagara Falls,

Birch Bay, and Kingston, where they organized, and then dispersed to their assigned checkpoints and field bases. This intermediary force (comprised primarily of Australian, British, Belgian, Spanish, Dutch, and German troops) worked with Canadian and American border officials to diffuse much of the border tension festering since the forty yard violation.

COINCIDING WITH THE KANGAROO TRIAL given to Canadian Alain Keating for his role in sabotaging Quebec hydro facilities (he was handed down a life sentence because he could not be given the death penalty), Secretary of State Colin L. Powell designated three new Foreign Terrorist Organizations (FTOs) in January 2002: the Real IRA, the AVC, and the Canadian-based Yukon Sprites.

The Sprites (originally a charitable organization) were designated an FTO on account of substantial evidence linking them to the sabotage of NORAD and American bases; their detonation of high-grade explosives at the Quebec hydro stations; for hijacking a US coastal defence vessel that had been assigned to protect Canadian and American "interests" offshore Vancouver island; for detaining and threatening discovered CIA operatives in Toronto and Ottawa, and for their potential involvement in the failed assassination of Harvey King. Bruce Kalnychuk's name appeared for the first time in the report, where he was listed as a suspected recruiter for the Sprites. This raised many graying eyebrows since Kalnychuk was an expatriated American with a proud military history.

A September 2001 US report showed that fifty groups and three-hundred-and-twenty people with ties to terrorism had lived in or traveled through Canada. January 2002 marked a terrifying milestone for Canadians: over two percent of the population was [allegedly] involved in terrorism, financing terrorism or harbouring terrorists (in the range of 650,000 to 800,000 people). The statistic was of course distorted by an American brand of paranoia. Nevertheless, the numbers, right or wrong, were enough to keep the Emergencies Act active (it needed to be renewed every 120 days). Additionally, Canada was held conditionally answerable for maintaining an American-style martial law under NORTHCOM, allowing US officials to finally and legally arrest, detain, and extradite Canadian citizens.

During the first wave of official American "excisions," the Canadian Alliance Party (the official opposition in the Commons) successfully lobbied to form a coalition with Chretien's Liberal government with hopes of giving the government a higher degree of legitimacy, and to ensure that the public did not need to worry about bipartisan politics in a moment of economic, legal, and social distress. The distinctions that previously divided the parties seemed trivial at this point in the conflict, made especially easy by the commonplace animosity curing all of the bleeding hearts.

ON JANUARY 16, 2002, a man disguised as an engineer detonated a suicide-bomb at one of the recently repaired Hydro facilities along the Quebec–New England Transmission Circuit. Within four hours, a hastily assembled UN force met the NATO intermediaries. This combined force worked to bolster checkpoints north of the border, anticipating a violent reaction to the dark and cold.

The press was denied access to the detonation site and the frontlines, because law and military officials were fearful that the different media outlets would exploit the scene and conflagrate their viewership with images of the destruction in order to secure future employment with a big messy war.

NATO forces were left at major intersections on both sides of the border, while Canadian and American forces, coordinating under NORTHCOM, worked ardently to provide firewood and provisions for districts suffering blackouts and rolling brownouts. Blackhawk helicopters equipped with heavy-machineguns and commando units dinned above southern Canadian cities and border towns, primarily around "hot spots," including: the southern Ontario industrial complex; the Quebec hydro facilities; the Alberta pipelines; the Halifax and Vancouver ports; Sault Ste. Marie; Windsor, and Niagara Falls. Although a warm January had given the northeast a respite, lives were nevertheless lost, fueling already passionate anti-Canadian movements.

Disguising the need for greater involvement in home defense, the Canadian Coalition Government—with the full support of the House of Commons and the Senate—set a mandate for increased youth involvement (i.e. recruitment). The third stage of this motion *required* men and women of able body, sixteen to thirty-five years of age, to *volunteer*—informally, selective conscription. The designation was "Home Defense Force One" (HDF1).

Realizing that Canadian arms manufacturers were insufficient to arm a force of this size, Chretien called upon non-American weapons manufacturers to equip the HDF1. Chretien sought Russian exports, and suggested to Russian President Vladimir Putin that the time might come where Russia's intervention might be required. Alternatively, France could provide weapons (including Exocet anti-ship missiles), but would commit no personnel or air-support. However, among the rather ineffectual UN Force were French soldiers who were able to smuggle weapons to the Canadians through for months.

Following the second Hydro bombing, the Bush Administration deliberated on the shift to "preventative war" contra "pre-emptive war." In Bush's 2002 *National Security Strategy*, he jettisoned containment and deterrence altogether, and embraced anticipatory self-defence. Russian supply ships en route to Canada were consequently obstructed for several hours by the US Navy. Foreseeing a potential complication with the Russians, who perceived the diversion as a blockade and thus a violation of international law (akin to the Cuban missile crisis that nearly sent the world to nuclear war), the States allowed the ships to continue to the B.C. Coast. Suspicious, however, of the contents (i.e. advanced weaponry) of the ships' containers and wary of the press' conflagration of the event—one headline read "From Russia with Shared Animosity" —Bush set another meeting with Chretien and Putin.

Excitement was at an all-time high when Harvey King's lawyer insinuated in a media scrum that King intended to issue a public statement on January 19. It would be televised on all major networks. Questions over whether or not he would make an on-air confession circulated widely, and the major news networks ran interviews of weary family members of 9/11 victims pleading with King to "do the right thing". In spite of the hype, King did not say a word. Two days after the second suicide-bombing, calamity befell the Can-American conflict's progenitor, guaranteeing his silence.

Harvey King and deputy sheriff Thomas Scott were shot in a convenience store by a masked man allegedly there to rob from the register. The store's surveillance tape told all: a man wearing a balaclava entered the store, executed the counter-clerk, and then proceeded to gun-down both officers before they could react to the initial gunshot. Only three shots were fired, each of which was fatal. The marksman, though carrying a bag—presumably for his loot— took off without actually stealing any merchandise or even cracking the register open. He escaped with his anonymity intact.

When the news reached Bush, the President promptly called off the planned tri-national summit, and heightened the national state of emergency (using an easily accessible colour spectrum). Under the assumption that "persons of interest" were being systematically executed, he took Air Force One to Camp David to safely ponder the country's next steps.

ANTICIPATING REVOLT and stressing the need for sustained martial law, the Canadian Military initiated the second phase of the recently recruited HDF1's training (i.e. in guerilla tactics). The HDF1 was subsequently armed to the teeth with dated Russian weapons (i.e. Soviet-era Kalashnikov rifles, SA-2 Grail surface-to-air missile systems, anti-tank weapons, phosphorous grenades, and mortars) and a selection of Cold-War-era Canadian armaments, since the better-alternative modern ordnances were already shouldered or fielded by the regular Canadian Forces.

Unlike the Regular and Army Reserve Forces who had top-of-the-line weapons, gadgetry, digital camouflage, and an unparalleled average IQ, the HDF1 was an unrefined, rag-tag force of patriotic youths drawn to bear arms for Canada against a Canadian insurgency. This force pooled at local armouries and Reserve-bases where they were organized into distinct groups by region, and then diffused by rail and the Trans-Canada Highway to temporary garrisons across Canada. The two major troop deposits in Canada-west were in Winnipeg and in Airdrie, Alberta. Unlike the Canadian Forces (proper), the reported average age of the HDF1 was nineteen, and it totaled 446,000 members, greatly outnumbering the combined totals of the Regular (66,210), Reserve (23,420), and supplementary (21,000) Canadian Armed Forces. HDF1 battalions fell in with the Reservists, providing the occasional support to Regular forces.

An armoured CF group was positioned in Field, British Columbia, and instructed to provide support to the western defenses. The Fifth Field Artillery Regiment, on high-alert at the revamped Victoria-Esquimalt Fortress, provided additional coastal defense, while CF Chinook helicopters (equipped with depth charges) flew circuits above the Salish Sea. In the east: Charlottetown, St. John's, and Halifax saw the erection of giant, temporary military installations, including towers (modeled after the Rafah Tower in Palestine) and berm-rimmed artillery dug-outs. One-third of the Canadian Reserve Forces were sent to northern British Columbia and the Yukon, while others were divided between Yellowknife and Churchill, Manitoba. The largest concentration of Regular Force troops was divided among Quebec, Newfoundland, and southern Ontario towns and cities.

Bush and Rumsfeld openly questioned the Canadian armament and mobilization, and deemed such posturing as distrust, "insulting to the integrity of the Can-American bond." Rumsfeld, in a Q&A session, suggested that the "Canadians should focus on mending relations in their urban areas and addressing border concerns, rather than bolstering their military. After all, what are neighbours for?" Mention of large purchases of Russian weapons again surfaced in the course of Rumsfeld's public scrutiny of Canadian militarism. He criticized it as a breach of economic and security loyalties and more: "a pivotal moment in diplomacy." This all came off as somewhat ironic, given Paul Celluci's earlier suggestion that Canada should bolster its Armed Forces and Canada's inability to purchase and ship American ordnances over the sealed border.

The leak of information regarding Canadian rearmament was in turn deemed by Canadian officials as "espionage" and "neighbourly spying." The dozens of banned CIA agents and the droves of FBI agents under Rob Mueller's command operating in Canada were consequently given ten hours notice to leave. Colin Powell, defensive about the accusation that US agencies were spying on their Canadian counterparts, insisted that all information brought to the attention of the American Government derived from approved intelligence agencies, and had been cleared by the Canadian government. Despite Powell's protest, the ban stayed in-effect. The arrest warrant for non-approved American agents did not, however, scare everyone out of Canada.

An unauthorized CIA agent on the RCMP's watch-list was found skulking around the Prime Minister's office after his ten hours were up. Irritated by his arrest by Canadian officials, the Administration bid the US Army to close all bridges and roads between nations to traffic, pending the agent's release. When the

Prime Minister's Office released a statement indicating that the agent would necessarily be imprisoned and interrogated, the border was formally sealed to all non-military personnel. Ex-pats on both sides of the border were refused access, regardless of rationale or necessity. Mindful of anti-Canadian coverage, Canadian border-agents repeatedly denied press access to *FOX*, *CBS*, and *CNN* reporters, who nevertheless managed to infiltrate the country embedded with their American military hosts (approximately six-hundred achieved entry).

Patience-sapped and humourless, neither government was prepared to tolerate any further deviance or disorder. Every domestic mistake and slip of the tongue now had international implications. For instance, a fishing-trawler leaving St. John's gave the US a reason to put additional pressure on eastern Canada.

In early February, several intoxicated fishermen toting stolen weapons from a HDF1 cache fired off the bow of a Canadian patrol boat. After a brief firefight, the Canadian Navy deployed gas grenades to subdue the fishermen, and boarded the neutered ship. The prisoners were brought to St. Johns, Newfoundland, and turned over to local law-enforcement agents. Since the local law-enforcement had American "supplementary staff" with them, the fishermen's statements during questioning found an international audience. In response to a question about their motivation for firing on a Canadian ship, one responded:

> Oh, sorry about that, boys. You know how it goes[?]. We all saw the memorial on the TV, and got so damned emotional…Well, see, Bill had his guns below deck, and Chris, well, he thought you were ganging on us, so he starting saying: 'Let's give this a go, eh.' We thought you were Yankees, after all.

In response to "mounting threats in [American] coastal regions," the United States sent a medium-sized naval fleet to Halifax. The CF at CFB Halifax and CFB Gagetown (i.e. those not yet deployed elsewhere) responded immediately by entrenching and creating a regional "net" in case things went sour. Commodore Drew Robertson met the US Fleet with three of his four ships. His fourth, the HMCS Halifax, joined them three hours later.

Within the week, another American fleet was stationed in staggered formation twenty kilometres off the Vancouver shoreline, in range of coastal Canadian batteries and the large guns on Galiano Island, and obstructed by strategically anchored Russian trade vessels (whose commanders had been well-compensated). CF in Esquimalt prepared to "receive" US Forces while the Royal Canadian Navy continued to keep the Americans at bay on the east coast.

RECOGNIZING THAT NORTHCOM played by Bush's rules could serve two masters, Canadian General Henault organized an operation to quash a terrorist operation in Detroit, which Homeland Security had willfully overlooked.

Canadian General Henault was greatly displeased with the ineffectuality of the Bi-national Threat Assessment Committee's evaluation of certain North American security threats. The committee had debated without resolution over whether several heavily-armed individuals, working out of a motorcycle-club-turned-auto-mechanic-depot in Detroit, actually intended Canadians harm.

Two of the suspects had relatives who died as a result of the November Bombings, so besides any ideological motivation, revenge was already cause. Henault, present at the debate, requested that the RCMP and CSIS launch a secondary investigation. The subsequent second-look produced damning evidence revealing that the Detroit Dozen (the term used by the *Detroit Free Press*) was in fact a militant group planning to bomb iconic Canadian sites. Since the Americans concerned gave the Detroit Dozen a low priority, Henault knew not to expect a speedy resolution initiated Stateside.

Minister of Defence Pugliese gave the Canadian Military the go-ahead, pending permission offered Stateside. The permission was given after-the-fact—a 'maybe' was initially offered, and the full 'go' was given half-an-hour after the street outside the depot was reopened to traffic. (The Detroit Dozen had plans to go out-of-state the evening of the planned Canadian operation, so time was of the essence.)

Four two-man teams were met by Detroit law-enforcement agents on the Ambassador Bridge. They were briefed by their ex-pat Canadian sheriff, Martin Shelling, who then escorted their convoy within ten kilometres of their destination. They left their American guard, and set up surveillance posts to guarantee they had: a) the right targets; b) entry and exit points to the compound; c) no civilians confused for perpetrators; and d) the best vantage points on the front and back yard. Once satisfied that the several would-be terrorists were all accounted for and that all customers were cleared, the JTF2 commando team signalled the local authorities to form a perimeter, preventing entry to all incoming traffic.

The team—wearing American designations—moved in, eliminated all targets, and secured the garage for explosive-teams to dismantle the twelve-hundred pounds of explosive materials, which included four one-gallon containers of thirty-five percent hydrogen peroxide, uranium, thorium, lithium metal, thermite, aluminum powder, beryllium, boron, black iron oxide, and magnesium ribbon. While heavily-armed, the suspects were subdued with extreme prejudice before getting a shot off at the Canadian team.

When word of the operation hit the news, Chretien attempted to spin it as an indicator that the terrorism "currently fought on Canadian soil has taken root elsewhere." Of the suspects killed in the raid, John H. Cummings—a family man from Belfast, Maine—was identified as one would-be terrorist. His father had left him a ten-million dollar a year trust, which he decided would be best-spent on a dirty-bomb. American pundits suggested Cummings and his accomplices intended their attack for a Stateside target, and explained away the Canadian ingredient in this State-sponsored counter-terrorism operation.

Members of the JTF2 task-force who undertook the counter-terror mission were subsequently awarded the Presidential Unit Citation in an effort by the American administration to suggest that the operation had been sponsored and organized by American government or Military officials, despite having actually outraged those employed in the West Wing. The success of the operation appeared to be a step in the right direction (i.e. for interoperability and efficiency in counterterrorism operations across the continent), although it was clear, from both from American history and Bush's comments, that the US was not to be bested at their own game.

♠

FINDING THE RIGHT WORDS

THE CUSTOMS AGENT drummed his short, dehydrated fingers on my passport photo. "So Mr. Danson, what was your business in Canada?"

"Profit by misfortune." He did not find this particularly funny.

I grabbed my bags and headed outside Reagan International, whistling, thinking about my mobility despite all that I had seen and circumnavigated theretofore and the unfocused resentment festering in my heart. A line full of men (coincidentally sporting nearly identical blue-striped dress shirts, blazers, and tacky ties) and women (again uniformly wearing grey dress-suits and brown leotards) —all toting ridiculously-sized coffees—awaited me, where I idled at a spot designated "taxi pick-up, drop-off" for fifteen minutes. When came my turn, I departed in a cab with a paranoid new American who'd demonstrated his patriotic zeal by decaling his car with a few hundred American flags.

Bound for the Washington Hotel on Fifteenth Street, just north of Pennsylvania Ave (a hop-skip-and-a-jump away from the White House), I surveyed New Rome on high-alert. The marble city was teeming with reporters, brush-cut secret service members (all ex-military), black SUVs, and press vans. As we drew closer to the Mall, I spied copious concrete barriers, evacuation-route signs, rooftop snipers, and heavily armed police enforcers. It was clear that Red Coats would not burn down the White House a second time.

Allocating superfluous military personal to the Capital was a clever plot: it served as a tableau vivant of a nation under the threat of attack. The ostensible extremity of the security in New Rome was used to simultaneously foster paranoia and a perpetual fear of terrorism, as well as prompt a lingering appreciation of reactive capability. Although the conflict was well contained, this continual show must have had a psychological effect on Washingtonians—on the policy-makers, the lobbyists, and those who missed the memo—and their ability to make rational decisions about what was predetermined as a threatening anti-American force.

The cab delivered me to the hotel. With the help of my driver—one critical comment away from breaking into a recital of the anthem—I dumped my bags off in the hotel lobby. I arranged with the bellhop, who'd identified himself as Boris, for my luggage to be brought up. After the elevator doors closed on Boris and my heap of bags, I returned to the front desk for a map. The map, a cartoonish re-presentation of the Mall and downtown Washington, seemed to suggest that it'd take me longer than expected to get around on foot. Anxious about this disproportionate space-time ratio (favouring the former), I bolted out the gilded doors. I was on the clock.

The Network had attempted to get me an interview with someone in the FBI with a sense of what—apart from sniper-fights and wide-roaming tank battles—was going on along the American-Canadian border, particularly along the Alberta-Montana border, but no one at the Edgar Hoover Building was willing to give me the time of day. Dejected, but still my old, utilitarian self, I instead marched along Constitution Avenue, deviating to the Lincoln Memorial where close to 120,000 demonstrators were out protesting the war.

Few among the crowd could tell me much more than the press had told them, so my efforts to solicit compelling interviews were all in vain, especially since I didn't want to complete the news circuit by covering opinions on the present coverage. That would have been far too self-referential for my liking. Nevertheless, I had time to kill before I could meet Charlie Kalnychuk.

The protestors were an eclectic mix of isolationists, constitutionalists, peace activists, and ex-pat Canadians. Among those I spoke to, there was a wide variety of interests voiced concerning the war. I met several gay-rights activists who were worried Canada's cultural-left was likewise under attack in the American sweep. I also encountered the inevitable crazies, drunks, rabble-rousers, and extremists. Some had a number of incendiary remarks about the United States to share; others had a hate-on for Bush, and the odd John Birch type was content to recycle historical Ron Paulisms, and then misapply them, utilizing them for all the wrong reasons. *Zealotry is a hard-sell with hard-headed buyers.*

I received a text from Charlie halfway into a Vietnam veteran's speech about the toxic nature of intervention and the average American's inability to play politics without recourse to violence.

Kalnychuk wanted to meet at the Matchbox Restaurant in Chinatown.

I hailed a cab, and rocketed over (my driver was probably setting records). Since I had beat Kalnychuk there, I secured a corner-booth, bordered by an embossed window and a red brick façade. There, alone—an inconsistent chiaroscuro figure strobed by an incandescent bulb past its prime—I welcomed the company of a few German beers. When Charlie finally arrived, I had socialized my way to a buzz.

Out of practice with the Kraut-beer, I couldn't contain my shock to have the world's most-wanted-man's son recognize me. Even more bizarre was the type of person he appeared to be: a well adjusted young man pushing thirty-five. No weird tattoos. No affected intonation. I had expected to sit down with an Osborne. Instead, I got a Kennedy. I got up to shake his hand, and we exchanged pleasantries.

"You look surprised to see me. What were you expecting? A Canuck?"

I scratched my head, searching for the right words. "Pardon?" He surveyed my face and the puzzlement inscribed on it, smiling.

"Don't be upset if I don't drip maple syrup like the old man." He sat down and waved for the waiter. A short, young woman with tar-black hair darted towards us, her hands buried beneath a stack of menus. "Good afternoon, my dear. Can I grab a car-bomb?" She nodded and smiled, surmising the kind of men we were with two quick scans. "Much appreciated," he howled behind her.

"Are we getting hammered?" I inquired, worried that the car-bomb may slow *us* down.

He pointed at my most recently emptied pint glass. "Oh, I'm just catching up," he chuckled. Sizing me up, he leaned forward to the point of parody, smiled, tented his fingers over his salad plate, and began slowly, "So Mr. Danson, you've traveled long and far to talk to me. I hope this not a colossal disappointment. I also hope you don't expect to learn much about the old man. It has been quite a while."

"Mr. Kalnychuk—" I pulled my notebook out of my pocket and conducted my syllables with the spine.

"Chuck. You can call me Chuck," he said, squeezing binocular vision out of a wince so that he could read the specials. He sat, shoulders back, running his long, boney index finger up the laminate. Charlie's gorgon hair was streaked with grey, which bled down into his beard. In the clearings where his visage broke through the heavy, black curls, there was some evidence of a weak jaw and a roundish face.

"Do you mind if I record our session?" I held out the Dictaphone, thumbed *record*, and began scribbling down notes.

"The calamari dish is supposed to be really good here." I turned the recorder off. With the click he jerked his head up. "Oh! No, I don't mind at all. On the record, yes? You mind if I smoke, on the record?"

"Not one bit." He pulled a pack of cigarettes out of his shirt pocket, and tapped himself a smoke. He motioned to return the box to its well worn groove, but then gestured it to me. I waved my notebook no, smiled, and then clicked record. "So David, it's David, right?" He bowed his head to catch the flame, and returned his gaze to its earlier plane, behind a curtain of smoke.

"David, Dave, whatever works," I said, flustered and off-rhythm.

"Not whatever, unless of course, you want me to call you Lucy."

"David is fine."

"So David, what do you want to know?"

"You may not have seen your father since the divorce, but you may have some sense of who he was—who he is." He squinted and pinched at his temple.

"Some sense. Yeah, you could say that."

"Would you care to expand on your answer?"

"He's a man's man: he sported a red and white hat and shirt, blue pants, big spectacles, and a walking stick." He smiled mischievously. "World hide-and-go-seek champion I reckon." I feigned a smile. Too many hipster-kids had beaten him to the punch-line for his witticism to elicit a real laugh. In fact, I think I'd *seen someone wearing the shirt at the Memorial.*

"Any additional information you can provide, however seemingly superfluous, might be helpful in constructing a proper biography. If we have a stronger biography, there's a better chance we can avoid caricaturizing your father in our media coverage."

"You mean for his obituary?"

"Do you mind elaborating on the disposition of your father?" My heart was racing. I was in the zone.

"Sure. Dad was—well, he was a lot of things. After my brother Aden passed, he was..." His gaze disintegrated, and he stared blankly over and past my shoulder. "An obsessive compulsive hermit, I suppose...You look for strength in your role-model. Up until then, he had been the picture of gallantry and courage. Used to tell us stories about the secret agent before bed. Aden and I always knew it was him—the man in the stories. Had to be. I mean, who else could hear a mark gurgle after an assassination and then tell the story? He was a liar, omniscient or the agent."

"It sounds like he told you some gruesome bedtime stories. A tad morose for children, no?" He waved my politically correct concern away like it was bad wind.

"Dad had no filter. Ma said it was because he lost certain sensibilities in 'Nam. I'm sure he saw kids fight, kids die. The world probably matured for him in the late '60s. After seeing that, what's a little horror story before bed, right?"

"I'm interested in this secret agent. Did he give you any details about any of the agent's operations?"

"Not that I can remember. I've always been dead to details."

"They can do that."

"Do what?"

"Kill you."

"Huh...Yeah, I just focused on the callous protagonist. The man'd do just about anything and everything for Fortress America. Dad later criticized government propaganda for sending Aden to the grave, when he was the most compelling source."

"You moved to North Bay when you were just young. How did that affect you?"

"God dang, Dave; you sound like my shrink." The waiter placed a half-pint of stout and a mixed shot of whisky and Baileys in front of him. He pointed to the shot-glass, "Here's the real cure." Chuck dropped the shot-glass into the pint and pounded the concoction back. He wiped his moustache dry along his sleeve. "North Bay's a hole. Weekends were cool though, in more ways than one. As dad was tasked with less and less to do at work, he took more time to teach us to hunt, fish, and be real men."

"Like the secret agent."

"Yeah, I suppose. Are you ordering food?" he asked, hungrily whipping his head side to side, stuck between two tasty options like the proverbial thirsty-hungry donkey before a feast and water.

"No. Not yet, anyway." He raised his eyebrows, and filled his cheeks.

"Calamari or pork knuckle?"

I really couldn't have given less of a shit about what he had to eat, but wanted his focus, so I pretty much shouted "Calamari!"

"The second before you answered me, I realized what I really wanted."

"Good."

"Not a fan of pork, Danson?"

"So you spent some quality time with your dad?"

"Business, business, busyness. Alright, Danson. I don't want to give you the impression that he was a bad father. He was terrific. Hell, some animals eat their children. Polar bears, lions, langurs, and baboons. Didn't Chronos consume his children—I mean, the Titans?"

"I don't follow too many sports."

"Anyway, people presume that I'm some sociopathic guy just because my dad's a terrorist. Ma raised me right. I went to school." He paused, and ran his finger around the rim of his glass. "Aden's death was tough on all of us, but certainly put an end to sibling rivalry." The upward curvature at the corners of his mouth evened out, and his eyes seemed to gloss over. "Aden was older, see. I was still a kid by some people's sun dials when he died. Fucking Iraq…Ma tried her best to shelter me, even though I knew what was going on. She spared me the imagery, though. Didn't let me watch dad fall into his rut. Probably was a good thing too. Even on the down and out, I'm sure he could have been mighty persuasive. Moving away likely kept me a law abiding citizen."

"And you are?"

"I try, anyway."

"Did any of your father's personal affiliations strike you as out of place?"

"Not that I can think of. It was always Canadian or American military-types. A few reporters I suppose." He leaned back to check his pager, and then coiled forward as though possessed. "Although there's a damn good chance he may have had an affair when I was younger."

I leaned forward, my pen grooving the paper beneath it. "What makes you say that?"

"Some blonde would come round the house when mom was at work." He gestured to the waiter for another drink. "I heard them fight about it in the kitchen once, while I starved sleep at the top of the stairs. But who knows? She could have been just another military official doing her patriotic duty."

"Do you know her name?"

"Sorry, David. No clue."

"I don't mean to return to the matter of Aden's death, because I know it must be painful to dredge—"

"Whatever. What've you got?" I took a pause to signal respect.

"When Aden died, was there anyone who regularly visited your father? I know you moved, but before you moved, did you know about anyone in particular contacting your father?"

"God, pretty much everyone: newspapers, *CNN*, our parish priest – everyone wanted to send condolences, get the scoop or ruminate over what to do."

"The reason I ask is that the Yukon Sprites had been around since the end of the Gulf War. Originally was a charitable organization. I'm curious if Bruce may have been introduced to someone in their network prior to 2001."

"You're alright, Danson. Very forthcoming of you to reveal intent before asking the hard questions. Ha, do you want another beer or are you just going to dry up over there?"

"I'll have another when the waitress comes back around."

"Lady on the phone warned me that you'd be pretty intense. What was the word she used, 'unsympathetic'?"

"The Sprites—"

"The Sprites before 9/11? Fuck, probably." Charlie scanned the room, looking for the waitress. "He was a lost cause to his friends, colleagues, and family. No one kept tabs on him. Ma had presumed him dead, shacked up with some whore or taking contracts from the mob. Probably the latter. If there was one thing he's good at, it's killing and lying...He didn't show his right hand what the left was doing, especially when it was wrapped around some poor guy's throat."

"No names came up? Nobody in particular?"

"I don't know what to tell you, man. His buddy Amir works at the State Department. Crowley died last September from a heart-attack. Hoff—I never saw him, but heard enough about him. Had some high-ranking military job. Apparently dropped by on occasion. Frequently called my dad back in the day, but always about work."

"Does Hoff have a first name?"

"My dad's business was only ours when he decided to share it, which was never." He leaned his cup over to stare at my distorted version.

"The next round is on me," I proposed.

♠

GENESIS: A HAPPY FEW

BEFORE SUBDUING a rogue Canadian state to initiate regime change, Bush first had to create one. Thus it was necessary to create an environment that would produce a reaction that could be conveyed to the American public as tyrannical. The threat of domestic violence was sufficient for police-action and a small-scale intervention, but didn't warrant the full might of the war machine, which the executive administration presumed necessary to eliminate the threat of northern Canadian militants. Nevertheless, Bush (now taking a direct line from his Deputy Chief of Staff Karl Rove) wanted to feel out NORTHCOM's territorializing potential.

In a closed meeting with select members of the Security Council, Powell suggested to Walter Stuetzle (State Secretary of the German Ministry of Defence) that a regime change may be necessary to change the tide in Canada, even though eastern Canada was relatively restrained. In the same meeting, Stuetzle apparently argued that the US needed to provide clear evidence of the Chretien Government's complicity in the recent terrorist attacks before a regime change could be initiated. Stuetzle vowed to fight the initiative at subsequent UN meetings if his condition was not satisfied. This attempt to reach out for third-party involvement was the last the US would try for years. While the US was losing European friends, Canadians ran down their list of potential allies, both international and indigenous.

SEVEN FIRST NATIONS protestors with Natives Against the Occupation (a.k.a. NAtO)—an Iroquois (from Brantford, Ontario), a Tsuu Tina (from Calgary), four South Peigan (from Montana), and two Ojibwa students (from the Hastings-Prince Edward)—were massacred in early February by machinegun fire when picketing at the waterfront in Sault Ste. Marie. Condi Rice relayed reports of their complicity in an attempted terror attack, and insinuated their use of Molotov cocktails against American Forces, but no evidence was ever provided to substantiate her aspersions.

Ross Emerson, representative of the Blackfoot Confederacy, was outraged by the unrepentant American government's response, especially when Jacquelyn revealed on *CNN* that the NAtO group had been unarmed when shot with lethal rounds from an armoured vehicle. On February 9, Emerson organized youth from the Blackfoot Nation, and proposed a special deal with the Canadian Coalition government. Further, he incited other First Nations to get involved. He remarked in a *CBC* interview:

> Why must all imperial aggression begin with violently silencing our countries' First Nations or Indigenous People? We cannot stand by and watch this aggression run its course. But we also cannot become pawns for either side in a war where white men will inevitably be the only winners. Only if promised an economic and socially beneficial ends, will the Blackfoot and our friends constitute a means to an end of this imperial aggression. What will Canada offer recent victims, keeping in mind its historical obligation, failings, and guilt? To the men on Parliament Hill: our ears and hearts are open, especially with the recent, unchecked aggression against innocents, but they'll just as quickly be shut if we feel we are being infantilized or not taken seriously.

The historical obligation and failings Emerson was referencing was the Canadian government's broken promise to protect the Shawnee's American-threatened-land after the War of 1812. Without the support of Tecumseh and his men (including "280 Mohawk and Kahnawake Akwesasne, another hundred Iroquois from the Grand River Settlement, and about three-hundred Ojibwa from the Thames River area"), British and Canadian Forces may not have been able to take the strategic American forts of Michilimackinac (Chicago), Detroit or Beaver Dams (Thorold, Ontario).[48] Their contribution helped to prove the annexation of Upper Canada too costly for the American invaders. Despite their support, the British failed to secure their land, leaving them with a thinned confederacy and scorched earth.

Members of other First Nation groups (the Tsuu Tina in Alberta and some of their Navajo-relatives in the American southwest, as well as Shuswap descendants under the American shadow in the Canadian west) watched the proceedings attentively, likewise agitated by the US treatment of the NAtO group's tragic massacre. A list of land, pensions, and social benefits was drafted and signed by the Canadian government, Blackfoot, and Tsuu Tina officials, as well as by individual volunteers from the other First Nations.

---

[48] Ray, Arthur J. Canada's Native People (Toronto: Key Porter Books, 1996) 138.

There was, however, dissidence within the Blackfoot Nation on account of the potential risk that Canadian support would have for their holdings of over one-and-a-half-million acres of land in Montana. Emerson forwarded the complaint to the Prime Minister's Office, and the Coalition Government responded with land guarantees. Although this quelled some of the discord amongst the Blackfoot, thousands decided to remain neutral, while those following Emerson arranged to support their Canadian relations. According to Emerson's deal with the Coalition Government, a special regiment would be designated for volunteers, attached by way of armoury and base to the Royal Edmonton Regiment. Cross-border initiatives were coordinated online.

Seeing beyond the obvious advantage of more able bodies, Chretien noted the importance of this dissent and the bond that grew from it on both sides of the 49th parallel. On the one hand, it made the American left (with their bleeding hearts and de-oxygenated brains) highly critical of their complicity, and demoralized many American war-supporters. On the other hand, it showcased a functional Native American-Canadian partnership.

Members of the special force were contracted with generous salaries, special reservations (with proposed, limited self-governance), and promised pensions upon one year's activation. Assignments were granted on a volunteer basis. Although the Canadian government had, in the past, mistreated its native population, its failings paled in comparison to the US, and Canadian propagandists harped on this disparity.

Two-thousand-five-hundred men illegally crossed the border from Montana into Alberta to meet hundreds of Canadian volunteers in Medicine Hat. In the daring cross, an undisclosed number of individuals were arrested by border officials, spotted in advance by the newly purchased US UAVs. Chretien conferred travel visas to all ex-American volunteers, and the Canadian government pressed for amnesty for those captured by American border guards during the migration.

On February 23, the missing body of a Mohawk teen from Akwesasne, separated from a related migration en route to Cornwall, Ontario, was "found" and paraded Stateside in an anti-Canadian rally. A cell-phone video-capture of this incident incensed Canadians, First Nations, and others around the globe. While Amnesty International flagged this as a morbid violation of a "whole-long list of human rights," a subversive human rights group affiliated with the newly emergent Sprites militant group targeted an American military barracks Stateside Sue Sault Marie, not far from the scene of the NaTO group's slaughter, in retaliation for the teen's murder.

The covert operation crippled several vehicles and claimed the lives of two soldiers. Officials from both countries condemned the operation. In the American condemnation of the attack, there was an insinuation of Canadian-Aboriginal complicity, without any specification to hone the contemptuous remark. This concretized the resolve of fence-sitters and those previously unsure of which flag to fly.

ALTHOUGH THE QUEBEC REGION of Saguenay-Lac-Saint-Jean had been the heart of a number of Quebecois secessionist movements prior to the war, the indiscriminate prejudice of the US towards Canadians drove many separatists to rally behind the collective Canadian cause. The Quebecois, fearful of having their province become the American lebensraum, voiced their support for the Coalition Government.

Premier of Quebec and Le Parti Quebecois leader Bernard Landry—who previously desired that an independent Quebec be born sooner rather than later—was fully aware, even before American troops set foot in Laval, that separation had ceased to exist as a positive opportunity for his province, and in the long run was a greater threat to Quebec sovereignty (i.e. to trade one federal government for another). Although popular largely on account of his advocacy of a supranational confederation of Quebec and Canada, he was forced to prioritize his loyalties. With Canada united and buttressed by new alliances, it had a shot at repelling the imperial advance.

♠

THE BATTLE FOR ALBERTA

He had brought them into the high country where the wind blows among the grass roots, where man's voice is a small thing, his shout but a whisper dying in the storm, and they and their horses only a few diligent morsels of life clinging precariously to mountain walls.[49]

– Howard O'Hagan

Washington, D.C.
November 7, 2005

THERE WAS A KNOCK at the door, followed by a throaty voice: "Mr. Danson? Your breakfast and your paper." I begrudgingly withdrew from the comforter's warm pockets, and sauntered to the door to let in the large, bottom-heavy man.

"Hello?" I responded, groggily.

"Good morning, sir." He lumbered in, leading with a tray and a paper, and returned to the threshold with my suitcases. "They'll be downstairs, sir. Wodja like yourself a cab?" I greased his hand, thanking him in the only language that matters.

"Yes—as soon as possible. To the airport."

"Naturally, Mr. Danson."

AIRPORT SECURITY had surpassed even the most cynical of Orwellian predictions. The sooner I got to the airport, the better. Reagan International was, on a bad day, twenty minutes away from the Hotel Washington, but I had to be prepared for a two hour wait at security, where they'd pat me down, rummage through my bags, and try on my shoes. I couldn't afford to miss my flight or waste any more time in Rome while the barbarians were kicking up dust on the other side of the wall.

Kalnychuk's brief cease-fire had come to an end after he realized that the US was simply using the time between Ottawa's peace talks to regain its footing in the western provinces. Although it would have been helpful to round out my perspective by spelunking for insight into the American agenda for Canada post-conflict or to

---

[49] O'Hagan, Howard. *Tay John* (Toronto: McClelland & Stewart, 2008) 99.

deviate from the Mall and see how they were doing at the Canadian embassy overlooking Congress, there were more pressing issues up north.

I had made huge strides with the Sprites in Ontario, but hadn't made any connections west of Kenora. Fortunately, someone who identified himself as Louis Vigeland, contacted *The Network* from a blocked number, offering to take either Stephanie McCorkell (one of my colleagues) or I to meet Kalynchuk in person. It was clear to the receiver at our tips-line that the man knew too much about the Sprites to just be another prank caller or attention-starved rebel. *The Network* was especially content with my submissions as well as the exploitative photographs I had salvaged, so they arranged for Louis to meet me at a rustic, dimly lit bar in Banff called the Magpie and Stump.

The Vigeland connection was tenuous, but opportunities were few and far between. They would have tossed the scoop to one of *The Network*'s better-groomed talking heads, Stephanie included, but there was not enough Kevlar in the world to coax the crisp and beautiful into a Sprite van headed northwest of the US firing line. Besides, if anyone was actually going to be permitted direct access to Kalnychuk and his compound, it was me.

CNN and the *BBC* couldn't get a real shot of the Sprites in action, let alone talk to them, because word of numerous journalist-source-compromises had spread early in the conflict. Jacquelyn's editor coined me *The Network*'s "Peter Parker" on account of the fact that I had made a name for myself keeping my mouth shut and eyes open. Recognizing I was potentially their ace in the hole, Sandy Myers at *The Network* booked my flight, obtained for me the necessary security clearance and press pass, and arranged for a fixer to track me down and put me back in touch with Vigeland in Banff once I landed in Calgary.

AS I INHALED A BACON sandwich and tossed more paraphernalia into my bag, I glossed the front page of *The Washington Post*. The headline read: "American Forces Avalanche through Sprite Stronghold." The photograph squeezed below seemed to substantiate the statement; however, on second review I was struck by the obvious disparity between the statement and the visual evidence appealed to: a depiction of smoke rising from a broken column of LAVIIIs outside of Canmore, Alberta. That's odd, I thought to myself: the Sprites had been primarily using stolen Leopard Tanks or avoiding armour altogether (chiefly because of the success of the US A10 "tank-killers"), whereas the official Canadian Forces tended to use LAVs.

One detail neglectfully unmentioned in Barbara Ostenso's article, was probably the most important: these medium-armoured vehicles had been remote-detonated by Canadian resistance guerrillas (not to be confused with the Sprites) to slow US ground-support. Furthermore, the American Third Armour Division was hardly avalanching. It was stalled south of Calgary, near Okotoks, waiting for a series of tactical strikes on anti-armour and anti-air groups in the foothills before it could press into interior British Columbia, and then north into the Yukon.

Ostenso, and others like her, were doing the US military's bidding: selling the war as successful. Much was at stake in the US military's western campaign. If the war became too costly to sustain (more than the projected seventy-billion dollars), then Bush would likely be pressured to withdraw his forces after a brief shock-and-awe campaign. No misinformed report or article could change the fact of the matter: the proverbial can of worms had been opened. Bush had stumbled into a war he'd ultimately be unable to afford or justify.

As US Forces continued to excise "evil" factions north of what strategists mused was the equivalent to "Hadrian's Wall for the Twenty-first Century," anti-Americanism grew more prevalent. Whether it was the end of the occupation or simply the beginning of a new phase, I had to be present to document what the Ostenso's of the world were content to distort with indolent conjecture. I wanted to meet the Green Legend: the Kurtz of the Yukon: Bruce Kalnychuk.

-EMBARGOED REPORT-

♠ *Banff, Alberta*
November 8, 2005

THE SPRITE'S GROWING RURAL INFLUENCE made American troops more psychologically vulnerable to intimidation (curiously not resulting in fear but in poorly directed escalation), despite their ridiculously disproportionate armament and claim to dominion over land, sea, and air. Moreover, the Americans spent huge sums of money to kill (with ease) comparatively innocuous individuals, but failed to generate much deterrent (statistically) with regards to further insurgencies. This conflict's asymmetrical nature placed the Americans in an especially precarious position. The United States is the type of country that could do total war better than any other nation or empire in all of human history. Unfortunately for the Bush Administration, they could not simply raze Canada to the ground. Restraint is a burden they've had to yoke, especially with the CFs keeping them in check. It's been a very expensive burden.

To better put it into perspective, the average cost of a Kalashnikov automatic-rifle round is twenty-five cents on the Canadian black-market, and the majority of the Canadian guerrillas are equipped with AK-47s ($250 each if purchased on the Scarborough or West Hastings black market). Weeks before I arrived in Banff, the *CBC* reported an Apache attack-helicopter downed near Shuswap Lake. The images had not surfaced in the mainstream American media—whether as a result of censorship or delays in circulation—but my fixer was able to obtain one of the flyers distributed to resistance-members. The flyer was a palimpsest of nationalistic blurbs above the soon-to-be iconic image of the shattered Apache wreckage, reminiscent of the '93 Blackhawk-Mogadishu incident.

Interestingly, the image—although a grainy photocopy—revealed a curious detail about the type of damage that brought down the chopper. It was neither stinger missiles nor flak-cannon-fire that brought the war-bird down, but rather, an eight dollar magazine fired from a guerrilla's AK. The rifleman damaged the fuselage and rotor blades to the point of inoperability. For the price of two coffees at a corporate cafe, Canadian rebels decimated a twenty-two-million dollar piece of equipment.[50] Gotfried drew my attention to the back of the flyer to read the details concerning the fate of the pilots: the pilots were freed, each carrying a dispatch to

---

[50] Taylor, Scott. *Spinning on the Axis of Evil: America's War against Iraq* (Ottawa: Esprit De Corps, 2003) 170.

their commanders, which stated: "the Sprites oppose the war machine's occupation of Canada, not the American people."

While the Sprites and the resistance were cost-effectively toppling multi-million dollar war machines, in its western campaign the US had not been so thrifty. Each Tomahawk missile used to assassinate a Sprite member or group costs three million USD. Already the Americans have launched thirty-nine of these precision-guided missiles, costing the government over $117 million. One journalist and ex-soldier of particular interest to me, Scott Taylor, took an interesting jab at the extravagance of such assassinations: "You can bet that whoever the dead man [is], he never thought he would be worth one-hundred million to the Pentagon."[51]

The frustration with paramilitary drops and air-support in the region encouraged the USAF and the Marines to dumb-down their use of "smart bombs." Success so early in the conflict clearly did the Sprites more harm than good. One frontline reporter suggested in late 2002 that: "Whatever they do, the last thing [the Sprites] want to achieve is any initial success against the US Forces…because the only thing more dangerous than the US military is the US military when it's scared."[52]

The western Sprites who had not yet received their expensive scalping committed to a campaign aimed at destroying infrastructure in the Rocky Mountain region. Without bridges, railways or clear roads, American armour and ground support lagged behind the USAF, making aerial-assaults and reconnaissance missions particularly dangerous. Hermetically sealed in the mountains, the Sprites could focus their attention on chokepoints. As of November 7, only nine of the sixty-five American paramilitary missions and airstrikes yielded satisfactory results according to a NORTHCOM report, meaning that the Sprites were enjoying moderate success.

Kalnychuk allotted reserves of anti-air mountain fighters (referred to as "Snowmen") throughout the Rockies, and assigned them with the task of distracting the American Airborne's long-range-patrols and Coalition Special Forces. Although ineffective in thinning the US and Coalition ground forces, Kalynchuk's

---

[51] Taylor 171.
[52] Taylor 168.

destruction of supplies and air-support offset their momentum. Coinciding with this effort, automatic weapons proliferated in the Rockies at treetop level, thus deterring support-choppers from flying low-level sorties. Since the concealed guns forced helicopters to fly higher, they consequently became targets for flak-cannons and ground-to-air missiles. Tunnel systems and remotely-operated AA guns likewise made it difficult for US and CF airstrikes to eliminate or exact any decisive toll on the Sprite's Snowmen anti-air teams.

Kalnychuk's Wraiths (i.e. his special mountain guerrilla commandos) managed to keep the Okanagan Valley and maintain a tight perimeter around the western portion of Banff National Park, due in part to a large stock of US Stinger missiles (purchased illegally, I imagine). Chopper sorties out of Washington State were cancelled, pending the destruction of Kalnychuk's anti-air teams. Javelin, Rapier, and TOW missiles were prominent in the region, as well as anti-air guns obscured behind high berms and beneath camoflauge netting.

Without consistent air-support, US and Canadian ground operations became especially dangerous. One US special operation sent a Delta Force group to a remote, Sprite-infested gully not far from the Washington border. One member later told a colleague:

> The planners think we can perform fucking magic. We can't. Don't put us in an environment we aren't prepared for. Next time, we're going to lose a company.

The Sprites' erratic guerrilla warfare warranted caution from the advancing Coalition Forces. The typical counter-terrorist's hubris was a danger to him.

AS THE SECOND WEEK of bombing [of Banff] continued, reports began surfacing that all was not going well and that the Bush Administration was not sure how to proceed. US generals were frustrated that their bombing had not flushed out more [Sprite] forces.

Those surviving forces were a constant threat to the invaders. Notwithstanding these setbacks, the ratio for battle-fatalities, insurgents to American/Canadian soldiers, was lop-sided: seven to two (in the Vietnam War, for example, the kill ratio was twenty VC per US soldier). As winter drew closer, however, the Sprites had more than tactical nukes to worry about. They had to stockpile supplies in the mines, railway tunnels, bunkers, and natural caves they had made home, otherwise there'd be no surviving into the New Year, given the cold and inaccessibility of fundamentals (i.e. food, oil, ammunition, etc.).

One curious ramification of the destruction of infrastructure in the region is that historic difficulties in crossing the Rockies, circumvented for a century thanks to the highways, railways, and their respective bridges, emerged once again. The mountains again constitute "an unbroken and unpassable barrier."[53] Whereas before, the ease of locomotive travel and transit along the Trans-Canada Highway mooted much of the immobility sensed by travelers, where "it was not a case of going where one wished to go or even where one ought to go, but of going where it was possible or at least not quite impossible to go…"[54], war in the region has reduced man and place to their barbarous basics, reviving resistance, difference, and adventure in even the simplest of journeys.

♠ *Jasper, Alberta*
November 9, 2005

TO REACH THE AMERICAN forward operating base (FOB) in Jasper from the Sprite lines in Banff (my trip to Banff was paid for by *The Network* for a frontline TV special), it took me over a day of driving, hiking, and cross-country-skiing along Icefields Parkway, not to mention the thirteen-or-more-hours I spent waiting at US, Canadian, and resistance checkpoints or in interrogations at "clearance-facilities."

After being stripped of my belongings and searched for "items that could aid the enemy" at the Saskatchewan River Crossing, I was re-issued my press pass, my wallet, and my gear, on the condition that I embed with the US 173rd Airborne. Although embedding with the 173rd was not in keeping with my mission statement and would certainly get me no closer to my Sprite contact, the United States' expeditionary forces managed to be very persuasive.

---

[53] Fraser, Esther. *The Canadian Rockies; Early Travels and Explorations* (Edmonton: M.G. Hurtig, 1969) 106.
[54] Edwards, Ralph. *Trail to the Charmed Land.* Hamilton (H.R. Larson, 1950) 12-13.

In Jasper, I was well received by the 173rd. They assigned me a bunk and permitted me access to their cafeteria. The majority of the men and women on base were extraverts, all wanting to give a statement or have their picture taken. I tried to inform them that I was there seeking answers, not playing paparazzi. You could imagine that this didn't do me any favours. "What questions do yah got?" one man belted, shaking his M4 assault rifle. "I got all your answers. We're killing bad guys. Simple as black and white." I didn't want to further investigate or historicize the soldier's uncomplicated sense of black and white. Instead, I went in search of Jasper's feudal lord: Colonel McAdams.

McAdams was strategizing on the hood of his personal Humvee. I introduced myself, and he offered me some bourbon. "This'll put some hair on y'ur chest!" he exclaimed. Using his hands to animate a great deal of the story, he explained the difficulties met by the Americans driving into Banff.

McAdams was surprised I didn't encounter any problems on the way. "You mean to tell me they couldn't smell the American on ya?" He directed my attention to some papers on the hood of the Humvee. "Here," he said, running his finger along Highway Two and Two-x on the map, "this is the Highway of Death. We carpet bombed the tree line here and here a week ago. We're not going to give the green light to the armour to head down to smoke 'em out until we're certain the anti-tank units are all cleared out. The whole thing's a bit of a catch twenty-two. We need our armour to take out the anti-air teams, but we also need airstrikes to take out the anti-armour. The air-force has already lost two F16s over the Park. Command is convinced that the only solution to our little dilemma is to send in a few squads. They don't seem to understand how counter-productive and suicidal attacking an entrenched, camoflauged force on their home turf would be. I still can't justify the risk to our forces when we can simply freeze the enemy out there. We've got them where we want them. "

The townspeople of Banff had all been evacuated in anticipation of a two-week firing mission on known Sprite locations. "We're going to take the highway south to Banff," suggested McAdams. "Our batteries are set up and clear to start pounding the shit out of the insurgents. Once we have Banff and a perimeter around the area—including Tunnel Mountain, including checkpoints here and here—we'll reintroduce the townspeople and designate it a safe-area. Then it's onto Yoho and Kelowna. By December 14, we should have the Sprites stuck, just where we want them. Our boys coming up from Spokane will clear the way, that is, once they're done cleaning up Colville[55]."

I was rather alarmed by the lack of distinction for who'd be considered a Sprite, an insurgent or a resistance-member. In any event, McAdam's assured me that bodies meant progress.

WHILE AMERICAN ARMOUR and artillery pounded "known-Sprite locations," which were simply strategic dug-outs along the highway, Kalnychuk had a group laying anti-personnel and road mines in the Park, easily disguised by gravel, moss, bushes or in culverts. Given the continued Sprite mining, McAdams found it necessary to continue indiscriminate shelling, highly contestable on account of the civilian cost growing unbearably high. "It has to continue," he suggested, "otherwise we'd be giving them an opportunity to regroup. That'd be unacceptable." The amount of unmarked, "invisible" mines and death traps scattered through the mountains is staggering.

Concerning the prevalence of mines and traps in the region, Private Lombari (with the 173rd) commented:

> Our CO passed on the order: 'see anything fishy, get outta Dodge.' These Sprites've been booby-trapping and nuisance-mining our wounded, dead, and supply drops, as well as the resources and pipelines we've been ordered to safe-guard. So far they've employed: caltrops, C3A1s anti-personnel mines, M16A2s, and M18 Claymores; time, pressure, pull, and tension-releases; and an assortment of other nasty things that maim and go boom, resulting in at least twenty percent of our casualties...
> My brother on active over in Red Deer said he saw some of th[ose] horizontal C14s. He was saying that they're hard to spot and they're usually packed to the tits with a Carl Gustav eighty-four millimeter. That shit can penetrate fifteen inches of Rolled Homogenous Steel armour, even if active. First time in a long time that a US tank commander's got something to fear other than friendly fire. This is the big leagues, boy. Most of us with the heavy step are now thinking twice about our surroundings. The bush's evil all over again.

---

[55] Colville had been the site of a small Stateside counter-offensive – the handy-work of Kalnychuk – intended to give the Banff-district Sprites time to regroup before pressing onwards to Kelowna.

Not all of the effects of Sprite mining have been direct. "Every once in a while," said US Major Mahmoud, McAdams's right-hand-man in Jasper, "we'll hear one go off. Go and check, and it's a bear, wolverine or a moose or what's left of one. If we're lucky, it's a Sprite who's tripped his own wire." Mahmoud quipped: "If it is an animal that's gotten unlucky, be sure not to eat it." Military officials have wizened to a deadly habit plaguing many of their frontier-warriors. Animals killed by mines or by American weapons should not be consumed or touched. Unfortunately, some individuals have already broken this convention.

Several men in the camp were diagnosed with uranium poisoning, and were waiting in the infirmary to be transported to see specialists at Rocky View Hospital in Calgary. Fatigue, paralysis, and blindness, have resulted from their consumption of animals shot with ammo containing depleted uranium. If Saeedy—the Iraqi scientist Jake and I consulted for our DU story—was right, the sickness plighting these men is incurable, and worse: their offspring will be horribly deformed, stricken with one or more congenital birth defects.

Morale is dwindling, suggested Colonel McAdams, despite favourable skiing conditions, clean mountain air, and good hunting. The alpine fun and games in safe-areas is frequently disturbed by sniper-fire, the odd mine or an encounter with one of the many punji stick-pits that have recently been exposed around the countryside. Some of the more reckless soldiers in camp take ski-dos up the hills and board down (in shifts).

"Our thermal imaging is cutting-edge," said McAdams, "but it is not flawless. Some of these bastards crawl for days, take potshots at our sentries or the boarders, and then crawl back through unmarked minefields…They certainly cannot sustain these efforts for much longer. That's the hope, anyway. A perseverant enemy is exhausting—a real pain in my ass." When I asked about the success of patrols in end-running sniper activity, McAdams shrugged, "I am reluctant to send out too many search parties on account of mines, booby-traps, and such. I much prefer to fire on the tree line or call-in airstrikes on our perimeter when necessary. It's enough of a deterrent to give us some peace of mind. Besides, time is on my side."

MY ATTACHÉ for the day (filling in for Gotfried who was literally sitting-out with a bad case of beaver-fever) brought me within sight-line of four smoldering vehicles, about a kilometre north of the US base in Jasper. When I met with Mahmoud later in the day, I inquired about the wrecks and perimeter security. The Major shook his head in disappointment: "A supply convoy was hijacked when it was about two hours out of Edmonton. I was notified when the driver radioed the wrong codes nearby Snaring. If you don't have the right codes and ignore the first, second, and third warnings, you're finished—classified as a saboteur. We shelled them. Haven't inspected the kill yet. We'll wait till Sunday when we do the prisoner-transfer."

"Are you suggesting that you intend to use prisoners as shields?"

"Remember, those prisoners are unlawful combatants. They're not prisoners of war. They're terrorists. And they're the only lives their buddies up in the hills'd waste an opportunity to kill us for. I'm doubtful they'll blow up their own men, and yes, I'll use that to my advantage."

"If armed and guarded," I impinged, "then how do so many convoys get toppled by the Sprites?"

Mahmoud looked uncomfortable. "A lot of the time, we can't tell who's who, which accounts for at least half of the civilian casualties. You have to realize that we—a lot of the American Forces out here—consider this a humanitarian mission. We're eradicating an evil group from a friendly country. I don't pay much attention to the whole regime-change party line. At the end of the day, we're helping these people. So when a mixed, non-threatening group approaches a convoy looking for aid, we can certainly shirk the responsibility of humanitarian rescue, but that doesn't mean we can justify being inhumane. No one wants to riddle innocents with bullets outright. You can imagine how our ethical mandate is a bit of a problem, especially with a lot of the Sprites starting to pose as civilians. That's an easy disguise to pull off...Let's them get close enough to use their anti-tank grenades. With enough firepower, they can punch holes in our Humvees, the Coalition Land Rovers, and the Canadian G-Wagons, and do a lot of damage. Their approach is the same every time: take out the first and last vehicle, and then when all is chaos, round everyone up." He insinuated that the round-up entailed massacre with a thumb across his throat.

I gulped. "Sounds awfully hectic."

Observing my uneasiness, Mahmoud motioned to reassure: "Just be thankful their rocket-teams have all nearly been wiped out. You should have seen this place a week ago. Whether it was their French or Russian connections, those pricks got their hands on AC 300 Jupiter's and LAW 80s. See up there?" He pointed to cleavage on a nearby ridge. "They were firing down on us, and we couldn't see any flashes. Camp was all ablaze, and we were running around like chickens with our heads cut off. It took us three minutes to get the exact coordinates on them, and by then, well—my guess is—they'd moved because there weren't any remains to indicate a kill; nothing but scraps of evidence to suggest they had camped up there for a while and had us under surveillance. Hell, they're probably watching us right now...Just makes my blood boil." He seized the mountains with an angry and determined stare. "Every other day we have to call in Apaches to clean up those mountain bunkers. Even if the choppers aren't actually smoking any out, the boys in camp buck-up when they see the spectacle..." He threaded his finger through a bullet hole in his jacket. "These aren't your run-of-the-mill third-world fighters, if you know what I'm saying. These are advanced fighters who think like we do."

"Third world people aren't advanced?"

"Don't mince words. I meant as far as modern warfare goes." I glared at him, my expression coded with disgust and expectation. "Answer me this, David: this morning, did a sea-skimming Exocet missile hit the USS Elliot off the coast of British Columbia or was it a band of thugs armed with machetes?" I adopted his angry stare at the range. "We're not fighting child soldiers. These are troops who know our tactics, have serious hardware, and have a geographic advantage...This is an uphill battle, and we're pulling out all the stops. We'll have to, anyway...These are top shelf bad guys."

"If you're fighting bad guys, would you say you're fighting a just war?"

He smiled. "I wouldn't say I'm fighting a war at all. It's closer to police-action than anything else." *How many police captains default in a firefight with an intercontinental ballistic missile?* "And it feels *just*, because it's not about hatred. We're fighting, not because we detest Canadians, but because we love America. When we succeed, it is for the benefit of both our nations. But make no mistake, America always comes first, and its security trumps all. That's why we're here. Ensuring American security is always a just cause. Eliminate all potential threats and when you're certain the homeland is safe, call it a day. Suffice to say, I've not had many days off this year."

I pondered over my failed objectivity and personal interest in Canada's "top shelf bad guys" while I headed to my bunk in Jasper's "press-gallery"—an old fire-station that had been converted into a restaurant, and then again augmented to serve as a rest area for the media and official guests of the American 173rd Airborne Brigade.

THE 173rd HAD BEEN DROPPED into the region with little notice and had expected to have been relieved by November. As a result of fierce guerrilla warfare in western Alberta, replacements were reallocated to so-called tension spots, leaving the 173rd with the command of Jasper-base until mid-January. They settled in and made themselves comfortable in the homes of recent evacuees. Since the 101 Airborne Division faced little resistance in southern Alberta after 2003, and therefore did not require the direct support of the First Battalion 320th Field Artillery, the 320th came in with three firing batteries to support the 173rd and their stake in Jasper.

Jasper would have been a convenient location in which to entrench, had it not been for tenuous supply lines and the severed rails. The train station was repurposed to serve as the 173rd's command centre. Where it bordered Connaught Street, it was invisible; buried beneath sandbags and razor-wire. A railcar on the east-side served as a mobile pillbox, which could be sent as support to either the north or south entrance of the town.

This once-peaceful tourist town had been transformed into a military stronghold overnight. Towers had been devised to better-manage the Yellowhead Highway, although they were rarely used on account of Sprite and resistance snipers (the primary tower on the south side of town was pock-marked by high-calibre rounds). Medium-sized cannons sat westerly facing on the northern ridge, and barbed nets had been lowered into the river that runs out of Jasper Lake to deter aquatic assaults. Along the tree-line, McAdams had his men lay anti-personnel spike-strips and mines. Heavy-wattage lamps lit up the river-valley. Notwithstanding all the precautions that the 173rd took to simulate a sense of safety, the shared sentiment in the camp was exposure. Outside the corona of the American vision, the myriad eyes of Sprite and resistance militants looked back with a hungry gaze.

To minimize risk to allied aircraft and recipients on the ground, air drops targeted the iced-over Pyramid Lake, just on the edge of the Jasper-township. The area had been cleared, first by a Canadian JTF2 group, and again by Rangers early in the fall. It has been highly monitored ever since. The supplies were trucked into town from Pyramid Lake, and divided into two stores: one for headquarters, and the other delivered to the primary barracks. McAdams had mentioned an enemy surveillance team camping on the ridge. I knew to keep my wits about me. As the days grew shorter and the weather colder, the Sprites would necessarily become more aggressive. With the boys from the 173rd amassing decent supply-stores, a raid was inevitable.

The Sprites had been testing the American perimeter defences, and engaging nightly in psychological warfare, launching rockets and rifle-fired Molotov cocktails into the base. Although highly predictable, Kalnychuk's Wraiths successfully and consistently encircled the camp, instigated confusion and chaos, and then disappeared back into the shadows with recon for further attacks.

Disadvantaged by their static defensive position, McAdams had engineers attached to the 173rd create dummy-targets in order to reveal Sprite firing-locations. To disorient potential attackers, many of these dummy-targets (a.k.a. "scarecrows") were coupled with "sound-posts"—loud speakers devised to run gunfire and armour sound-effects when motion-triggered. A number of these scarecrows were also equipped with inflatable decoy tanks and troops, which could draw fire and intimidate opposing forces.

McAdams, unable to use his bishops, knights or rooks, had to line up his pawns with Kalnychuk's, and prepare for slaughter. The longer I spent in Jasper, the better the chance I'd end up as collateral damage, without a sense of by whom or why.

♠ *Jasper, Alberta*
November 10, 2005

MAJOR MAHMOUD WOKE me early in the morning. "Get your ass out of bed!" I hadn't yet rubbed the dream-silt out of my eyes when he started-in with the intensity: "We have some questions about your whereabouts last week and how you came to us."

A big uniformed brute with "MP" markered on his helmet came to help me out of bed. He ushered me out into the street, not even half-dressed. Cold bombarded me—cutting through my long-johns to my more vulnerable areas—while Mahmoud addressed his men. "Meet me in the gift-shop. I'll wait on the fax, and then catch up with you."

The military policeman led me into a store on the main drag. Behind shelves of Canadian kitsch and Jasper souvenirs, I waited for Mahmoud. I fooled around with the snow globes and drawstring Mounties. The MP cuffed me. "If you move, I'll fucking blow you away."

"Right away?" I smiled.

Before the meathead could *show me how serious he really was*, a cold gust shot through the room with Mahmoud in tow. The MP crossed his arms. Mahmoud nodded to my guard, and flicked a wad of papers nestled in the crotch of his arm. "Danson, we have to talk."

I told the Major and his entourage that I had already been interrogated at the clearing facility, where I had given a full testimony and signed an affidavit. I explained that I didn't want to repeat myself unless they were particularly interested in hearing the whole story told again.

"Well, Danson, I don't give one goddamn whether you care to repeat yourself or not. We're going to talk about your testimony." Mahmoud turned the papers to show me a transcript of an earlier grilling where I'd been charred. "You mentioned to Sergeant Engles at your briefing that you encountered Sprites along your way up Icefields Parkway. Is this correct?"

Although I had come from a Sprites encampment, those I had met along my journey were actually resistance-members unaffiliated with the Sprites. I told Mahmoud that I had encountered civilians and resistance members, but apart from one Sprite on his way to Colville, I had not heard or seen them.

"We have reason to believe that there is a terrorist group amassed near Lake Louise. We have no viable intelligence on account of the enemy's surface to air missiles (SAM). Their SAM-launchers are chipped into the glacier so that we can't get any thermal reads for a cruise missile strike. It's hard to figure out how to melt them out, especially when they're putting down every fucking lead. I really hope you've got something for me."

I shrugged my shoulders.

"Prior to engaging a potentially unarmed group, we need to know the facts. Don't want to do with a gun what we could alternatively do with a handshake."

I informed Mahmoud and the committee of wary eyes gathered around me that these were neither terrorists nor Sprites, but members of the resistance, unaffiliated with any officially designated foreign terrorist organization. "There are women and children among them," I stated, "and they are operating only defensively." I posited my guess, stabbing at the map tented on the register: "These are probably remnants or deserters from the Canadian Forces' encampment at Field, British Columbia. Non-combatants. The Sprites that are hugging civilian groups for safety are further south."

"How far south?"

"I don't know. South. They're constantly moving. I'd be lying if I told you I knew their precise locations."

"Did you see any anti-air weapons when you passed through?"

While I'd already compromised so much in terms of journalist-source anonymity, I was not prepared to play double-agent and weigh-in further, especially when the next answer could mean annihilation for the entire resistance group. "I am not sure. Major, you have to understand that I am used to being a weather reporter. This is all one bad storm to me."

Mahmoud scoffed, and instructed one of his soldiers to get "the weatherman the fuck out" and grab me a coffee for my troubles. Mahmoud disappeared into the HQ, joined a moment later by McAdams.

STILL SHAKING in my long-johns, I guzzled an oily red-eye and suffocated a cigarette. As I counted how many smokes were left until I was empty, the camp was swept up by a sudden commotion, spiraling out of the barracks on the other end of Connaught Street. Fits of yelling chased a dozen or so jeeps and Humvees past me and out the south gate. I dashed across the road toward the 173rd's HQ where two officers were conversing. "Where the hell is everybody headed in such a hurry?"

One officer picked at chew wedged between his molars and burbled: "Hunting!" Three armed-to-the-teeth Apache-support choppers whipped overhead, past Marjorie Lake, towards Henry

House. Those birds of prey, like the ground-support on their way to Lake Louise, were not out to shake hands.

-EMBARGOED REPORT-

APART FROM THE WIND, which howled and scraped away at the fire station's temporary metal sidings, Jasper was eerily quiet. I squeezed a warm cup of coffee between my legs, and reviewed my notes on my bunk. Gotfried, my convalesced fixer, was growing frustrated with his wind-up radio. After struggling again through pitches of static and crackles in an attempt to convey some "Sympathy for the Devil," he angrily switched it off and began rolling an "after-dinner joint." I knew if I partook or vacuumed some second-hand smoke, I'd be dead to rights, and the night'd be lost, so I bound my ravings with an elastic band and bid him farewell.

I straggled to the north side of town, just past the rail-bridge, and readied a cigarette for a quick nicotine delivery. As I tried to coax a flame from my lighter, a bullet ricocheted off the iron suspended above me. A primal yell announced: "Sniper!" Before the warning had a chance to echo, the perimeter alarm was sounding.

I froze-up, unsure of which angle to cover against. Explosions—likely McAdam's mines—went off sporadically along the far ridge, while brass started to pile up ahead at the barricade as US gunners unloaded a seemingly unlimited supply of full metal jacket into the unknown. The 173rd forward-defense was creating a lot of thunder but little or no locative lightning.

Initially, a few ostentatious soldiers with the 173rd rushed pass me, firing at the ridge without cover. Once projectiles started to whiz by en masse and chew through the surrounding pine, even the gallant hit the dirt. Apart from the occasional tracer-round indicating a static firing position, the American retaliation had no focus—nobody to shoot. The base's floodlights illuminated the roadway only up to the tree line. Beyond, Sprite snipers fired safely under the cover of darkness. McAdams sent men up to the plateau overlooking the north-gate to cover the two-squared kilometre clearing. Mortars sounded off, pinging like cash registers on Boxing Day.

The novelty of *pkt-pkt-pkt* wore off after the first series of close-calls. A rifle-burst raked the "maximum fifty" sign inches away from me. I veered behind a nearby mound of sandbags, and pulled my tattered notebook out of the open. The base was all roaring engines and gun-checks.

A second US mortar team dug in behind the rail-bridge, and started sending shells into the river valley. Despite the death and destruction raining down over Henry House and Old Lodge Road, the assassins sustained their seemingly erratic firing pattern.

Recognizing the ineffectuality of their M16s against ghosts in the darkness, the Americans ordered-over an auto-cannon fitted on a Humvee. The armored vehicle slowly rolled past me toward the barricade, reciprocating metals into the night. As soon as it had delivered its first barrage, a rocket-propelled grenade screamed past the barricade, twisting right into the Humvee and ending in a handclap explosion. Groans and coughing prefaced the driver's collapse out the door. "Medic! We need a medic down here." Fire and smoke poured out of the Humvee, waving over the gunner's body, crumpled inside.

Soldiers peering through the slot on the furthest berm started yelling, "Smoke! Smoke on the horizon! Focus your fire on the smoke!" as a number of smoke grenades obscured the roadway and concealed a running-assault. Using infra-red lenses, US snipers on the bridge and the plateau called down to us, confirming kills, and yet, the attack nevertheless continued.

The 173rd's support Apaches were nowhere to be seen, likely on account of their commitment to the hunting-mission in Lake Louise. The 173rd were also without artillery support since their in-base howitzer and Pyramid Lake guns were under relentless fire. The FOB was separated from the rest by systematic rocket fire and the rear had been compromised. Molotov cocktails pelted Connaught Street, pressing the rail-mounted pillbox to guard the HQ. Within minutes of the initial barrage, Jasper had become an inferno, leaving the Americans divided and encircled.

Major Mahmoud strode down, trench side, with his radioman in tow barking "Do not fire! Hold your fucking fire. Do not make me repeat myself. Hold your fucking fire!" Bullets continued to hail-in, some pimpling the cement barriers running parallel to the road.

"Sir, permission to engage?" yelled a soldier propped up against the mound opposite me, incoming-bullets spilling sand over his shoulder. Mahmoud threw him a look of disdain, and then full-turned to address the men, asphalt fissuring around him.

"There are friendlies out there. Hold your fire until instructed otherwise." Two firebombs mushroomed over the Trefoil Lakes across the river, while just fifty-feet north of us mortar shells of unknown origin began raining haphazardly, churning up the far side of the highway.

"Mahmoud! Major Mahmoud, who's out there? Who's firing?" I screamed. He smiled at me, and cupped his hand over his ear, poising to listen as fewer and fewer small-arms responded to the cannon.

"Armour! Armour at nine o'clock." The sand-covered soldier equipped his LAW rocket-launcher. "Sir! Permission to fire."

"Hold your fire," insisted Mahmoud. He pushed the tube into the soldier's lap. "I will not repeat myself again, soldier."

A harsh staccato drone resounded in the valley ahead of the creak of some invisible machination. Through the dissipating smoke and carnage rolled a battered and screeching Leopard tank, cutting eights. The drone accompanying the metal-on-metal screeches took on a unique, haunting pattern of harmonics and discordant whines. Thirty, forty well-camoflauged men followed the tank in loose formation—all firing on the insurgents attempting to retreat to the tree line. A G-Wagon dragged behind the group with a piper leaning out of the gunner's hatch.

The man leading the charge signalled to the G-Wagon, and then waved at us. Mahmoud waved back, and the storm troopers sprinted for the 173rd's north gate. The white-clad troops passed the barricade and the rail-bridge, and piled into the 173rd's mortar trenches. A red-cheeked, block-headed man sprinted towards Mahmoud. The Major got to his feet to address him. "Welcome to Jasper, Captain."

"Major Mahmoud! Ah, it's nice to be back. Hope you don't mind if we crash at *your* place tonight." He winced, and turned around to acknowledge the fuss. The tank's cannon fired repeatedly, each time illuminating death on the forest's fringe. "We're on our way to Field. Going to tent infantry and armour tonight, then dig in behind Kicking Horse Lodge tomorrow."

"How many tanks do you have tasked?"

"Just the one at the moment." He aimed his finger at the tank just in case Mahmoud had missed it. "Thankfully, they've taken their heads out of their goddamn asses, and given me what I asked for. We've had that relic fitted with a Bushmaster cannon. Using armour-piercing shells. Turns Kalnychuk's Swiss Guard into Swiss cheese. Damn crucial too. They've acquired some armour, as I'm sure you've heard."

"Did you see any out there?"

"No. All you're dealing with at the moment are guerrillas with some anti-tank gear. They had a few support vehicles—technicals[56] fitted with Browning machine guns—but as of this evening, they're no more. As for the tanks we've seen ... they've all been stationary jobs; buried up to the turret and utilized as batteries. Some new, some old. Saw a T-72 in British Columbia. With antiques like that, really makes you wonder, eh? That reminds me: I'd really appreciate it if you'd order your men to fire on Henry House."

Mahmoud turned to his radioman. "Instruct artillery: light 'em up. Three o'clock... Coordinates?"

"Abley!" The Captain waved over a lanky soldier. The young man ran into a salute, and then yanked out a map. "Give Major Mahmoud the coordinates." He circled the target in red, and confirmed the firing coordinates. The captain seized the map. "Check Henry House: five-two-dot-eight-seven-eight-and-neg-one-one-eight-dot-zero-six-three-niner. Go ahead, Orion." The captain turned back into the conversation, and resumed his normal speaking voice, "Fantastic. Is there a service road in? I don't feel like leaving the Mercedes in the open with only a lo-jack for protection."

"Certainly, Captain. We'll open the gate on the south side."

"Splendid. Now, have you anything to eat?"

"Plenty." A ricochet off the bridge sent both men into three-point-stances. "How many verified?"

Explosions flooded the forest on the opposite shore. The screaming and shooting stopped, as if a tap had been shut off. Two Apaches powered over Mount Colin, rocketing Sprites retreating north on the Yellowhead Highway.

"Ah, the cavalry's arrived...I'd say thirty or so, equipped with RPGs, assault rifles, and a few mortars. Sound about right?" He

---

[56] A technical is an improvised fighting vehicle; more often than not, an open-backed civilian pickup-truck or full-wheel-drive with a machine gun or anti-air gun.

glimpsed through one of the holes in a ragged "maximum-fifty" sign. "Looks like it got thick around here. How bad?"

"I suppose we'll find out together," said Mahmoud staidly, "and then look into getting some grub." Mahmoud surveyed the damage. "Although, I regret to inform you that, for whatever reason, they fail to deliver in under thirty-minutes." Both men laughed. Mahmoud turned to go, but saw me cowering in the corner of his eye. "Oh, there you are. Danson, meet Captain Steely, Calgary Highlanders." I had failed to notice his Canadian designations, matted under his camoflauge.

I threw out my hand. "It's a pleasure."

"Danson, eh? What the sam-hell are you doing all the way down there?" He grabbed my hand, and lifted me to my feet. "You must've missed the show!"

"I'm just happy I'll live to catch the re-run."

"And a re-run's the best you can hope for. We've thinned out the cast quite a bit."

A group of men piled by us en route to reconstruct the northern barricade, while medics went to tend to the wounded. I made my way through the outward flow of panicked support-forces with Mahmoud and Captain Steeley, and headed towards the command center.

Gotfried, red-eyed and smiling, intercepted me on Connaught Street, and pulled me aside. "Hey man, I have to show you something."

"Not now." He tugged on my jacket-sleeve.

"Seriously. You've got to see this."

I motioned to go. "Later." Mid-step, I saw Mahmoud and Steeley disappear into the 173rd's field HQ. I turned to Gotfried, "Hey, where the fuck were you when all hell broke out?"

"I was pinned down!"

"Pinned down or rolling pinners?"

"Listen man, I've something to show you." Impatient and still somewhat shell-shocked, I broke his grasp and stormed off. Gotfried stammered behind me, "Asshole."

-EMBARGOED REPORT-

A ROADSIDE BOMB claimed the lives of three soldiers from the 173rd and one from the Calgary Highlanders on their way south to Banff (McAdams sent units to assist the Highlanders in circumnavigating a known Sprite minefield). The retaliation involved a couple-dozen daisy-cutters and non-stop shelling from noon to nightfall. "Kill everything in the red-zone that moves," was the order from McAdams. While doubtful that the retaliation would change anything, McAdams knew that the deaths of American and Canadian troops by "faceless cowards" could not be trivialized by inaction.

I handed Mahmoud a few cigarettes and he caught me up on current affairs in the camp. Pressing my luck, I pressed the Major about a certain double standard: "And what of the American covert missions?"

He replied, rather angrily: "And just whose side are you on? And who the fuck do you think you are? You're an awful long way from Malta, aren't you Danson?"

"I was just asking. And I've been a long way from Malta for a long time now. Full-fledged Seattlite by even my toughest critic's criteria. Have lived there for two decades." With another cigarette pocketed, he had the luxury of tossing his lit cig down in disgust.

"Well, that just makes your dissent all the more troubling." He continued, but his disdain was muffled—something about "west-coast hippy scum."

Despite having an arsenal of petty remarks for a stinging retort, I realized I was a guest of the 173rd and it was not prudent to begin to challenge the contrived moral balance appealed to by American Forces in the Canadian west. I apologized, and whisked off with my tail between my legs to see if I could get some better shots of the smoldering remains of the pockmarked battlefield.

♠ *Jasper, Alberta*
November 13th, 2005

THEY SAY THERE IS NO CURE for the common cold, but I think I've found one. Ancillary equipment and munitions had been trickling into Jasper for the artillery crews from the 320th for weeks. Someone had decided that in addition to the three cannons operating outside of Jasper, they needed an M119 in-town. Unaware that the gun was ready (I had thought it was more of a set-piece lain in the center of town for show), I walked past it without consideration as three men bustled about.

An enormous bang sent me wheeling through the air. The sound bounced from one rock edifice to another, growing in volume and intensity as it climbed higher and higher. Once it had conquered the mountains, the sound relinquished its power over the valley in a Marabar boom. Below mountainous ramparts streaked by regiments of trees, I lay in the snow with my hands reddened by frost, and my ears deafened to all but a high-pitched drone. Though mucous frosted my beard, I ceased to care about the cold I had been nursing and its effects. The ringing in my ears dampened all my other senses. With every appendage numb, I had no idea what body party I could be missing.

"Ah-ha-ha-ha! David, you never told us you were afraid of guns. Boys, keep your firecrackers to yourselves…Get up. It is alright." Shepherded by the laughter of countless others, Mahmoud surrendered his rifle to a soldier in his entourage, and offered me his hand. "If the *Manifest Destiny* is enough to knock over a man such as yourself on this end, just imagine what it's doing miles away in enemy territory. Where you headed, son?"

The gun reeled back again, spilling smoke into the air. One soldier adjusted the angle, while the other two lugged another shell into the feed, stood back and then plugged their ears. I stood stammering and embarrassed before an audience of hardened veterans. I've convinced myself that I was stuttering because I was cold, though I am not entirely sure. "I was h-headed to the c-convoy to get some pictures." The laughing subsided and the crowd dispersed. Mahmoud called on his satellite phone to McAdams, who emerged from his HQ and nodded, indicating consent.

"Alright. Boss says yes. I'll assign Brody to keep an eye on you. He's a sniper. The best. Boy has an eye for trouble. You must be quick and no lollygagging. Grab your stuff. You'll head out in ten." Coinciding with Mahmoud's good-natured order, the cannon erupted again, stabbing the azure sky with rancorous possibility.

WHEN I RETURNED to the town centre, the gun was unmanned. Mahmoud, reduced to a silhouette, was waiting for me beneath a flickering orange orb, likewise contested by the storm. I trudged up to him in the snow, and he handed me a cigarette—perhaps as a reward for managing to stay on my feet. "Dave, I've got some bad news: more insurgents have been spotted by one of our reconnaissance drones. They're going to attack the base again tonight or tomorrow morning. It's not going to be such a cakewalk without any armour support."

"What about the Apaches?"

"After their little show the other night, the birds had to return to Airdrie for rearmament. They've since been grounded. Jasper's been designated a no-fly zone, so it's just us. Hence, we're taking all the necessary precautions...I'm sending our wounded out, back to Calgary. You're going with them. This is non-negotiable. If you are found by our men or theirs, we cannot—we will not protect you. Take care of yourself David."

I argued with him, told him I had military experience—had been a beat journalist with the Marines during the Gulf War—but he wouldn't budge.

"It was good having another hard head on site. You know, one can get carried away out here in the wild. If you're staying north of the 49th, keep your wits about you. Venturing anywhere in Canada is the equivalent to playing Russian roulette with two bullets." *And in Canada post 9/11, there was a good chance those bullets would be Russian too.* He grabbed one of his men by the shoulder, and turned to me. "David, hand me that camera. Private Blake's going to get a picture of the two of us together for your scrapbook." We puffed our chests and brandished our canines.

I RETURNED TO the fire station. Some of the less-seriously injured had packed in and were dressing their wounds. The chef was preoccupied with handing out soup and buns to those who could stomach his cooking. Gotfried, on the other hand, was bundled up with a book and a tin of hot tea. His glasses, fogged by the heat off the cup, straddled the edge of his nose. They rode up when he recognized me, his scowl transforming into a smile. "David!"

"Gotfried..." I grumbled. "You look cozy." His cheeks rode up, squeezing his eyes into tiny, crescent moons.

"David, check it out." He pointed past me. Turning slowly, I followed the aim. Wind whistled through several holes cut through the metal siding of the building. The metal around the punctures curled inward, leaving little mock flower petals. "I told you, David," he guzzled his coffee, "I was pinned down." He kicked the blanket off his legs, and swiveled on the bed. "Look, check this out." He slouched forward and grabbed my bag. Lifting it above his head on an angle, he stared up at me through the ragged burlap. "Through and through, man...That joint saved your life. Shit. You're so lucky, man. I was just chilling, and out of nowhere, it was all bing-bang-boom around here."

"No kidding."

"Then Sergeant Fulworth told me to get in the corner. I'd have come out, but I couldn't. An order's an order."

"I wouldn't attribute my good fortune to a joint, Gotfried. But, alright." I snatched my bag from his hands, and inspected the insides. "Oh goddamn-it."

"What?" inquired Gotfried, feigning concern. I pulled out my fractured Dictaphone. "Are the tapes okay?"

"Yeah, looks like it. Ah, come on! This is—this was my second in... fuck!"

"Dude, you have to relax. It could have been worse. A whole lot worse." Gotfried snuggled into his bunk.

"Okay, Get packed. They're giving us the boot." I scrambled my belongings together.

"What? Where are we going?" The sadist in me enjoyed his panicked and confused reply.

"Cowtown. Have you gotten in contact with Vigeland?

"No word yet."

"Keep trying," I demanded on my way outside.

My old friend, the Howitzer, was again repopulated, and poised to begin its cantankerous cadence. Though I would be unable to capture the Battle for Alberta in its prime—where and when it counted—I determined that exile to Calgary might prove as interesting.

♠

GENESIS: WAR PLAN RED

STILL AMBIVALENT about the Canadian government's complicity in the terror-acts, Bush waved the declaration of war. Instead, he increased the number of American troops along the border and at Canadian checkpoints. Additional US Marines and naval units were deployed in the Great Lakes (breaching a long list of historical treaties with the Canadian and British governments forbidding any nation to do so) in order to ensure greater efficiency regarding their crack-down on terror. Despite its mandate, the US Military was not, however, keen on preemptively eliminating *all* forms of cross-border terrorism.

Canadian railway lines west of Winnipeg were damaged in an overnight raid by "crossers" from North Dakota on February 25. The CF, with the combined effort of the Royal Regina Rifles, the Queen's Own Cameron Highlanders (sent from Ottawa), the Royal Winnipeg Rifles, and the Fort Garry Horse, were able to eliminate a large number of the southern militants, capturing only a few. Prisoner-interrogations carried out by the CF revealed that the swift Canadian Military response had saved most of the raiders' intended targets.

The CN Railway Bridge on the Assiniboine River was among the structures ruined, probably the most successful sabotage of the raid. Anticipating more of the same, the Third Battalion of the Princess Patricia's Canadian Light Infantry (Regular Army) was sent from its Edmonton base to defend southern Alberta and the Second Battalion was dispatched from CFB Shilo (near Brandon, Manitoba) to an FOB in Killarney, twenty kilometres north of the American border. Aging Leopard tanks were taken from Wainwright, Alberta to Lloydminster, where officials feared an unofficial American "sweep." Funds were secured to update the Leopards to C2s to ensure their success, while dozens of heavily-armed LAVIIIs patrolled the damaged highway and rail-lines.

Since the US Second Fleet had tightened its hold on the Halifax Pier the day before the raids, coinciding with reports of submarines in the St. Lawrence, security analysts in the Canadian media suggested that these official and unofficial escalations were harmonized. Chretien, furious with the allowance of northbound raiders into Canada by American guards and increased coastal pressures, demanded assurance be given that the US would continue to seek the best for both nations: "We are now committed to bi-national solutions under NORTHCOM. Why, then, do you still act without communicating, communicate without elaborating, and engage without warning?"

The CF (with American attaches absent) were briefed on responses to an American escalation on February 27, 2002. This warning had obvious complications given the integration of the two militaries. Bush reacted poorly to the briefing. He interpreted the CF's defensive posturing as hostile, consequently remarking: "Militant hostility against our country will not stand." This allusion to his father's war speech, wherein Bush Sr. had said: "this will not stand, this aggression against Kuwait," indicated to all that war was inevitable.[57] In the same address, Bush also remarked:

> Our responsibility to history is already clear: to answer these attacks and to rid the world of evil. War has been waged against us by stealth and deceit and murder. This nation is peaceful, but fierce when stirred to anger. This conflict was begun on the timing and terms of others. It will end in a way, and at an hour, of our choosing.

Bush's wallop on the drums of war worked well to win him favor in the polls. After the statement was released, Bush's approval ratings shot from fifty-one to eighty-six percent.[58]

Depictions of Canadian animosity and exaggerated threats of Canadian-initiated escalation were discussed ad nauseam in the American coverage in order to concretize a warlike resolve across the country. Eighty-one-year-old Toronto Star writer Dalton Camp remarked on the fear campaign:

> It is not surprising that the American media—from *CNN* to *The New York Times*—would join so fervently in the task of preparing the American people for a war of undetermined length against a catalogue of hypothetical enemies. In such an endeavour, critical judgment becomes consumed in patriotism while being terminally suspended.

---

[57] Feith, Douglas J. *War and Decision: inside the Pentagon at the Dawn of the War on Terrorism* (New York, NY: Harper, 2008) 3.
[58] "David Ryan - 'Image, Rhetoric and Nationhood': Framing September 11: Cultural Diplomacy & the Image of America." *49th Parallel: An Interdisciplinary Journal of North American Studies.*

AT THE OUTSET, the American campaign planned for "rescuing" Canada-west (sold to the public as police action) sounded promising, specifically in addressing what Bush had identified as "danger areas" or "targeted zones" (i.e. major northern cities; coastal cities; mountain cities, etc.). Apart from the central states and the south, Americans—coached to believe they were perpetually "under the threat" of the Canadian cancer spreading south of the border—fully supported increased intervention.

On March 1, 2002, Bush set a mandate for Chretien: martial law must stay in effect until violence subsides; American prisoners must be released (there were no remaining prisoners in custody apart from the spy who had broken into the Prime Minister's Office), and members of the Sprite terrorist organization must be captured at all costs. If these items were not addressed by March 25, the United States would send a US Marine Expeditionary Force to major Canadian cities to support in these efforts, far and beyond their current commitment, all extra to existing NORTHCOM arrangements.

Bush's outline suggested that he desired to protect Canadian sovereignty during this short period of tumult and unrest, contra the American directive outlined in War Plan Red (an archaic American contingency plan for Canada de-classified in the seventies), which states: the US would initiate the war, and even if Canada declared neutrality, the US would still invade and conquer it, planning to hold in perpetuity all and any territory gained and abolish the dominion government. The proposed coalition of American and Canadian Forces (with particular provisos stressing the congruity of the joint task force, its mutual interests, and its objectives) would quash terrorism. On the condition that by mid-March the primary terrorist factions were gelded, the Americans would leave after an additional six months of mandatory support (channeled through the Coalition), leaving Canada to mend and defend, rather embarrassed and emasculated.

According to the US Under Secretary of Defence for Policy Douglas Feith, the ultimatum was initially going to permit high ranking members of the Sprites (Kalnychuk included) to live in exile. They worked on an "action plan" for the ultimatum strategy, and drew up a list of candidate countries for asylum and a draft UN resolution.[59] The Bush Administration decided, however, that they would not negotiate with terrorists, and that Kalnychuk must be captured or eliminated.

Wary of the increasing "coast guard" on the west and east coasts, and his severed rail and national highway, Chretien hesitantly conceded to the action plan after weeks of discussions, knowing full-well that the CF would refuse to kill the majority of Canadian citizens who had been designated as terrorists on account of the notoriously dodgy American "intelligence." This patriotism bred resistance.

Chretien, although vilified by many Canadians today, had done his successor a great service: he had bought the Canadian Armed Forces, resistance fighters, and the HDF1 over two weeks to organize, arm, strategize, and position, by slowly acquiescing in a not-quite-so negotiable agreement with Bush.

Exactly two hours after Bush's address on March 1, the Canadian government appealed to the UN, requesting additional peacekeeping forces. The Canadian Forces were "ready and primed to address" what Canadian Brigadier General Fraser called "any unnecessary escalation or aggression." The UN force was appealed to merely to "cool everyone off" and to mediate hostilities.

This lightly-armed UN force was owed Canada or to any other "state that fe[lt] threatened by an armed attack by another state."[60] Since the request was unilateral, the force would have to remain inside Canada—on the Canadian side of the border. This request complicated the ease of passage for the American surge. Although not a permanent fix, it ensured that a full-scale war would not break out—not immediately anyway. "While we have no doubt that our allies have our best interests at heart," claimed Chretien:

> It is important to maintain certain divisions, especially those that pertain to security and sovereignty. For this, we appeal to a neutral third party, afforded to both our nations by the UN. North of this complementary buffer force, the Canadian Military, with the invited help of an American counter-terror taskforce, will eliminate the terrorist threat.

---

[59] Feith 304.
[60] Naidu, Mumulla Venkatrao. *Perspectives on Human Security: National Sovereignty and Humanitarian Intervention* (Brandon, Mb: Canadian Peace Research and Education Association, 2001) 131.

It was clear, however, that despite the buffer provided by the committed UN countries—composed by a variety of nations east of Greenwich—the United States would still be waiting for Canada in the playground after school, especially with the CF flexing and building some self-esteem.

Canadian General Ray Henault (Air Command) termed the tension a "medium intensity type 'A' conflict." Accordingly, the new forces were trained and briefed on operations that would:

> Establish, regain or maintain control of land areas or populations threatened by guerilla action, insurgency, rebellion, dissidence, communal violence, civic disturbance or other tactics aimed at internal seizure of power or changes to the established order by illegal, forceful means.[61]

Due to the nature of the classification, training was adjusted to hone in on dealing with guerilla fighters in unconventional and asymmetrical warfare. With the HDF1 looking more battle-worthy and having enough time to dig in, the CF could fill the bag with a little more wind before droning into any potential future firefight.

THE MAJORITY OF THE NEWS correspondents I spoke to in late winter 2003, were convinced that Canada was ready to fold and take a big spanking from an American expeditionary force. If war was on the horizon—I don't think Chretien had imagined it worsening to such a level—Canada couldn't afford a violent *tête-à-tête* with the United States. The CF had to chaperone the American Forces, and hope that they eliminated the Sprites before this friendly intervention devolved into a full-on occupation.

MAJOR GENERAL Chris Vokes, a Canadian soldier, once argued that:

> The enemy must be beaten only to the point where he has no more desire and capability to fight. But a foreign nation must believe that attacking Canada would be like sticking its finger into a buzz saw.

Although the chain had aged a great deal and suffered a lot of wear and tear since Vokes' day, the saw could still bite.

---

[61] Issued on the Authority of the Chief of the Defence Staff "Canada Training for War" (*WikiLeaks*. November, 1992 Web) 19.

In addition to innovative training, cutting-edge weaponry, and world-class personal equipment, the Canadian Forces were experienced. CF18s flew over 678 combat sorties of nearly 2,600 hours in Kosovo, and dropped 532 bombs. This particular example is interesting because it reveals recent aptitude but also is undercut by a vignette about Canadian dependency. While the CF18s ran these sorties successfully, the Canadian Air Force (CAF) had to borrow one-hundred general purpose bombs and two-hundred laser-guided bombs from the USAF. The CAF, like the CF in general, was placed in the position of a superb NASCAR driver behind the wheel of a Pinto, which would need to be refuelled at an American pump with Canadian gas.

The domestic requirement for the American intervention to appear just and justified was an interesting equalizer. Despite their staggering numbers and potential force, "[the US'] vast armada of missiles and planes [was] largely useless" on account of the asymmetrical nature of the Canadian conflict, and the US Military's reluctance to incur too many civilian casualties.[62] Some strategists argued that the difficulties faced by the US in Canada were not unlike those met in Vietnam:

> But as Vietnam proved, when the US Military's goals and technology met unanticipated challenges, the US escalated step-by-step and its initial war strategy and political objectives became counter-productive.

Like the Vietnamese, there were extra-national supporters secretly bankrolling and arming Canadian resistance groups, and later, the Yukon Sprites. The US did not technically engage with Russian, Chinese or French fighters, yet it fought their proxies—the barbarian horde—on Canadian soil. With Canadian and US interests and military distinctions so muddled, the US was again faced with a war with, "no front lines," where the "enemy [wa]s both everywhere and nowhere."[63]

Adam Lowther suggested in his book, *Americans and Asymmetric Conflict,* that these muddled distinctions resulted in less precise American engagements: "It is unlikely that there will be a clear

---

[62] Kolko, Gabriel. *The Age of War: the United States Confronts the World* (Boulder, CO: Lynne Rienner, 2006) 91.
[63] Sully, Francois. Age of the Guerrilla: The New Warfare (New York: Parent's Magazine Press,1968) 182.

distinction between the good and bad guys as America's adversaries are likely to change."[64] Although Bush's rhetoric set up a number of straight-forward binaries, such distinctions were scrambled on the field, where: the Canadian Military was working with American Forces to subdue the Sprite threat, but also periodically supporting the resistance in places where American operations were clearly too heavy-handed or misguided by bad-intelligence; and resistance groups supported the Sprites from time to time and vice versa.

THE KEY OBJECTIVE for the CFs in 2002, it seemed, was to put down the Sprites and protect Canadians, whatever the cost (i.e. put up a fight where it was required), until political unity occurred, especially since Bush had initially declared the Canadian Coalition Government a "regime that continually fail[ed] to represent the Canadian people" and a "rogue government." International and civil war broke out in flourishes, prompted by humanitarian rescue or revenge.

If the United States thought it was worthwhile in terms of reparation and subduing dissenters they would roll over on Canada as Anne Coulter wanted from the start. The fact was that the cost and perpetuity of such a war would bankrupt the United States and run holes into its social stability.

Cine-romantics among the chief mainstream-journalists felt compelled to suggest that Canada's peril was analogous to the Liechtenstein-like country's goofy standoff with the US in *The Mouse that Roared*. Despite the insensitivity of the parallel, it seemed that like the dwarf nation in the Peter Sellers' film, Canada showed the first signs of legitimate hostility (i.e. if you discount the whole American invasion). The strategy, however, was disparate from that employed by the country in the film. There was, after all, no world-ending bargaining chip with which Canada could gamble. The situation, instead, was more akin to the method employed by Tay John (Howard O'Hagan's prominent Shuswap-turned-legendary-hero) in his encounter with a gargantuan grizzly bear in the Canadian Rocky Mountains.

While covering the western offensive, I embedded with a Sprite faction, and dwelt among them in their northwestern, subterranean

---

[64] Lowther, Adam. *Americans and Asymmetric Conflict* (London: Praeger Security International, 2007) 78.

base. There, I was subject to many folksy-tales from "unlawful combatants" piecing together their broken lives and stunted culture between patrols. I wouldn't be surprised if the boys were reading Canadian literature out of some new sense of nationalistic pride, because on numerous occasions I heard the Sprites specifically associate the story from O'Hagan's *Tay John* with the calculated machismo inherent in the (let's call it the) "Chretien Manoeuvre." Thus, I raise this anecdote from *Tay John* because it contains imagery *embraced by* (as opposed to haplessly *applied to*) North America's latest subaltern group, and hell: I think it's a damn good one worth repeating.

Tay John, a mixed European-Shuswap Indian, lived in the Rocky Mountain range, drifting from story to story in western Alberta and eastern British Columbia. He was a mountain guide in the Rockies as well a hunter and a serious mountaineer.

Since the Canadian Pacific Railway had not yet harnessed the mountains, the Rockies remained formidable: an awe-inspiring fortress that one did not traverse, so much as risked all in order to pass. Without the conveniences or securities present to most people of his time, Tay John faced a perilous, unsympathetic wilderness alone.

His hard life produced in him an unparalleled calm (often perceived as stoicism). This internal principle was manifest in the serenity of his leathery façade, later marred by three vertical trenches. Although he was obstinate, he was also patient, unrivalled as a survivalist, and a genuine badass.

For a while he was content with merely surviving as a shadow in valleys not yet bookmarked by the human imagination or heavily trodden with repetitious patterns in the snow, though one spring, greatness found him. While hunting for pelts on one of his less frequented mountain trails, Tay John found a baby bear.

Before he could drape the hide over his shoulder with the other acquisitions from the hunt, he first had to gut the corpse. Diverting from his carefully plotted path, he went to a mountain stream to go about his cleaning. He leant his rifle and gear against a young pine tree overlooking the surging white water, which pounded granite boulders and an assortment of small, rust-coloured stones. He also left his furs and jacket so that they would not be soiled at the water's edge. Tay John decided to keep his trousers, his headband, and his knife, on his person.

He went to the shore and noticed footprints in the mud. They were erratic and deep, seemingly deeper due to the puddles collected there. He knew they belonged to a large creature, most likely a bear. He was unsure because the prints had been eroded by runoff.

The cleaning must be expeditious, Tay John determined. After cutting the sinews and flesh from the hide with his hunting knife, he held the skin to the water's surface to wash off the residual markers of flesh, and let his hands grow numb in the rippling cold. The sun, reflected on the perpetual power running through his red fingers, illuminated the eagerness, satisfaction, and pride on his weathered face. Content with the foot-rug-to-be, he started back for his gear. He would treat and cure the skin later; somewhere safe, he decided.

He trudged toward the tree line, but was taken aback by an off-beat in the natural rhythm that was his living soundtrack. He paused and listened at full attention. Some powerful force was dashing through the bush, snapping branches as it plummeted down, towards the water. The crack of whips sounded in unison with the tremors that shook dirt from exposed root. Tay John, wise to the source of the commotion and its prerogative, threw the pelt—still dripping red—to the tree line.

An enormous grizzly emerged from the forest, vehemence written into every step and motion. Tay John drew his knife. The she-bear was rifling towards him at a suicide pace, the fearsome growl emanating from its dark centre.

Tay John knew he had to buy himself time to think. There is no projectile at the water's edge with any stopping-power that I can launch in time, he thought. And no branch close enough to fashion into a weapon! No rock, jagged or heavy enough. Not violence, not yet, Tay John determined.

He took a moment to think, bowed, and then exploded into a full-spasm, screaming so that his voice clamoured up to the heavens, his presence not far behind. Thundering above both opponents, the sound intensified in a chorus of echoes. The bear, affronted with the overpowering though illusory threat engrained in Tay John's throaty dissonance, stopped in its tracks. Its quick deceleration launched a small shower of rocks into the air. Behind the shower of pebbles, it too broke down into an aggressive posturing, and threw its head sideways into another awesome growl.

The she-bear was simultaneously beautiful and terrifying. The dark, matted fur around its eyes concealed the rage that meanwhile channeled through its pulsating shoulders. Its body began as chestnut brown at the rear, which blended into the crème fur padding it neck. Aflame in the sunlight, the bear—glorious and in its prime—stared hungrily at the feast-for-vengeance limp in the fore.

Tay John, afforded a moment's peace to calculate the particular equation for his success, threw his headband forward so that it glided over the bear. The bear pitched itself onto its hind legs, and swatted at the headband. With its powerful arms overextended at the benign article, the bear's chest was exposed to the sun. Tay John barreled toward the bear, leading with his gleaming blade. He plunged the blade into the bear's chest, just missing the heart, and embraced the bear as tightly as he could.

The cold metal awakened the most primal of all impulses in the bear. Ferociously, it swiped its mighty paws at Tay John and the sky, now seemingly malevolent in this time of crisis. Its left paw came down across Tay John's face, raising flesh and scratching bone. Tay John, focused on his objective, overcame the pain and ignored his instinctive flee-response. As shock set in, he received one more adrenalin kick. Tay John pulled the knife out of the bear's throbbing chest and plunged it on-target. At one with the weapon, he searched for the animal's heart. The bear clobbered Tay John's bare-back. With a click, Tay John lost his sight, and sank into the warm fur.

Tay John regained consciousness beneath six-hundred pounds of decommissioned, wet fur. His arm was dislocated, and his face brutally disfigured, but he had survived. The last breaths from the bear had long been spent into the shallow run-off diverted from the stream into a green pool rimmed with crimson. Tay John, a broken man, dragged himself to the water's edge. There he washed his face, and cleaned another skin.

Besides the obvious bravado, the Sprites who recited this story had paid special attention to the rudimentary yet effective tactics involved in Tay John's rather costly victory. The initial time-out afforded by the Chretien Manoeuvre was not wasted on a uncritical reaction, but a plan. The plan involved a distraction, which left the enemy exposed and divided its focus. Although this entailed a sacrifice (Sun Tzu suggested the plum tree for the peach tree), the substitution gave greater gravity and position to the preserved.

The next step was getting too close for a proper head to head. Ill-equipped to deal with an animal at least three times heavier and more powerful than himself, Tay John ventured into the enemy's comfort zone. Delivering a crushing blow to momentum and proving capable of a sustained asymmetrical conflict was essential to the hunter's cause. The grizzly was a powerful animal, but as with most powerful creatures, its large body was relatively cumbersome, and its power was in short supply. Without energy, the beast spent its internal drive and its means of violent application before delivering an effective, finishing blow.

The final step promises a resolution or negotiation. Tay John succeeded with a very permanent resolution—he resolved to cut the beast's heart out. Canadian resisters would have the opportunity for only one stab, and then would have to settle for a more political, consensual resolution after an unsightly disfigurement.

The Sprites take-away: use your time and distractions wisely, get too close to be a traditional target, and kill momentum. If the over-bearing hostile presence (i.e. Occupiers) can only sustain a quick battle, plan for a long scrum.

I thought the heart imagery might correlate to a Sprites operation Stateside, but they suggested southern-retalliations were not a component of their mission, that is, so far as Kalnychuk's instructions were concerned.

Unlike the mytho-poetic imagery that *Tay John* provides, there was nothing romantic about each of these steps as they were carried to fruition in the Can-American crisis or in Sprite-guerilla warfare. There was nothing redemptive about the sacrifice of troops to slow the American war machine, just as there was nothing redemptive about the Sprites' perpetual war legacy.

During the first stage of the Chretien Manoeuvre, the Canadian Military retooled so that they'd be technologically competitive. The HDF1, led by experienced soldiers, transformed the landscape with garrisons, road blocks, anti-aircraft weaponry, and bunkers. The thousands of new recruits were not concentrated in any one area, but instead armed and enabled to coordinate defensive and aggressive measures with the Reserves and Regulars across the country.

The sporadic dispersion of a good amount of these new troops (fresh out of basic) indicated an inclination to asymmetrical warfare from the get-go. Modern communications technology enabled, to a point, coordinated action across a country 9,984,670 squared kilometres. American strategists were wary of an engagement with a diffused and embedded fighting force, noting the inevitable exhaustion of US supplies, troops, and patience.

Lessons from the past were not very encouraging. Just thirteen years prior to the outbreak of this conflict, the Russians had been pushed out of a country fifteen times smaller than Canada by a poorly trained, poorly equipped group of fighters (sponsored by the US). Although thirteen years was long enough for the United States to develop some advanced toys for dispatching such a group, the fact was that Canadian militants were fighting on home turf with similar geographic advantages over their invaders with weaponry on par with the Americans'. Moreover, the sort of technology developed for US operations was best suited to a head-to-head, which they were robbed of in an engagement with guerilla warriors hugging civilian areas.

The Americans "focused first on providing security to the host population and second on isolating the enemy from the population."[65] American troops hugged the host population and worked towards the ideal: winning the confidence of the people while providing protection for the integrated Canadian Forces and constabulary officials. Unfortunately, their hugs were not widely appreciated. In close proximity with mixed crowds, the US Forces placed themselves at extreme risk of assassinations, kidnappings, and worse.

AFTER A STRING of large-scale engagements alongside and, at times, with the Americans in 2003, the Canadian Military— entrenched throughout the countryside—was coaxed by their

---

[65] HQ US Special Operations Command 23.

Coalition Government into a cease-fire with US Forces, recognizing the need for all members involved to save face.

During this pause in the fighting, the Canadian Prime Minister hoped to establish the Canadian government in the media as a single, legitimate entity, thus reassuring the world that Canada remained a sovereign nation. The Prime Minister and members of the Coalition Party met with Bush and members of his administration at the Royal Over-Seas Club in London, England, and negotiated reparations, prisoner exchange, oil, energy, lumber, and possible follow-up to address war crimes. Meanwhile, the Yukon Sprites and factions affiliated with the Canadian Sovereignty Movement were inundated with foreign and domestic input, support, and volunteers. The quick war had left victims, many with nothing to lose.

♠

THE GREEN LEGEND

> I tried to break the spell—the heavy, mute spell of the wilderness—that seemed to draw him to its pitiless breast by the awakening of forgotten and brutal instincts, by the memory of gratified and monstrous passions. This alone, I was convinced, had driven him out to the edge of the forest, to the bush, towards the gleam of fires, the throb of drums, the drone of weird incantations; this alone had beguiled his unlawful soul beyond the bounds of permitted aspirations.[66]
>
> — Joseph Conrad, *The Heart of Darkness*

Calgary, Alberta
November 25, 2005

THE SOUND of Colonel McAdam's Manifest Destiny grew fainter as our convoy pressed east, out of the shadow of the continent's backbone. Wind beat on the canvas, replacing the murmur of war with a synthetic applause. The cognizant wounded and I stared out through the truck's plastic transparency at the pockmarked foothills, enshrouded with bloody scab-like mounds and disabled vehicles, turned to noodles by the US advance. My mind buzzed with should-haves and could-haves, and I agonized over my failure to document the war as it was, not as the elite willed it to be recorded. All that anxiety was exhausting.

Amidst the mortal cries of those with whom I shared the small compartment and my internal cacophony of guilty considerations, I somehow managed to fall asleep. Had I become immune to reality and the pain of others—a Greg Marinovich? Every time I had reached this threshold in the past, I would say to myself: "This is the last time, David. No more." The lie sat like bile in my mouth. "No more."

I spent the morning in a cafeteria off Glenmore Landing in Calgary next door to a Laura Secord ice cream shop, taking drags off cigarettes driven-in from the Indian reserve. American smokes had been boycotted, so I had to settle with tongue-rot to

---

[66] Conrad, Joseph. *Heart of Darkness.* (New York: Dover, 1990).

accompany my gut-rot—some brown, hot liquid, reminiscent of coffee.

Jacquelyn had booked me a room at a nearby motel, after seeing my stream of texts and emails indicating that Vigeland was a no-show, Banff was a no-go, and that my forced-return to Calgary was imminent. *She's always been a life-saver.* "David," she said, "Get some sleep. When I get to Philadelphia, we'll figure out a new course for you to take."

Sleep felt like too much of a commitment—the kind of inaction that only amounts to surrender. I couldn't retire to my room, not yet anyway. Besides, my nap on the drive to Calgary could sustain me for days. Ever since the Gulf War, I'd been convinced that I got my best work done when on the down-and-out.

"Oh, and David, Audrey left me a message for you." *What does she want?* "She says she can no longer take care of Chomsky."

"What? So what does she plan to do with him?" I could hear my shouting echo back to me over the phone.

As sad as it sounds, that dog had been a consistent marker of my sanity through a failed marriage and multiple depressions. Together, Chomsky and I had watched Bush Sr. condemn Saddam's aggression on Kuwait, all the Bond-films, and several women walk out of our lives. That little patch of fur licked me out of one-too-many whisky comas. Once he got past his vindictive "I shit wherever I want" phase, we got along famously.

"Sh'ays, 'pick him up in ten days or I'll take him to the pound.' Her words, not mine."

"Okay Jacquelyn, well, I can't exactly fly back at the moment... Fuck! That no good bitch... Where are you right now?"

Jacquelyn was stern: "Don't you yell at me like I'm your goddamn gofer. This is all your fault to begin with."

"Sorry," I whispered.

"I am working on the pipeline-story."

"Oil, Direct to China?"

"Yup. David, listen. About Chomsky—"

"I'll figure something out."

"Well, I have a friend in Seattle. She's a teary-eyed empty-nester. I'm sure she'll snatch up any opportunity to have something give her the time of day. I'll call when I know."

"Thank you Jake. You don't know how much...thank you."

"David, get some sleep."

TABLING MY EXHAUSTION and frustration, I decided to waste the daylight reading the despair written onto the faces of the Canadians in my company. Word of brutality in Canmore unsettled those around me, glued to the wall-mounted television:

> Canadian Forces have managed to eliminate the Sprite threat in Yoho National Park, but have been unable to rendezvous with American Forces outside of Banff, on account of Sprite anti-tank and anti-air teams. The American bombing campaign has been less than successful, leaving Sprite encampments and defences unscathed...US troops now face some of the heaviest firefights in their western campaign...Yes, that's right Susan...The liberation of Canmore has been difficult, compounded by the efforts of renegade ex-Canadian Forces, especially for many of the refugees camped behind the American lines waiting to return to their daily routines. Much of the fighting we've seen here today will leave many homeless, and it comes at a particularly inopportune time: the temperature continues to drop and heavy snowing continues.

I wanted to thank the war-journalist for the weather report.

> Even in this most recent engagement, revenge is cited as motivation by many. The American troops, seen behind me, have not forgotten the evil that killed more than a thousand civilians in November...

IT'S INTERESTING HOW the Bush Administration and the media were content to manipulate the memory of the victims of terrorism in order to plug farther into Canadian territory. Eliot Weinberger describes this trend in *What Happened Here* (2005):

> No longer murder victims, [those killed directly and indirectly by the November Bombing's] will now be portrayed, by both sides, as having died for a cause. By avenging their deaths with more deaths, Bush and Cheney and Rumsfeld and Rice and Powell are murdering their identities and, above all, the innocence of our dead as they murder abroad.[67]

The revenge factor and the US Military's utilization of misplaced anger were especially disheartening when US Forces toppled Sprite-free towns. There's no question of whether this mentality was systemic. Major General Charles Swannack promised his troops

---

[67] Weinberger, Eliot. *What Happened Here: Bush Chronicles* (New York, NY: New Directions, 2005) 49.

they'd use "a sledgehammer to smash a walnut."[68] Worst of all, the majority of the civilians trampled and tormented by the invaders had initially supported Canadian and American counter-terror efforts and condemned the Sprites. It was clear to me that the American sledgehammer was ineffective in the short-run and likely destructive in the long-run, given the US track record and patterned behavior, where "military reprisals for terrorist attacks (Libya, 1986; the Sudan and Afghanistan, 1998) killed civilians, strengthened anti-American sentiments, evidently did nothing to stop terrorism, and probably added new sympathizers to their ranks."[69]

BEHIND ME, a woman, hunched over a disarray of sickly-looking eggs and bacon, was sobbing heavily. There was a crescendo in her blubbery gasps, and the wet bellows eventually evolved into angry, semi-articulate outbursts: "That sunuvabitch Bush'll sacrifice paradise just to put an honest Canadian in'a ground. My Mike's out there!"

My phone rattled on the table: "Dave," said Jacquelyn, sounding slightly distressed on the other end, "just so we're clear, I didn't book that hotel room so you can go nomad on my dime." I played ignorant, himmed and hawed. "Are you crying?"

"No, no, no worries. That's someone else." I could feel the mewler staring daggers into my back.

"Sure... Check in. Relax. Take a bath. You probably smell like shit. Something will turn up eventually. Kalnychuk is not going anywhere."

I told her not to use his name on the phone, and then asked her if she was able to get me the Klein interview.

"Again, and I'm fucking tired of saying this: I'm not your agent. Call O'Malley. Doubt he'll be able to get you the interview, though. Haven't you been watching the news? The Alberta Premier has been taken into American custody. They're calling him a 'rogue politician'."

"Klein?"

"It's bullshit, no? You give any Canadian a few beers, and they're bound to say something scathing about the occupation. He's off

---

[68] Weinberger 149.
[69] Weinberger 46.

limits to the press. Apparently, he had Reaper affiliations. Provincial and Federal g-men couldn't afford Powell reconsidering them for a collective spot on the FTO list. Instead, they threw Klein under the bus."

Jacquelyn was grasping at straws and fighting to keep my sanity with busy-work. "There are some Sprites being held at Rocky View Hospital, under the strict supervision—"

I cut her off. The article on their capture was coffee-ringed before me. Their injuries were so extensive that they were incapable of speech (i.e. nearly de-cerebrated), let alone the cognitive capacity to tell me what I needed to know.

"Dave, I'm trying to help. Don't be so fucking pernickety. "

"Sorry."

"There is one fellow being held at Spy Hill whose story might pique your interest."

"Spy Hill?" I inquired.

"It's a correctional facility, a prison, in Calgary. It's been commandeered by one of Cucolo's guys. The 10th Mountain Division is killing time *rebuilding* Calgarian institutions until they get the go-ahead on Banff. Anyway, they have Colonel Schmidt. The wake around this guy ripples east to west, and all the peaks suggest a Sprite involvement." I jotted down the details on Spy Hill and Schmidt, thanked Jake, and drained my imitation-coffee.

The last time I had asked for consent, I lost a two-hundred-dollar recorder. I had no intention of handing over my third recorder in six months. With the Dictaphone saving voices and ambience to be deciphered and manipulated later, everything was on the record. Fuck ethical reporting, I thought. No one else was playing by the rules.

I registered as a member of the press at the front-counter, and was offered to speak to a number of prisoners from the Governor General's Horse Guards. I felt like I had walked into a bordello from a sleazy Western film. Pick the prettiest from the line-up, and have your fifteen minutes.

"No that's okay. Kevin Schmidt. I would like to speak with Kevin Schmidt." A TV crew bustled past me, led by a boom and an oversized camera. Someone had caught their eye.

"Sorry sir, we don't do requests," stated the obstinate young officer. He towered over me with a bright florescent halo. His suspicious gaze held me in its umbra. I felt simultaneously guilty and rebellious, perhaps the latter sense accounting for the former. "If you want to wait, you can talk to a few of the Blackfoot militants we captured in the Cypress Hills." I pretended to check my pulse, and I squeezed my tongue.

"Everything alright, sir?"

"I thought so, but now I'm not so sure."

"What's the matter?"

"Well, for one reason or another it doesn't seem I can *fucking get through to you*. I would like to interview Kevin Schmidt."

"You've made that evident to me sir. We do not do requests. Are you a friend or a relative?"

"Would it make a difference if I was either?"

"No," he laughed. "We don't do requests." His commanding officer entered the room, separated from the front lobby by reinforced glass and bars. The higher authority approached me in fragments.

"Mr. Danson. I overheard you request to speak to one prisoner in particular…"

"Yes, that's right." I smiled wickedly at the young soldier and answered the CO without trading glances, "Mr. Schmidt."

"I see." He cocked his head and scanned his underling's frustrated expression. They looked at each other knowingly. "Any particular reason for the specificity of your selection?"

"He was the most charming in the catalogue."

The officer smiled. I could tell he was dying to kill me. He fed his tie back through the gold clip toothed into his shirt, threw the rest of his attention at me, and continued: "Wait one moment please." He reviewed my press pass and papers. "I will have Sergeant Callaghan brief you. Just so you know in advance, you may not bring anything into the room with you. You will have just a few minutes to ask questions, and then you will leave." He opened the log book and dragged his fingers along the rows until he found my name. "I see you've called ahead. I'll need an additional piece of identification. A driver's license, a passport or a travel visa should suffice." I handed him my wallet. "Fantastic, I'll have this processed while you speak to Mr. Schmidt." The CO ordered Callaghan out with a whisper. "And Mr. Danson, if you intentionally disobey any of the rules, you will be held accountable." The recorder had begun to burn a hole in my pocket. "This is neither the time nor place to press your luck."

I WAS UNABLE to confirm the veracity of one story I was fed en route to Spy Hill, but it nevertheless intrigued me. Apparently the CIA had an interrogator dress up in a bunny costume and beat the shit out of suspected terrorist-facilitators at Spy Hill in order to obtain signed confessions. Those obviously not guilty of the charges, demonstrated by one too many rounds with Bugs, were released.

The CIA and the complicit guards were unimpeachable due to the ridiculousness of their technique. If anyone was to approach another government agency or NGO complaining of mistreatment at the hands of American operatives, they would inevitably lose the confidence of their confider as soon as they were to mention "the big pink bunny." I wouldn't be surprised if the anthropomorphized rabbit was secreted behind one of the many doors I passed on the way to meet Schmidt.

CALLAGHAN BROUGHT me down a cinder-block corridor, and ushered me into a dimly-lit foyer linked to three doorways. He unlocked the middle door with the swipe of a key-card and cranked it open. "The room is down the hall on your right. Number one-hundred-and-four. I will bring the prisoner into the room once you have taken a seat. You will take note that neither Private Wright nor I have brought any harm to the prisoner."

"And Private Wright is?" I inquired.

"One of the men who's helped oversee Schmidt's stay with us. Regarding the prisoner and his wellbeing—"

"Oh, he's well, is he?"

Disregarding my comment, Callaghan continued, "His earlobe and his upper cheek were grazed by shrapnel long before he encountered us, and his limp is due to his violent resistance at the time of capture. You will note that the prisoner has received medical attention and has been fed regularly since his arrest. You, under the supervision of Private Wright, will be able to ask the prisoner questions. You may not touch the prisoner. You will not hand anything to the prisoner. So far as engagements go, this one will remain strictly puritanical—purely immaterial. Do you agree to the terms of the interview?"

"Yes. One question, though. Since he's in Calgary and not Guantanamo, I'm assuming you haven't been able to finger him as a terrorist."

"That's less of a question and more of an assumption, Mr. Danson, wouldn't you say?"

"I'm looking for a simple 'yes' or 'no'."

"I'm afraid such information is above my pay grade, and I am not in the business of fingering anyone." He smirked.

"The prisoner is secured, Sir," chirped the Private, leaning out of the doorway at the end of the hall.

"Okay Mr. Danson. Change of plans. He is already waiting for you. You will follow me into the room. The prisoner is handcuffed to the table. You will not touch the handcuffs. You may rest your hands on the table, but refrain from crossing the line."

"What line?"

"You'll see it. It's designated with duct tape. Follow me." Wright entered the room ahead of me. Callaghan chimed in, out of sight, "You may now interview the prisoner. You have ten minutes."

The room was small and furnished with a table—really just a glorified gurney—with two metal chairs, and a wall-mounted intercom. It was musty and cool. Having no visible ventilation, I imagine the room was only fed fresh air when someone entered or left. The ten-minute limit on my conversation with the Colonel was likely for our benefit—so we wouldn't suffocate.

As Wright pulled the door closed, I heard another slam shut. The wall fitted with a ceiling-to-waist-level-mirror shuddered as if possessed. I winked at the mirror, and then settled into my seat.

"Hello Colonel. I've heard a lot about you." I adjusted my collar, and surveyed the mug on the body before me.

He stabbed me with his lobotomy eyes. "Who're you?"

"David Danson. From *The Network*."

"Hmmm." If I was a doctor, a nervous nurse would have informed me, "You're losing him, doctor." *I pulled out the paddles.*

"Kevin Schmidt? You were stationed in Regina, yes?" I fanned my fingers out on the table, and ran them in circuits as if I had projected his file before me, thumbing through his history and future.

"I was an engineer." *Go time.* I had committed my questions to memory. I had to make every syllable count.

"Under the command of Mikhail Kossorov, you managed to find your way to the Sprite compound. How? Why?"

"If my marks were high enough, I was going to do an M.B.A. Sell instead of create. It'd probably have been wasted on me, though. I really just wanted to use my hands." He ran his fingers over his bruised and misshapen knuckles. "To build something. Now all I use them for is staying alive." His pupils bled black onto the irises that roped them back. Those big dark saucers vacuumed my inquisitive stare.

"Colonel Schmidt, why did you defect from the Canadian Forces?" He rolled his eyes, and then looked out, through the small Plexiglas window, past the glare, into the grayish blur beyond. "Did you meet the manufacturers of Green Legend? Did you meet Kalnychuk?"

"Listen, asshole: what d'you think this is?" *Flat-lining.* "Some big fucking mystery?"

"Well, Colonel—" I stammered.

"Listen up! If I so much as saw the Legend, you think I'd be talking to you right now?"

"But you must have—"

"See this fucker over here?" he pointed to Wright, who feigned deafness in spite of the remark. "If that chump or any of his friends had any inclination or sense that I knew something, there'd be no way in hell that I'd be allowed to talk to you. They'd find my secrets. You know? The ones you think you're looking for." He jerked forward and poised as if to whisper, but instead, raised his voice: "All they'd have to do is what they've always done on the side: cut holes in my teeth; drown me slowly; open me up. After a few rounds of that *Marathon Man* shit, I'd blab. Everyone does, eventually. And once you've blabbed, you're no good to anybody. No good to your friends, to your enemies or to your family." The black had completely subsumed the brown coronas bordering his eyes. Although rendered innocuous by chains, zip-ties, and exhaustion, he still seemed physically threatening.

"So what took their sights off of you?"

"What?"

"Why are you suddenly off the US Army's radar?"

"I'm under surveillance twenty-four-seven," he sneered at me, and flipped off the ghost lurking in or behind the mirror.

"But you've said so yourself: if you knew anything, you wouldn't be permitted to talk to me. You'd be wet and wincing with every cool breath, nursing a freshly stitched wound. How do they know that you know nothing?"

"I'll tell you what I told them: I've neither seen nor met Bruce Kalynchuk."

"Then who was the Sprite that initiated you?"

"Initiate? It's not the boy scouts or the Skulls. I was clearing out bungalows in Crowsnest Pass with my group." *We have a pulse.*

"Crowsnest is near Regina?"

"No. I was attached to a special team ordered to clean up hamlets on the BC/Alberta border. We had met heavy resistance. A bunch of us ended up digging-in and fighting a merciless battle with some rebels on their home turf. There was a great deal of collateral damage. It got to the point where we were doing more harm than good. Anyways, when things calmed down, I did a walk-through. Turned over some bodies to confirm sniper kills, and it was the same story again and again. We were killing kids. Worst of all, we were killing *our* kids. Rebels, Sprites, pissed-off landowners: all of them Canadian. I couldn't do it anymore."

"So you turned?"

"Not right away. But I'm a firm believer that if someone's going to wear the hometown's jersey, he ought to at least shoot in the right direction."

"If you haven't encountered any Sprites with higher tiers within the organization, then how did you rise to the rank of Colonel?"

"I met like-minded folk once I went underground. After successfully leading them through some rough times, I earned their respect. By earning their respect and keeping it, I took the title." Schmidt crooked a half-smile and leaned back, a little more at ease. "It's an appeal to an authority I don't actually command until the shit hits the fan. But when it does, and it always does, everyone always seeks out the leader. A title's only as good as the truth it signifies and the confidence it inspires."

"And Kossorov?"

"Kossorov's a phantom, an invention." He grinned and crows-feet bracketed his eyes. "He was a character created for the sole-purpose of sending the enemy off chasing specters. It's a cheap way to tie up their resources."

"What, besides the true nature of Kossorov, did the Americans ask you about in your interrogation?"

"One of them asked me which bases I visited. Makes me think Kalnychuk's all over the place." The guard shot a discerning look my way. "Hidden somewhere in the mountains or tucked away in an arctic sub. Off of their maps completely. Fuck, he could be right here in Cowtown or leaving Vancouver in a trawler. They expect me to have all the details because I'm a Colonel. In Kalnychuk's army, rank's as good as a dollar-store sheriff badge. They want— they need—a link between Kalnychuk and the Canadian Forces to pull out the heavies." Callaghan barged into the room.

"Mr. Danson, this interview is over. Please stand back against that wall until we've moved the prisoner." An additional guard stumbled in to join Wright and Callaghan in subduing Schmidt.

Schmidt, twisting between the sentinels, concluded: "They think we're a bunch of dysfunctional scoundrels. There're still tens of thousands of us hidden with Uncle Sam in our sights, and we're anything but inept. We're still in this."

"This interview is over," bellowed Callaghan, red-cheeked. *Call it, nurse.* The door squeaked behind Schmidt and his captors. The consequent rush of air waved through all of my projected notes. Sitting in that pale cell alone, I knew, just as well as the voyeurs lurking on the other side of the one-way mirror, that I was nowhere closer to the Legend. I had wasted the opportunity.

-EMBARGOED REPORT-

I WAS ESCORTED off the grounds by a polite young officer who mapped out a few of Calgary's less rowdy bars in my journal. After god-knows-how-long standing there, watching her fill the page, smiling dumbly at the first soft face I'd encountered in days, I thanked her, and set out to walk off my frustration, sexual and otherwise.

The prison gates closed behind me, and I tapped myself a cigarette. While fiddling around in my pockets in search of a lighter, I registered the scornful gaze of a dozen people. Given what I'd heard about the hate-crime statistics (i.e. against people suspected of facilitating American objectives in western Canada), I wasn't quite sure whether to feel fear or discomfort. More than anything, I felt defensive. "No!" I wanted to yell. "I'm not here to bury you, but to praise you!"

On the way to Spy Hill, I shared a cab with a correspondent from *The Herald*, who had mentioned rampant vigilantism turning out more corpses in Calgary than piled by the US Army outside

Airdrie after the airstrike mishap. He insinuated that anyone seen leaving an occupied penitentiary out of uniform would raise the suspicion and attention of passersby and locals, especially with the recent talk of "fur traitors" betraying the trust of resistance groups. This was a country increasingly undecided about enabling Americans in Canadian cities, he explained.

I had expected to raise a few eyebrows leaving Spy Hill without a camera, an arm band or handcuffs, but not to this extent. I bowed my head to light a smoke and, in so doing, subtly surveyed the scene, noticing one onlooker whose constant stare set him apart from the rest. Clutching a newspaper in one hand, and making a fist with another, he plodded along, parallel to me. Squinting unabashedly over, eyes garroted by fat, carmine cheeks and a Neanderthal brow, he caught me returning his glance. The connection unnerved me. I jolted into a draw from my smoke. My quick aversion brought a smile to his face. He began to whistle at me. Assuming it to be flirtatious, I began walking briskly, with purpose, towards the next bus stop, and when it persisted, I broke into a light jog.

"Danson! Eh Danson!" I am not reputable enough of a reporter to be recognized in Seattle, let alone abroad, so his familiarity simultaneously intrigued and discomforted me.

I delivered my response while in motion: "Yeah? Can I help you?" He abandoned the sidewalk and branched into the street.

"No. But you can sure pay me to help you. You want to meet the chief?" He stopped in the middle of road, indifferently splicing an onslaught of military-personnel vehicles and weary commuters, their horns the greater nuisance.

I waved him over. He shuffled towards me, just barely avoiding the side-swipe of a US Humvee.

"If so," he began, just close enough for me to get a contact-buzz off his malty breath, "Mister Danson, then you can come with me."

"What exactly do you know or mean to tell me?" I barked, approaching him cautiously.

He laughed, deflating my staidness. "There's a lot that I know that I wish to tell you about, my friend. But it is what I can do for you today that you might be interested in." The brute could have been a pimp, a thug, and a murderer—I didn't know him from Adam. The only qualities I could discern were superficial and damning.

160

I knew I was leaning his way before he even gave me the hard sell. I reeked of desperation and failure. His booze-laden, hand-knit, out-of-season, wool sweater insinuated more of the same. We had something in common, besides an interest in today's news, but it was hardly an icebreaker. His moustache twitched, as if triggered by the scent of another wanderer. The fur, left untamed by shower, comb or a finger's caress, shuffled frenetically above his upper lip, curling out his pitch.

While *The Network* had given me some play money, I was running out of time, and I still hadn't made contact with Louis Vigeland of the Prince George Sprites. If the Americans tightened the noose anymore, I'd have lost the big story, and my remaining play money would quickly become the last real cash I'd see for a while.

"How much do you want? Where will you take me?" He cocked his head sideward like a spaniel over the prospect of time alone with a lamb shank.

"Did you plan on finding him in that fucking prison?" He wheezed and coughed. Mucous disappeared into his moustache and the pubic growth on his chin. "The chief's not in Calgary. Ah! You've got a problem, see?"

I didn't want to play into his rhetorical sales-pitch, but I also didn't want to interrupt the stream of potential intel. "Oh yeah? What's that?"

"You are in Calgary. You have get up north. But you cannot get up north by yourself, and you are certainly not getting into the Yukon from Alberta. Those good ol' American boys have Bitscho Lake all the way to the wetlands under lock and key, making damn sure they have got the water that NAFTA has neither granted nor secured for them, and they have heavily fortified anything that looks, smells or feels like oil. Man, you have got to go through *the mountain-way*!" What he proposed seemed easy enough, especially since we modern travellers had a leg up over explorers like Palliser and Grant on account of more than a century's worth of roads, paths, and trails blazed through the seemingly impenetrable Rocky Range.

He had me beginning to think that some things in life are free— a premature consideration arrived at on the grounds that he hadn't disclosed why he was a means to the end of my journey. "But if you don't have an in with the Sprites, you will not make it far in the mountains. No sir, you will not. And, if I may be so bold, sir, you will not make a handsome corpse either." He laughed again; this time it thundered from the depths of his gut.

"I've interviewed the Sprites. I know the jargon and the right names, so passing through shouldn't be a problem." I already had a fixer who could take me, probably wincing off a hangover somewhere in the city, and now I had a direction. Another guide would put an unnecessarily big dent in my wallet, already pretty banged-up. "Thanks for your time and the heads-up."

When I motioned to turn he seized me by the shoulder: "Which group of Sprites are you referring to? Out west? East? Where? In Toronto or Valcartier? That means shit-all to these guys. This is a nation divided. There're factions within factions governing one patch of land, and entirely different groups reigning over another. Sprites? They've grown out of a single group—out of their allegiances to Kalnychuk. It is an ideological movement now. Kalnychuk —" *He* muted himself as if a horrible curse had been uttered, and quickly surveyed the area. In a softer voice he continued: "He could give a fuck about your southern-Ontario or Quebec Sprites. He probably considers them a threat, especially now that everyone needs a martyr to get the ball rolling." I still had to figure out how he knew me, but in the event that he was right, I'd need someone or some way to get my foot in the door. The gamble—hitching my wagon to a crazy horse—was a chance I had to take, otherwise I'd let the Legend get away.

"Well... you already know my name."

"How rude of me." He threw out his hand. "Mister Danson, my name is Frogner."

A CANCEROUS-YELLOW aftermath swallowed the churns and metallic murmurs let loose by Frogner's "baby," a '99 Black Cadillac Deville, as it whipped out of the parking lot and careened towards me. Its breaks whined as Frogner pulled it over to the curb. The car's all-black aesthetic was marred by a dozen silver squares on the passenger side of the car—duct tape covering bullet holes. Its hubcaps and the brand inscribed thereon were masked by a thick layer of mud, much like everything else found below the waist in occupied Calgary.

A loud click emanated from the back of the car. "Trunk's open," Frogner shouted. I neatly fitted my shredded luggage between

Frogner's gas canisters and his rifles. Automatic rifles and gas: *just the usual.* I suppressed my unease and slammed the trunk down over my bags, loosing sheets of ice and snow-pack from the windows and roof. I put out my cigarette and waltzed over to the passenger's side. The door was locked. Frogner cracked the window. "Get in, get in." I tried the door again, but it was still locked. He complimented my effort with a Cheshire-cat grin, and unlocked the door. "If at first you don't succeed... You good to go, Danson?"

"I should be fine."

"Excellent." He shot a determined look down the sight-lines provided by the Cadillac laurels and kicked the beast into action. With the governor disabled, the car growled as we accelerated seamlessly to one-hundred-and-ninety-clicks-an-hour. While the car skated across the asphalt, it likewise kicked up the salt and gravel lining this and all of Calgary's streets. Little dings were our soundtrack until we hit the highway.

When the scraping beneath the car died down, Frogner, cued by silence, decided to fill the cab with an intolerable selection of music, drawn from a foot-tall stack of burned-CDs, all strung together with a mutilated earphone cord. The music made me especially suspicious of my guide. *Who of sound mind actually enjoys Celine Dion?* I was under the impression that she was one of those toxic exports used as a cheaper alternative to white-noise-machines in office buildings. Sensitive, however, to my host's feelings, I decided not to recommend we listen to some Kyuss, Truckfighters or Metrokueen to foreground our excursion northbound.

"So David, I'll call you David, okay?"

"Yes. That's fine."

"It is a very bad habit you have—getting into strangers' cars. What would your mother say? Trust should not be so easy to come by."

"I never said I trusted you. You just hit all the right buttons." There must have been blood dripping from my ears, because Frogner, otherwise unprompted, began smashing radio-presets and turning the dial through canyons of static. "I'm not important or rich enough to hold for ransom, and I'm no good to anybody dead. If you wanted the contents of my wallet, you'd have saved both of us the charade. Frogner, I'm assuming you're a legitimate business man. I'd appreciate it if you didn't prove my assumption erroneous." He stopped tinkering with the settings on the dash, satisfied with a crackly oldies station.

"Ah, no worries my friend. You will meet the Legend! No worries!" The more he said it, the more I felt like I should have been worrying. "Your friend in town—"

"Gotfried?"

"Yes. He can join us further down the road. A friend of mine will be in touch with him, and will let him know where you'll be at all times."

"How did you know about Gotfried?"

"David, it pays to know these sorts of things."

"Who pays?"

"Well, you for one."

WE THREADED THROUGH Jasper National Park along Highway Ninety-three. The US soldiers who let us through the heavily-fortified checkpoint were from the 173rd, but no one I recognized. They were clearly battle-hardened, haggard, and drawn, and seemed preoccupied with more pressing concerns than a reporter and a half-pissed Francophone. Tired though they were, the soldiers seemed genuinely interested in our safety. One soldier recommended, "Be careful."

Another soldier orbited the car, and probed each bullet-hole as he passed. He knocked on my window and signalled for me to roll it down. "Just in case you don't already know, there're snipers ahead. Proceed with extreme caution." We wished them both a good day and rolled on unscathed. The snipers failed to materialize.

Past the checkpoint, the highway—marred by mortar fire and artillery strikes—was especially bumpy. I threatened Frogner with the prospect of car-sickness all over his leather seats, and he pulled over. While I took some pictures of the wildlife, Frogner decided to make a phone call.

Assuming he'd let down his guard, I inched towards him, camera out, pretending to focus on the mountain vista. "Yes, we are coming," he said, phone hovering at the side of his head, his hand on his hip. "He just needed to stop…No, he was vomiting like a sophomore…No, it's alright… Yes, yes, I have it." When I tried to eavesdrop, he reverted to French. Discouraged, I slugged off, and threw some stones over the pass. "Danson, get the fuck back here!" Noticing fresh earth turned in the fore, I scoured ahead.

"What's wrong?" I yelled back, focused on getting a glimpse of the gulley on the other side of the hill. "Just give me a minute!"

He closed the phone. "Stop throwing those stones. You are like a child. We have to go now, this very instant!"

I hadn't felt like a child until he scolded me. I returned to the car, and wedged my way back into the passenger seat, pouting. As we traversed the bridge, I saw a heap of corpses not far from where I had been pitching the stones. A group of three or four men were pouring gasoline over the bodies. "Frogner—look!" I ripped off my seatbelt and struggled to open my window. "What the hell're they doing? I need to get down there. Frogner, stop the car."

"David, you are a very morose individual." He examined me in the rear-view mirror. "Has anyone ever told you that?"

"There must have been twenty, thirty bodies lying out there. Why—that's a mass grave! Turn this piece of shit around," I demanded.

"We have no time. We must keep to our schedule."

"Schedule? Stop the fucking car." He accelerated, and the bodies disappeared in the rearview. "Since when do we have a schedule? May I see our schedule?" I impinged.

"It's okay, David. I will get you to your destination safely and on time. You are paying me to get you to the Legend, not to sight-see. Don't you worry; you'll get your money's worth."

"Frogner, how did you know about the bodies back there?"

"David, I did not know there were bodies back there, but I do know that there are bodies everywhere, if you look hard enough." Frogner had done a poor job reassuring me. I dug into my pockets nonchalantly, feeling for my keys. I found them, fitted them between my fingers, and balled my hand. I'd have only one shot if things went sour.

WE HEADED NORTHWEST to Mount Robson National Park along the Yellowhead. A few dozen bison-burgers later, we were speeding west to Prince George. From Robson to Prince George, I was surprised to find that the majority of the American checkpoints had been abandoned, and were now manned by Sprites or Canadian Forces (rarely both, given the CF's evolving hate-on for any remaining cause warranting an American presence). Man-sized, black plastic bags heaped here and there indicated a struggle, although everyone we spoke to neglected to mention any fighting.

Now that I knew to play the Romeo, it was rather easy circumnavigating the abhorred checkpoint cavity search. Frogner, conversely, was prey to many pat-downs and mini-interrogations because he couldn't keep his trap shut. Unsure myself, I was keen on listening to his answers, hoping for inconsistencies in his back-story to justify my suspicions. Pointing to his ass, he joked, rather anxiously: "David, man, I swear to god! I should booby trap this thing."

When we reached the Upper Fraser River, Frogner had me help him build a snow-garage for the car, "The battery'll be dead, but no matter. Better dead than stolen." He sealed the garage with ice blocks and did his best to cover our tracks. After marking a tree so he'd know where to look for his car upon his return, he announced: "The bull will drive again."

All of the bridges in the area had apparently been transformed into death traps. Wanting to circumnavigate them altogether, Frogner determined to take the road less traveled by. The difference could be measured in centigrade. Dressed in the hip-waiters he'd acquired as a bonus with his infrared-binoculars purchase, we forded the river, bags above our heads. I was feeling cocky and demanded that we make the most out of the day's trek, but Frogner warned against hypothermia: "It'll get you at your bravest. The sun'll be down and take your newfound courage with it." Jacquelyn and Frogner would get along swimmingly, I decided. We set up camp on the north shore, and built an unruly fire right on the forest's edge.

I AWOKE TO FIND FROGNER cooking some bacon he'd stolen away in his pack, humming an enchanting old melody. Attempting to get up, I knocked the prop holding up my lean-to. "Ah!" He exclaimed, still with his back to me. "Good morning, David. It is so good you did not freeze to death."

"Ah-ha," I responded, brushing snow off my back and spitting out evergreen needles.

"My guy—the man with our equipment—requires fifteen-hundred dollars for the snowmobiles. Without the money and the transports, we have no chance of making it to Bear Lake."

My wallet was already too light for comfort. I couldn't afford any more surprises. Reluctantly I surrendered a roll of fifties, and signed a cheque for the remainder (approximately three-hundred-and-fifty dollars). Frogner failed to tell me that gas was extra, but was content to cover the first leg of the trip.

"David, keep watch and tend to the fire. I'll be back soon enough." He disappeared with my money into the woods. I stared at the sliver in the thicket into which he disappeared, afflicted with some irrational expectation that he'd emerge almost instantly and that all would be well, like someone hunched over a gap in the ice clinging to the hope that their beloved will surface alive. Minutes and hours passed, and there was no sign of Frogner or the snowmobiles. Discouraged, I began collecting wood in case I'd have to spend another night wedged between an arctic river and a sinister-looking forest in war-torn western Canada. When satisfied by the size and crackle of the fire, I huddled close and transcribed some of my interview with Schmidt.

Frogner came back just before nightfall to find me in the middle of a panic attack. The fire had begun to wane and my feet were freezing. I had no idea where I was and had no preserves to speak of. *He was right on time.*

"Hey, relax David. It's okay man. A promise is a promise!" He patted me on the shoulder, took his mittens off, and then stuffed them under his arm. With hands half-raised over the yellow tongues as if in benediction, Frogner continued firmly: "I will get you to the Legend. My guy said 'two guys need only one ski-do', but I told him that was unacceptable. This is not Newfoundland, eh?" He grinned, dispelling his serious tone, and made profane hand gestures suggesting something questionable about the nature of Newfoundlanders. "We have to go claim them now."

"Where?"

He directed my attention to a range of hills northwest of our little camp.

"People actually live out there?" I inquired.

"This is a land of eyes," Frogner replied. His gelatinous pearls provided a secondary pit for the flames. "You are never alone."

We packed up camp, and hiked over the ridge to a little ice-enveloped shack, fenced-in by two cords of wood, stacked high in an l-shape beside the ski-dos. "Where's your man?" I asked. The question was less of an articulation and more of a pant.

Frogner suggested that his contact didn't want to be seen, especially since he didn't know me.

"And who are you exactly, Frogner?" I was still struggling with my guide's opaque identity.

"A light in a dark place," he said, erupting into a mixture of laughter and coughing. "Be careful you don't snuff me out with too many questions."

The juddering of the snowmobile scrambled my eggs, prompting me to vomit on a number of occasions. Frogner was convinced that I was a "city-boy." As my patience dwindled, I began to agree. "Eh tenderfoot! Do they have real men where you're from?"

Crossing a particularly bumpy clearing on the way to the lake, I was forced to dismount to blather wet obscenities onto a snow-bank. Sweating and teary-eyed, I lost my bearings. I began to stumble about, attempting to regain dominion over my esophagus. Mid-heave, ten fat digits dimpled my skin, jabbing-in to the point of smarting, sending me toppling over. I hit the ground, and writhed around to see Frogner panting.

"What the fuck, Frogner?" I tried to lift myself up, but he kicked at my legs. "What the hell are you doing? Why'd you have to push me?" Cheeks maraschino red, Frogner wheezed and fought to catch his breath. He drew a finger, stretched it to the sky, and then wielded it down with both our eyes following it. He ran it through the snow, tracing a line.

"Sorry, my friend." He pushed my foot away from the line with his other hand. "Look!" He continued the line to a little ice patch a few inches away from where I was spewing. He wheezed a rhetorical question: "See that?"

"What, Frogner? What is so goddamn important?" He kicked the patch of snow he'd designated with his finger, shattering a false-floor and exposing a hole about three-by-three-and-seven-feet-deep. Thirty to forty pointed sticks protruded from the sides, the majority angled on a downward slant. There were two horizontal bars across the pit fitted with pike-adorned wheels.

"David, you have seen these in your research, yes?"

"Punji sticks? What the fuck are these doing out here?"

"Danson, you know as well as I: force of arms cannot win every battle. These traps target the hearts and minds of the enemy."

"Legs, feet, and armpits, by the looks of it. All part of Kalnychuk's asymmetrical war-faring?"

"To survive, the Yukon Sprites feel the need to live up to the cruelty of the previous group to reject the American transplant. They're extremely effective, even if not immediately deadly." He reached into the chasm and shook one of the stakes. "Dipped in shit so that if you survive the injury—and I don't see how you could get out in the first place—your wounds'll become badly infected. This one's modeled after the Viet Cong's clipping-armpit-trap."

"How fitting. . . " I probed my armpits for phantom pain.

"Regardless of which way you fall through that bramble of spikes, the axels will catch you under the arm. With no strength left in your arms, you're stuck for good."

"I am not going to ask you how you knew it was there."

"Finally, a good idea!"

Had it not been for Frogner's friendly push, I would be spewing out of more than one orifice. The near-death experience was enough to shock my system into keeping the bile down. We snacked on some of Frogner's cured meats, and then buzzed along, unhindered by traps or icy obstacles all the way to Bear Lake.

AT BEAR LAKE, we met with Sprite reinforcements, headed south on an anti-armour mission. Their group had been seriously thinned by Tomahawk strikes and CF snipers, but they maintained high spirits. The Sprite commander recognized Frogner, and they spoke privately, pointing on two occasions in my direction. I motioned toward them and Frogner belted, "Eh Danson! Rest a while."

Around a fire with thirty-odd unlawful combatants, I was fed moose jerky, propaganda, and stories about unbelievable encounters. One Vancouverite attested to having broken into an American compound and slain all of its occupants. Unlike his envious comrades, I knew that Braveheart was lying. He was referring to the 173rd's base in Jasper, still relatively unscathed by the Sprites' savage, nightly attacks. Although I was uncomfortable watching falsities converted into group history, I was consuming my first warm meal in days and couldn't justify complaining.

We drank moonshine and whistled flames. One of the senior officers supplanted a soldier sitting beside me, and filled my mug with rotgut. "Hear anything from Ottawa while you're there?"

"Actually, I came up from Calgary."

"Calgary you say? I got stitched up in Rocky View Hospital. You know?" He jabbed me in the ribs. "Rehabilitated overlooking the puddle and Heritage Park. That's the one with the big 'H'. The 'H' stands for *howdy*. Ah, Calgary's not too shabby."

"Yeah, it's not too bad." I was too cold to offer much of a critical review.

"Beats the hell out of Medicine Hat for damn sure! But who knows how long it will last. The city as we know it, I mean. My guess is I won't be able to recognize it by the time the US is all done *helping out*...Someone was telling me they're calling our government 'rogue' now. You hear about that in Cowtown? You think Canada's a rogue state?"

"First I've heard of it and no, not really."

"Me neither. See, I know full well this is just that nasty side rearing its head again. Yankees have this horrible multiple personality disorder. They can be so goddamn noble, and then—no warning—your home's on fire and your people are dead. It's just engrained in 'em. Indians were their test case." The only difference between this officer jabbering away and the protestors I met at the Mall was a rifle and a death sentence. "You know that in the last half of the twentieth century, the US helped overthrow a bunch of real, democratically elected governments? Brazil, Iran, Guatemala, Dominican Republic, and Philly."

"You mean Chile."

"Tomato, tomat-oh."

The soldier's indifference marked the onset of my own. He'd stopped pretending to care about the other tragedies once they provided a context for his.

"Were those rogue states?" he rattled on. "Maybe. But Goddamn! If they install some Vichy government in Canada—with their track record—we're fucked. You're a reporter. I know. The boys told me. You know full well how Kissinger was the kiss of death in Indonesia. You know how Clinton fucked over Somalia and alienated the Arabs who wanted to play ball when he was releasing his poisons with interns. You know all about the nasty dictatorships they arranged in El Salvador, Panama, Ecuador, Bolivia, Columbia, Iran, Indonesia, and the Philippines." He may have been the one talking, but I was out of breath. "Who's tied your fucking tongue all this time? It's so goddamned awful."

I wanted to shut him up with: "Yeah, so you've read Chomsky; you and every other angsty teen with a library card," or a definition of compassion fatigue and the reasons why I can't endorse his scattered message with tears, but instead, I submitted to mental laziness and permitted him to continue to blow hooch into my ear.

"So what does somebody like me do? What should I do? I am no terrorist. But my unit's been disbanded. These boys know they're Canadian and that they ought to protect what's theirs, especially with the CF preoccupied with American missions...No one is gonna take on the elephant. Just going to placate it with peanuts and hope that it won't throw a tantrum and kick up more dirt. Problem is that the damage can no longer be localized. There'll never be enough room for an elephant of this size and appetite."

"You should start a blog." He must have thought I was sincere because he responded with a goofy smile. "The CF providing you guys with any support?"

A man limped into the conversation, the steel of his arbitrator gleaming in the light from the fire: "Cain, you've had too much to drink. Reporter doesn't care about you or me. See?" He pointed to my bags. "He's on his way somewhere. Somewhere as in *not here*. Doesn't care about your elephant. Doesn't care about 'The cause'." He swiveled on his porcine legs, and turned to me, spitting indignation. "Just wants to eat our food and drink our reserve. Isn't that right, mister reporter?"

"I feel entitled to a little bit of your gruel," I said, my tone bordering on snarky. "I almost ate it back there, thanks to one of your fucking death traps."

"That moose you're happy to gobble down—we caught it in one of those traps. They're not for men, but for animals."

"That's fucking nonsense and you know it," I snapped back. "Why would you want to plug your dinner with sticks dipped in feces? Catching sasquatches with those armpit traps?"

"Know your bounds, boy," shouted another, stepping into our conversation.

The other Sprite continued: "Do you think we have time to leisurely hunt for venison? We're at war. Unless we trap, we have to rely on American supply, and that, I can fucking assure you, would require 'death traps.' There's no such thing as a free meal up here." He slapped the jerky out of my hand. "You're entitled to nothing, reporter. This is not your country. This is not your war. We are not

171

your friends. And that food—" he waved his finger at the ground, "is for men of conscience."

♠ *Yukon-bound*
November 27-29, 2005

BEAR LAKE REMINDED Frogner of the boreal fringe, northeast of Wabasca, Alberta. The comparison didn't seem to hold, although the idyllic place in his description was not veiled in snow and ice. Snow-blind, lips chapped, and red-skin flaking, I decided that I simply didn't care. I just wanted to reach my destination.

From Bear Lake, Frogner and I met with a group of civilians who agreed to take us north in their rust-bucket Silverado pickup through blizzards and treacherous winds to Mayo, Yukon Territory, via Dawson, where the American presence was minimal, and where resistance groups had some serious networks throughout the countryside. Our agreement stipulated that Frogner and I should drive, relieving the road-weary travelers, who'd been driving non-stop from Vancouver, and further, that we each pay one-hundred-and-fifty dollars for gas. Those in our company had business in Mayo, so the expedition benefitted all.

Two out of the three (i.e. Sheila and Wilfred) were researchers from the University of British Columbia. The third, D.W., I was not so sure about. While he fit the stereotype of an academic (i.e. awkward, tangential, stubborn, cynical, and quick to remind you of his designation), he seemed too rough-skinned and fidgety to be constrained by the demands of the position (i.e. marking, reading and research). I was convinced, very briefly, that he was a frontier doctor, but later decided, after seeing his hand-writing, which was quite legible, that he was, in all likelihood, a professor-cum-tradesman.

Frogner pitted us against the night and up the snow-swept Alaska Highway at a suicide pace. I was crooked sideways in my chair, talking to Tom and Sheila. D.W. had no interest in our conversation. He was unconscious, plastered against his window, mouth agape like a trout resigned to its fate, snoring. Apart from what Tom and Sheila had heard on the news or secondhand from friends, they had very little sense of the extent and gravity of the war. They were, however, ripe with statistics and insights into the consequences of the new North American paradigm on trade and supply, with a special focus on the Tuchone people in the territories. Although sweet people, Tom and Sheila bored me to tears, such that, when we arrived at the first US checkpoint in Whitehorse and could no longer speak, I counted my blessings.

We underwent our checkpoint ritual (i.e. smile, obey, and "sir-yes-sir"). Frogner, again failing to emulate a Romeo, had a rough time with the US guard. The soldier was convinced Frogner was a match to one of the personalities depicted on the US military's standard issue deck of most-wanted Sprites (he mistook Frogner for the ten of clubs). After several soldiers came and scrutinized Frogner's likeness, they finally let us go.

We managed to head north on the Klondike Highway—probably the most tedious leg of the journey—with few obstacles. The checkpoint debacle made our hosts suspicious, but I assured them of our media affiliations and distracted them with stories about the Middle East. As I switched roles and bored Tom, Sheila, and D.W., we vaulted deeper into Yukon Territory, ushered in by undulating hills, ice-capped lakes, pines, and deciduous trees bowed by heavy snow dumps. We should have driven slowly on account of the two-lane road's poor maintenance, but Frogner insisted on speed, and D.W. agreed, suggesting that time was of the essence.

ON THE BRINK OF SLUMBER, Frogner flicked my ear. It was my turn to drive the truck. My predecessor and I dialed clockwise around the shouldered Chevy to occupy one another's spot. The seat was uncomfortably warm, but the ride was smooth. An eternity of snow-swept tar disappeared beneath the beast as I pressed the pedal and watched the hand inch towards one-hundred-and-fifty-clicks-an-hour effortlessly. You know when bombs are falling left, right, and centre, no one is going to care much if you speed in a seventy or ninety-zone. Liberated from consequence, I wrinkled the pleather on the steering wheel and tapped the gas. With the four-by-four option enabled, I felt like a road god, disdaining every "don't speed" sign and the horizon—eternal and unconquerable.

By about three-thirty in the afternoon, baby blue had chased the burgundy remnants of the day behind the mountains and buttes, leaving layered, purple clouds imbued with the legacy of the sun. By four, their expressions were veiled in twilight. The halogens from a second car chased my reds and stared me down in the rearview mirror. After an hour of cat and mouse, I put the Vortec V8 to the test.

In our lone ship, we peeled down a deserted path into the Yukon kaleidoscope: barbed, white, coiling nothingness, stretching over islands of pale green and rock, all shrouded in darkness. I fought off sleep while my passengers snored a grunge opera, exhibiting an unconscious indifference to the world of the living and the not-quite-dead.

With one hand on the wheel, and my left foot pigeoning the gas, I rifled through my jacket for a smoke to inaugurate daybreak. Out of the corner of my eye I spied an animate shadow on the side of the road. I plotted my right where I imagined the brake should be, but found nothing. "Fuck!" I screamed as I scrambled back into my seat. The brown obstacle on the horizon grew exponentially before the car. I hammered my foot against the pedal. My seatbelt caught my calm, and the massive jerk awoke those in the cab, sparking a sense of panic and primal fear.

"What the devil, Danson?" The car skidded to a halt, only feet short of the blob, far more ominous in focus than as an abstract entity. The blob, a mule deer, struck an alpha pose and poised as if to ram the truck. Frogner grabbed the stick: "Eh David, your first ambush?" He put the car into park and turned off the engine. My heart was racing. "He's not afraid of you. Why is that?" Frogner sounded the horn and the buck disappeared into the bramble hugging the road. Frogner slammed the dashboard. "Cause he's used to a malevolent nature. Nothing that manages to live up here lives afraid."

"Yeah, and what if I fucking hit him?"

"In all likelihood, his aggressor would likewise be slain in the accident; thus, he'd die a good death in the Yukonian sense. 'Those who have rifles will use their rifles; those who have swords will use their swords; those who have no swords will use spades, hoes or sticks,' mules will kick and coyotes will holler. Everything must endeavor to oppose the colonialists and save his country."

"A tad ironic that you should quote George Washington..."

"Would be if I had; however, that was Ho Chi Minh."

Gelded in front of the group, I was deposed from my position as road king, and forced into the back seat where I begrudgingly talked soil with D.W. who, to my chagrin, had a lot to say.

"Solid rock and a foot of soil prevents many tree types from taking root round here. No cover for those goddamn terrorists. You'll for sure see some other-worldly firs and pines shoot up, though; right out of the fissures in the rock. See?" He pointed outside to a skinny, top-heavy pine, which blurred into collective memory. "There's not many around here, but when you see them, you know they're ancient warriors. They chased off the glaciers with the lichen."

"No kidding," I yawned.

AFTER TWO HOURS of polite nodding, I concluded that D.W.'s wonderful social stamina was less of a gift and more some type of retardation. I took the first interruption in his stream of encyclopedic regurgitations as my cue to disengage. As he drew mouthfuls from his canteen, I closed my eyes. My passive aggressive alternative to confronting the man on his dreadfully mundane fascinations swiftly led to unconsciousness.

I dreamt about Audrey, and then wandered into a distorted memory of my dad warning me about American women. Apparently I couldn't escape being lectured even in the deepest of sleeps. I awoke to a grading barking: "Look alive, Danson." I molted my melancholic dream-state and sat up into disappointment.

"Where are we?"

"Whitehorse."

"How long is the stopover?"

"Two checkpoints, a few shakedowns, a gas-up, and a Tim's-run."

"And then?"

"Up the Klondike to Carmacks. There, a friend of mine is letting us stay the night. Tomorrow we'll break in Pelly Crossing, break with the Klondike, head east—hold on." He began dodging in and out of the small-town traffic, leaning out of his window to emphasize his impatience. "Learn to fucking drive!" He pulled back into the cab. "I swear to god, Danson: if it's a bad driver, you can sure you're dealing with one of the Five O's."

I feigned half-interest with a shrug of the shoulders.

"Old, ovaries, on-the-phone, on-the-run or—I always forget that last one. Anyway, after we get some coffee and donuts, we'll head east along the Silver Trail. You want to do a mountain hike? Eh David, do you want to see more deer?"

"I'm hiked-out Frogner. How long until we meet—" I hesitated, realizing that mixed company called for censorship, "Reach our destination?"

"Mayo? A day-and-a-half if roads and traffic continue in this fashion."

"And when we get there, will—" he began talking over me.

"David, David. It is all good. I've gotten you here without a bump on your head or punji sticks up your asshole. Relax. Here," he said, digging into his satchel. He tossed me a paperback. "Feed your head."

Sheila leaned over and patted me on the knee, "That one there's a good read!"

I thumbed my way through the timeworn poetry anthology to a creased and dog-eared page, and read Robert Service's "The Law of the Yukon," superimposing fantasy on the passing blur:

This is the law of the Yukon, and ever she makes it plain:
Send not your foolish and feeble; send me your strong and your
sane;
Strong for the red rage of battle; sane for I harry them sore;
Send me men girt for the combat, men who are grit to the core;
Swift as the panther in triumph, fierce as the bear in defeat,
Sired of a bulldog parent, steeled in the furnace heat.
Send me the best of your breeding, lend me your chosen ones;
Them will I take to my bosom, them will I call my sons;
Them will I gild with my treasure, them will I glut with my meat;
But the others—the misfits, the failures—I trample under my
feet.

IT WAS ABOUT FIVE p.m. when we rolled into the outskirts of Mayo: a town hidden unto itself by bush and forest; essentially hamlets interconnected by dirt roads. Dilapidated shacks and burnt shells of cars lined the road in. Seemed like the kind of sight you'd expect to see after a nuclear holocaust or a zombie invasion.

Frogner pulled onto the shoulder, and stopped the car. "One moment, ladies and gentlemen." He pulled a zip-lock bag out of his jacket pocket containing a different cellular phone than the one I had seen him use before. He punched a number into the phone from memory, and after three pulses, he was agreeing to commands from the other end. "Alright...Yes. No, they're dropping us off at the school. Sure, we'll wait. Okay, see you soon." Frogner took the battery out of the phone, tossed the SIM card into his satchel, and then handed me the cannibalized phone. "A souvenir." He arched his neck and addressed the peanut gallery: "We're going to let ourselves off at the high school and that'll be it. Appreciate your patience."

He started us along a goat path to the centre street, where there was a semblance of a permanent settlement. Blue and pink neon cut through the twilight letting all of Mayo's ghosts know that it was open for business.

Mayo had a church, a post office, a health centre, the recently added J.V. Clark School, and some little businesses. The upkeep reaffirmed my sense that anyone who got rich off of the Gold Rush had left the Yukon altogether. We parked in front of the school. Frogner and I disembarked.

"You mean to tell me he's teaching grade school now?" I balked. "Finger painting?" I added in an attempt to amuse myself.

"Who's the painter?" inquired Sheila.

"Oh, just a friend of ours," I replied. "A jack of all trades, you could say."

Frogner did not respond. He was either nervous or playing a part he had previously written for himself in Mayo. With a steely stare, he signalled me to follow him. I waved goodbye to D.W., Sheila, and Tom. Frogner and I trudged away from the school, and crossed the road to a warehouse. Our ride sleuthed away, kicking up ice and gravel as it vanished around the bend.

"David, you must be very cool, otherwise they will not trust you. Just be honest and patient." He knocked on a side-door. Two men surprised us from behind. They were both unshaven, dressed in military fatigues, and wearing red bandanas.

"Who the fuck are you?" barked one of the grunts behind the butt of an AK.

"Frogner. We've come to talk to Qi." He identified me with a tap from the back of his hand, "This is the reporter."

The thuggish guard seemed to recognize Frogner. "Ah, it's been a while. Qi is not here. Now...fuck off."

"Hey Frick and Frack, I just spoke to Qi, and he said that this was the place. He's going to take us to see the Legend."

Frick kicked me to the ground, and prodded my chest with his rifle barrel. "This reporter's already seen too much."

Frogner seized *Frick*'s firing-arm and poised to strike him. "That's not for you to decide," growled Frogner.

Frick, surprised by Frogner's defensive maneuver, fired several shots into the ground, just missing my legs. *Frack*, responding to the commotion, aimed his AK at Frogner's head, and began screaming: "Don't fucking move!" All four of us were gripped in a frenetic struggle for our lives.

As I clamored to my feet, *Frack* began to wallop on Frogner's sides. I lunged for the guard's firearm, unsecured in its holster, wagging right in front of me.

It had been a while since I had last held a gun. The power was heavy and unfamiliar in my hands. I yelled: "Get off of him! Or I'll—" but before I could finish, there was a high-pitched screech behind me—the sound of one metal surface resisting another—and then a second noise: the sound of a bolt being pinned back. I nevertheless kept the gun fixed on the guards, resolved to shoot pending any escalation. The door swept open, stiffening all of the hairs on my neck. I knew immediately that I was exposed and at the mercy of whatever strange darkness lurked behind me.

"Enough!" *Frick* and *Frack* eased off of Frogner, and turned, standing at attention. "Son, lower that weapon before you hurt yourself." I cocked my neck to the side very slowly and saw him: a tall, gaunt man whose white hair waved wildly in all directions away from his Easter Island-esqe face. "Anderson, Mr. Graham: help Mr. Vigeland up." Frogner puffed his chest, and launched a bloody spit across Anderson's bust. "Hello Louis. It's been a while."

Frogner's face lit up. He wiped his mouth and shook the stranger's hand. The stranger—muscular and weathered—released the shake and slapped Frogner playfully on the shoulder. "It's okay, boys," said the stranger. "These are friends. Tom, you remember Louis. All is well." The men eased off, but maintained their glowering train on Frogner and I. The calm personality led us inside, into the dark.

HE STRODE with a wide gait. His heels clicked with a metronomic precision. He was a picture of confidence. "Louis, I believe your friend would like to speak to me alone." Frogner—who had been keeping pace beside me—stopped in his tracks. I overstepped and pivoted, looking as if I was trapped between two irreconcilable poises.

"I'll see you in a bit, I suppose," I said.

"Yeah, sure."

"A light in the dark, huh?"

"I realize that was a little dramatic. How about: *the right man for the job.*"

"Suits me just fine, *Louis.*"

"Washroom working yet?" inquired Vigeland. The tall man, cocooned in the darkness ahead stretched his hand into a blade of ambient light indicating the way. He turned to face me and smiled wryly. I felt as though I had met him before. *The apple does not fall far from the tree.*

"Mr. Danson, I understand you'd like to meet the Green Legend." He reached into his jacket. I half expected him to plug me right there—in a dark room in the middle of nowhere. He pulled out a pipe with one hand and procured from his pants' pocket a little bag with the other. He tapped the pipe on his forearm, finger-cleaned the bowl, and packed it with some green leaves. "Or did you come to take in all Mayo has to offer."

I chuckled nervously.

"No? I didn't think so. Follow me."

WE DESCENDED a set of stairs to a seeming dead end manned by a different pair of goons armed with AKs. Both saluted, and the one closest to me barked: "Sir. Good afternoon, sir." With a nod from my escort, they shouldered their weapons, and together pulled open a hidden, heavy door, disguised by graffiti. The artifice concealed a metal gate. Embroidered in smoke, he coughed, and searched his pockets.

"Oh, where did I put those damn things?" He reached into his sleeve, pulling out a set of keys. "Always the last place…" He unlocked the gate and took his beret off. "Stephen, hold this for me, will yah?"

"Yes sir." The guard folded the beret, and inserted it into his passant.

"You both be sure to call me if you hear anything upstairs. Louis is home, safe, and sound, but you never know—he could have been followed. See that he wasn't." The two men nodded, and then slung their guns with rehearsed pageantry.

Behind the door lay a few kilometres of tunnels of varying height and width, but almost always a tight fit. There were no lights, and from what I could tell, no machinated air-pumps. Save for small tunnels that snaked to the surface every hundred feet or so, there was no fresh air. That being said, I was not surprised to find myself greatly fatigued when we surfaced from the Sprites' subterranean passage.

He knelt at the end of the tunnel, waiting for me as I schlepped forward. "Now David," he belted down to me. "Do you mind if I call you David?" He scanned my face as I emerged into the light, looking intently for a reaction.

"Hum? Yes. David is fine." We entered a burrow walled on three sides with loose cinderblocks tearing up with mud. Serpentine roots and rock protruded on the fourth side. A generator shuddered in the corner of the room. Wires branched up from the machinery to the ceiling where they disappeared into pink insulation. Where they were exposed, they swayed with the infernal rhythm of the power source, energetic enough to make the single hanging bulb flicker. Having lost all sense of depth and location in the tunnel, I tried to make sense of my surroundings. "Where are we?"

"We're in my basement. I'll formally welcome you once we're upstairs and have these filthy shoes off." The stairs were constituted by rotted wood too soggy to creak. A tall Tuchone woman answered his knock and let us in.

"Oh, you better be fucking kidding me... Take off those shoes this very instant! I just mopped." She spied me lurking behind my guide. "And who's this?" she inquired bluntly, pointing at me indecorously as if I was a hock in a deli.

My escort swept up her arm, kissed her hand, and whispered to her. She scrunched her nose and went into the kitchen.

"Always bringing the lost and the damned in here," she shouted. "Why don't you make some nice friends for once?" The door to the kitchen whined behind her, and he winked at me. Through the sliver in the door, shrinking geometrically with each swing, I spied her put a kettle on the stove.

"David, would you care for something to eat?"

I was starving, but I didn't want to start the interview a dependent. "No, thank you."

180

"Are you sure? Jason caught some pike and graylings just this morning. If you like white fish, you should try the tezra—it's absolutely scrumptious."

"Perhaps later on, if the offer still stands."

"Certainly. I understand completely. Make sure you try the salmon before you go. It too migrated up here for a good death. Hmm. A cup of tea then?" he adjusted the wings of his moustache, which cut across his high, bony cheeks and pointed to his Slavic blue eyes.

"That would be most excellent. Thank you." My caffeine withdrawal had left me with an excruciatingly painful headache. It had been a day since my last Tim's run, and the sweets that Frogner had fed me on the ride-in were all unnaturally sweetened, and thus of no use to an addict.

"Brucie! Can you turn off the lights out there? We're going to overload the generator," piped the woman from the kitchen.

"Damn it. I always forget," he whispered to me. "Yes, dumpling," he whinnied to the kitchen. His quick shift in tone—when speaking to me and the Tuchone woman—made him seem appear schizophrenic, which was especially distressing because I was not sure which was more genuine, more dominant. He led me down a hallway to a circuit board, and switched off power to the floors marked "one" and "two." "Welcome to my home. The lovely femme fatale in the kitchen is my secretary, Anna. She's very protective. You can't blame her for being a little rash."

I indicated my indifference with a shoulder shrug.

"I promised her father that I'd take care of her. He died of injuries he sustained while fighting-off American forces with friends in the Na-Cho Nyak Dun in Mayo. Like her father, she's very loyal."

"Of course."

He drew his finger as if to speak, and controlled a moment of silence. After standing motionless for a minute or two, he swept his finger like a sword in play, stabbing the dead air between us with a dramatic point. "Soon their suffering will be at an end. While our tea steeps, let me take you to where you'll be sleeping tonight. Your *kamra singola*, yes? Is that how you say it?"

It took me a moment to realize that the garbled slush he was shoveling at me was an attempt at my native tongue. "Sure. How did you know?"

"Hmmm?" he threw his head back to drain the tea from his cup. "How did you know I was Maltese?"

"Oh." The question had caught him off guard. "Louis told me."

"And how do you know Louis?"

Anna belted from the kitchen: "Brucie, she left another message on the machine. Sounded urgent."

"Yes, yes," he replied. "Thank you, I'll check it later." He ran his finger along the rim of his cup. "David, you may ask any question that you want—till you're blue in the face—but let's get settled first."

UP THE SECOND FLIGHT of stairs was a corridor lined with several doors, ending in a *cul de sac* marked with a laminated Canadian flag. As we trudged down the hall, I leaned into the doorway of one of the rooms for a gander. Blinds had blotted out all but a few bands of pale light, which played visual tricks with the topography of the peeling wallpaper. A soiled mattress sat on the floor covered in bloody and tattered rags. At the foot of the bed, a man sat, legs akimbo, bending a blind with a scoped rifle. This deep into the conflict, there was no buffer-zone between public and private, domestic and political, battlefield and bedroom.

My guide gently grabbed my shoulder and said in a low voice, "Come, come. Your room is just down here."

"Is he on watch?" He smiled.

"We're all always on watch. He who closes his eyes is already dead. Isn't that right Jason?"

Slowly, the man identified as Jason turned his head and stammered: "Sir, yes sir." The answer haunted the quiet that followed it. The premature crows-feet carved into his mug indicated an internal strain and struggle to stay awake.

"You're a heck of a man doing a heck of a job. Keep it up, Jason," ordered my guide.

The bedroom contained several bunks; each a six-foot metal frame fitted with two-inch-thick bedding. The solitary window, which had been boarded up and halved by sandbags, loosed a few muted, triangular bands. There was a sink stained pinkish-brown in the corner with a space above for a mirror, and a painting of John Paul II hanging crooked on the wall.

Noticing a couple pairs of boots under a number of the cots, I asked my escort: "Will I meet those men?"

"No, unfortunately; those men closed their eyes." He winced, and thumbed his moustache. "Leave your belongings here. You can take your pick of the cots. We will have tea, get acquainted, and then you should rest. I imagine the trek here was less than luxurious. Tomorrow, when we're both at our best, I'll tell you whatever it is you want to know or came to learn."

"So you'll tell me about the Legend?" Although Anna implicated the man as Bruce, I decided to play coy so long as he was content to.

"Legends have no meat. I will tell you about the man."

♣ DEEP BACKGROUND

BRUCE KALNYCHUK was born on April 13th, 1937, in Ann Arbor, Michigan, to Stefan and Mary Kalnychuk. He was the second eldest of five children (three boys and two girls). Mary worked as a gym teacher and Stefan was a city bus-driver.

Matthew, Bruce's older brother, suffered from an acute respiratory disorder and low bone density forcing him indoors most days and rendering him immobile most of the time. (Bruce attributed this to his mother's alcohol abuse during her pregnancy.) From an early age, Bruce was a zealous extravert, compensating for his brother's weakness. He focused on becoming physically intimidating, despite his asthma.

The boys' father celebrated Bruce's athleticism and aggression in the gym, on the field, and with his friends. Though benevolent and affectionate with all his progeny, Stefan doted chiefly on Bruce, while Matt was forced to append himself to Bruce vicariously and waste away by the attic window, neglected and abhorred like a proud sinner's portrait. Despite obvious resentment, Matthew appeared positive about Bruce's success, so long as it remained physical, leaving him to dominate intellectual space in the family.

Bruce took notice of his brother's hate-love pending the sanctity of some tenuous balance he had imagined/projected onto their social dynamic. Bruce recounts:

> There was one evening after football practice in November. I was just getting home. Matt was sitting on the veranda reading a book. He did not say hello. He pulled a sheet from beneath the book. He started fanning it about violently and screaming at me. Told me I was supposed to be 'the fucking family meatball.' He

183

had some sense of a bodily-mental symbiosis we had—some ludicrous rationalization that entitled him purpose or a perceived social weight in the house. He swatted the paper at me. I pushed him. I've always regretted pushing him. Wasn't fair…Matt was crying. I don't know if you've ever seen a pale-faced black-eyed kid cry, but it's terrifying. I remember him poking me and yelling with the conviction of the martyrs, 'You're a nothing! A nothing!' He vanished into the house, leaving the piece of paper at my foot. It was my grade nine report card. I achieved my first 'A' average. Prior, I had been having a great amount of difficulty, especially with English. Dad spoke a lot of Ukrainian in front of us, so I grew up with a schizophrenic grasp on language. Mom was considering homeschooling…Ah, poor Matt. You know we were really good friends growing up? He was a good older brother, when he was able.

Impelled to academic success, especially after his encounter with his brother on the steps of their Michigan home, Bruce worked diligently at his studies. Although convinced he had to foster his cerebral energies, he nevertheless maintained the fierce barbarity his father had celebrated when he was younger. (One high school guidance counselor had figured him to be a psychopath: "quick to anger, quick to cool.")

Wanting to study German in Berlin, he practiced until he became proficient. He preferred his Nietzsche, Leibniz, and Freud in German. Unable to afford the trip to Berlin, he instead enrolled in an English night-class to "improve his accent." Every second weekend, Bruce accompanied his German-speaking friends to chess tournaments. Alternating weekends, he destroyed his opponents in English debating.

After placing first in a State debating tournament, he was invited to follow around his congressman for a day, during which he made "quite an impression." This fated meeting proved opportune because it allowed him to pursue a path where his seemingly disparate interests could converge. The congressman's nomination, in combination with a portfolio of records indicating his mastery over three languages and his competitive grades, earned Bruce a spot at the United States Military Academy at West Point. His fellow students noted him an extremist: "capable of much, determined to do more."

In Bruce's second year of schooling (i.e. the fall of '58), Matthew Kalnychuk died in a car accident. While Matthew's passenger (i.e.

Mary Kalnychuk) suffered only bruises and scrapes, the impact was enough to break his neck. Matt's death sent Bruce into a deep depression.

After attending the funeral, Bruce returned to school, ostensibly unaffected. Privately tormented by his brother's death, however, he became fixated on mortality—on dying. Lapsed on his religious heritage, he began to favour a more nihilistic and haphazard approach to people, life, and death. Bruce recalls fixating on Sartre's "Nausea" and finding that, in undermining the theoretical value of life and the Christian determination to live peacefully and abundantly (buried in the Kalnychuk mausoleum), it made it easier for him to justify living selfishly and guiltlessly.

An exemplar, as far as his soldiering was concerned, he was called upon for military service in the early sixties. With his schooling behind him, he expected action to harden him above and beyond what he had endured at West Point. Already an Army second lieutenant, he looked forward to fast-tracking through the ranks.

VIETNAM WAS NOT at all what Bruce expected. He shipped out in '67 and returned prematurely in April '68 as the result of a "serious injury sustained in active theatre." He lost friends and (my sense is) he began to see the dark underbelly of the American empire. The logic was: "If they had a gun, they were a VC. If dead, they were VC," tested his resolve at first, still managing a sliver of ethical sense.

In 1967, Bruce wrote to his girlfriend at the time, Marsha Miller (ellipses wherever segments were censored by the US Army):

I don't like seeing these guys turn feral. They become wilder, better fighters, but only to a point. *Your* lord gives and then he takes away, does he not? Obedience to authority is tenuous when instinct is calling the shots...We lost five guys yesterday. Sonny doesn't look like he'll make it through the night. Dysentery doesn't help him any. Oliver and I knew morale was low, so tonight we sent a message [in the Quang Nam province]...We found a little village. It was really pretty. If you didn't have qualms about the heat, we could easily move here after this shit dies down and be happy. I could teach our dumplings how to fish, and you could build a library for your books...When we got into the village, it was clear that either all the men had fled or they were with those who had died defending the ridge yesterday. There were only women and children left. I ordered Jamie to take a walk; more specifically: I told him to search for anyone who required medical attention. Not everyone could handle what we're doing...I don't know what to do with myself anymore. We killed everybody and everything. Women, children, cats, and dogs. While Jamie was fussing around with some kid with shrapnel in his leg, I helped Oliver and the boys mow down the rest of the villagers, high on grass and bloodlust. Sonny's brother went around mutilating bodies afterwards. It was horrible...[70]

Notwithstanding his disillusionment, Bruce managed to make a name for himself over the course of his tour. In addition to rising to the rank of major, he was awarded the Medal of Honor for "conspicuous gallantry and intrepidity at the risk of his life" for his actions mid-January 1968, days before the Tet Offensive put the fear of god into the American Forces.

Called upon to relieve a shell-shocked officer, Bruce met a platoon under heavy fire from North Vietnamese regulars. With the support of the First Battalion 69 Armour, he burned through the jungle ahead of his men. An ambush cut him off from his unit, forcing Bruce to take refuge in a recently exposed VC foxhole. The hole was not, however, a dead end. Realizing that he sat at the mouth of one of the heavily populated tunnels reported by South Vietnamese spies, he reloaded his Colt 1911 and crawled a few yards in to investigate the extent of the burrow and to counter a possible attack from behind.

By the time Bruce had reached about twenty feet into the tunnel, the USAF, responding to orders to fire on the tree line, dispatched several F4J Phantom fighter-bombers, which proceeded to fire on the VC battalion top-side. The explosions revealed more of the tunnel entrance. Advancing American troops recognized the open tunnel as an opportunity and invitation for retribution, their herd having been thinned in the ambush earlier.

Seizing this opportunity to infiltrate the tunnel plexus, a US flame-thrower team was ordered to advance all the way through the tunnel system. Fleeing the inferno behind, and facing ahead dozens of bayonets and Soviet weapons, Bruce charged the next tunnel exit.

---

[70] Bruce Kalnychuk to Marsha Miller, 8 Feb. 1968.

Low on 1911 ammo, Bruce took an enemy weapon and surfaced on the 69th's right flank, carving through an enemy bazooka team. Fire erupted behind him, alerting nearby US troops to a silhouette of a man toting an AK47. Private Alowishus Freind fired on Bruce mistaking him for a North Vietnamese soldier, wounding him in the groin and belly.

When the smoke cleared the battlefield, Freind led a medic to Bruce, who apparently still had some fight in him. He was rushed to a preordained extraction point and med-evac'd by Huey Hog to a temporary field hospital set up to receive wounded from the Dak To area. He was honorably discharged and sent packing, back to the USA.

Bruce prayed for deafness after hearing 'duty, honour, and country' rattled on back at home. He couldn't reconcile *his* America with the reckless violence, fragging, and malice he'd witnessed overseas. His experience poisoned his imaginary. Honour had failed him, and the America he loved seemed annexed to some romantic imaginary. Only duty remained.

The experience in Vietnam scrambled Bruce's resolve and invested interest in spreading the *Pax Americana*. Nevertheless, he proved himself as a strategist and a patriot in the eyes of his brothers in arms. When his tour had concluded, Bruce received, in addition to his Medal of Honor, the Purple Heart. The extent or consequence of the wounds he sustained did not come up in any detail in his recollection of the events (to me).

DURING THE 1970's, Bruce was involved in a number of black-ops in South America. Although Bruce sat proud and stoic, he winced when I asked him details about where he fit in.

> What was the United States to do when these developing countries discovered they could nationalize or worse: democratize their commodities and resources? Well, they couldn't stand for it. The rationale for intervention was often clouded by rhetoric. Instead of terrorism, as is the case today, it was communism that called for the swift hand of justice. *You're with us—for a price—or you're against us.* Regime changes and interventions are cheap when the new authority picks up the tab. [Pointing south to the columns of smoke on the horizon] I was on the other side of that imperial muscle. The cause paid well and made sense.

I found it troubling for Bruce, a self-aware and cautious man, to have served without issue for so long. How many men, just like him, were poised to vanquish the remaining "Canadian marauders"?

-EMBARGOED REPORT-

IN THE SPRING of 1980, Bruce was moved to the NORAD base that bustled above North Bay, Ontario. Since the base was primarily concerned with air defence, particularly over the arctic, Kalnychuk's extensive ground/urban combat experience seemed superfluous. It was clear that he was assigned there to serve in a thuggish capacity: to direct security for the base, which was nothing more than a "strict perimeter detail," with only the slightest "hope" of a Soviet confrontation. He joked that after learning how to stage massive American battles and fighting in classified wars in South America for the US, he ended up fighting for elbow space in a Canadian cafeteria and scaring intoxicated adolescents off the ridge. His stint in North Bay was supposed to have only lasted a year, though he suspected that he would be asked to treat it as a permanent move.

Life on the hill wasn't completely abysmal, however. His neighbours and colleagues were fond of him and they genuinely respected his input. Furthermore, he had won favour with his joint supervisors, who had satisfied his ambitions with the promise of promotion. Despite the sugar-coating, Bruce realized that he was tethered and going nowhere fast. *The US military had put one of its best on ice.*

There was, however, some excitement to go around, when pernicious groups within the Soviet Union, with ears to their emasculated nation's death rattle, began playing hardball. The prospect of the Soviets sending a Mig-team or a missile over the arctic as the result of an overnight *coup d'etat* kept things interesting. Bruce snuggled in and waited for the apocalypse.

This working opportunity also afforded him time with his family, which had grown out of its convenient bubble. Bruce was granted dual citizenship in 1981, after which he began flying his wife Katherine up to visit him monthly.

Katherine, reluctant to become too invested in her lacklustre home away from home, nevertheless committed to writing the

Ontario bar exam. On her second writing, she passed with flying colours, and moved into a military row house in Hornel Heights—the satellite town above North Bay—with their two boys. She practiced matrimonial law, which was slow-going in North Bay and a constant reminder of her own inevitable divorce.

When I asked him about home-life with Katherine, he responded: "home life? Home kept me at work. I was working two full time jobs, neither of which was particularly fun." He insinuated that Katherine shared this sentiment. (She could not be reached for comment.)

Katherine and the boys rarely utilized the sports complex, confectionary, grocery store, movie store, theatre, and bowling alley developed for the military personnel living on "the mountain." Instead, they spent the majority of the time in their foster town below. Their move north to be closer with Bruce revealed how little time his family actually wanted to spend with him. He had imported disdainful strangers.

Resentful of working in a *cul-de-sac* position with NORAD, Bruce requested new tasking or placement. Apparently someone had it out for him: hearing that he was disgruntled, they planned to move Bruce and Katherine to Anchorage, Alaska. Pleading for a "better" alternative, he was sent, via a NATO exchange program, to CFB Edmonton to instruct a class on "war and strategy in the modern city." Katherine's practice, likewise dismally slow, was not worth becoming a single parent over, so she rallied the kids and followed in tow.

The family moved into a house on the south side of the Iron Bridge in 1986. There Bruce celebrated his 49th birthday. Candles melted and the cake sagged while the Kalnychuks bickered in the kitchen and the boys fought over the television remote in the basement. Bruce began to resent the Lady Macbeth he had married in haste—whose ambition had outgrown their Edmonton bungalow much quicker than it had their military row-house—as well as their two boys who had inherited their mother's spite without question or reflection. He didn't have to think twice about spending six nights a week with his second dysfunctional family.

Since the United States Air Command took advantage of the old RCAF Namao airfield—renamed Lancaster Park during the Cold War—which was in the neighbourhood, Bruce's old friends would often drop in on him. Much to Katherine's chagrin, they'd take him drinking on Whyte Avenue where they frequently roughed-up Fort McMurray tough-guys for fun. By the end of their first year in Edmonton, the Kalnychuks had determined to sleep in separate beds and lead separate lives.

In Edmonton, Bruce began to appreciate the subtle differences between Canada and the States. He grew fond of a number of the Canadian officers who attended his class, and published a plethora of articles on foreign affairs issues as well as on Canadian and American military strategy. He also cycled through worst-case scenarios as well as possible ways of solving them, confident that he'd "manage a tight ship in choppy waters." Anchored in his home-office, he exorcised the solider inside, and instead became a one-man think tank (not that the two are mutually exclusive; Bruce just thought he had abandoned his roots). Barnacled, tired, and graying into C-Class, he began to grow restless.

IN 1990, ADEN, HIS ELDEST SON, returned to Michigan. There he enlisted in the army. Bruce agonized over his son's desperate pursuit of his respect and affection, which he noted he had bestowed in perpetuity (and evenly among the two boys, reacting to his father's preferential treatment of one son over the other), despite spending less and less time with them as his marriage disintegrated.

As a boy, Aden had devoured Bruce's highly censored and romanticized stories of war and bravery. He grew to covet his father's experience of war, and like his father, sought a spot at West Point. Despite the cronyism and nepotism enacted on Aden's behalf, he was not admitted on first try due to "interesting findings" on a psychological evaluation. Like his father, he perceived failure to be worse than death. Edmonton, still largely considered a pioneer city, was constricting Aden. He did not want to attend a civilian university, so he packed his bags for the States.

When January came around, Aden—in waiting at Harrison—was selected for early deployment to an American base in Central Europe, with Bush's war in Iraq still pending. January 16 rolled around, and the Gulf War erupted. Bruce received letters and photographs in the mail, detailing mass Iraqi surrenders and boring faux-humanitarian assignments.

After a brief shock and awe campaign, March came. Aden was killed by a road-side mine. Bruce, who had been collaborating with planners at Fort Wainwright, Alaska, heard the news days later. Devastated, he flew to the American base in Turkey where the body was being temporarily held with a host of others.

Prior to collapsing into a five year bout of alcoholism, delusion, and self-abuse, Bruce first obsessed over the details of Aden's death. He analyzed the photos of his son's wrecked Humvee, and concluded that the striations and external damage to the vehicle could neither have been exacted by a mine nor a rocket propelled grenade.

The twists in the metal and the origin of the blast suggested an outer-breach as opposed to an internal explosion or under-breach. Bruce pointed out that the type of explosion was inconsistent with an Iraqi RPG. Furthermore, the residue left by the blasting device was also inconsistent with the enemy weapons supposed responsible in the report on Aden's death.

American weapons manufacturers developed depleted uranium (DU) munitions in the '80s, "whe[n] they realized the density of this nuclear waste had armour-piercing capabilities. Far cheaper than other dense metals such as tungsten, DU had the additional property of igniting on impact…transforming the interior of an enemy tank into a skin-removing fireball of radioactive particles."[71] The DU residue on the Humvee suggested that American or NATO weapons had been used.

Aden's death was allegedly the result of a shelling that was planned and coordinated with one or more insiders. Concluding thusly, Bruce began to draft a list of potential allied suspects who may have been culpable, beginning with local artillery groups and tank commanders.

Investigating Americans during wartime was career suicide. Kalnychuk's zeal in his detective work would have incurred legal ramifications had it not been for a pass granted by Aden's commanding officer, also agitated by the mysterious death. Bruce resigned his temporary Alaska post and returned to Edmonton, short one son.

More and more, Bruce began to lose his grip on reality. As the correlation between despair and drinking became too obvious to

---

[71] Taylor 82.

dismiss, his peers and friends attempted an intervention. The intervention failed horribly, leaving two individuals badly injured— one with a fork-into-eye wound. Bruce's rants and violent outbursts estranged him further from the social circles he had endeavored to excel in. A lieutenant colonel at the time of the intervention, Bruce's actions ensured he'd never be addressed as general by lawful combatants.

Katherine, fearing for her safety and Charlie's, filed for divorce in 1993, citing Bruce's Hemingway-esque descent into madness as "potentially dangerous." She moved out of their Edmonton house coinciding with one of Bruce's visits to a local leftist-fringe radio station, where his sob-story was plugged as an indictment of the American "war machine."

The anarchical show-hosts excavated Bruce's delusions and guilt, and circulated his belief that American Army officials had killed Aden to anger his father to the point where he would re-enlist as a private mercenary and wage a one-man war on foreign aggressors. "A killing machine never dies. They put me on ice in Ontario, and then locked me out when I turned middle age. Why would they kill my son? To wake the sleeping giant?" Paranoia and ego, it seems, served to alienate Kalnychuk and drive him further into depression and isolation. When prompted by the show-hosts to commit the giant to action, Bruce finished with one line and left the studio: "The US Army killed my boy. That's unacceptable."

THE FAMILY WAS GONE. The boys' bedrooms were empty. He wasted forgotten hours etiolating in hazy bars or lost in his mess of a room, eroding as a volitional agent little by little. I am uncertain of whether he composed himself in front of a broken mirror in a moment of strength or weakness or just woke up one morning with a mission instead of a hangover. However he righted himself or whoever gave him the nudge and direction, it was exactly what he needed to make a name for himself.

He quit binge drinking and smoking the ounces of marijuana he was rifling through weekly. Clean and focused, he departed from Edmonton's salt-lined streets and headed for northern British Columbia, where he worked solitary forestry jobs until 1998.

Kalnychuk was rather elusive when it came to talk about Hoff's involvement in his Phoenician rise to a new calling and what he meant to him. It was nothing intimate, he suggested. "Was more of a mentor. Activated me." (Bruce chose not to follow up on either statement, and I failed to pry, thinking nothing of the ambiguity and implications of the term "activ[ation]" at the time.)

Bruce procured for himself the appearances of power and purpose (with Hoff's assistance?). He had a plan or at least referenced one, and people who found themselves waiting in a political vacuum for strength and answers latched on. It's doubtful any of them could discern whether he had been a platoon leader in Vietnam or a drug addict. Regardless, most of his army came looking to be recruited.

Notwithstanding the hordes of willing and pliable denizens at the ready, Bruce needed infrastructure to direct resources and momentum. The opportunity presented itself when a group with a charitable and environmental mandate lost half its executive board. They were meeting a potential donor at the Downtown Visitor Information Centre inside the WTCE when eviscerated by Harvey King's blast.

John Qi, the founder and CFO of the Sprites, first encountered Bruce in 2000, at the Drunken Goat in Dawson City. Amid dizzied Dawsonians gobbling calamari and skewered lamb, Qi overheard fragments of a quintessential Kalnychuk rant about duty and one's obligation to remedy social imperfections. They became acquainted over coffee, and Qi, recognizing Bruce as an intelligent man on the down-and-out, employed him on the spot as manager of the Sprite's soup kitchen.

The sudden deaths of Meghan Redding and Kevin Phan in the 9/11 bombing left more than an emotional scar on the organization: their spots needed to be filled. After observing him do a fantastic job for two months, Qi alerted Bruce to one of the openings. Bruce seized it before Qi could field other applications or appeal to elections.

With his new managerial position and temporary executive position, Bruce had access to a small press, a base of operations, and a direct link to Dawson City's addicts, poor, and hungry—a winning combination of volunteers.

As you could imagine, most Canadians did not initially condemn the actions of the Sprites. The Yukon Sprites were a regionally isolated group (initially a non-profit organization that had made its name operating the longest-running food drive in Dawson City), and their message to the world was localized in terms of action. Coinciding with Bush's first ultimatum, crime (particularly riots and looting) began to decline in western Canada. Despite localized terrorist threats, Canadians were attempting to return to normalcy.

Kalnychuk, Hoff, and an up-and-comer militant, Jason Fresno (later the primary international recruiter for the Sprites), used the ultimatum to focus anti-Americanism in small northwestern towns. The timing was perfect. The threat to Canadian sovereignty seemed to be at its zenith, and people were not thinking rationally. Would-be criminals and rioters finally had a focused group to rally behind instead of wasting time and oxygen yammering at the deaf along frosty Canadian streets.

In the past, Kalnychuk would find himself crushed by the hellish world of other people; however, once he began to articulate direction to his early followers, he realized numbers and bodies as essential to his success. Moreover, he recognized one truth he had perhaps failed to absorb at West Point: *words are power*. In an asymmetrical conflict, words used effectively and in an appropriate tone command attention, hope, obedience, and organized action— even if unrelated to war or fighting. Although versatile in strategy and rudimentary command, he lacked charisma. With his copy of the *Penguin Book of Speeches*, he pieced through the most influential speeches and memorized the most effective lines, patterning great speakers' cadence into his.

Bruce's carousing went unmitigated in the Sprites' kitchen; after all, Qi saw eye to eye with Bruce on most issues. The loss of Meghan and Kevin had left Qi with a chip on his shoulder and an antipathy for all things American. Qi's resources were Kalnychuk's.

-EMBARGOED REPORT-

WHEN WE DISCUSSED this especially dark period of his life, Kalnychuk distanced himself from the man he was—from "the man who'd said those things." (His earliest speeches drew upon an ultra-violent image base and were rather inflammatory with regards to the "American Empire.") He did, however, have a sense of humour when attempting to reconcile his two selves. "That's not me. My story is not over yet." In an effort to elucidate what he meant, he drew a parallel between the 19th Century Canadian rebel Louis Riel and himself.

> Riel went crazy. Saw the face of God. The guilt of war threatened to destroy him. He went down south where he was harboured by Americans until he rejoined reality, and before being quickly snuffed out, he took a stand. Sure, you could remember Riel as a lunatic. Alternatively, you can remember him as a Métis hero.

Dissatisfied with his parallel, I inquired whether he would label Riel a terrorist. He opened his mouth as if to speak; instead, a thick column of white smoke spilled into the ether. "If he was, I suppose we should remember that the United States gave him amnesty. He wasn't a terrorist, though…Problem is, a historian among his enemies lived to tell the story, and of course the guy failed to paint Riel in a positive light."

Despite his best efforts to connect himself with his foster nation's past, Bruce was far more than a shit disturber attempting to rectify a governmental *faux pas*. He was a head-case turned warlord (not that the two are mutually exclusive).

I followed up with a question: "How do you think historians will depict you? How do you want them to depict you?"

"Well that all depends, David. American historians will likely argue that I was a hero-turned-traitor; some veteran who lost the light and killed innocent people. Canadians? It's hard to tell. Eastern Canadians, save for the boys in Halifax and Cape Breton, would likely call me a harbinger of death—the bad apple that managed to delay more than one welfare check. Others? You ask members of the resistance in Okotoks or Airdrie, and they'll tell you: Kalnychuk's the "no" wagging in the wind before the unending imperial 'yes', bold and magnetic, attractive, perfect, malevolent. 'He's our guy, they'd say.'"

"What would you say?" I asked.

"Oh, well I don't care all that much. I suppose I'm not too picky. From what Louis has told me, you're gearing up to be our wordsmith. Throw something together. I'm sure you can find the right words."

♠

GENESIS: STATE TECTONICS

> President Bush will pursue re-election by insisting that his hands
> are clean and that the forces of darkness are behind every door.
> If this blindness and these lies persist, the long-term prospects
> are too desperate to contemplate.[72]

– Tariq Ali

DRAWING A PARALLEL between Russian brutality in
Chechnya and American incivility in Canada, Russian President
Putin argued that the Bush government was isolating itself from the
international community and hypocritically making the same errors
it had criticized Russia for in previous years. Other governments
began to criticize US tact and intention as well.

Chinese President Jiang Zemin, "called the leaders of France and
the UK, both of whom were soon to meet Bush. He told Blair and
Chirac that any military action against terrorism should be based on
'irrefutable evidence and should aim at clear targets so as to avoid
casualties to innocent people.'"[73] China, with oil to gain from a
cooperative and thankful Canada, voiced support for a complete
withdrawal of foreign forces from Canada's western provinces and
territories. Even British Prime Minister Tony Blair, who had
donned the role of American cheerleader after the Quebec bombing
and the subsequent blackouts along the north-eastern seaboard,
agreed with Zemin, distancing himself from the militaristic agenda
for Canada.

Blair had become "very steely, very focused" after the 9/11
WTCE bombing and in response to the terrorist problems plighting
the United States.[74] It was apparent from his reluctance to intervene
in any major way between the American war on terror and the
resultant sporadic beatings Canada was taking, that he perceived
Canada too far gone to purge itself of freedom-hating extremists
and too weak to fight its own battles. "This is not a battle between

---

[72] Ali, Tariq. "Tortured Civilizations: Islam and the West In the Brutal Aftermath of the War on Iraq,
a Genuine Clash of Civilizations Has Emerged. Could It Have Been Avoided?" *The Walrus* Sept. 2004.
The Walrus Magazine. The Walrus Foundation. Web. 10 Apr. 2012.
[73] Bennis 119.
[74] O'Carroll, Lisa. "Tony Blair Knew Immediately That 9/11 Terror Attacks 'changed Everything' |
World News | Guardian.co.uk." *Latest News, Sport and Comment from the Guardian | The Guardian.*

the United States of America and terrorism," Blair remarked, "but between the free and democratic world and terrorism." Given the compelling history of constitutional democracy and freedom in Canada, the 'democratic world' he referenced in his statement was intended to be inclusive, but it served the American mission in another way: that is, dissolving Canadian political agency.

The impetus to stop terror turned rational leaders into crazed, Manichean fanatics. Blair, commenting on the American intervention, noted: "There is no meeting of the minds, no point of understanding with such terror. Just a choice: defeat it or be defeated by it. And defeat it we must." Indirectly and resentfully, Blair endorsed the American go-ahead by his inaction, despite one-and-a-half-million demonstrators in London (the biggest protest in the history of Britain) who, gravitating around the Canadian High Commission in Trafalgar Square, protested the US attacks on Canadian soil as well as the British Government's tacit consent. Despite their numbers and zeal, the protestors in England were not effecting any real change. The Coalition Government had not expected any official support from the English. They were well aware that the umbilical cord had dried up and disintegrated long ago.

Blair's later back-tracking did little to earn Canadian confidence. Blair had said earlier in the conflict that "the United Nations…could help with political legitimization for military action [in] Canada, but its role is not to provide legal authority, for 'states do not need UN approval to act in their own self-defence'."[75] He changed his thinking by the time the Flathead Massacre in southern Alberta made the news (where an American pilot shot up civilians, mistaking birthday-fireworks for surface-to-air missiles), stating: "the United States may want to work through the UN to achieve its anti-terrorism goals in Canada." *Too little too late.*

The British neutrality ended in a Canadian leaning in 2004, when British NATO troops, carrying out a routine exercise at the Canadian Forces Base Suffield in southern Alberta, were accidentally hit by an American cluster-bomb—a regrettable mistake for the USAF and for American-British diplomacy. The event further fractured NATO, and prompted Blair to begin

---

[75] Feith 306.

brainstorming ways to step into the fold without being too heavy-footed. Like Americans at the Canadian border in the Second World War before 1941, Britain would serve as a silent benefactor. (It was no coincidence that Rapier missiles flooded the Canadian black-market soon after the Suffield victims were shipped home.)

CANADA WAS BEING TREATED like a patient, presumed ignorant of the causes for and required means of the procedure. The grown-ups and doctors debated and cited questionable statistics concerning some great tumour—greatly exaggerated in consequence—that required excision. Soon, they would administer the gas, and all means of participation would be rendered null, notwithstanding pacts made in relation to NORTHCOM, NORAD, and NATO. Canada had to resist the gas and spot out new or unexpected allies.

Putin had feigned sympathetic with both the Canadian and American quandaries. He foresaw negative consequences for Russian security and trade if Canada was annexed to the Americans. Taking a nuclear gamble on America shying away from another world war, Putin, alongside the relatively anti-American Jacques Chirac, considered ways of helping Canada maintain its sovereignty, mess with the Americans, or at the very least, to put up a fight.

Christopher Hitchen's sense that Chirac was preoccupied with "extracting advantage and prestige from the difficulties of [his] allies," and that France's inadvertent support of Canada during its American cleansing amounted to the "rat that roared," was right on the money.[76] France's support to Canada was treated with contempt in the States. The extent of the animosity was supercilious: fast food chains and street vendors referred to French fries as "freedom fries," and popular French goods saw boycotts across the nation.

China, alternatively, was still thinking about how, in the event of a fleeting love affair with Canada, it could get its hands on Canadian resources and further drive the wedge between the US and Canada. (Canada's resources were quite desirable. It ranked first globally in potash production; second in uranium; fifth in nickel; fifth in zinc; sixth in diamonds; sixth in oil; seventh in wheat; and eighth in gold.)

---

[76] Hitchens, Christopher. *A Long Short War: the Postponed Liberation of Iraq* (New York: Plume Book, 2003) 65.

The reciprocity lay in China's investment as protection. Chinese workers could be diffused as untouchable sovereign individuals in contested geopolitical regions eyed by the same southern interest groups that lobbied for war. It was understood that killing or detaining Chinese engineers could turn the conflict into a legitimate, multilateral cold war.

The Canadian-Chinese deal also meant that Canadian resources and "international zones" were safeguarded by a bloodless blockade that had the political potential to short the American advance in ways that the UN forces could not. Thanks to the ambiguity of what properly constituted an "international zone," the Canadian government was able to micro-manage key areas (i.e. chokepoints, checkpoints, armouries, weapon-caches, etc.) and prevent foreign tampering, kidnappings, and seizure.

Continental Europe committed to circuitous and innocuous debate over the issue; the Trudeau-Cuba love affair was a distant memory; and other South American countries were content to steer clear of an involvement in what Bruce Kalnychuk referred to as a "first world brawl." Russia, France, and China, were invaluable to Canada as it played its hand.

The game changed when Tom Ridge, on behalf of the Department of Homeland Security, acquired and relayed intelligence concerning heavily armed militant groups amassing in southern Alberta. Recall: post 9/11, 'homeland' extended past international borders to American areas of special interest. Bush decided to exercise his new pre-emptive/preventative war doctrine, irrespective of Canadian condemnations. He believed Americans lives were at stake and that the only way to contain the Canadian threat was to advance until all hostile potential was neutralized.

Condoleezza Rice publically disclosed the American counter-terror strategy in Alberta: a special American force would "eliminate Yukon Sprite caches of chemical/highly-destructive weapons, their means of delivery and associated programs, to prevent [groups within Canada] from breaking out of containment and becoming a more dangerous threat to the United States." Notwithstanding their puzzlement again at the Bush Administration's inconsistency (the US helped arm Canadian law enforcement officials, but wanted to put out all the fires) and their shock at the fallacious nature of Rice's "chemical weapons" accusation, the Coalition Government made the Edmonton City Airport available to the American force.

Alberta Premier Ralph Klein, who "had it up to here with all the goddamn floundering and rhetorical bullshit," greatly favoured the notion of sending an armed welcoming committee to seize US hostages Rohmer-style at the Edmonton airport, and somehow talk the Americans out of a wasteful engagement. Despite his vehemence, the American group was ultimately received peacefully and in good humour.

KLEIN'S NEWFOUND ANTI-AMERICAN disposition put him at odds with the Coalition Government, which was attempting to put a lid on all the controversy spilling out of Alberta. Prime Minister Potter initially begged Klein's silence, and secured it with the promise that, if worse came to worse, Klein could utilize some of his more unsightly connections (i.e. those developed in shady bars), including those of his acquaintances who patched over from the outlaw Grim Reapers Motorcycle Club to the Hell's Angels (HA).

While Klein had often been at odds with the HA during his political career and had attempted to prevent the patch-over of two Alberta bike clubs to the HA in 1997, he was induced by his political gagging to build himself an army, drawing on old foes. He used criminal-forgiveness for a number of individuals detained under Canada's new terrorism-laws to win himself friends in low places. In an interview with the CBC, Klein remarked, with regards to his use of felons as soldiers, "In a country with no death penalty, one does what one can."

Under the impression that Canada's military had to play by the book, Klein gave the Potter government access to mercenaries: guys that that could run guns, unofficial recon, and information, between military and resistance groups, all the while remaining illegitimate. This alliance was tenuous given the divided loyalties of the bikers, who had ties to both Canada and the United States. Klein's Killers, nevertheless, had a strong hand in the 2003 Canadian-sovereignty-movement. (Motorcycles have since become a favourite mode of transport for resistance members and Kalnychuk's Wraiths.) This off-the-books arrangement was cited in American intelligence reports as one of the instances of corruption in the Canadian government that warranted remedy.

THE SMILES AND SUGARY RELATIONS in southern Alberta began to sour the evening Bush went public with a new ultimatum: surrender or pay the price for terrorism. He called for the elimination of those in the "Alberta stronghold," and made a number of references to the binaries and terms outlined in his "Axis of Evil" speech. It was another polarizing accusation to the world. Canada's tumour was showing, and the United States felt obliged to operate. Bush pledged in his speech: the purpose of a campaign in Canada is to "destabilize a localized regime that engages in and supports terrorism...that attacks US Forces almost daily and otherwise threatens vital US interests."[77]

The rhetoric employed in the "Axis of Evil" speech had some American approval for the intervention, although a strong minority opposed the language and direction their government was taking. Bush's enhanced-Texan-drawl alerted Americans to a cowboys-and-Indians set-up as well as to their new *Other* in American politics: Canadians, a group of half-devil, half-child miscreants bent on turning the American dream into a nightmare.

This propaganda aired unexamined in most media-discussions of the war. Networks like *NBC* were busy showing off American hardware developed by their affiliate General Electric (a major military contractor) effecting their "magic" on Canadian vistas.[78] Other powerhouse networks were merely providing myopic detailing on a victimless war.

US Senator Kucinich singled out news agencies complicit in Bush's spin on the war. In his February, 2002 speech, he remarked:

> We licensed a response to those who helped bring the terror of
> the [hydro-bombings]. But We the People and our elected
> representatives must reserve the right to measure the response,
> to proportion the response, to challenge the response, and to
> correct the response...
> We did not authorize the invasion of [Canada].
> We did not authorize the invasion of [the Yukon].
> We did not authorize the invasion of [Alberta].
> We did not authorize the bombing of civilians [in Ontario and
> British Columbia].

---

[77] Feith 52.
[78] Kellner, Douglas. *Media Spectacle and the Crisis of Democracy: Terrorism, War, and Election Battles* (Boulder, CO: Paradigm, 2005) 67.

We did not authorize permanent [Canadian] detainees in Guantanamo Bay.
We did not authorize the withdrawal from the Geneva Convention.
We did not authorize military tribunals suspending due process and habeas corpus.
We did not authorize assassination squads.
We did not authorize the resurrection of COINTELPRO.
We did not authorize the repeal of the Bill of Rights.
We did not authorize the revocation of the Constitution.
We did not authorize national identity cards.
We did not authorize the eye of Big Brother to peer at [our neighbours] from cameras throughout [their] cities.
We did not authorize an eye for an eye. Nor did we ask that the blood of innocent people, who perished senselessly in the [November cold], be avenged with the blood of innocent citizens in [Canada].
We did not authorize the administration to wage war anytime, anywhere, anyhow it pleases.
We did not authorize war without end…
…This has nothing to do with fighting terror. This has everything to do with fuelling a military industrial machine with the treasure of our nation, risking the future of our nation, risking democracy itself with the militarization of thought which follows the militarization of the budget… [79]

Despite the prevalence and authority of this criticism and those like it that were widely circulated, coverage continued to shelter the American leviathan with simple, moralized binaries and warring patterns of pity and fear in an effort to starve anti-war sentiment. In the southwestern United States, recruitment centres were packed with military registrants, especially in poorer neighbourhoods. The media's diligent efforts to prime American paranoia and bloodlust were relatively successful.

WHEN THE CONFLICT reached the apex of the carnage and chaos, the United States reiterated its resolve to preempt Canadian threats to the thirteen bordering states; stop the Canadian government's alleged involvement in Sprite-enabling; cut Canadian

---

[79] Bennis, Phyllis. *Before & After: US Foreign Policy and the War on Terrorism* (New York: Olive Branch, 2003) 222.

links and sponsorship of international terrorism (e.g. eliminate their unofficial link with the Grim Reaper MC and the HA); curb the burgeoning drug trade in western Canada that was funding Sprite operations, and maintain Canada's unity and territorial integrity.

Condoleezza Rice's paper, entitled "Canada: Goals, Objectives, Strategy," concluded with the proposed commitment of the American people to "liberate the Canadian people from tyranny and assist them in restoring their constitutional democracy, with a special emphasis on moderation, pluralism, and transparent government." Condoleezza expressed the need for Canada's constitution, which apparently lacked the aforementioned traits, to be rewritten just as Japan's had been in 1945. Without the ease of total-war that led to Japan's surrender, however, Canada's re-inscription/saving proved extremely difficult.

A US army colonel remarked on the Bush Administration's oversight concerning blow-back and resistance: "It was a big mistake to discount the [Canadian] resistance. If someone invaded Texas, we'd do the same thing."[80] Brigadier General Vincent Brooks notified the world that the American Military would escalate its troop presence from 35,000 to 100,000 on account of the efficacy of reactionary groups who were persistently targeting American security officials and vital infrastructure (e.g. Edmonton's high and low level bridges, the Capilano bridge, and Groat bridge were all severed by reactionaries equipped with industrial-scale cutting-explosives in order to prevent American armour from easily crossing the Saskatchewan River, providing resistance groups the tactical footing they needed to secure the northern quadrant of the city).

Ambushes became prevalent in southern towns and cities, but were inconsistent and unaffiliated, so Bush could not condemn all Canadians outright, though he (without recognizing the irony or historical significance) cited instances of Canadian violations of the Geneva conventions (i.e. the use of Viet-Cong style death traps in British Columbia, Alberta, and the Yukon; mistreatment of prisoners; use of civilian institutions as bases for military operations, etc.).

---

[80] Ali, Tariq, and David Barsamian. *Speaking of Empire and Resistance: Conversations with Tariq Ali* (New York: New, 2005) 70.

-EMBARGOED REPORT-

FOR DETAILS *pertaining to the Canadian engagement of invading American Forces and Major General David Fraser's phenomenal military success at the head of the First Canadian Division, see David's collection of essays and interviews in* Xenophobia *(2005) or Carl Ethelbridge's delicate analysis of the war in* Top Dog *(2004). Ethelbridge's discussion of the Quebec counter-offensive (specifically the Van Doos and Black Watch) is particularly interesting in his detailing of the price of war faced by civilians, using Laval as a case-study. Conversely, in* Xenophobia, *David draws a less analytical event-chain, extrapolating from interviews, journals, video documentation, and the pertinent third-party statistics. For elucidation of the nature of this war and the quality of the Canadian insurgency, also see his paper on the Canadian counter-offensive at Sherbrooke, the Battle of Three Hills, and the hostage situation at St. John's, Newfoundland, printed in the University of Toronto's* 49 Degrees of Hostility *special December 2004 issue.*

♠

THE LAW OF THE YUKON

> But would his legend crack upon the mountains?/There must be
> no retreat: his bugles knew/ Only one call—the summons to
> advance/ Against two fortresses: the mind, the rock.
>
> – E. J. Pratt

> By bowing to the public pressure to be shielded from the
> pictorial representation of death, the media relies upon
> metaphoric and metonymic images which obscure the full nature
> and extent of horror, so that—especially in the social context of
> these horrors being distant and foreign—the photograph cannot
> easily provide the full accounting of horror that might provoke a
> strong reaction.[81]
>
> –David Campbell, "Horrific Blindness"

TWO DAYS AFTER their first extensive interview, Kalnychuk took off for Dawson City to arrange a second deal with the Russians for Stinger missiles, essential to the success of his next trip east. The Russians would not tolerate any unfamiliar faces at the meet (they didn't want to compromise their supposed neutral-standing), so Kalnychuk insisted that David stay behind at one of his better defended bunkers in the interim.

*Classified location, near Mayo, Yukon Territory
December 14, 2005*

I LAY AWAKE for the greater part of the night thinking about how the doctor was vaporized in yesterday's mortar strike. Gotfried, likewise a witness to the violence, was callous after the fact, save for a whisper, revealing his diminished sense of agency: "It's so fucking horrible. Mark another one for Uncle Sam."

The Network would never air footage of such blunt and unwarranted aggression. Airing this variety of abstract violence is not conducive, the argument goes, to producing any positive reactions amongst the viewership, and it alienates sponsors and corporate investors, many of whom share American foreign

---

[81] Campbell, David 'Horrific Blindness: Images of Death in Contemporary Media', Journal for Cultural Research, 8: 1, (2004) 55 — 74.

interests. On the other hand, it produces the secondary traumatic distress order otherwise known as compassion fatigue. Accordingly, if one sees too much killing, then they will ultimately feel powerless to effect change, and would thereafter perceive such violence as commonplace and unpreventable. The major networks find grisly violence counter-effective because it demoralizes anyone who should endorse the action.

A cloud of human cinders is not personable enough to drive viewers to tears or complaint, so it is instead relegated to subversive-shock websites, which capture the unsanitary spillage from engaged reporters and amateurs in the field. My current network appeals to *CNN* as the gold standard for "managed" reporting. As a result, *The Network* is supposed to turn a blind eye to this sort of abstracted violence.

The chairman of *CNN* reminded their guys early in their coverage of the conflict that it is "perverse to focus too much on the casualties or hardship in [Canada]."[82] If a reporter commits the atrocity of revealing that the war is not bloodless, and displays victims or "shots" as individuals (i.e. full-fledged personalities with histories and domestic lives outside the causal net of the broader issue that subsumes them and their particularities), then viewers may begin to wonder what else is lost in a network's ideological sieve.

Spun in the American news, the good doctor, Johannes Ralston, was a "looter killed while thieving." What if the public knew that he was and always had been a good man? Not a thug, but rather a outdoorsman; a father, husband, and musician—prone to story-telling and a loud snorer—who got caught fulfilling his Hippocratic oath during an imperial sweep, keeping secret all his knowledge of the men, women, and children who confided in him with their injuries and death rattles.

Real context is abhorred by viewers and news agencies alike except when it serves to substantiate their benefactor's policy and propaganda. No one wants to be left to clean the shards when a progressive reporter shatters the one-way mirror and fractures the "us" and "them" mentality. The news seems less and less justifiable

---

[82] Blum, William. *Freeing the World to Death: Essays on the American Empire* (Monroe, Me.: Common Courage, 2005) 107.

in its present form when it continues to treat the suffering of the Other as surreal and theatrical, and imperial ambitions as perpetually warranted.

Had I been able to document the incident from beginning to end with my camera and provide a visual account of the doctor's selflessness, the outcome—delivered raw and unapologetic—would stem all possibility of offering a rationale in defence of the blind-firing on the Sprite's encampment near a civilian town.

THE DOCTOR WASN'T ARMED. In fact, he'd never fired a weapon in his life. He was simply foraging for medical supplies in town. Although injured militants needed painkillers, the supplies were primarily for the women and children housed in a logging-camp-cum-infirmary situated ten kilometres outside of the Sprite "Hobbiton" base.

In Mayo, the clinic was fairly empty, and had been since the surge. Ostensibly devoid of purposeful materials, it temporarily housed local scavengers and broken glass. The remaining drugs in the clinic's plywood coffers were, however, the most valuable, missed because of the inexplicably misleading medical names on the bottles and jars. Anything that one could use to get stoned with certainty was gone—taken in the first hours after the initial attack.[83] Left behind in the drawers and the shelves were a number of antiseptic and anti-bacterial ointments, cortisone, insulin, adrenalin, and a handful of painkillers. The clinic's nitrous tanks had all been exhausted or wheeled away, and there was no sign of any easily recognizable feel-good 'scrips.

When the mortars resumed kneading the town, the good doctor had already filled his pockets with life-saving medicine. Arms brimming with bottles, jars, and dressing-rolls, he set a course for the water treatment facility at the northeast corner of town, wherein he would connect with the YS tunnel system. The shells broke the concrete around him, throwing rock and debris into the air. Clouds raised by the explosions swallowed the sky, and churned every-

---

[83] An Apache had raked the main street with explosive rounds, and then fired missiles into the hardware store where Sprites had been said to have gathered. The town was mistakenly designated as a hotspot because a collaborator, unwilling to surrender the location of his mixed camp, misled his interrogator into thinking the town harboured fugitive Sprites. This misinformation was passed on to a nearby Apache gunship, and repeated later for a nearby American mortar team. The speed of the attack and the density of the town meant only one thing: massacre.

which-way. The figure of the doctor vanished in a robustuous body of smoke, unraveling outward and then back into itself. The cloud spilled into the Legion and into the barren Tim Horton's opposite, already lacerated by tongues of flame in the previous onslaught.

Emerging panicked from the expanding flow of particulate, bloody but agential-still, he regained his momentum and pressed forward through the car cemetery. Nearly past the lights in front of the cinema, Ralston tripped. Before the consequence of his descent became fully apparent to him, he dematerialized before my eyes in a snap—in some cruel coincidence of thunder and flash. The red mist quickly dissolved into the tawny cloud.

The suddenness of his departure and the resultant sense of immateriality deferred his shock to me: his surrogate. Unable to be witness to the nature of his own abrupt passing, annexed to some dislocated existence, I inherited his fear. Only right, it seems, for the voyeur—who safely watched a good man turned into confetti through binoculars from a safe distance—to be burdened with the cynicism rejected by one too brave to give it any credence.

Time, something I felt I had much more of all of a sudden, became, simultaneously, a curse and a gift. His fear was mine to bear and the lesson (if there was one) was mine to pass on. A good man died. A simpleton survives to tell you that more good men will die in the event the imperial thrust continues its trajectory, seemingly indifferent to civilian/combatant distinctions.

We reached Hobbiton after nightfall. Since a "no lights" order had been given, there were no campfires or incandescent smiles to greet us or take our minds off of the horror we'd witnessed earlier. I resigned to my quarters and tried to sleep.

HOURS PASSED where I, alone, was witness to an inner chorus of primal screams, always panicked: "I need more time!" "Save me!" "I don't want to die!" My cot dripped sweat as I feverishly tried to calm myself with rationalizations and montheistic appeals to universal justice and Providence. I sensed that I was going mad trying to secure some sort of inner-silence.

Frustrated with overlapping thoughts of death in the dark, I decided upon a more constructive activity, and determined to go out for a smoke. Though my eyes were open, I was still in Erebus. Confined to quarters, I had to cry out, locate and bang on my door like a dog desperate to be walked.

Still clouded by sleep, my temporary military attaché, Sergeant Tristan Foller, let me out, into the muddy foyer, and begrudgingly led the way to the bunker door. "You know you can piss in your sink, right? There's really no need to go outside, unless you're claustrophobic," said Foller.

Claustrophobic seemed less cowardly and more irrational than the truth. "Oh yeah. It's pretty cramped."

He fiddled with the locking mechanism. "You wouldn't be the first to choke on the darkness." Foller, had found his way to the Yukon Sprites in early 2002, after hearing that members of his regiment were being arrested en masse.

When he pried the iron open, the smell of smoke flooded the stairwell. Once the cloud dissipated, Foller and I emerged from Kalnychuk's Hobbiton into morning half-light. We were met by laughter and the promise of new dawn. The sun was about to break its horizontal seal.

The cigarette seemed less important as I surrendered myself to the landscape. The day had advanced its emissaries. Faint bands of red and neon orange chased the turquoise up to the zenith, where the colour matured to a navy blue. In the distance, batteries were discharging morning glory, effectively forwarding the question, "Had enough?" The rejoinder was constituted by the *pkt-pkt-pkt* of AK47s and small arms fire. This indefatigable conversation resounded through the southern forest, stirring winged-life in the slanted canopies.

Glimpsing a heavily armed rabble laughing in unison around a bonfire as if they were one refulgent, organic composite, I headed over in search of a cigarette. (Someone in the barracks had taken both my Jackson's and my Stripes, and I would not dare accuse anyone lest I find out it was the poor doctor who had taken my smokes, thus sullying my tidy idealization.)

The majority of the cigs on the base were hand-rolled, biked straight from the Indian reservation. Although easily purchased or swapped for city-affectations, I always felt swindled afterwards. They offended the palate and left a residue comparable to battery acid on my tongue. Not everyone was so critical, however; Foller suggested that the men were more covetous of a pack of cigarettes than sexual partners or toilet paper.

The fire had outgrown its rudimentary confines. "Sarge, don't you think that your boys' fire may attract some unwanted attention?"

Foller, too, was fixated on the fire. "Hum?"

I pointed to the inferno.

"The boys are wearing the new CadPat. The Amies can send ten thousand drones over our heads and they won't pick up a single signature." (This turned out to be a fatal misconception. CadPat reduced a soldier's visibility to night-vision, not infrared.) Satisfied with his vindication, the pyre once again seized his attention. "Besides," he said, his back to me, "the sun's just about up and over. Let the boys enjoy their moment of warmth and peace."

"And the smoke?" I inquired, the good doctor's fate pressing on me.

Foller turned to me, slightly inflamed by my persistence. "Hear that?" It sounded like a construction crew driving piles. "That's our M777 shelling Coalition armour, airfields, and artillery. If it's still there—and trust me, that's the biggest target out here—then you can defer your fear of impending doom." Taking my silence to mean dissent, he continued: "Furthermore, we have a division of men in full camouflage, armed to the teeth with TOW and Rapier missiles, assembled for a week's scrum. There'll be no planes flying overhead unless every last one of those men is dead, and the chance of that happening is *highly* unlikely. The stealth bombers, on the other hand, nick us here and there during the night, but those shades are mainly targeting burnt-out cars and vacated bunkers. Doing a poor job, unless they are intentionally spending millions simply to keep us awake at night. All those toys and no brains! Ha!"

He handed me a lit cigarette, and I encouraged him to continue with an embellished nod.

"The Snowmen and the Wraiths leave only one treachery for us to worry about: those goddamned UAVs. Can you fucking believe those things?"

"I saw a few above Jasper, and more around Whitehorse."

"Doesn't surprise me. They have those fucking things everywhere."

"All the more reason to put out the fire." He completely dismissed my comment.

"Now, a Tomahawk is a killer, a real hunter. Its job is to search and destroy. The drones have Hellfire missiles. They're no fun. But the fly in my ointment has to be those toy planes. They call them Pioneers, but they're nothing but goddamn mosquitoes. Buzz around and make our positions. Buzz, buzz, buzz. Toy planes under Amie's employ, and they're driving us up the creek."

"Precisely my point! What if they spot the fire? A pillar of smoke's bound to look more suspicious than a burnt-out car."

"Danson, this whole fucking country looks suspicious. Your threatening bonfire over there'll look like just another successful firing-mission executed and forgotten by the Amie war machine. Who knows? Maybe one of the airstrikes started a brush fire. Shit happens. They can't justify nuking every smoldering heap, right?" He took a long draw from his cigarette and flicked it toward the fire. "Sometimes you have to catch their attention too. You know, go out of your way to rouse suspicion. It can be advantageous, trust me."

"Kalnychuk was going on about victory through defeat... Is he sending out kamikazes?"

"No. Not kamikazes, but we'll send a squad or two to kick the hornets' nest, or draw straws for raiding parties to throw them off the scent. It's enough to give our boys a chance to move their artillery and guns around without worrying about being under the undivided attention of the warring eye. This is a psychological war now. If they can't sleep, then we're fighting a sloppy and exhausted first world army. It's a leg up."

"Will you continue your raids through the winter? What do you think about the prospect of losing connection to your supply lines?"

"You know what I think? I think you think too much. Lighten up, David."

He was a confident officer, and acted the part. When his CO was hanged with defectors from the Pats, Foller picked up the slack.

"Remember: economy of effort, David. That's what I tell my boys. Can you fix the problem? If you can't, solve another. If you can't fix that one, have a beer and say a prayer. You have to be a team player or you're out." Foller came across as sincere and reassuring, which meant one of two things: he was a madman, fearless and over-confident; or conversely, he was a liar—the kind of propagandist the doomed crave when their backs are against the wall. In either case, he was a leader to the core. Foller patted me on the shoulder, shivered out of his morning stupor, and disappeared into the huddle in search of another cigarette.

I STOOD FOR A WHILE where Foller left me, perseverating on the fire, watching the cinders disappear against the corona of the rising sun. Men came and went, disappearing over the hill or back into the bunker, emerging from the woods dressed in earthly colours like ents, always maintaining a full cast around me. The fireside was full of commotion and laughter. All warmed up, I pressed my way further into the circle. "What's so funny?" They were reluctant at first, but the most visibly affected grabbed me gently by the arm and sat me down.

"It's always the reporter who needs to ask what's funny!" He quipped.

As soon as his smile peaked, the laughing subsided and a forest of weary eyes trained-in on me, their detached observer. They were clearly interested in my fleeting encounter with *their story*. While the bard, identified by the myriad waiting eyes, wet his lips and cleared his throat, the rest of the good humour dissolved into the smoke and sparks, likewise fading.

"You probably think we're all barbarians. Fighting an endless war of attrition. Hurting innocents haphazardly and branding ourselves machismo. These men and I...we try to be level headed individuals. We just want to live normal lives. Normal is out the window, though. You can't have normal if you have to ID yourself to foreign nationals and wait in line just to see your nephew play ball. Normal is not having your job and resources squandered by foreigners. Normal is not getting roughed up because you were out past seven. We've been stripped of our sovereignty and our dignity. You can't beat and starve a dog and expect it to remain docile, can you? No! Its stomach will flip or the dog will turn." He began weaving in other analogies. "Sure, we could surrender, but why fold your hand before the river-card's been turned? It seems we're all-in."

"Isn't that premature? Do you even know your opponent's hand? How he might be willing to play it?"

"We have seen..." he made sure to speak inclusively since everyone had their ears glued to our conversation, "Forget it. Honestly, poker is not my game, but I know Westerns, and I know that in Westerns, if the hero's been cheated a hand and doesn't want to be cheated again or perpetually thereon in, he shoots the fucker."

"And there's been plenty of shooting."

"Right." He stared expressionless at my ID-badge. "Oh!" he exclaimed, sentience re-entering his visage and animating his eyebrows. "How rude of me; my name is Vargas." He offered me his hand, swaddled with red-tinged bandages, and gripped mine. "I am supposed to be the chaplain on site; however, I've grown to hate so much and so many people that professing love, truth, and redemption has begun to sting my lips. It's a pleasure to meet you."

"Likewise."

"You are Canadian?"

"No," I replied.

"American?" he inquired, voice wavering, oily face alight with the fire and agitation.

"Eh Vargas, don't go spilling the beans to some fucking Yank."

"I'm actually Maltese. Grew up in a town called Had-Dingli," I hastily added.

"I don't know where that is."

"The town?"

"No, the country."

"South of Sicily and west of Alexandria."

"So, near Italy?"

"Yeah. Not much different from these hills."

"Really?"

"No, of course not. It's extremely different. Usually mild." My breath, visible against the fire and morning blue, chased out my comparison. "There, you'd never see this kind of cold." Vargas laughed away my smarm.

"What do you get out of this, reporter?" barked one of the men, intently watching me from behind a cigarette dripping amber.

"Don't mind the boys." Vargas turned to my heckler. "Andrew, you're not on a raid right now because, according to what you've told us, you've gone deaf. Do us all a favour and act the fucking part."

The man identified as Andrew swatted away the pithy mashing of lips and then feigned the onset of sleep.

"Do you know the real story of Romulus and Remus?" asked Vargas. "Eh? Have you heard it?"

I had, in fact—one too many times. "Depends on whether Remus dies in your story." Vargas smiled.

IN THEIR SEARCH of easy ways of allegorizing a conflict irreducible to simplistic metaphors, the primary news channels affixed themselves to Roman imagery and mythology to break down the necessity of the occupation. Accordingly, Romulus and Remus were to represent or signify the mighty US and an affected Canada.

The Cain and Abel story resonated poorly with American audiences, for they could not reconcile themselves with the fact that Americans were killing Canadian innocents without just cause, so Romulus and Remus stuck. Since authority was not given to any particular strain of the myth, both Americans and Canadians were free to modify it, accentuating either the grandeur and civility or Rome or conversely, deriding Rome as a war-mongering, uncontained threat, doomed to implode. (The US-as-imperial-Rome analogy sometimes found interesting parallels. For instance, one commentator compared the initial US defeat in the Okanagan Valley, British Columbia, to the Battle of Teutoburg Forest, where Germanic tribal-fighters defeated Quinctilius Varus' Roman legions in densely forested, swampy terrain.) In contrast to the Roman giant, Remus seemed a suiting symbol for Canada: a multilateral pacifist, living past Hadrian's Wall, doing its own thing, its own way. In the Sprite tradition, Remus supplants Romulus and exacts brutal revenge on his followers.

WITH THESE TWO countries intertwined in this ugly, violent confrontation, the ratio of influence is no longer ten to one, US to Canada. The occupier-occupied relationship has had serious ramifications for both groups. Bush assumed that he could contain the moral and psychological decay symptomatic of an unjust war. Despite the concrete road blocks, razor wire, and machine guns nests erected all over Canada, the sickness continues to spread south like a cancer.

In his study of (resistance to) the American empire, Tariq Ali noted the impact of occupation on an empire. By crossing the Canadian border, the United States provided a unifying factor for previously partitioned groups as well as a shared objective. The longer they remain, the stronger the resistance grows. Tariq argues:

> But when you occupy those countries with your own troops, all that technology is irrelevant: you have to confront a sullen and embittered population, which is what American soldiers are now

fighting. Then cracks begin to appear in the empire that once seemed invincible. You begin to realize that when it comes to people, you aren't that strong after all, because they refuse to accept what you're imposing on them. This is how resistance begins, and this resistance shapes the consciousness of the occupied and that of the occupiers and their countrymen as well. Occupying empires perpetually provoke resistance, and eventually this resistance has an impact inside the empire itself.[84]

When a misguided and misled government begins to make mistakes on behalf of a self-professed free people, the leviathan wakes up from its coma with a moral conscience and rechecks its complicity in reckless aggression. One potential consequence is positive change from within the empire. The price of a long, violent occupation has been clear over the past several years in the deflation of morale and support (both individual and economic), evidenced by the mass troop defections from the US army in 2004, and by the debilitating economic recession in the US.

If the Yukon Sprites cannot push the US out of the northwest and the rest of Canada, then the American people will. The costliness of the war (in terms of lives, bombs, cruise missiles, fuel, aid, food, etc.) is a discouraging factor, and has not taken register with the masses, largely because it is a topic circumnavigated in the news. Broken records (i.e. Ron Paul) have underlined how Americans permitted policy to be skewed by fear and anger and have been frequently ignored. I am curious what will happen once the reaction hits critical mass. Might it simply be a matter of force pairs on a global-stage? Wherefore every action, there is an equal and opposite reaction?

For the Sprites and for most Canadians, their losses are beyond quantification. The men around the fire, like their tongue-in-cheek, mythic progenitor Remus, were borderline feral. In these mountain prisons, they are cut off from the civility we take for granted. The constant threat of death creates an air of paranoia and sobriety, despite the fact that the air is also often heavy with the acrid aroma of marijuana (aka "Green Legend"), which the Sprites sell to Americans via cross-border tunnel systems to finance their northern operations. In coping with this trauma, many of the soldiers have

---

[84] Tariq Ali.

resorted to amphetamine addiction, others to faith, and the good majority to a cavalier disregard for life and living.

♠ *Classified location, near Mayo, Yukon Territory*
December 23, 2005

AT THE NEW OLD CROW compound, I watched three men take their chances with their golem—an angry grizzly—while another man mounted on a horse calmly covered their lunges with a rifle. The 275 kg bear would normally have been hibernating, but life in the Yukon was deregulated for man and beast alike. Artillery and airstrikes messed up the bears' instinctive cycles, sending many of them venturing about.

The Sprites' "bear-wrestling" forced me to recognize the intensifying apathy for life, self, and others, manifest in the mountain camps. This reduction to primal-base may be isolated to these resistive enclaves of Canadians because, unlike their imperial counterparts, the men in the camps possess only their cigarettes, ammo, and dried meats. With nothing to lose, everything to gain, and little or no religious drive, the Sprites and other rebel factions constitute a frightening nihilistic force, making rural Canada a dangerous place.

The Sprites were not salaried in any traditional sense, but Kalnychuk made an effort to address their principle needs and concerns. He made sure that every man had ammo, so that all of his soldiers would be confident in their ability to effect change. He ensured that all of his men could eat and wash, so that they'd have a reward for returning to base alive. He made an effort to know each of their names, so that they'd aspire to make their monikers memorable. (Vargas suggested, "If the chief doesn't know your name, you're not trying hard enough.") Finally, Kalnychuk consistently reminded his men of what they'd lost as a result of the American invasion. Besides the oath, essential to becoming a Sprite, and his effective leadership, Kalynchuk's men fell in line because nobody else would take them alive.

Machiavelli's particular theories of command were moot for Bruce. He realized that there was no fear left for him to manipulate. Those remaining fighters had all crossed the Rubicon *for him*. There was no going back, not that they'd have anything left to return to.

Legally they were dead to the world. Mahmoud, back at the 173rd base in Jasper, suggested that if a Sprite surrendered or was captured by Coalition Forces, survival would be an unlikely outcome. If one was somehow captured alive, he would never see freedom. Ironically, the "give me liberty or give me death" crowd in the US has been unable to comprehend what many in the press have referred to as a "suicidal garrison mentality."

Vargas had personally buried seventy-two Sprites and civilians since the war began. Johannes was number seventy-three. Before his transfer west in May, Vargas had been positioned near Mayo. There he helped manage a field hospital and a graveyard at a classified location off of the McQuesten River. As doctor and chaplain, he took on the role of saviour. The odds weren't in his favour:

> The coffins were often double-packed due to overcrowding. Because we can only dig so deep in certain spots because of the rock and permafrost, and depending on when we're burying them, we often have to double-stuff. Feels like a meat packing plant. You talk to these boys, eat with them, swap stories, see pictures of their kids, and then you end up going through the motions, thumbing through your Catechism with their guts hanging out all over the place and then, an hour's passed and you're slinging them into the ground. A conveyor belt could do my job better. After the first five, ten or twenty, the words just began to grind against each other. Got to oil the machine [he brandished a mickey and took a swig]. I've become an actor. If I make-believe, the kid whose light is fading before me can take comfort in the potential of something better. I have to play preacher and bang my book or these kids die with nothing. It's fucking maddening.

Vargas conducted the service for the doctor's burial (purely symbolic for the lack of a body). After laying a dozen or so wooly louseworts from Keno Hill on the mound, he exclaimed: "Let us rejoice! He is in a better place, for he is no longer in hell."

♠ *Fort Ross River, Yukon Territory*
January 1–2, 2006

I CELEBRATED the New Year with Bruce and his Wraiths in Fort Ross River. The particular group of Wraiths boarding with us were a commando unit comprised of defectors from the Royal Canadian Regiment; the 48th, Seaforth and Calgary Highlanders; the Red Devils; the Queens Own Rifles; guys from the 62 Field Artillery Regiment; the Queen's York Rangers; the B.C. Dragoons; the First Canadian Ranger Patrol Group, and the Princess Patricia's, all of whom had been handpicked by Kalnychuk to wage psychological warfare on American troops.

In an ambush on an American supply-convoy, the Wraiths had procured champagne, some brie, bacon, fish, and coffee beans. The civilian prisoners were permitted to walk back home through the storm, while the soldiers accompanying them were killed in a short, defensive firefight. No longer deluded by my belief in a distinction between the sort of reporting I had embarked upon and thano-tourism—or the ability to remain objective for that matter—I embraced my new role as an engaged documentarian. Thus, I had no issue wolfing down tesra browned in bacon grease or gorging on a platter of stinky cheese with the Sprites. *A guy's got to eat.*

The minus-fifty-seven-degree chill and the accompanying blizzard meant we could hibernate without fearing any heavy confrontation. Thanks to the food reserves, no one was required to hunt for caribou and moose or trap marmots, and no one was obligated to head out to fight, at least not right away. The Sprites were more than happy to have the Americans freeze without action for a day. However, Kalnychuk knew that a comfortable army was an army at risk, so he told his Wraiths to prepare to head out January 2. Their mission: disrupt the short repose with more psychological warfare.

With the intent of demoralizing and exhausting US Forces, Kalnychuk's special team had committed to a series of loud assassinations. After eliminating a given target, they would goad opposing forces into following them through a booby-trapped and mined wild (inspired by the old Chinese stratagem: *disturb the water to catch the fish*). The mines were not in keeping with Canada's promises at the UN, although Bruce assured me that the Hague's inability to provide more than hollow gestures and scrutiny from the sidelines undercut their expectations, and further, there were no limits to what the resistance and the Sprites were willing and able to do (hence the punji sticks that almost annihilated me en route to meet Kalnychuk). I pointed out to him that it didn't matter, given he was a terrorist already, and that's a category one can't simply good-will himself out of.

While the Sprites were well-equipped and experienced to handle the extreme cold and unpredictable precipitation, support- and supply-lines were negatively affected, creating an obvious disadvantage. Replacements and supplies reached US troops from Fairbanks, Alaska, daily, whereas the Sprites depended primarily upon the reserves stockpiled during the Chretien's Manoeuvre. Road blocks prevented humanitarian missions from heading north from Dawson City, so Kalnychuk's Northern Alliance had to depend on other rebel factions (those who didn't have any direct YS affiliations apart from resource exchange, including members of the Grim Reaper MC) for mail and food drops. These drops were carefully observed by American reconnaissance flights, though the runners were usually successful in disappearing, honouring the secrecy of troop positions and Sprite encampments. This vanishing act was enabled by the tunnel systems carved through the cordillera. When one tunnel was compromised, there was always one or two more that led to safe, alternate openings. This plexus, often referred to as the "catacombs," resembled the work of termites on a dying tree. There were, however, serious hiccups in access and supply.

Two Canadian groups were compromised when one runner, working under the assumption that American equipment malfunctioned during the Aurora Borealis, traveled top-side from Old Crow to their base. The USAF tracked the individual's movement via an UAV, and an Alaska-based Tomahawk found the base, reducing it and all inside to ash and rubble.

Incorrectly assuming that John Qi—a prominent figure in the resistance movement—had been rendered smoldered remains by the tactical strike, Bush announced: "the Jack of Spades has been eliminated, and the deck is, once again, lighter." (Each key Sprite member or facilitator had a correspondent card given to American troops so that they could identify crucial kills or captures.) John Qi narrowly escaped the attack, only to be captured two months later after his convoy was destroyed by Hellfire missiles fired from a Predator drone. With New Year behind them, the Wraiths lived with the expectation that their next respite would be accompanied with a card-draw.

THE SPRITES' twenty-three-millimeter automatic anti-aircraft cannons rattled off flak into the air in a futile act of defiance against the drones and low-flying bombers raking suspicious structures wedged in the Yukon's nooks and crannies. The Sprites and I had taken refuge in an old mining camp, hidden in a snowy cove populated with spruce, fir, and aspen. In the camp, the far-off thunder was overcome by the murmur and excitement of a poker game, and somewhere nearby a kettle whistled.

The weight of my Kevlar jacket and the four lagers I had with dinner did a fine job of coaxing me into a sleepy stupor. I knew that I'd succumb and that there wouldn't be much of a delay, especially since I'd grown accustomed to the *pkt-pkt-pkt* of assault rifles and the quake made by exploratory artillery shells.

Kalnychuk, on the other hand, stayed up all night writing grandiose battle schemes with a Kalashnikov on his lap. When daylight broke, he walked around, energizing his boys with one of his many party lines about sacrifice or victory through defeat, always with the reminder that: "the US didn't pull out of Mogadishu because of a high-tech armoured threat."

-EMBARGOED REPORT-

DAVID ASKED ME *to stricken components of this segment to avoid complicating his case with ambiguous details that could potentially lead to a graver prison sentencing.*

Kalnychuk, unable to reach one of his chief strategists in Ontario by satellite-phone or email, planned to meet him in person. David elected to join him on his trip east. En route across the vast Canadian expanse to Toronto, their convoy was ambushed by US Marines. Since the ground-orders for American troops when confronting Sprites was to kill everything and anything that moved, David was forced to bear arms to defend his life. This involved blind-firing around a corner to create a window of opportunity for a lengthy escape to the first safe-house off their east route.

In transit
January 23, 2006

BRUCE AND I, with survivors from the ambush, met a Sprite contact in Winnipeg who took us to a resistance camp in Sault Ste Marie. After recharging our batteries and rearming, rebels from the camp took us south in separate civilian vehicles.

The ride would have been far more pleasant had we not been required to lie perfectly still under a false second-floor for hours and hours. I was initially surprised that they felt the need to conceal a reporter, but our Charon revealed that *The Network* let inquiring US Forces in on the secret that I had potentially tracked down the Green Legend. If I was identified, they'd have some sense of where to start looking because there's no specific legal protection granted to wartime journalists who wished to keep their sources confidential. Getting caught would mean a lost opportunity to learn more about Kalnychuk. I realized that where embedded journalism is concerned, journalist-source anonymity means erasure—ceasing to exist autonomously as whoever you were before. You become some benign growth on an interesting personality.

When we arrived at the first of several safe-houses near Toronto (we parked a block away), we found a RCMP horse tied to a fire hydrant, neighing and kicking wildly. Behind the crazed horse: a bullet riddled façade. We crept past the bestial excitement, circumnavigated the bungalow, and found the backdoor. The doorknob had been smashed off, and the door was ajar. Kalnychuk instructed Jason (his enforcer) to take point and lead us inside.

The walls were rife with gashes and bullet perforations, which offered tiny glimpses into the adjacent rooms. Whoever's story had been written along the main hallway was long gone, leaving behind only dusty outlines and empty frames. Jason pressed down the hall with the butt of his gun buried in his gut, taut at the ready. He turned into the kitchen and stopped. The aggression written into his posture left his body in a dispirited sigh.

"Jason, what is it?" inquired Kalnychuk, drawing his pistol.

"Boss, it's...no good. It's no good." Kalnychuk cautiously approached Jason, and peered over his shoulder."

"Oh God! No, no." Kalnychuk threw Jason aside, and disappeared around the corner. I could hear Bruce mumbling incoherently. Curious, I inched closer. As I approached Jason, recomposed but still stunned and standing at the threshold, I was hit by a repellant and familiar smell.

The crimson streak indicated she had been dragged across the tile and left there, a fetid worm pie in dark-mirror pools. Choking on the stench of the decomposing blonde, I knew—by his expression and shortened list of friends—that Kalnychuk's days were numbered and that I was in over my head.

Kalnychuk, misty-eyed, knelt beside the corpse, and rocked back and forth haplessly. His arms were as limp as the body that lay before him. As he repeated the motion with dirty fingers turned up, the metal of his gun growled against the linoleum. "Fuck!" he erupted. He shook his gun, and then whipped it into the nearby china cabinet. "How did they find you?" he sobbed. He ran a finger through her hair. This was the first time I'd encountered the real Kalnychuk. Before, he was a mirage of some indestructible ideal. He'd outlived his legend. Now, he was just a man.

Bruce placed one hand on her stomach and the other on her shoulder, and slowly turned her over. I angled to get a good look at her face. She had been pretty, at least before the maggots found her. She was middle-aged, freckled, and marked by a large mole on her cheek. The face stopped turning. Kalnychuk froze. He held her like she was about to break, about to shatter.

"Okay, David. I'm going to need you to—" A sharp click sounded, overriding his request. "Oh, fucking hell."

(I later found out that the body had been booby trapped. A grenade had been rigged so that if someone moved the body, a string nailed to the floor would pull the striker lever [unsecured by a pin] off the grenade, fitted in the deceased's shirt pocket.)

Registering the click of the lever as a good time to run, Kalnychuk piled over and threw the two of us into the adjacent hallway. An evanescent cloud of drywall and smoke enveloped our motionless bodies while shrapnel and shreds of flesh volleyed towards us. I tried to open my eyes, but it was all darkness...Something was wrong.

When I regained consciousness, I was squirming about involuntarily. All my thoughts were clouded by mortal panic. The concern in Kalnychuk's voice nearly sent me into convulsions: "Oh holy fuck. Those goddamn bastards! It's okay Dave. We're going to find you some help. Jason! Jason! Get the doc on the satellite phone, double-time. Hey David, can you hear me?" I could barely make out his voice amid the sounds of glass shattering and the hail-like raking of bullets against the outer walls. The explosion had ruptured my right eardrum (it had been facing the blast), so a painful ringing made it especially difficult to distinguish voices from the violent ambience.

There was something soothing about his voice, however; something reductively paternal. "David? Hey Danson I'm talking to you!" When he gripped my hand I knew something was seriously wrong.

Is there something wrong with my face? I thought. Oh god, something hurts terribly. How horrible would it have been to end up nutrients in a shallow grave somewhere in Ontario, mouth choked with worms, all for nothing! *Audrey had been right all along.*

Signals were going out to my fingers and legs, and pinging back. I ran my tongue along my gums to ensure I hadn't fallen prey to the same horror suffered by Dalton Trumbo's pitiful war victim. "Sit up. There you go." He leaned me against a wall. Once Kalnychuk elevated me, warm fluid began to drip down over my cheek. It was not accompanied by the stinging pleasure of tears. Instead, a palpable sense of horror lingered behind the flow. The topography of my visage had been altered. The stream was interrupted by divots on its way to my chin. Phrases, poetry, and promises long unrecalled came back to me: he "will swallow up death in victory...and wipe away tears from off faces."

I raised my fingers to my cheek to inspect the damage. Kalnychuk grabbed my wrist. "Don't touch it, Dave. Just hold on buddy." Wood splintered around us, tailed by the crunch of some far off gun. "Sniper! It's a fucking ambush. Jason! Get the fuck in here and give me a hand. Out the back! Out the back! Corporal!"

"Yes sir," said another man whose face I could not make out.

"Quit pussy footing, and give me some fucking cover fire." Hot shell-casings trickled down over me as the Sprites snapped a retort. "Throw him in the chair. There. Grab it." I was elevated above the heads of Kalnychuk and his right hand man, Jason, and escorted out of the blood-soaked kitchen, a blind king. After a brief sprint, they dropped the chair, draped me over the horse's back, freed it, and then ran alongside it towards the car, hell hot on their heels.

SHRAPNEL FROM THE GRENADE had found me on my cartwheel into the hall, resulting in a "full-thickness entry wound" and "corneal abrasion." Other pieces had also diced Kalnychuk's neck and forearms, but not to the extent or severity of my injuries.

Metal pellets, bone fragments, and scrap, were imbedded in my cheek as a result of the explosion. In total, fifteen fragments were extracted from my cheek, jaw-bone, and eye, by Kalnychuk's physician, who guaranteed me my HMO wouldn't come close to covering the damages.

Since neither Bruce nor the other members of his team could afford exposure, they decided to avoid taking me to a real hospital altogether. Instead, I received my reconstructive eye surgery in a dank basement cellar in Vaughan, north of Toronto. Kalnychuk suggested, while helping me down into a leaky basement that made his place in Mayo look like Shangri-La, that, "Where emergency eye surgeries are concerned, one cannot get stuck on appearances."

Covered in my own blood and apparently speaking only in Maltese, they decided I was too far gone to have a say. *Call it an occupational hazard.* Lacking proper anesthetics, the "surgeon" administered heroine for my pain, which had crept in after the shock from the object-penetration, just as the concussion began to wane. I've been told that if I received professional treatment sooner, I could have saved up to fifty percent of vision in my right eye. With less than ten percent vision in the right eye post-op, half my world is shadow, but then again, wasn't it before?

WHEN I EMERGED from my heroin-induced coma, the first thing I saw was my dad. His silhouette hung on the wall behind a dark figure revealed in fragments by the occasional flick of a lighter. After an hour or so of moaning and excruciatingly painful spasms—while having my eye dabbed with Polysporin—I recognized that the Maltese patriarch cast against the wall was merely a phantasm, and again, I was alone.

I slipped in and out of consciousness for a duration of what felt like days (though I am told it was only hours), waking up finally with enough sense to recognize I was no longer alone in the cellar. Kalnychuk, looming over me, fed his pipe with a jet lighter. He looked through me with glassy eyes and exhaled.

"We found one of the shooters—loose ends in a basement somewhere by now, after what he did to you. Hell, my arm's not looking too good either. He didn't say much, the shooter." He puffed and exhaled through his nose. "Everyone talks eventually. A man's courage is only as good as the body parts he has left. Still, I'm surprised. He didn't say much. Just enough to establish that he's part of that rapid assault group out of Fort Drum. Those boys aren't paratroopers and they're sure as hell not Marines. They're here to play the war our way: a decisive guerrilla war." He snuffed his pipe on the bedside table, and sprung to his feet. "Now, they were one step ahead of us back there, which means one of two things: our friends are selling us up the river or I have become too predictable." Kalnychuk stabbed the drapes drawn closed with bony fingers, releasing an intense golden belt of light. Someone had covered the windows, either to hide the wretch inside or to conceal a worse reality outside. It was sometime in the afternoon, and we were in a half-buried, unfinished basement. "Goddamn-it...That's not something for you to worry about. This is not your war, after all. It's going to be okay, son."

"My ear—" The pain was unbearable. He injected something into my IV.

"God, is that a bubble?" I had no energy to resist whatever fateful concoction was en route to my heart.

He laughed. "Kill my favourite reporter? What am I? Some kind of monster?" He chortled and returned to his seat. "The doc can't do anything about your ear right now, but we'll find you someone with a knack for it once we get to Toronto. Sound good? Oh, sorry. Worst case scenario...you'll have to wear a hearing aid."

"What!?"

"Relax... Nobody has anything good to say anyways. You'll be fine, you'll see."

"And you?" I slurred, drool chasing out each syllable. "Why don't you just get the fuck out of here? Next time you meet your Russian pals, just take a ride home with them. Disappear."

"No, no, no. David, this is home. Every day you spend in any one particular place is the equivalent to drops of hemlock into your cup. You can't just walk away when the cup's full. Besides, I'm beginning to develop a thirst."

♠

GENESIS: A CALEDONIAN RESPONSE

> It always surprises and grieves us to learn that other countries
> are sometimes incapable of appreciating the true beauty of the
> world system Americans are trying to build.[85]
>
> —Walter Russell Mead

THE RULES OF ENGAGEMENT and detention were
relatively clear when the US was only fighting the Yukon Sprites
and Canadian resistance groups; however, by late 2002, the United
States was effectively and simultaneously fighting a war with both
unofficial and official Canadian Forces (without any formal
declarations), and was consequently party to the Geneva
Conventions invoked in an earlier address by Bush.[86]

Ambiguity was introduced into the detention and treatment of
Canadian prisoners, particularly those with connections to the
Sprites, on account of the argument voiced from Washington that,
"Canada is a [compromised] state, not a sovereign country.[87] The
former Canadian government, working with the Sprites, should be
deemed an armed gang engaged in a civil war, and not a proper
government."[88] Reacting to this stance, Canada went to the World
Court, which condemned the US for "unlawful use of force" and
for violation of treaties. The court ordered the US to terminate its
crimes and pay for reparations. The US rejected the World Court's
judgment.

Canada, quickly running out of viable options, next went to the
UN Security Council, which voted fourteen to one for the
application of the Geneva Conventions to the Canadian occupied
territories. Of course, the United States voted no. Without its
enforcer, the Security Council was impotent to effect change. There
was weeping and gnashing of teeth.

---

[85] Bert, Wayne. *American Military Intervention in Unconventional War* (New York: Palgrave MacMillan, 2011).

[86] Feith 160.

[87] There was a great deal of hesitation in determining whether the Canadian Government was corrupted at the Federal level (thus demanding economic and social sanctions) or if the terrorist collusion was provincial. If provincial/regional, the States would declare Alberta, the Yukon, British Columbia and Saskatchewan rogue states/hostile territories, severed from their eastern counterparts in mission and political intent.

[88] Feith 161.

In the first months of 2003, the US Southern Command prepared plans for the construction of an unconventional and extrajudicial detainment and interrogation facility in Guantanamo Bay Naval Base, Cuba. By the time Bush gave his ultimatum, three-hundred-and-seventy "Sprites" had been confirmed as arrested (taken into US custody), and transferred to Guantanamo. Anyone complicit in terrorist activity could be detained and transferred to this facility.

When American border patrol agents found and collapsed 265 tunnels connecting Sprite and Grim Reaper-drug runners with the American market in Washington (state), a number of those in the neighbouring towns with no direct connection—but rather a sense of the happenings—were taken to Guantanamo. [89] NATO allies found the US rejection of the application of the Geneva Convention for their detainees an egregious fault. They were also enraged by the findings in Meagan Churchland's September 2003 report on the "Cost of War," which revealed that docile Canadian border towns in British Columbia were being targeted by an American bombing campaign intended to discourage drug trafficking.

Despite the poor favour garnered by the campaign, the US had not fully isolated itself: the Japanese Prime Minister Junichiro Koizumi supported the occupation and the Americans' use of third-country facilities to "win the war on terror." Tony Blair, conversely, refused to meet Bush to talk "containment," indicating a growing fissure between American and British interests and direction. It became clear that an aging but indomitable Monarch was exerting intense pressure on her British government to aid her Great Dominion. But for her preoccupation with personal issues and tragedy, the Crown would have doubtless changed the international dynamic.

WHILE "NORMAL" PRISONERS were covered by the Conventions, the majority of the Canadian Forces who supported the Canadian Sovereignty Movement (CSM) and other resistive factions were not. The SD&G Highlanders, the Sudbury Irish, and other Reserve groups, for instance, were held in contempt for

---

[89] From interview with Red·Cross Representative.

aiding and abetting supposed terrorist factions (i.e. shooting down a gunship that had been firing on a mixed crowed, and aerating a US submarine in the St. Lawrence).

American accountability was scrutinized in extra-national reports, but little changed. Bush promised transparency, although he neglected to disclose any official reports about Guantanamo or the Oregon and Montana detention centres receiving bad press on account of allegations of the construction of torture chambers. The UN High Commissioner for Refugees (Lubbers) demanded that the US show more restraint:

> Those who are planning military action will understand that it has to be targeted at ending terrorism, and at those who protect terrorists, and that it should not become a war against Canadians.[90]

Bush's "whatever it takes, whatever it costs" mentality was a curse for many Canadians, evident from the US treatment of prisoners, and the blatant disregard for life it demonstrated (e.g. 767 Canadian civilian casualties were reported in the first eight weeks of the American Operation 'Red Dawn' in 2003). The number would have been exponentially higher if it wasn't for Brigadier General David Fraser's decision to put the First Canadian Group on alert and in a reactive position: if NORTHCOM did not provide ample support and evidence for a given operation, Canadian Forces would "not permit the activity" and would "protect Canadian civilians to the end."

The Canadian Forces, fighting an asymmetrical war with a conjoined force, were, in a number of separate instances, viewed as complicit in anti-American violence. Further, their targeting of hostile US operatives, when conducted near civilian centres on the border, was viewed as terrorism. Components of the Canadian Military were transformed via political rhetoric into a "terrorist force," depending on "bias demonstrated through action." Thus, Canadian troops—well aware of the inhumane treatment of captives designated as terrorists—were taking a huge risk when donning their CadPat.

The American presence in Canada effectually resulted in the "disintegration of the state…and a condition of anarchy throughout

---

[90] Bennis 144.

the remainder of the country."[91] Economic sanctions and America's blanket condemnation resulted in food shortages, which worked their way to epidemic levels. By the end of 2003, three-and-a-half-million Canadians were short of food and at risk of starvation, said a UNCHR official, and not for an actual lack of food, but lack of access. With roads blocked, railroads cut, and air drops strictly monitored, food was late in coming (especially to isolated enclaves), and frequently short in supply despite stockpiles along the border.

Debates ensued over whether Canada would return to its former autonomous self or slowly wean off a strong American presence until stable enough for self-determination, and whether the US was entitled to special territories for military bases intended to strengthen Northern Command and the rule of law. Timelines for troop withdrawals were withheld or postponed, and Canadian sovereignty with them.

It seems that, at some point or another, Bush genuinely wanted to help Canada, but couldn't ignore the tantalizing potential of adopting Canada's fatherless resources (oil, lumber, and most importantly, fresh water). Given Bush's conflict of interest, Canadian academic Nilks Orvik's statement seemed especially prophetic:

> The security and defence efforts of smaller states constituted a 'defence against help' strategy. By taking care of their own security, smaller powers can ease the security concerns of larger neighbours. This contributes to the maintenance of the smaller power's sovereignty in a crisis, and minimizes the danger that a larger power would believe it necessary to violate the sovereignty of a weaker state to protect its own interests.

Too often we dismiss the soothsayer and his ravings. Canada's failure to beef up its military spending before 2001 was an invitation for help, regardless of the ramifications that such assistance might have. Dick Cheney and Donald Rumsfeld seemed excited over the prospect of their patient developing Stockholm syndrome as they nursed it back to good health and standing.

The primary objective of the occupying force tended to be bathed in the language of "resource management." US officials sent groups to protect oil facilities around the oil fields, the nickel mines in Sudbury, and trans-national fuel reserves, since these "would be

---

[91] Blank, Jonah. *Foreign Affairs* (September 2011) 156.

absolutely crucial to [Canada's] postwar recovery and development."[92]

CHRETIEN FELL OFF the map in early 2003 due to undisclosed medical reasons. Some media-speculators suggested stress had exacerbated his Bell's Palsy, but his family friend disclosed to the press that he was in fact recovering from a double-bypass surgery. His successor, James Potter, was a rather sombre man from Nanaimo, British Columbia, who had lost family to an American cruise missile during the initial stages of the western offensive. Pugnacious, patriotic, and prone to yelling, Potter handled himself well in the company of Americans.

Rumsfeld, highly skeptical about Potter's intentions (he came off as vengeful and mysterious), cited evidence drawn up in a State Department report, which linked the Yukon Sprites to Potter's government. The report referred to Potter as an extremist; a "dangerous ideologue" who had indirectly financed terrorist organizations hostile to American forces in the past. Perhaps Rumsfeld was referring to the Government's funding of the country's military; but in any event, this tentative connection permitted the American administration to refer to Canada behind closed doors as an international threat: it had become a "rogue state." After first being referred to as a "rogue state" in the *Washington Post*, Potter's colleagues began punning on his rogue-initiatives. The papers drew a cartoonist parallel between Potter and Robin Hood, fighting a feudal power from "the forests of Canada, eh!"

The de-centralization effected by the US government in Canada let the Americans regionalize the country (treat each province as its own state), and to give and take accordingly. If the government installed by the US and the early elections produced the "wrong" result, then an American presence would be required to remain in Canada. Consequently, the US made sure that they could destabilize Potter's government. The more instability the new government faced, the more Bush could overstate the threat to American security in his re-election campaign. Things got worse in the west, and even more muddled in Ottawa.

---

[92] Bow, Brian. *The Politics of Linkage* (Vancouver: UBC P, 2009) 151.

In March, 2003, Lewis Paul Bremer III was appointed the US administrator charged with the oversight of the American occupation of western Canada. He first served as Director of the Office for Reconstruction and Humanitarian Assistance (ORH). The ORH, based out of Vancouver and Montreal, was transformed into the Coalition Provisional Authority three months later, turning Bremer into the chief executive authority in the country, notwithstanding Potter's contested handle on things. Wary of the cost of the war, and the inverse relation between American presence and Canadian support, a number of officials in Washington wished to back and transfer authority to the Potter government, which they had just undermined with evidence of "great malice" and other misdoings.

Bremer offered a plan-of-action in a *Washington Post* article he penned entitled "[Canada's] Path to Sovereignty", which was not in keeping with the Administration's policy of early transfer of authority in Canada. According to the seven-step plan "on the path to full [Canadian] sovereignty," Bremer suggested a method that would slowly strengthen the Canadian government, restore Parliament and the House of Commons, and result in a elections, mid-2004.[93] Apparently the article had undercut Rumsfeld, who had initially considered handing full sovereignty over to the Potter government. After all, his reasoning went, the quicker the US ends its occupation, the quicker Canada can jump-start its own affairs and begin piping energy to the States on its own volition. Of course there was the matter of reparations, but as Bush had suggested in his debate with Al Gore years earlier, the US was not in the business of nation building.

Bremer's plan incensed Canadians, for he stipulated the necessary presence of an American administrator to oversee the reformation and purging of the Canadian government. Further, Bremer's resolve (shared by other civilian and military officials, including General John Abizaid) to disband non-conforming components of the Canadian Army by issuing Order Number Two frightened many Canadians on account of the dissolution's potential rhetorical transformation of the existing resistance and remaining Canadian Forces into unlawful combatants. Canadians rallied

---

[93] Feith 453.

behind their troops and demanded immediate sovereign authority for the Potter government.

Colin Powell backed Bremer's sentiment and argued that more time was required to ensure governmental legitimacy prior to elections, and elections were required to complete US withdrawal. Bremer postulated in the fall of 2003 that, in the event of Kalnychuk's capture or surrender, a transfer of authority would be rushed, especially since the US had begun "to look like an occupying power, which [impeded its] ability to accomplish the primary US mission of destroying the [Sprites in Canada]."[94] US officials believed that "it would become harder and harder for the US to withdraw [its] forces, without raising the spectre that [Canada] w[ould] relapse into internecine warfare if [they] left."[95]

The flippancy of the American demands left many caught in the middle feeling utterly hopeless. Keen on changing the social climate, Potter manned up, especially important in the wake of the war's heaviest insurgencies. He re-established the three levels of government, and saw to repairs on the trans-Canada highway and the railway. He sought a greater UN presence to supervise the proper allocation of aid and supplies, and hailed the many diverse resistance groups in an effort to bring fighting to a close. Unfortunately, due to the extremity of the violence and the resistance fighters' severance from social connection with eastern Canada as well as current events, violence persisted.

In an address to occupying forces, Potter recognized the Canadian Forces and their defensive protocol as legitimate: "Leave us to mind our own, and you will protect your own." Potter's strength did not do him any favours. It came across as threatening, enabling the Bush Administration to justify many of their previous fallacious "rogue-state" charges.

THE CONDUITS TO PEACE remain open (and there is no surprise concerning what the possibilities are, given they've been the same in every post-Cold-War debacle). The conflict will end in the west if:

---

[94] Feith 145.
[95] Feith 145.

232

a) it becomes apparent to the Bush Administration and his generals that they're locked into a mutually hurting stalemate (MHS), in which the loss of life, damage to property, and diminished morale amounts to a worse political and social nightmare than the issues targeted in the first place; or

b) the US succeeds in its objectives, and conquers all remaining pockets of insurgents, terrorist splinter-cells, reactive-ex-Canadian-Forces, and rabble-rousers; or

c) the Potter government acquiesces to the extensive list of terms and demands issued from the Pentagon and White House, effactually signing the death warrant for the western resistance movement; or

d) UN troops grow some balls and properly enforce the promised cease fire, so that peace talks and negotiations can commence; or

e) third parties (i.e. the PRC, Britain or Russia) [continue to] intervene on behalf of the Canadians or facilitate peace-talks; or

f) the US withdraws all forces from the Occupied Canadian territories.[96]

Until then, the state of affairs remains a nightmare for both countries, and all those (e.g. yours truly) caught in the mix.

♠

---

[96] Cochrane, Feargal. *Ending Wars* (Cambridge: Polity P, 2008) 34.

A WOLF IN SPRITES' CLOTHING

> We made dumb our anger and our honour; but that has not
> brought us peace.[97]
>
> –G.K. Chesterton

Great Falls, Montana
March 2, 2006

JACQUELYN POSTED BAIL. I was led out of my holding-cell
by a hefty guard, whose shirt held on desperately to its buttons, all
yanked to the limit of their yarn, to reclaim my clothes and personal
items from the prison bureau. Cold sunshine filtered through
clouded glass, painting the room with a grid of sterile light. The
guard took my handcuffs off, and left me at the counter.

The room was spliced in two by a plain white plaster wall.
Horizontally, along the middle, ran a ragged hardwood countertop
with a dimple beneath a glass division, where they'd slip my
personal paraphernalia. The glass divider, stained onion-yellow
from age, was reinforced with metal netting. It sepia-ed the desktop
computer screens and the blinking lights it reflected.

A capped gentleman transpired out of some dark crook in the
room beyond, and met me at the glass where we were separated,
lawman and supposed villain. His shoulders were active, but I could
not see what he was handling. My suspicions were quelled when my
box of notes, mangled recorder, and watch, clamoured into the
depression beneath the glass ahead of his spidery fingers. I quickly
snatched up my items, and he provided me with a receipt indicating
what I had deposited upon arrest, and he made me sign for the
items.

As I closed the clasp on my watch, I saw another man enter the
room, discard a handful of papers behind the counter, then
disappear into the dark. My stomach instantly went into a knot. The
similitude between his stature, swagger, and basic features, and
Kalnychuk's was distressing. "Excuse me; do you know who that
was?"

---

[97] Chesterton, G. K. *The Crimes of England* (New York: John Lane, 1916)
<http://www.gutenberg.org/ebooks/11554>.

"Sir, you'll have to speak through the microphone. I can't read lips."

I found the microphone, caught it between my fingers, and recited my inquiry. "Do you know who that man was? The one who just was here. Walked in through that door."

"I didn't catch a glimpse of him," he said apologetically.

Unsatisfied with his response, however sincere, I kept prodding: "Do you have any idea who it could have been?"

"No. We have a lot of traffic through here. Besides, I do not— cannot—identify any of our staff unless requisitioned by a higher authority. You're not a general, are you?"

"No, I'm—"

"Good day sir." The capped gentleman likewise disappeared into the darkness. Prison procedure assured quick remedies for erratic behaviour, so I thought it best not to chase my white rabbit down the corridor and into an asylum.

The guard who had unbound my hands returned. He caught me staring down the hallway. "Everything alright, Mr. Danson?"

"Yes. Everything is fine."

"Mr. Danson, the officers outside will take you to the hotel room the State's provided. If you subvert any of the provisions you've agreed to in any way, then you're coming straight back to us, and honestly, we'd prefer not to see you again. While we can't detain you indefinitely, since you technically do not have any formal terrorist affiliations, the American government would very much appreciate your patience and cooperation. *Capiche?*" I shook my head to sign agreement and externalize my puzzlement with the elusive figure.

Whether blinded by Stockholm syndrome or the tunnel vision reporters sometimes develop when focusing too hard on a particular subject or story, I had neglected the possibility that Kalnychuk was not the blunt and neurotic man I interviewed for hours over the course of days and lives. My Ahabian obsession with the man could have had me seeing Bruce anywhere and everywhere, which was especially easy given my diminished faculties. I could not be sure that the man in the prison was not Kalnychuk, just as I could not be sure that Kalnychuk was the man I came to know. The possibility that he was free and alive stung like the divots on my cheek.

L. PAUL BREMER, the US administrator in Canada, had announced on January 27, 2006: "Ladies and gentlemen, we got him," to a room full of relieved American and Canadian military officials and politicians, as well as the usual horde of reporters scrambling to their blackberries.[98] "The tyrant," Bremer continued, "is a prisoner." Major General Ray Odierno substantiated Bremer's claims, suggesting: "He was caught like a rat."

Bush released one statement with regards to the demise of the Sprite leader. He shuffled to the center of the White House's briefing-room stage, and tapped the microphone. Oblivious to rolling cameras, Bush helloed Tom Ridge and laughed away an out-of-order question from Jake. He shuffled his prepared speech on the podium and his smile washed away. Sternly, he began:

> Good evening. Tonight, I can report to the American people and to the world, this past Friday at 9 a.m., US and Canadian military forces—following intelligence intercepted by a joint task force manned by CIA, CSIS, and RCMP agents—captured Bruce Kalnychuk, leader of the Sprite terrorist group, alive. He was found barricaded in his Toronto safe-house. Fierce fire fights ensued between the Coalition Forces and the Sprite remainder. After seeing all of his troops eliminated and captured, Kalnychuk attempted to commit suicide; however, he failed, and was brought into American custody. And now the leader of the Yukon Sprites will face the justice he denied to millions.
>
> Bruce Kalnychuk lived to account for his malice. He survived to answer for the lives of American soldiers killed in Canada. He survived to answer for the men, women, and children who froze in the November Bombings. He survived to account for the rift he has caused between Canada and the United States of America. Today is a momentous occasion. It marks the end of the road for Kalnychuk, and for all those who bullied in his name.
>
> Since Prime Minister Potter's government, my administration, and I, knew that a public trial would permit Kalnychuk an opportunity to communicate to potential Sprite terror cells—thus endangering our people and nullifying our chance to establish a durable stability and security in western Canada—we instead saw to a closed-to-the-public tribunal before Canadian and American officials.

---

[98] Bret Baier, Rita Cosby, and Jim Angle, *[Bruce Kalnychuk] Captured 'Like a Rat' in Raid*, http://www.FOXnews.com/story/0,2933,105706,00.html.

> Yesterday, Saturday, January 28, 2006, Bruce Kalnychuk heard his sentence, and at 11 a.m. this morning, he was executed by a firing squad.
>
> This achievement marks a victory for America, for people who seek peace around the world, and for all those who lost loved ones as a result of the November Bombings and in the events that followed.
>
> I have a message for all Americans and Canadians: the capture of Bruce Kalnychuk does not mean the end of violence in western Canada. We still face terrorists who would rather go on killing the innocent than accept the re-emergence of liberty. Such men are a direct threat to the North American people, and they will be defeated.
>
> Let the Sprite leader's demise serve as a grave reminder to all those who wish to do our nation harm: if you murder Americans, you will be hunted, you will be found, and you will be brought to justice.

Bush's zeal and the ostensible gratification he took in delivering Kalnychuk's post-mortem had me convinced. I hadn't scrutinized the time frame or veracity of the death-claim. I hadn't interviewed anybody from the firing squad or looked into the Canadian officials present for the tribunal. All I had was President Bush's word that Kalnychuk was dead. I wanted to see the body. I needed closure.

Even if he was dead, there was still the question of why the American government was so prompt to kill him, and why not a public trial and execution? None of the remaining Sprites followed his lead anymore, anyway. The security claim was bullshit. The world had watched this war unfold on television and on the internet. They watched and stomached massacre, murder, torture, and international crime, and yet, the climactic execution of justice was for some reason forbidden to the public. What would Kalnychuk have done before a vengeful audience to have made the G-men in Washington hesitant about televising the spectacle? More importantly, what would he have said?

The Legend could have been an American pawn as opposed to a Canadian king. This prospect corrupted the nice-and-tidy history I had been contently committed to. I did not see him burn. I did not see his execution. For all I know, the Legend may have been the baseball thrown into the neighbour's yard to permit the uninvited entry and all this turmoil. But if that is true, then his testimony—my big exposé—would be the scraps thrown to potential conspirators or dissenters in order to hide a worse truth from the world.

Bruce had been rather ambiguous about his activation by Hoff. The guy could have either given Bruce a hand during a rough time in his life or, conversely, turned him into a ticking bomb. If he was an American plant (used to whatever ends), was he conscious of his role? Had he been acting the entire time?

THE NETWORK arranged for me to work on *Faultline 49* until the court released or charged me with something more damning. As a result, I could edit my manuscript in beautiful Great Falls, Montana, in my room at the Best Western, not far from where the progenitor of this conflict grew up.

The phones in the room were wire-tapped. I could not get within ten feet of the elevator or stairs without being slammed by the law-enforcement officer assigned to care for the three offenders on my floor. The internet on the public computer had remote locks on what could be accessed and fire walls preventing me from contacting particular individuals. My immobility aside, I still needed to get more information on the elusive Hoff. I needed to talk to Jacquelyn.

As I rifled through what looked like confetti—an eclectic mishmash of phone numbers and names of people who could potentially supplement Jake's findings—I pondered motivation. While the Americans would have loved to get their hands on Canadian resources and territories, they knew too well it would not be a simple matter, and that the consequences of blow-back would outweigh any benefits of a sweep. There was also the issue of public support: you can gain popularity and secure votes with a quick win. Conversely, a long, ugly war can only lead you to losing friends and alienating people. Besides, too many lives were lost to justify such greed. It was out of the question. It wasn't an official operation, if an operation at all. Who would want a North American conflict?

In 2001, multitudes of stung Middle Easterners wanted to strain America's relations with her allies and sap her resources. But who and why specifically? The strong Canadian and US relationship with Israel was enough to prompt Arab/Islamic antagonism, but apart from Al Qaeda and Hamas, which were ruled out, intelligence could find no linkage between the Middle East and 9/11, the November Bombings or any of the subsequent terror-incidents that cropped up during the Can-American conflict—that is, apart from a single condemnation/boycott.

Saddam's people discussed messing with North American affairs, particularly Canadian affairs, after Canada continued to support bombing attacks and sanctions on Iraq. Scott Taylor's note in *Spinning on the Axis of Evil* alerted me to this antipathy: "Canada was now the only country to receive a 'double X' boycott rating from the Iraqi government."[99] If the resentment grew to be enough, they may have supported some dissent in one way or another, but there is no way – especially with his uncertainty concerning the cause of his son's death in the Gulf War—that Kalnychuk would have intentionally made a deal with anyone in Iraq.

The Sprites did, however, pre-exist Kalnychuk's rise to command. Perhaps he was pressed—by Hoff[?]—into their embrace; subtly persuaded to envision himself as their rightful ruler; and then utilized by those he once considered enemies to carry out their goals and objectives. Would Kalnychuk have seen this coming? If Saddam was trying to set a wedge between the US/Canada and their allies, how did he manage?

Until the Sprites have been erased from the western cordillera, few people will want to pick at the scabs for fear of provoking some disastrous continuation.

JACQUELYN'S VOICE was a comfort, and quieted the ringing that rented my hearing. "Hey jailbird! You've sprung your cage?"

"Yes. I've got a new one now, but it's far more comfortable. Minimal threat of being raped when I'm off guard—a definite plus. I have you to thank for that."

"You would have done the same. I'm actually boarding my flight to Atlanta in ten. I'll call you back when I touch-down. Everything okay?"

"Yes. Well, not really… Jake, I need another favour."

"No kidding."

"I know it might not be a good time."

"Yeah, David. It really isn't." The kerfuffle and heavy-breathing on the other end suggested she was walking somewhere briskly.

"Jake, just give me a minute."

---

[99] Taylor 67.

"One minute. Okay. I'll see what I can do. Alright, what's up?"

"This Hoff fella—"

"Going to stop you right there."

"But I still have at least forty seconds."

"Yeah, you do. But your fella is a lady."

"What? No. *He* was in deep with Bruce."

Jake clicked her tongue against her teeth to emphasize her negation. "Yeah, and I did some digging after you brought her up in your call from Washington. She was the affair Charlie mentioned in your interview. She's deep in it. I can't tell whether she was with the CIA or the NSA because I hit a brick wall querying her name, which got me thinking. Since most of her history is classified, she's either a player or a referee."

"Jake, what does she look like? Any identifying marks? Any tattoos?" Kalnychuk had tacked a picture of a blonde on the wall before the arrest—the same woman we found face-down in her own blood on the way to Toronto. I was praying for a mole on her face.

"Just ask her for her number, Romeo."

"God, Jack. Her number's been called. If I could only ask her for her number, I wouldn't need your help with a visual description, now would I?"

"She's actually your type: a blonde. Big Marilyn Monroe smile. She even has the mole – on her left cheek." *Bingo.*

"Freckles?"

"Maybe. Actually…yeah. I'll fax her profile and the rest of what I've collected when I get in."

"Gee, no kidding. Hoff is a woman."

"Yes, I know," she laughed. "So, now do you have what you need?"

"Other than a name and a corpse, I've got nothing. I'm betting this Hoff is a keystone in the conflict."

"Take a breather, Dave. Return to it when you've gotten your shit together. Did you ever get around to crying?"

"Thanks for everything. Seriously."

"Don't mention it. Oh, David… You there?

"Yup."

"Audrey's back in Seattle with Samuel. So, if you want to see your son…"

"Gotcha. Bye Jacquelyn." I tossed the cell phone on the bed.

My mail was on the dresser. Besides a few letters and a dated newspaper with a headline story about Louis Vigeland's capture, there was a large package on the dresser: a big cardboard box addressed to me, with Robert Wharton's name marked as sender. He had arranged for me to meet with Charlie Kalnychuk, which, in turn, bought me enough credit with *The Network* to gamble on a big story in western Canada. I ran a pen along the tape, opening its rib cage, and subsequently tore into it, terror and panic shaking my hands through a white and brown frenzy of corrugated paper.

Enclosed was the most recent issue of *Time Magazine* featuring Wharton's article on the Hell's Angels' involvement with the Sprites' drug and gun running. It was aptly titled: "Fairies and Angels." The article was a full four page spread. Fantastic black and white combat photographs accompanied the story, complete with emphasized key phrases in bold (e.g. "Killing is our business. You can tell we were not downsized with the border close…"; "it's not about sovereignty. It's about money…"; "pirates…" etc.). Good for him, I thought, wringing my palmed jealousy and bitterness. Apparently one of our careers will survive this gong show.

Beneath the magazine was a small laptop—one of those eight-hundred-dollar-heavy jobs—fitted beside a bottle of Canadian Club with a note:

> Dear David, thank you for the *in*. Hope Washington was what you needed. Jacquelyn told me about your Toronto incident. They say bad luck manifests in threes. Here's hoping that you'll harpoon your whale before 'three' is cocked and loaded. Fondest regards, R.W.

Not before this whisky I won't, I thought to myself. So far as luck is concerned, I was convinced it had left that wasteland.

I HAVE ATTEMPTED to live up to an unattainable pedigree set by attached journalists for attached journalists, and succumbed to an extreme position within the discipline: participant. A modicum of separation, my experience suggests, is necessary to avoid entirely becoming a character within one's story. The loss of that separation inspires a shift from journalism to autobiography (Joe Sacco or Anderson Cooper's toothy, character-driven styles, for instance, are situated somewhere between the aforementioned two). My current predicament is resultant, in other words, of becoming an active cast member on Kalnychuk's show. This means I've violated the essential divisions barring me from those I have attempted to research and threatened the objective followed by most attached journalists: to give the point of view of the appendage personality or group and to contextualize a wider view, ultimately providing a stereoscopic account.

How could a cast member properly judge a show he's on, when his interests and actions must be called to question without bias? Enough would have been to enter the lives of the Sprites to the extent that *us/them* distinctions would be diffused, but maintained in terms of action, and tell their story from a point of view unique to their nuanced circumstance without mediation by the American Military. That is not the case, however; not with this story.

I thought I could fall down the rabbit hole with my camera and notebook, and get out unscathed, but the truth is that I jumped without a rope. Worst of all, when I landed, I took shelter with the lot of them: bandits, terrorists, thugs, freedom fighters, and outlaws. I've lived with the interviewees, drank their tea, and played video games with their kids. The story has become a thing: it's beaten and scarred me; searched and patted me down at checkpoints; it's held my hand and cried; it's bled on my shoes.

It is my ardent desire to put a thousand miles between me and this place, and salvage what I can. What have I left but my sanity? That too has come under siege in these past few months. And for what? To get an interview with the king of a Canadian terrorist organization who jammed me with more pressing questions concerning two potentially sizeable Sprite operations named Arachnid and Northern Lights in addition to a body rotting in a safe house? A name that's nothing more than a whisper in the wind? I'm stuck with recurring nightmares about meat-hooks and shallow graves. Eyes open, eyes shut—*it's all darkness.*

Jacquelyn is right. Recalling Marouf's poignant and prophetic cartoon, it is apparent that the flood will not stop when the cause of breach is found, to the beaver's chagrin, but only when the dam is fully rebuilt. Until then, it remains a nightmare.

♠

EPILOGUE: IN MY FEAR IS PEACE

Toronto, Ontario
January 26, 2006

AMBLING ABOUT the mansion off kilter, still getting used to a dim world full of muffled voices, I followed the sound of hammering to find Kalnychuk boarding up windows. "Think that'll be of any use when the time comes?" I asked, slinging my voice across the room.

"Probably not, no. But one always gives his all, even in the shadow of the inevitable." He continued hammering the wood into place. He plotted a nail and hesitated. "When we were talking epitaphs, I had to hold myself back from laughing." All I could manage to see of his face was a pinkish-gray form eclipsed by the room's competing shadows.

"Why? Were you being disingenuous?" Kalynchuk turned ever so slightly into the light, smiling deviously so that the wings of his moustache quavered right below his eyes.

"No. I simply found humor in the futility and erroneous practice of self-definition, all things considered. Soon enough, everyone will be focused on individually reacting in the present as opposed to historicizing or retracing steps as a group. History only resumes after the last cannon fired goes cold, and you can be sure that the truth of it will have been lost by the time this bombardment is finished or left to be found in shards and pieces by the victorious, if winning is at all possible."

"What exactly does that mean?" I approached him slowly, and lowered my voice, "What will people be reacting to?" He was silent. "Are you aware of future terror attacks?" The question pained my ribs, and I keeled back.

"Don't strain yourself!" He resumed hammering. Still under the dirty reign of illicit painkillers, my attempted intensity had exhausted me. Knees bent and panting, I resigned to sit. "Hey, would you pass me those nails over there." With a grunt, I leaned forward and picked up a few palmers.

"These ones?" Kalnychuk nodded. I whipped them over. Kalnychuk smiled and turned around. He started to reinforce the board with additional wooden beams.

"I was drunk and stoned."

"Pardon?" I responded, comfortably inserted between tattered cushions on a red armchair.

"All of the time." He gestured for me to pass him more nails. "I drank and smoked my goddamn insides out in order to escape, but that just made it worse. The heavy cynicism that accompanies smokers' paranoia weighed down on me, in addition to everything else—no, the long ones." I was trying to find the right nails and screws by touch. Bruce tried guiding me from afar. "No...there we go. Thanks. Those days weren't pretty or memorable. It was cold. I was cold." He moved onto girding the next window. "I lived on guard, through weeks and weeks full of introspective highs. World was out to get me."

"That's hard to imagine," I sneered.

"Well back then, it was a different world. All that threat was in here," he said, pointing to his head. "I knew that my reality would be hyper-subjective—extra to the standard anomaly—but I didn't think it'd estrange me from my peers, friends, and family as much as it did...Those relationships didn't stand a chance. It leaves you there, alone—the drugs, I mean. Chemically and socially isolated in a hateful circuit. With remembering came hate, and the preamble to forgetting was destruction. My boy was dead and I knew who did it...But before I could pursue justice in my own way, I needed to clean up and man-up. You'd be surprised what doors a suit and a shave open for you."

"And then you took over the Yukon Sprites."

"Yeah. The Sprites...A fucking soup kitchen when I found it. A bunch of peaceniks and hobos: all of them disinterested in politicking and hard work. Now, it was chance or fortune that Hoff should show up again, start in with the old 'Hey Brucie,' and then throw me a shaving kit, an address, and a hand. It was too good to be true. So damn good, that I knew it had deep-seeded-evil-fucking-shit written all over it. And you know what I did? Hey David, you know what I did?" He stood up, and stomped across the room to the point where he could literally talk down to me. "I took that fucking hand without batting an eye," said the pinkish-grey blur. I wasn't the quivering, pathetic audience he likely wanted, so he disengaged his stare and started pacing. I slouched back and watched him pace as if I were a wallflower in the house of flies. "It was too late when I realized what I was doing. I let it blind-sight me because I was caught up in how well I was doing it. Danson, they all swore an oath to me. A fucking blood oath!" Kalnychuk kicked at the foundation. "When I'm gone—that's it; till death do us part. Whatever group emerges from the dissolved Yukon Sprites is no longer indebted to me. Arachnid, Northern Lights—whatever they've got planned. I had no hand in any of that."

"Arachnid? Northern Lights?" I inquired.

"I'm not shirking the historical role of instigator or failed ideologue...I just know that I was unable to restrain the monster I unleashed or delineate its efforts, and now it's made a mess of everything I loved. Everything..."

"Are those military operations? What do they involve?"

Bruce picked up the hammer and poised to resume garrisoning the mansion. On the first swing, he missed the nail and struck the side of his thumb. "God damn it." Kalnychuk held out a trembling, bloody hand. He put the hammer down, and scouted for a place to sit. Cornering the couch opposite me, he continued, dripping crimson onto the hardwood: "David, forget about it." Kalnychuk saw me staring warily in his general direction. "If I seem uneasy, make no mistake: it is not because I resent or fear the logical conclusion to North America's *Kalnychuk problem*, but the fact that it is not a conclusion at all. Not even remotely." I caught myself nodding—not to sign agreement, but rather my attention. "I may not be stroking a cat and laughing maniacally, but I might as well. It doesn't end with me. My dear vodianyk[100] and I have had a loveless marriage, and now our malevolent spawn is poised to de-rail everything. God, the events to come—can you just imagine?" He let out a nervous laugh. "Fuck. I am uneasy because I get off easy. The rest of them? You? Well, I guess that's not my fucking problem. But hey, Danson—business will be good for the carrion-flies: the arms dealers, the morticians, the preachers, the journalists...and you." I could tell he was smiling at me, though I wasn't entirely sure. He ended his gaze with a slap against the arm-rest. "Sorry."

The apology stung. How many families affected by the November Bombings were due an apology from this mentally-ill

---

[100] Sprite-like creatures from Slavic mythology. They would break dams and drown people when angered.

man? "Doesn't faze me," I replied. "Although, I thought that you'd, at the very least, consider me a higher-order scavenger."

"A hyena?"

"Or a coyote," I proposed.

"So you reckon yourself a trickster?" He crossed his legs.

"Certainly more so than a worm."

"Again, I didn't mean it as a slight," Kalnychuk reassured. He leaned his head back and examined his disemboweled fortress, looking past piping and insulation into the master bedroom. "You know this used to be the German Consulate?"

"Nope."

"At another point it was an artist's house."

"Now it just looks like bad art. *Guernica*, maybe."

"Before that, Al Capone used it as a hideout. Each era left behind its traces. All of these clues—all of these layers subducted beneath one another, piling high with only the present showing—make up history. I know you can appreciate how deceptive history is for one who's only studied the ground immediately beneath his feet...Some particularly aware folks privilege the democracy of the past and spend their lives as archeologists and geologists, drilling with the promise of understanding the base on which they stand and the benefit of foundation. Others—the seemingly free and powerful oligarchs of the present—build high their Babylonic towers, which lack the security of stability and underpinning, and are, therefore, as good as sand in the wind." He dug his pipe out of his pocket, and started scratching at the resin laminated to the bowl. "It's always there—the past, I mean. We may forget the details about its true nature, but," he laughed, "calling a volcano a mountain is a dangerous game of semantics. Beneath the surface, sometimes hidden...Aden. Matt. Hoff. My parents. Capone. They're all right there," he signalled the chipped hardwood floor, "erupting; screaming out for justice and haunting every decision we make. David, you'd be wasting your time if you scoured the sand and topsoil for answers. Dig deep and you'll find your truth. And when you do, take it and share it, regardless of the cost. Give them the facts."

♠

NOTE FROM THE AUTHOR

The simulacrum is never that which conceals the truth—it is the truth which conceals that there is none. The simulacrum is true.[101]

—Baudrillard

BY CONSIDERING the socio-political and individual implications of the terrorist attack in New York City on September 11, 2001—as well as the context that gestated this violent episode—and replacing it instead with an attack of equally unquantifiable gravity, I have attempted to illuminate elements of 9/11's effects—effects that we now take for granted as inevitable or happenstance.

As well as drawing a dissonance between realities for the purpose of estranging us to forces and ideas that we may find difficult to accept, I have utilized the distorting qualities of fiction to present a buffer-world: one that could theoretically have existed, though thankfully doesn't. My relief, although sincere, is short-lived, because our reality is plighted by an alternative chaos. While I've interrogated certain real-world elements—post 9/11 civilian and military doctrine; globalization; national sovereignty on the fringe of the American empire; media representations of the self and other; international integration and division in North America, etc.—by using estrangement via re-contextualizations and fabrications, I recognize now that the very cultural and legal phenomena that I wish to focus on exist only in our present context, which is, paradoxically, something that I had to sacrifice to enable the events and agents that populate this buffer world.

The product of this estrangement is something fractured: more than a sexed-up political essay, the story above is willfully comprised from shards of truth, epiphany, despair, and criticism, which constitute a larger thought experiment. All the research is there, cited at the bottom of each page, but often the data is filtered and demonstrated through fictional players of significance. Because of these new players, rudimentary real-world facts have taken on other meanings.

---

[101] Baudrillard, Jean. *Selected Writings* (Standford: Standford University Press, 1988) 164.

In writing *Faultline 49*, I had no intention of:
  •trivializing or profiting from the pain, tragedy and loss suffered by many Americans and foreign nationals as a result of the 9/11 terrorist attacks or the innocent lives lost in related and subsequent events;
  •condemning the American people or their [domestic] way of life;
  •mystifying or insulting those real elements/entities invoked;
  • or damaging aspects of this reality through the fictional one invoked herein. In fact, this is the last thing I would ever want to do. It is precisely our reality that I wish to better understand.
In an effort to achieve another view of the cultural, political, and social ramifications of the September 11 terrorist attacks, I've used *Faultline 49* to decentre, de-familiarize, delocalize, and derail the prevailing, popular social imaginary in order to study it, from the outside, looking in.

–David Danson, June 2012

♠

BIBLIOGRAPHY

"About U.S. Northern Command." *About U.S. Northern Command*. Web. 08 Jan. 2012.

Ali, Tariq, and David Barsamian. *Speaking of Empire and Resistance: Conversations with Tariq Ali*. New York: New, 2005. Print.

Ali, Tariq. "Civilizations: Islam and the West In the Brutal Aftermath of the War on Iraq, a Genuine Clash of Civilizations Has Emerged. Could It Have Been Avoided?" *The Walrus* Apr. 2012: Web. June 2012.

Allan, Chantal. *Bomb Canada: And Other Unkind Remarks in the American Media*. Edmonton: AU, 2009. Print.

Andreas, Peter, and Thomas J. Biersteker. *The Rebordering of North America: Integration and Exclusion in a New Security Context*. New York: Routledge, 2003. Print.

Axworthy, Lloyd. *Navigating a New World: Canada's Global Future*. Toronto: A.A. Knopf Canada, 2003. Print.

Barber, Benjamin R. *Fear's Empire: War, Terrorism, and Democracy*. New York: W.W. Norton &, 2003. Print.

Barnett, Roger W. *Asymmetrical Warfare: Today's Challenge to U.S. Military Power*. Washington, D.C.: Brassey's, 2003. Print.

Baudrillard, Jean. *Selected Writings*. Ed. Mark Poster. Stanford, CA: Stanford UP, 1988. Print.

Bennis, Phyllis. *& After: US Foreign Policy and the War on Terrorism*. New York: Olive Branch, 2003. Print.

Bert, Wayne. *American Military Intervention in Unconventional War: From the Philippines to Iraq*. New York: Palgrave Macmillan, 2011. Print.

Blank, Jonah. "Invading Afghanistan, Then and Now." *Foreign Affairs* 90.5 (2011): n. pag. Print.

Blum, William. *Freeing the World to Death: Essays on the American Empire*. Monroe: Common Courage, 2005. Print.

Bolkcom, Christopher C., Lloyd DeSerisy, and Lawrence Kapp. *Homeland Security Establishment and Implementation of Northern Command*. [Washington, D.C.]: Congressional Information Service, Library of Congress, 2003. Print.

Bow, Brian J. *The Politics of Linkage: Power, Interdependence and Ideas in Canada-US Relations*. Vancouver: UBC, 2009. Print.

Campbell, David. "Narratives of the Bosnian War." *Review of International Studies* 24.2 (1998): Print.

Campbell, David. "Horrific Blindness: Images of Death in Contemporary Media." *Journal for Cultural Research* 8.1 (2004): 55-74. Print.

Canadian Defence and the Canada-US Strategic Partnership. Ottawa, Ont.: Canadian Defence & Foreign Affairs Institute, 2002. Print.

Cellucci, Paul. *Unquiet Diplomacy*. Toronto: Key Porter, 2005. Print.

Chesterton, Gilbert K. *The Crimes of England*. 1916. *Project Gutenberg*. 13 Mar. 2004. Web. 14 Dec. 2011.

Chomsky, Noam. *9-11*. New York: Seven Stories, 2001. Print.

Chomsky, Noam, and David Barsamian. *Imperial Ambitions: Conversations on the Post-9/11 World*. New York: Metropolitan, 2005. Print.

Chomsky, Noam, and Noam Chomsky. *Media Control: The Spectacular Achievements of Propaganda*. New York: Seven Stories, 2002. Print.

Chomsky, Noam, John Junkerman, and Takei Masakazu. *Power and Terror: Conflict, Hegemony, and the Rule of Force*. Boulder: Paradigm, 2011. Print.

Chomsky, Noam. *On Power and Ideology*. Montreal: Black Rose, 1987. Print.

Chossudovsky, Michel. "Is the Annexation of Canada Part of Bush's Military Agenda?" *Is the Annexation of Canada Part of Bush's Military Agenda?* Web. 08 Jan. 2011.

Cochrane, Feargal. *Ending Wars*. Cambridge: Polity, 2008. Print.

Conrad, Joseph. *The Heart of Darkness*. New York: Dover, 1990. Print.

Crowley, Brian Lee., Jason Clemens, and Niels Veldhuis. *The Canadian Century: Moving out of America's Shadow*. Toronto: Key Porter, 2010. Print.

Dyment, David. *Doing the Continental: A New Canadian-American Relationship*. Toronto: Dundurn, 2010. Print.

Edwards, Ralph. *Trail to the Charmed Land*. Hamilton (Canada): H.R. Larson, 1950. Print.

"Emergencies Act." *Department of Justice*. Government of Canada, n.d. Web. 08 Dec. 2011. <http://laws-lois.justice.gc.ca/eng/acts/E-4.5/index.html>.

Feith, Douglas J. *War and Decision: Inside the Pentagon at the Dawn of the War on Terrorism*. New York: HarperCollins, 2009. Print.

Findley, Rick, and Joe Inge. "North American Defence and Security in the Aftermath of 9/11." *Canadian Military Journal* 6.1 (2005): Print.

Fraser, Esther. *The Canadian Rockies; Early Travels and Explorations*. Edmonton: M.G. Hurtig, 1969. Print.

Gotlieb, Allan. *Disarmament and International Law; a Study of the Role of Law in the Disarmament Process*. Toronto: Canadian Institute of International Affairs, 1965. Print.

Herstien, H. H., L. J. Hughes, and R. C. Kirbyson. *Challenge & Survival: The History of Canada*. Scarborough: Prentice Hall, 1970. Print.

Hitchens, Christopher. *A Long Short War: The Postponed Liberation of Iraq*. New York: Plume Book, 2003. Print.

Hurtig, Mel. *The Vanishing Country: Is It Too Late to save Canada?* Toronto, Ont.: McClelland & Stewart, 2002. Print.

Joffe, Josef. *Uberpower: The Imperial Temptation of America*. New York: W. W. Norton, 2007. Print.

Kellner, Douglas. *Media Spectacle and the Crisis of Democracy: Terrorism, War, and Election Battles*. Boulder, CO: Paradigm, 2005. Print.

King, John. "Bush: Join 'coalition of Willing'" *CNN*. 20 Nov. 2002. Web.

Kolko, Gabriel. *The Age of War: The United States Confronts the World*. Boulder, CO: Lynne Rienner, 2006. Print.

Lapham, Lewis H. *Theater of War*. New York: New, 2002. Print.

Linebarger, Paul M. *Psychological Warfare*. 2nd ed. New York: Duell, Sloan and Pearce, 1954. Print.

Lowther, Adam. *Americans and Asymmetric Conflict: Lebanon, Somalia, and Afghanistan*. Westport, CT: Praeger Security International, 2007. Print.

Luciani, Patrick, and Rudyard Griffiths. *American Power: Potential and Limits in the 21st Century*. Toronto: Key Porter, 2007. Print.

McGillivray, Brett. *Canada: A Nation of Regions*. Don Mills, Ont.: Oxford UP, 2006. Print.

Morton, Desmon. "National Defence: A Little Common Sense." Empire Club of Canada Address. Fairmont Royal York Hotel, Toronto. 17 Apr. 2002. Speech.

Naidu, Mumulla V. *On Human Security: National Sovereignty and Humanitarian Intervention*. Brandon, Mb.: Canadian Peace Research and Education Association, 2001. Print.

O'Carroll, Lisa. "Tony Blair Knew Immediately That 9/11 Terror Attacks 'changed Everything'" *The Guardian*. Guardian News and Media, 10 Sept. 2011. Web. 08 Jan. 2012.

O'Hagan, Howard. *Tay John*. Toronto: McClelland and Stewart, 1985. Print.

Pratt, E. J. *Towards the Last Spike*. Toronto: Macmillan, 1952. Print.

Rather, Dan. *America at War: The Battle for Iraq : A View from the Front Lines*. New York: Simon & Schuster, 2003. Print.

Ray, Arthur J. *Canada's Native People*. Toronto: Key Porter, 1996. Print.

Roach, Kent. *September 11: Consequences for Canada*. Montreal: McGill-Queen's UP, 2003. Print.

Rohmer, Richard. *Ultimatum*. Toronto: Clarke, Irwin, 1973. Print.

Ryan, David. "Rhetoric and Nationhood': Framing September 11: Cultural Diplomacy & the Image of America." *49th Parallel: An Interdisciplinary Journal of North American Studies* (n.d.): Print.

"Saddam Captured 'Like a Rat' in Raid." *Fox News*. Web. 08 Nov. 2011. <http://www.FOXnews.com/story/0,2933,105706,00.html>.

Scowen, Peter. *Rogue Nation: The America the Rest of the World Knows*. Toronto: M&S, 2003. Print.

Simpson, Jeffrey. *Star-spangled Canadians: Canadians Living the American Dream*. Toronto: HarperCollins, 2000. Print.

Sokolsky, Joel J., and Joseph T. Jockel. *Fifty Years of Canada-United States Defense Cooperation: The Road from Ogdensburg*. Lewiston, NY: E. Mellen, 1992. Print.

Stein, Janice Gross., Colin Robertson, and Allan Gotlieb. *Diplomacy in the Digital Age: Essays in Honour of Ambassador Allan Gotlieb*. Toronto: Signal, 2011. Print.

Sully, François. *Age of the Guerrilla: The New Warfare*. New York: Parent's Magazine, 1968. Print.

Taylor, Scott. *Spinning on the Axis of Evil: America's War against Iraq*. Ottawa: Esprit De Corps, 2003. Print.

Thompson, John. "Canada's Post-Kandahar Military: Now What?" *SITREP* 71.5 (2001): n. pag. Print.

Tirman, John. *The Maze of Fear: Security and Migration after 9/11*. New York: New, 2004. Print.

"The Unguarded Homeland." *How Did This Happen?: Terrorism and the New War*. Ed. James Hoge and Gideon Rose. New York: Public Affairs, 2001. Print.

"US Troops Deployment in Canada." *US Troops Deployment in Canada*. Web. 08
    Feb. 2011. <http://metaexistence.org/uscanada.htm>.

Weinberger, Eliot. *What Happened Here: Bush Chronicles*. New York, NY: New
    Directions, 2005. Print.

Welsh, Jennifer M. *At Home in the World: Canada's Global Vision for the 21st Century*.
    Toronto: HarperCollins, 2004. Print.

Winterdyk, John, and Kelly W. Sundberg. *Border Security in the Al-Qaeda Era*. Boca
    Raton: CRC, 2010. Print.

Wright, Robert A. *Virtual Sovereignty: Nationalism, Culture, and the Canadian Question*.
    Toronto, Ont.: Canadian Scholars', 2004. Print.

Made in the USA
Lexington, KY
30 March 2013